ILUSTRADO

ILUSTRADO

*

MIGUEL SYJUCO

HAMISH HAMILTON
CANADA

HAMISH HAMILTON CANADA

Published by the Penguin Group

Penguin Group (Canada), 90 Eglinton Avenue East, Suite 700, Toronto, Ontario, Canada M4P 2Y3
(a division of Pearson Canada Inc.)

Penguin Group (USA) Inc., 375 Hudson Street, New York, New York 10014, U.S.A.
Penguin Books Ltd, 80 Strand, London WC2R 0RL, England
Penguin Ireland, 25 St Stephen's Green, Dublin 2, Ireland (a division of Penguin Books Ltd)
Penguin Group (Australia), 250 Camberwell Road, Camberwell, Victoria 3124, Australia
(a division of Pearson Australia Group Pty Ltd)
Penguin Books India Pvt Ltd, 11 Community Centre, Panchsheel Park, New Delhi – 110 017, India
Penguin Group (NZ), 67 Apollo Drive, Rosedale, North Shore 0745, Auckland, New Zealand
(a division of Pearson New Zealand Ltd)
Penguin Books (South Africa) (Pty) Ltd, 24 Sturdee Avenue, Rosebank,
Johannesburg 2196, South Africa

Penguin Books Ltd, Registered Offices: 80 Strand, London WC2R 0RL, England

Published in Canada by Penguin Group (Canada), a division of Pearson Canada Inc., 2010
Simultaneously published in the United States by Farrar, Straus and Giroux,
18 West 18th Street, New York 10011

1 2 3 4 5 6 7 8 9 10 (RRD)

Copyright © Miguel Syjuco, 2010

*Publisher's note: This book is a work of fiction. Names, characters, places and incidents either are the product
of the author's imagination or are used fictitiously, and any resemblance to actual persons living or dead,
events, or locales is entirely coincidental.*

Manufactured in the U.S.A.

ISBN: 978-0-670-06395-6

Library and Archives Canada Cataloguing in Publication data available upon request to the publisher.
American Library of Congress Cataloging in Publication data available.

Visit the Penguin Group (Canada) website at **www.penguin.ca**
Special and corporate bulk purchase rates available; please see
www.penguin.ca/corporatesales or call 1-800-810-3104, ext. 2477 or 2474

For my siblings: J, C, M, C, and J.
And of course, for Edith

In response to the warnings received while researching this book, the author hereby states that all perceived similarities between characters and people living or dead are either purely coincidental or a skewered nerve in your guilty conscience.

    –from the extant title page of *The Bridges Ablaze*, by Crispin Salvador

ILUSTRADO

PROLOGUE

The Panther lurks no longer in foreign shadows—he's come home to rest. Crispin Salvador's fitting epitaph, by his request, is merely his name.

—from an unattributed obituary, *The Philippine Sun*,
February 12, 2002

When the author's life of literature and exile reached its unscheduled terminus that anonymous February morning, he was close to completing the controversial book we'd all been waiting for.

His body, floating in the Hudson, had been hooked by a Chinese fisherman. His arms, battered, open to a virginal dawn: Christlike, one blog back home reported, sarcastically. Ratty-banded briefs and Ermenegildo Zegna trousers were pulled around his ankles. Both shoes lost. A crown of blood embellished the high forehead smashed by crowbar or dock pile or chunk of frozen river.

That afternoon, as if in a dream, I stood in the brittle cold, outside the yellow police tape surrounding the entrance of my dead mentor's West Village apartment. The rumours were already milling: the NYPD had found the home in disarray; plainclothes detectives filled many evidence bags with strange items; neighbours reported having heard shouts into the night; the old lady next door said her cat had refused to come out from under the bed. The cat, she emphasized, was a black one.

Investigators quickly declared there was no evidence of foul play. You may recall seeing the case in the news, though the coverage was short-lived in the months following September 11, 2001. Only much later, during lulls in the news cycle, was Salvador mentioned at any length in the Western media—a short feature in the arts section of *The New York Times*,* a piece in *Le Monde*† on anticolonial expatriates who lived in Paris, and a negligible reference at the end of a *Village Voice* article about famous New York suicides.‡ After that, nothing.

At home in the Philippines, however, Salvador's sudden silencing was immediately autopsied by both sides of the political divide. Both *The Philippine Gazette* and the *Sun* traded blows with Salvador's own *Manila Times*, debating the author's literary, and indeed social, significance to our weary country. The *Times*, of course, declared their dead columnist the waylaid hope of a culture's literary renaissance. The *Gazette* argued that Salvador was not "an authentic Filipino writer," because he wrote mostly in English and was not "browned by the same sun as the masses." The *Sun* said Salvador was too middling to merit murder. Suicide, each of the three papers concluded, was a fitting resolution.

When news emerged of the missing manuscript, every side discarded any remaining equipoise. The legend of the unfinished book had persisted for over two decades, and its loss reverberated more than its author's death. Online, the blogosphere grew gleeful with conjecture as to its whereabouts. The literati, the career journalists foremost among them, abandoned all objectivity. Many doubted the manuscript's existence in the first place. The few who believed it was real dismissed it as both a social and personal poison. Almost everyone agreed that it was tied to Crispin's fate. And so, each trivial tidbit dredged up during the death investigation took on significance. Gossip cycloned among the writing community that Salvador's pipe was found by the police, its contents still smoking. A rumour circulated that he long ago fathered and abandoned a child, and he'd been maddened by a lifetime of guilt. One reputable blog, in an entry titled "Anus Horribilis," claimed extra-virgin olive oil was found leaking

*Natalia Diaz, "Filipino Footnote," *The New York Times*, May 6, 2002.
†Carla Lengellé, "Les guérilleros de Paris: de Hô Chi Minh à Pol Pot," *Le Monde*, July 22, 2002.
‡Anton Esteban, "Grand Central Terminus," *The Village Voice*, August 15, 2002.

out of the corpse's rectum. Another blog surmised that Salvador was not dead at all: "Dead or alive," wrote Plaridel3000, "who would know the difference?" None among Salvador's colleagues and acquaintances—he had real no friends—questioned the suicide verdict. After two weeks of conjecture, everyone was happy to forget the whole thing.

I was unconvinced. No one knew what I knew. His great comeback was scuppered; the masterpiece that would return him to the pantheon was bafflingly misplaced and the dead weight of controversy buried in his casket. The only remaining certainty was the ritual clutter inherited by those left behind—files to be boxed, boxes to be filled, a life's worth of stuff not intended as rubbish to be thrown out for Monday morning pickup. I just about ransacked his apartment searching for the manuscript of *The Bridges Ablaze*. I knew it was real. I had witnessed him typing away at it at his desk. He had spoken of it, puckishly, on many occasions. "The reason for my long exile is so that I could be free to write *TBA*," Salvador had said, that first time, spitting out the bones of chicken feet we were eating in a subterranean Mott Street restaurant. "Don't you think there are things that need to be finally said? I want to lift the veil that conceals the evil. Expose them on the steps of the temple. Truly, all those responsible. The pork-barrel trad-pols. The air-conditioned Forbes Park aristocracy. The aspirational kleptocrats who forget their origins. The bishopricks and their canting church. Even you and me. Let's all eat that cake." But what remained of the manuscript was only crumbs: the title page and a couple of loose leaves scrawled with bullet points, found sandwiched and forgotten in his disintegrating *Roget's Thesaurus*. Missing was twenty years of work—a glacial accretion of research and writing—unknotting and unravelling the generations-long ties of the Filipino elite to cronyism, illegal logging, gambling, kidnapping, corruption, along with their related component sins. "All of humanity's crimes," Salvador said, spitting a bone atop the pyramidal pile in his bowl, "are only degrees of theft."

I, of course, believe the conspicuous lack of clues is stranger than the disarray of the domestic scene from which he was mysteriously absented. Ockham's razor is chipped. Every bone in my body recoils at the notion Salvador killed himself. Walking through his apartment afterward, I saw his viridian Underwood typewriter loaded, cocked, and ready with a fresh blank page; the objects on his desk arranged in anticipation of writing. How could he have brought himself to the river without passing his conscience reflected in that Venetian mirror in the hall? He would have seen there was still so much to do.

To end his own life, Salvador was neither courageous nor cowardly enough. The only explanation is that the Panther of Philippine Letters was murdered in midpounce. But no bloody candelabrum has been found. Only ambiguous hints in what remains of his manuscript. Among the two pages of notes, these names: the industrialist Dingdong Changco, Jr.; the literary critic Marcel Avellaneda; the first Muslim leader of the opposition, Nuredin Bansamoro; the charismatic preacher Reverend Martin; and a certain Dulcinea.

*

That you may not remember Salvador's name attests to the degree of his abysmal nadir. Yet during his two-decades-long zenith, his work came to exemplify a national literature even as it unceasingly tried to shudder off the yoke of representation. He set Philippine letters alight and carried its luminescence to the rest of the world. Lewis Jones of *The Guardian* once wrote: "Mr. Salvador's prose, belied by the rococo lyricism and overenthusiastic lists of descriptions, presents a painfully honest picture of the psychosocial brutality, actual physical violence and hubris so acute in his home country . . . His vital works will prove timeless."*

In its efflorescence, Salvador's life projected genius and intellectual brazenness, a penchant for iconoclasm, and an aspiration to unsparing honesty during obfuscated times. He was, even until his death, touted as "the next big thing"—a description he could never transcend. "From the early age of self-consciousness, I was told I'd been gifted gifts," he wrote in his memoir *Autoplagiarist*.† "I spent

---

*Lewis Jones, "The Salvador of Philippine Literature," *The Guardian*, September 21, 1990.
†Crispin Salvador, *Autoplagiarist* (Manila: Passepartout Publishing, 1994).

the rest of my life living up to expectations, imposed by others but more so by myself."

Such pressure, and a strong belief in living a life worth writing about, led him through many roles and adventures. His autobiography read so much like a who's who of artistic and political icons that readers wondered whether it was fiction. "I've lived nearly all my nine lives," Salvador wrote. His work borrowed liberally from and embellished each of those lives: his upbringing as the son of a sugar plantation owner, the sentimental education in Europe, Mediterranean evenings spent womanizing with Porfirio Rubirosa or drinking zivania with Lawrence Durrell, the meteoric fame from his scoops as a cub reporter, training with communist guerrillas in the jungles of Luzon, the argument with the Marcoses during dinner at Malacañang Palace. The group of influential artists Salvador cofounded, the Cinco Bravos, dominated the Philippine arts scene for years. Yet it was the internecine intensities of the local literati that gossiped Salvador's life into chimerical proportions. Among the stories: he gave Marcel Avellaneda that scar on his face during a duel with butterfly knives; he drunkenly, though surreptitiously, vomited in the seafood chowder bowl at a George Plimpton garden party in East Hampton; he danced a naked moonlit tango at Yaddo, with, depending on who is telling the story, Germaine Greer, Virgie Moreno, or a dressmaker's dummy on casters; Salvador was even said to have insulted conductor Georg Solti after a performance at the Palais Garnier (it's alleged he shook the maestro's hand and chummily called him "a smidge off at the start of the second movement of Rach Two." Note: I've been unable to confirm that Solti ever conducted the Second Piano Concerto at the Garnier).

Salvador's early work—most agree—possessed a remarkable moral vigour. Upon his return from Europe in 1963, he began building his name with reportage focusing on the plight of the poor—producing subversive stories famously at odds with his father's philosophy of political toadyism as a means to the greatest social good. In 1968, Salvador declared his international literary ambitions with the publication of his first novel, *Lupang Pula* (*Red Earth*).* The story of

Lupang Pula (Manila: People's Press, 1968).

the charismatic Manuel Samson, a farmer who joins the communist Huk Rebellion of 1946 to 1954, the book earned some acclaim and was later translated for publication in Cuba and the Soviet Union. (Salvador's true first novel, *The Enlightened*,* released in the United States three years earlier, won prizes before it was published but could not live up to the fairy-tale hype. About his grandfather's role in the 1896 Philippine Revolution and the subsequent war against American invaders, it was a work Salvador hoped would be forgotten. He once told me his portrayal of his grandfather had created "shoes too big for me to fill.")

Despite his having been unanimously awarded the Manila Press Club's coveted Mango de Oro Trophy for his exposé of police brutality during the Culatingan Massacre, it was the young writer's milestone essay in the January 17, 1969, edition of *The Philippines Free Press*, titled "It's Hard to Love a Feminist," which incited uproarious controversy. To his own surprise, the attention thrust him into the consciousness of Philippine pop culture. Radio talk shows nationwide carried his voice, its studied enunciations characteristically losing form and rising in pitch when excited; television screens bore the images of his lanky frame seated insouciantly with a leg tucked beneath him, black pomaded hair parted severely, finger wagging at the other members of the panel discussion—a grab bag of effeminate academic men and thick-waisted female activists. He energetically debated with feminists on the television and radio, delivering froths of invectives that at times required intervention by the host. Salvador justified his work as "not chauvinistic, but realistic for a poor country with greater bêtes noires than those raised at that recent symposium, 'Changing *His*tory into *Her*story.'" In October 1969, in the same magazine, Salvador published an essay, "Why Would a Loving God Make Us Fart?" This earned him the ire of the Catholic Church and further enshrined his intellectual infamy.

Salvador left Manila in 1972, a day before Marcos declared martial law. He hoped to make a name for himself in New York City, but success there was more coy than he would have liked, or was used to. He lived in Hell's Kitchen, in a coldwater studio "so sordid even the

---

*The Enlightened (New York: Farrar, Straus and Cudahy, 1965).

buzzing neon sign outside my window no longer lighted up." To make ends meet he took a job at the Petite and Sweet Bakeshop in Greenwich Village. At night he wrote short stories, some of them finding print in small magazines like *Strike, Brother!* and *The Humdrum Conundrum*. His next milestone came with publication in the March 12, 1973, issue of *The New Yorker*, of the short story "Matador," a piece reportedly "not disliked" by the magazine's editor, William Shawn, but pointedly chosen for its relevance to the ongoing war in Vietnam. An allegory about the toll of neocolonialism, "Matador" drew on Salvador's experiences as a banderillero in Barcelona during his youth, presenting the United States as the matador and the Philippines as the brave but ultimately doomed bull named Pitoy Gigante.* After this success, Salvador had hoped closed doors would open, but his agent and publisher queries returned slowly, each demurring, though expressing interest if he should happen to have a novel. He started work on a new manuscript. A book attempting to provide a vivisection of loneliness, it was to be based on the unwitnessed drowning of a close friend and the effect the death had on the Salvador family.

In May of 1973, Salvador fell into a tempestuous relationship with Anita Ilyich, a Belarusian ballerina, disco queen, and early advocate of the swinging lifestyle. One stormy autumn morning following a party at The Loft, the couple, each of them reportedly under the influence of one too many gimlets and Quaaludes, had a jealous and theatrical fight there on Broadway in front of David Mancuso's apartment building. Salvador, convinced it was "just another one of those tiffs," returned to their home after a palliative walk to find his possessions dumped on the sidewalk to soak. Among his stuff were the translucent pulpy pages of his nearly completed novel.

That afternoon, Salvador quit New York for Paris, a city he'd frequented during his university studies. He swore off both women and literature, settled in a leaky *chambre de bonne* in the Marais, and worked as an assistant to a pastry chef's assistant. Soon after, he

* The story is renowned as the first fiction published by a Filipino in the magazine since Carlos Bulosan's "The End of War" in the September 2, 1944, issue. Marcel Avellaneda called "Matador" "over-earnest faux Ernest" and "a chapter edited judiciously from *The Sun Also Rises*."

broke his vow to teetotal the comforts of the softer sex, but it would be two full years before he returned to literature. Ultimately, both poverty and his restless spirit brought him back to writing in the summer of 1975; he took freelance assignments for *The Manila Times* and *The International Herald Tribune* and began work on what would become his popular *Europa Quartet* (*Jour, Night, Vida,* and *Amore*).* Written one after the other between 1976 and 1978, the quartet follows the life of a young mestizo gadabout in 1950s Paris, London, Barcelona, and Florence. It was a hit with housewives in three countries.

Buttressed by new success, Salvador returned periodically to the Philippines to undertake research, appear on panel discussions, stump for election campaigns, and work with other artists. In 1978, he began "War & Piss," his long-running weekly column in *The Manila Times*. His recently out-of-print travel guide, *My Philippine Islands (with 80 colour plates)*,† despite its unabashed subjectivity, was described by *Publishers Weekly* as "the definitive book on the Philippines [*sic*] people . . . entertaining and brave, chock-full of vivid anecdotes infused with a local's intimate knowledge . . . It situates the tropical country in the context of the rest of the world, retrieving it from the isolation and exoticization it is oftentimes suffered to endure." Later, in 1982, Salvador published *Phili-Where?*,‡ a satirical travel guidebook that charted his country's fall from "gateway to Asia" and proud U.S. colony to a plutocracy ruled by an "incontinent despot." The book was banned in the Philippines by the Marcos regime and thereupon enjoyed decent sales abroad.

The 1980s—the decade of global stock market greed, of beehived matrons meeting for weekly Jane Fonda workouts, of Corazon Aquino's People Power Revolution—was a new dawn for the Philippines. It was in that climate of moral contrasts that Salvador finally found the respect for which he'd intensely yearned. He published widely and often. His career peaked in 1987 with the publication of *Dahil Sa'Yo* (*Because of You*),§ an epic account of the Marcos dic-

---

Jour, Night, Vida, and *Amore* (New York: Grove Press, 1977–1981).
†*My Philippine Islands (with 80 colour plates)* (New York: Macmillan, 1980).
‡*Phili-Where?* (London: Faber and Faber, 1982).
§*Because of You* (New York: Random House, 1987).

tatorship that included a pointed indictment of the opportunistic cronies responsible for the couple's rise and fall, epitomized by Dingdong Changco, Jr.* Salvador re-created the tumultuous era through a mixture of press clippings, radio and TV transcripts, allegories, myths, letters, and vignettes from the various points of view of characters, factual and fictional, intended to represent Filipinos from all walks of life. The book spent two weeks at the bottom of the *New York Times* bestseller list; it was reprinted three times and translated into twelve languages. It earned acclaim abroad, and therefore also in the Philippines, and placed him on the long list for the 1988 Nobel Prize in Literature (he thereafter often said: "I'm the first and only Filipino to be in contention for a little award called the Nobel Prize for Literature").† The award went to Naguib Mahfouz.

Salvador, like other prolific writers of extraordinary breadth and reach, was well acquainted with such disappointments, as exemplified by the various publications that made the literati doubt his abilities. Critics consistently judged the less successful works to be long-winded, messianic, or derivative. (Avellaneda called his oeuvre "a dirty cistern filled with feces that has not been well formed. Objectively speaking, it's the sort of crap that sparks fears of outbreaks of amoebic dysentery.") The most memorable of these unmemorable works were: the 43,950-word essay *Tao (People)*,‡ which Salvador meant as "a catalogue and homage to the glorious diversity of our race, our rich customs, and our beautiful women"; *Filipiniana*,§ an ambitious but idiosyncratic survey of Philippine literature in English, which included most of Salvador's short works, but only one each from other writers; and an early book-length epic poem about Magellan's cartographer and translator, Antonio Pigafetta, entitled *Scholarly Plunder*.‖ Attempts to justify the latter in 1982 by transforming it into *All Around the World*, a disco opera, resulted in bankrupting failure.

---

*Dingdong Changco, Jr., sued for libel. Salvador famously told the court: "Whatever truths you find in my fiction are only universal ones." The book was banned in the Philippines after only 928 copies were sold nationally.
†Interview by Clinton Palanca, *The Paris Review*, winter 1991.
‡*Tao (People)* (Manila: Passepartout Publishing, 1988).
§*Filipiniana* (Quezon City: Ateneo de Manila University Press, 1990).
‖*Scholarly Plunder* (Manila: Ars Poetika, 1981).

What irked Salvador most—more even than Avellaneda calling his life abroad "a metaphor for an anonymous death"—was the critics' claim that *Because of You* was his literary swan song. And so began whispers about an epic book that had been in the works since the early 1980s: *The Bridges Ablaze*. But what Salvador published next surprised the country, establishing him as a much-read writer but giving credence to what local books columnists called his "flimsy literary prowess." *Manila Noir*,* the most popular of his crime novels, presented Antonio Astig, a swashbuckling mystery author investigating Jack the Ripper–style killings of pretty women from shantytowns (the real-life murders were a sensation in 1986 and '87: the police investigation was regarded as a sham and the murderer rumored to be a prominent "confirmed bachelor" politician). *The Bloody Sea*,† a five-hundred-page rip-roaring nautical saga set in the Philippines of the 1500s, pitted the dastardly Chinese pirate Limahong against the dashing Spanish captain Juan de Salcedo, and proved to be amazingly successful at home and in Britain. (The book, along with rumours of a sequel and prequel, fuelled, to Salvador's delight, public disdain from Patrick O'Brian.) And aiming to reach younger Filipinos, Salvador wrote the *Kaputol* (*Siblings*) trilogy,‡ a magic-infused offshoot of the YA tradition of Franklin W. Dixon. Following the adventures and coming of age of Dulcé, the tomboyish leader of a group of young boys in martial law–era Quezon City, the trilogy became his most enduring work, remembered and loved by a new generation of readers.

That period of his life, full of prolificacy but lacking in gravitas, plunged Salvador into a deep depression that made him lash out indiscriminately, though his behaviour during both defeat and success had long elicited eager mockery. His mania for collecting subjected him to accusations of being "a closet bourgeois." He famously wrote letters in purple ink, in grandiose longhand. With the advent of e-mail, to which he took early with extreme enthusiasm, he began sending long tirades to newspapers—intent on skirting the judg-

---

Manila Noir (Quezon City: University of the Philippines Press, 1990).
†*The Bloody Sea* (London: Chatto & Windus, 1992).
‡*Kapatid*, *QC Nights*, and *Ay Naku!* (Manila: Adarna House, 1987–1990).

ment of the editors of his column at *The Manila Times*—placing in his crosshairs such targets as our cultural crab mentality, or the hope that expatriate Filipinos will help rather than abandon their country, or the bad service at the Aristocrat restaurant and how in such an old institution it represented the passing of a more genteel society. The periodicals refused to run his missives, so he collected and self-published them in the book *All the News the Papers Are Afraid to Print.** Salvador's fastidiousness of manner also opened him to rumours of homosexuality, yet he was criticized for being a womanizer "with the lascivious energy usually found in defrocked clergymen." And he could never live down his 1991 TV commercial which showed him being served lunch in a book-lined study, shaking a cruet over his food before turning to the camera to deliver the now immortal words: "Silver Swan Soy Sauce, the educated choice."

On June 2, 1994, Salvador held a book launch at La Solidaridad Bookstore in Manila. The event had been wrapped in secrecy, and excited literary watchers expected *The Bridges Ablaze*. Salvador instead unveiled *Autoplagiarist*, yet another self-published book, a memoir that refracted through his life's story a history of the Philippines from the start of the Second World War to the end of the millennium. The 2,572-page volume, perhaps the most ambitious and certainly the most personal of his books, won him angry responses. One local critic said: "The Oedipal impulse was so ambrosial, [Salvador] fucked his father and killed his mother." Another said: "Dear old Crispin might have done better had he put his money where his mouth is and cleaned up Smokey Mountain [garbage dump]." Abroad, Salvador's literary agent could not sell *Autoplagiarist* to publishers, and even ultimately terminated their professional affiliation. Worst of all, the memoir's frankness destroyed what had long been a tenuous relationship with his family and friends at home. Salvador was suddenly a true exile. "You're lucky your parents are dead," he once told me. "The people who love you," he said, while moving his bishop to take my queen, "will only see their deficiencies in your work. That's the strength of good writing and the weakness

---

*Crispin Salvador, *All the News the Papers Are Afraid to Print* (Manila: Passepartout Publishing, 1993).

of the human ego. Love and honesty don't mix. To be an honest writer, you have to be away from home, and totally alone in life."

The cut ties saw Salvador settle permanently in New York, and inexorably into a period of deep silence. He dropped his newspaper column. He gave up writing. That he became well known as a teacher attests to his oh-so-very-Filipino resilience. As he said in "War & Piss" on many an occasion: "If life gives you lemons, have your maid make some lemonade."

Much of his life was apocryphal, so it may well be that this next bit was, too. Shortly after clipping the last review panning *Autopla-giarist* and pasting it into an album, Salvador went out by the Hudson River and burned the scrapbook, along with his diaries, in a public trash receptacle. It was in the wee hours of a summer night. Two policemen happened upon him while he was relieving himself into the conflagration. "I'm just trying to put it out," he told them. Salvador was taken downtown and charged with misdemeanours for drunkenness and public urination. The event was somehow reported in the Manila papers and elicited the habitual snickers from those who remembered him.

But it was in that fire, Salvador later told me, that he rediscovered what it is like to be intoxicated by your own anger, to find the solace of destruction. The following morning saw him returned to his desk with frightening intensity. He had retrieved, from a locked drawer, the three black cardboard boxes containing the unfinished manuscript of *The Bridges Ablaze*.

*

At the end of the first week of last February, Salvador left for home. The purpose of the visit, his first in years, was for him to accept the Dingdong Changco, Sr., Memorial National Literary Lifetime Recognition Prize, or, as it is widely known, the DCSMNLLR Prize. The afternoon he arrived in Manila, Salvador ate a late lunch at the Aristocrat restaurant before going to their comfort room to change clothes. In front of the mirror, he adjusted the collar of his formal barong and practised his speech. Outside it was raining heavily, and he took a taxi to the Cultural Center of the Philippines. The audience was composed of the old guard, mostly members and officers of

PALS, the Philippine Arts and Letters Society. They leaned back in their plastic monobloc chairs, smirking magnanimously, faces serene and satisfied, as if at a much-awaited funeral. (The DCSMNLLR Prize is historically given to writers at the end of their careers.) Salvador bounded up the steps onto the stage, shook hands, posed for a picture with PALS deputy vice president Furio Almondo, and stepped to the podium. He looked admiringly at his gold medal—an ornately filigreed circle made of sterling silver. He poured himself a glass of water and drank it. Finally, he spoke. "Literature," he declared, "is an ethical leap. It is a moral decision. A perilous exercise in constant failure. Literature should have grievances, because there are so many grievances in the world. Let us speak frankly, because we're all peers here. Your grievances with me are because you say I have failed. Though I only failed because I extended myself further than what any of you have ever attempted." The boos and jeers came suddenly, then peaked savagely, as at a crucifixion. "I accept this award," Salvador continued, shouting to be heard, "ahead of what I will achieve. Next year, I will publish my long-awaited book. Then you will see the truth of our shared guilt." The boos and jeers turned into laughter. "History is changed by martyrs who tell the tru—" The microphone was disconnected.

The author walked through the audience and out of the CCP building. When there was nobody to see him, he began to run, splashing headlong into the torrential rain. He caught a flight out that evening—just missing the unseasonable supertyphoon that would flood vast swaths of the city—and returned to New York via Narita, Detroit, and Newark. I saw him the morning of his arrival, the day before Valentine's Day, when I rushed to his apartment on the pretense of dropping off a folderful of students' essays from his missed classes. He was seated in his study, bedraggled but radiant, banging away at his typewriter. It sounded like machine-gun fire. He had not even bothered to change out of his ruined barong. Beside him, there it was: yesterday's *Philippine Sun*, turned to the deaths and births page. Though the paper's website had run an erratum, blaming an intern for accidentally running Crispin's from their stock of prepared obituaries, you could almost hear the self-satisfied chuckles swooping in on the westerly tradewinds. I didn't know how Crispin had taken it, so I asked if he'd had a good flight. And what had got him all fired up. Crispin smiled at me brightly. "Death," he said, "in Manila. I apparently have nothing more to lose."

That was the second-to-the-last time I saw him.

Then silence too soon for one whose most pernicious enemy was silence.

If our greatest fear is to sink away alone and unremembered, the brutality that time will inflict upon each of us will always run stronger than any river's murky waves. This book therefore shoulders the weighty onus of relocating a man's lost life and explores the possible temptations that death will always present. The facts, shattered, are gathered, for your deliberation, like a broken mirror whose final piece has been forced into place.

—Miguel Syjuco, en route to Manila, December 1, 2002

1

A battered wooden chest in the bedroom, its inlay shedding, its key finally found in a locked desk drawer. Inside: A recent diary (orange suede cover, hand-burnished a smooth caramel [inside: translations, riddles, jokes, poems, notes, other]). First editions (*Autoplagiarist*, *Red Earth*, *The Collected Fictions*, *The Enlightened*, et cetera). A dilapidated overnight suitcase (white Bakelite handle; stickers from hotels long shuttered [the lock is forced open with a table knife: the scent of pencil shavings and binding glue, a sheaf of photographs {slouching at the edges}, his sister's childhood diaries held together by a crumbling rubber band, pregnant manila envelopes {transcripts, newspaper clippings, red-marked drafts of stories, official documents <birth certificate, vaccination records, expired passports, et cetera>}, a canvas portfolio {charcoal, graphite, ink sketches <horses, facades, portraits, cutlery>}, a battered set of Russian nesting dolls {the innermost missing}, other assorted miscellany {a Parker Vacumatic fountain pen, inherited medals from the Second World War, a lock of amber hair, et cetera}]).

*

My friend and mentor was quite alive the night before. The door cracked open, only his nose and eye visible. "I'm sorry," he said. "I'm sorry." The blue door clicked shut, unapologetically. The dead bolt slid in with a finality I did not at the time recognize. I left and had a bacon cheeseburger without him, irritated by his uncharacteristic rudeness.

What could I have said to him? Should I have forced open the door? Slapped him twice across the face and demanded he tell me what was wrong? Days, weeks later, all the fragments still would not click together. The events seemed unreal, confusing. Some nights I'd tiptoe quietly out of bed, cautious not to wake Madison and risk igniting her anger; I'd sit on the couch, deep in thought until the sky turned lilac. Both suicide and murder seemed like two sides of the same prime-time seduction. In retrospect, this was healthy for me to feel. Clichés remind and reassure us that we're not alone, that others have trod this ground long ago. Still, I could not understand why the world chose to take the easy way out: to write him off simply, then go home to watch TV shows with complicated plots. Maybe that's the habit of our age.

Then, at four weeks after Crispin's death, I was telephoned by his sister (her voice as thin and pale as a piece of string) and asked to divest his life's possessions; I entered his musty apartment as if it were a crypt.

At four months, I found myself unable to sleep at night; I'd sit and listen to Madison's breathing, thinking, for some reason, of the parents I never got to know, and how I missed Crispin, with his stupid fedora and strong opinions.

At six months, I began Crispin's biography; the long hours in the library, the idea that his life could help me with mine, somehow kept me sane.

At eight months and one week, Madison left me for good; I hoped she'd call but she didn't.

Late in the night of November 15, 2002, nine months to the day after Crispin's death, I was watching my in box for any e-mail from Madison. With a bing, three new messages appeared. The first was from Baako.Ainsworth@excite.com. It said, in part: "Sharpen your love-sword rubadub soundess. Help that breeds arousal victories. How to last longer making love and have more feelings." The second was from trancejfq22@skaza.wz.cz. It said, in part: "GET DIPLOMA TODAY!If you're looking for a fast way to next level,(non accredited) this is the way out for you." The third e-mail was about to be trashed when I noticed who sent it. The message said, in part: "Dear Sire/Madame . . . I was informed by our lawyer, Clupea Rubra, that my daddy, who at the time was government whistleblower and head of family fortune, called him, Clupea Rubra, and conducted him round his flat and show to him three black cardboard boxes. Along the line, my daddy died mysteriously, and Government has been after us, molesting, policing, and freezing our bank accounts. Your heroic assist is required in replenishing my father's legacy and masticating his despicable murderers. More information TBA." The sender was crispin1037@elsalvador.gob.sv. I brought up a blank message to respond. I wrote: "Crispin?" The cursor winked at me. I hit "send" and waited.

The next morning, I bought my plane ticket.

*

See the boy getting on an airplane. He's not a young boy, but a boyish man, as he would describe himself. He sits in his middle seat, notebook open, pen in hand, en route to Manila (I almost wrote "home," he thinks with a smile). It is a trip he hates, both the voyage and arrival. He writes at this moment, "the limbo between outposts of humanity."

As the airplane is towed backward, he thinks of what he is leaving. Thinks of his lost friend and mentor, seated at the typewriter, working away in a slow accrual of letters, words, sentences, puzzling together pieces shed like bread crumbs on the path behind him.

The boy will return, heartbroken, lonely, dejected. His three brothers and two sisters are all abroad, free from home—atop a hill in San Francisco, washed under the big Vancouver sky, hidden amid the joyful noise of New York City. His parents, whom he cannot remember, are in graves he cannot bring himself to visit because he knows their bodies are not there. The grandparents, who raised him as best they could, are in Manila, though he no longer has contact with them because of the emotional violence of their last departure. He is coming home, though he doesn't dare admit it. He knows well what empty houses are and the mischief memories can play when cast among unfamiliar echoes.

In the long hours spent in the airplane, he tries not to think about how his parents died, and therefore that is all he can think of. He flips through the Philippine newspapers, obsessively. He studies his files of notes, clippings, drafts. He unscrews the fountain pen he took from his dead friend's possessions. Tries to write the prologue for Eight Lives Lived, *the biography he wants to write about his mentor. He fidgets. Thinks. Observes his fellow passengers. Judges everyone, in the traditional Filipino sport of justifying both personal and shared insecurities. He reads some more, searching for a point of reference in a world that has never felt entirely his. He writes some more, trying to explain things to himself. He scribbles an asterisk.*

*

Salvador was born to Leonora Fidelia Salvador in a private room at the Mother of Perpetual Help Hospital in Bacolod. Present were his eight-year-old sister, Magdalena (nicknamed Lena), his six-year-old brother, Narciso the Third (shortened to Narcisito), and their yaya, Ursie (no record of her real name). Their father, Narciso Lupas Salvador II, known to family and friends as Junior, was aboard the De La Rama Steamship Company's M/V *Don Esteban*, en route from Manila, where he had been engaged with the Commonwealth Congress.

The newest Salvador came into the third generation of family wealth, acquired through a blend of enterprise, sugar, politics, and celebrated stinginess. The four years before the Japanese invaded would prove formative: throughout his life the familial roots in the Visayan region represented something promising and pure.

—from the biography in progress, *Crispin Salvador:*
Eight Lives Lived, by Miguel Syjuco

*

. . . eyewitnesses reported two explosions, the second occurring thirty seconds after the first, both on the third floor of McKinley Plaza Mall in Makati. According to a spokesperson for the Lupas Land Corporation, there were no fatalities. No group has claimed responsibility for the . . .

—from *Philippine-Gazette.com.ph*, November 19, 2002

*

INTERVIEWER:

You wrote in the late 1960s, "Filipino writing must be the conquest of our collective self divorced from those we fear are watching." Do you still think this true?

CS:

I used to believe authenticity could be achieved solely by describing, in our own words, one's own fragment of experience. This was of course predicated on the complete intellectual and aesthetic independence of the "I." One eventually realizes such intellectual isolationism promotes style, ego, awards. But not change. You see, I toiled, but saw so little improving around me. What were we sowing? I grew impatient with the social politics that literature could address and alter but had until that time been insufficient in so doing. I decided to actively solicit participation—you know, incite readers to action through my work. I think of the effect of José Rizal's books in our own revolution against Spain a century ago. I think of the poetry of Eman Lacaba, who traded his pen for a gun and lived and died in the jungles with the communists in the seventies. "The barefoot army in the wilderness," his famous poem called them. The epigraph of that piece was wonderful. Ho Chi Minh. "A poet must also learn how to lead an attack."

INTERVIEWER:

Was there something that made you want to lead that attack?

CS:

Pride and fear of death. Truly. You smile but I kid you not.

INTERVIEWER:

Your return to the polemical is a criticism often cited. Did you . . .

CS:

It's viewed as two steps backward. Erroneously. When you reach farther and farther, sometimes you come full circle. The task then becomes all the more difficult, false steps more likely—though the eventual outcome may become more pertinent. This of course opens you up to accusations of being quixotic or, worse—or perhaps better—messianic. Mind you, pretension and ambition are different words for the same thing. Truly, it's the artist's—the true artist's—desire for causality that trips critics up.

—from a 1991 interview in *The Paris Review*

*

Three more hours until I arrive. At Manila. I almost said "at home."

It's a trip I hate, both the voyage and the arrival, the limbo between outposts of humanity. Remember when air travel was fun? Toy pilot wings and smiling stewardesses showing you the massive cockpit? Now they separate us from our valuables and herd us through security gates, shoeless and anxious; they scare us with tales of deep-vein thrombosis; they pack us in like animals, then run Keanu Reeves on screens on the seat backs to lull us into a squirming stupor. Soon after we fall asleep, they wake us. I bet anyone who is still a Marxist has never had an economy-class middle seat on a packed long-haul flight like this one.

Around me, in this tin can, my fellow travellers: we, the acquiescent, unaware insurrectionists; we who have left and returned so constantly throughout history our language has given us a name—balikbayan. Sloped-shouldered we are, freighted by absence; our hand-carries bulging with items that wouldn't fit in overweight luggage, all the countless gifts for countless relatives—proof our time away has not been wasted.

These are my people. (Crispin once called them the "splay-toed, open-hearted.") Beside me, a stocky, sturdy man in an acid-wash denim jacket and a slipping eyeshade, his head thrown back to snore efficaciously. Likely a construction worker, one of the millions-strong diaspora indentured by the persuasiveness of dreams. To my other side, two older ladies, sisters by the look of them, fidget and flip through the inflight magazine for the sixteenth time. Their inflatable pillows around their necks remind me of yokes on water buffalo, if that's not too obvious a metaphor. One has a rosary wrapped around one hand. With the other, she turns the pages to the photographs. Her sister complains she's going too fast. Across the aisle, a petite Filipina with towering shoes rests her blond head on the shoulder of a Texas-big American, his glasses low on his wedgelike nose, reading Dale Carnegie in a pool of light. A snake-and-dagger tattoo slithers up his forearm. Behind sits a spry, elderly Caucasian, his white hair, warm-up jacket, and khakis rumpled in the fashion of intrepid Jesuits or vacationing pedophiles. To his side, a duet of tirelessly gossiping domestic helpers continue their nine-hour run. Their heads, wrapped in eyeshades that hold back their hair, peck at morsels of hyperbole, like pigeons at rice dropped on the pavement of park promenades every Sunday, day off to the maids who flock by the thousands in the big cities of the world. I've twice heard about what Minda did to Linda and thrice cringed at the horrible thing Dottie said to Edilberto. I took notes, smiled, when I heard one complain: "She stabbed me in the back and my back wasn't even turned." The women's bluster and brusqueness are crystallized by years of servitude, unconvincing confidence, irreconcilable distance from the things to which they once clung closely.

I myself didn't see what Crispin had become to me until he was gone. My own lolo, Grapes, had been always too remote, the way grandfathers often are, to make up for my father's death. He was hardly more than a ghostly silhouette I'd glimpse through the glass doors of his home office, writing letters at his desk or reading ribbons of paper from his telex until mealtime, when he'd come to the table and kid with me. The jokes had always seemed forced, and I laughed because I yearned for a connection. I keep telling myself nobody's to blame. They'd already raised their children. By some accounts, they failed even in that. And suddenly they have six more. New orphans from Manila, shipped wholesale to Vancouver, disrupting my grandparents' premature retirement—an exile which they had just learned to love.

Maybe the Filipino sounds in our English phrases, or the different ways we each looked like my father, reminded my grandparents too much of the life they had before the institution of martial law that drove Grapes from politics at the height of his career, that deprived Granma of her mahjong parties and battalion of maids, that turned them both into just another couple of doddering slant-eyed fools moving too slowly in the soup-cereal-baking aisle of Safeway. I had just turned five when we six arrived. My grandparents tried their best, gave up the small home they had built, moved into an ugly McMansion, hired a nanny to help with us. Grapes and Granma were intent on Canadianizing us, to prepare us for the melting pot into which we'd been thrown, and they prohibited us from speaking Tagalog lest we never master English. Even they cast off their traditional names, adopting my little brother's mangling of "gramps" and "grandmom": the man we knew as Lolo in the Philippines became Grapes ("sour," he liked to say); Lola became Granma ("Like the boat that ferried Castro's rebels"). As we all came to discover the limitations of assimilation, we grew closer as a family. I remember one time, after school, Granma and I stopped at St. Thomas's to light a candle, as she did daily, for all souls gone and present and not yet born. A man sat up suddenly in a pew and started shouting at us. "Go back home, you gooks!" He must have been drunk or crazy, though at the time I didn't know such distinctions. "We're not gooks" was all my grandmother could say. "We're Filipinos." On the drive back to our house, Granma was quiet, ignoring my questions, as if I'd done something wrong.

I also remember, years later, us six kids with our grandparents in front of the TV. Dinner on the table had long gone cold as we watched images of Edsa Boulevard thronged with people in yellow T-shirts, praying and singing, nuns linking arms to stop armoured personnel carriers, a young girl placing a flower in the rifle barrel of a soldier who was struggling not to smile. The CBS anchorman was saying: "This could be as close as the twentieth century has come to the storming of the Bastille. But what's remarkable is how little violence there has been." A small woman in glasses was shown talking to the people. "That's Cory Aquino," Grapes explained to us. The anchorman continued: "We Americans like to think we taught the Filipinos democracy. Well, tonight, they're teaching the world." Helicopters land and soldiers join the singing masses, everyone smiling. Then Granma said, tears in her eyes: "We can go home."

I've been old enough for a long time, but only now do I begin to understand. Around me on the plane, I hear what she meant: the sing-song of Ilonggo from the aisle seat nearby, the molasses accent reminding me of the way my grandmother said things. From farther down comes the clunking consonance of Ilocano by the lavatories, Bicolano by the bulkhead. A stewardess is speaking Tagalog to an elderly fellow, a man the age of my own grandfather, telling him all the places she's been to. He nods at each, as if he's been there, too. Maybe these people are coming home to make a difference. Maybe I can be like them.

My seatmates glance at me as if I were a foreigner. I save my Tagalog words for the proper time, to surprise them with what we share. Their accented imperfections remind me of my own, like that time in class, my first day at Columbia, when I pronounced "annals of history" as "anals of history" and how I'd wanted to flee the room, though nobody had seemed to notice. I eavesdrop on my countrymen, on their tentative English spoken to the cabin crew, never quite perfected despite years in the West: f's still often traded for *p*'s, vowels rounded, tenses mixed, syllables clipped—only the well-practiced Western colloquialisms wielded with conviction. Like those phrases, we're a collection of clichés, handy types worn as uniforms over our naked individuality. We are more real than that philosophical conceit of humanity as the milieu of light: we are the milieu of sweat. Our industriousness, our inexpensiveness, two sides of our great national image. That image the tangible form of our communal desire for a better life. Someone kicks the back of my seat as a reminder to quit being so profound.

On my left, my seatmate has long capitulated in the battle for the armrest (involving my performing many a subterfuge and feint, about which he didn't even know), and I relish my elbow's lebensraum. When I tell the stewardess my meal choice, I feel my neighbour observing me from the corner of his eye. He chooses differently, oppositely. When our food is passed down and unwrapped, I immediately regret my beef and covet his chicken. I slather my hands with alcohol disinfectant gel. My neighbour looks at me and smiles. I pass him my little bottle and he cleans his hands as well. Then he nonchalantly puts the bottle in his breast pocket. We eat our rectangles of food as if our elbows are fused to our sides. I pretend to be deep in thought and stare into the darkened screen of the TV in front me.

On my agenda, visit Crispin's childhood home.

Interview his sister and aunt.

Investigate those names found in his notes: Changco. Reverend Martin. Bansamoro. Avellaneda. Dulcinea.

Sift through the ashes of the bridges that he burned.

Reassemble his many lives.

I know when we touch down in Manila my fellow passengers will all clap at the pilot's landing skills. I know they will all jump, the plane still taxiing, to claim possessions from overhead compartments. I know a voice will reprimand them over the public address system and peeved stewardesses will swat at their upraised hands and shut the compartment doors. Always the same. That's good, isn't it? These fellow travellers have logged thousands more miles than most in the world, hugging hello and goodbye, working and saving, remitting money each payday, writing letters on onionskin paper to save on postage, telling their clan they'll soon be home, finally; they'll arrive unrecognized by unrecognizable children, to spouses whose kisses have become ostensible and indebted. It's like that aphorism of Ovid's that Crispin once shared with me: Everything changes, nothing ends.

Me, I'll arrive to nothing. That's really how I prefer it.

*

He doesn't know what he prefers. When the pretty stewardess rolls up with the drink cart, he wants a ginger ale but orders a "triple" Scotch. Drinks on international flights, you see, are free. Thrilled like a child at having his own screen on the seat back in front of him, he forces himself to stay awake to catch up on the latest Keanu Reeves movie. As the end credits roll, he tastes that exasperation we all know after we've prostrated two hours of our lives to be pillaged. Again and again he pilgrimages to the rear galley, to avail himself of free ice cream bars and tiny bags of snacks. He turns on his overhead light, tentatively, worried it will glare and awaken his neighbours. He reads the in-flight magazine. In an article about Bali, the photographs of Eurasian girls in day-glow bikinis lounging on white sand and triangular silk pillows excite him visibly, and he squirms beneath his seat belt and holds the magazine strategically, feeling as if he were thirteen and not twenty-six. He looks around. A few rows down there's a sexy Hong Kong Chinese girl he'd wanted to help stow her backpack as they filed into the plane. But he didn't have the guts, and so he stood in the aisle and waited for her to finish doing it herself, surreptitiously studying her ass and the way her shirt rode up to reveal the tempting concavities above her waist. He cranes his head to see her now. He thinks, Something about cabin pressure makes me horny. He blames the long-haul boredom. Eroticism, after all, exists to break life's monotony. What if—he thinks—she feels the same as me? What if I just took her hand and brought her to the lavatory? The worst she could do is say no. He looks over but cannot see her. He does spot her naked foot sticking out from where she's tucked it under her leg and her armrest. He marvels at its rabbitlike beauty. Madison had manly feet. I haven't touched another person in so long. The way Madison held him when they made love often seemed his main purpose for sex. It was like hands slowly being washed in warm water—needful, complete, and it cleansed him of that one thing he kept secret from her.

He rubs his stubbly chin, a silent-film villain deep in thought, and his watch reflects a locus of light that flies onto the walls, the seat backs, the faces of his slumbering seatmates. He covers his wrist, worrying his neighbours will see the crown insignia, wondering if they'll think it a Mong Kok fake. He examines it in the light. His grandfather had given it to him on his twenty-first birthday. This was years after the whole family had returned to the Philippines, years after things had begun to curdle, years after his grandfather had returned to his politics and his women. Stainless steel, pearlescent white face, Oyster Perpetual DateJust. His grandfather has one exactly like it. Almost. The boy's is a counterfeit, even if premium—real bevelled crystal rather than flat Perspex, but with Rado interior works. His grandfather had courageously followed a toothpick-chomping dealer, who he'd said reminded him of a hissing lizard, down an alleyway off Tung Choi Street and up three flights of narrow ramshackle stairs, to fork over two hundred U.S. dollars for the most real fake ever seen. A dedication to his grandson was later engraved on the back, and because of that the boy has treasured it. That and the savoury memory of lost family dinners when the two would unclasp watches and trade and compare and marvel. The boy for so long now has passed his off as genuine that even he has forgotten and has allowed himself, along with everyone else, to be fooled.

*

He bursts in, like a bomb, the pearl handle of his Midnight Special glinting. "It is I," he shouts, "Antonio Astig. Reach for the stars!" But the room is already empty. The window open, its panel swinging tauntingly. He crosses the room like a hungry tiger suddenly uncaged at lunchtime. Looking outside, on España Boulevard, he sees Dominador's bald head bobbing below. He is swimming across the flooded street to a stranded flatbed truck. Dominador fights desperately against the raging current, debris hitting him at nearly every armstroke. Antonio hears shouts of men from behind him, the clatter of their shoes running up the stairs, down the hall. The police! Antonio leaps out the window and into the flood. The water tastes like the tears of all Dominador's virgin victims. When he surfaces, he sees Dominador on the back of the truck, cutting the ropes of a tarp with his footlong switchblade knife. Above Antonio, police crowd the window, aim their pistols at him. He dips below, swimming like a shark. In the murky water, their bullets cruise past him like torpedoes. He surfaces in time to see Dominador pushing a yellow-and-red Jet Ski off the truck. Its engine roars like a grizzly and Dominador speeds away, weaving through the stranded cars and jeepneys. Antonio spots a second Jet Ski on the truck. He swims toward it. Bullets zip by. They make popping sounds into the water. Antonio pulls himself onto the truck. In a single motion he pushes the Jet Ski off and starts it. He speeds over the flood-water, the wind fresh on his face. Through foggy shop windows, panicked people watch the commotion. As Antonio blurs past, he gives them his most winning smile.

—from Manila Noir (page 53), by Crispin Salvador

*

E-mail from me to Crispin: Gee whiz, Mr. Wilson! I can't help but think Madison could've paid me half what she paid her therapists to diagnose her borderline personality disorder. It kills me how these days everyone has clinical justification for their strangeness. My lolo was recently diagnosed with Freudian narcissism. He then had his secretary do research on the Net. Instead of finding all the bad in it, of course he saw only the good. "All great leaders are narcissists," he exclaimed to my grandmother. So rather than buy all the books about how the disorder can be overcome, and how they hurt the people around them, he bought *The Victorious Narcissist*—a book about the triumphant qualities of Nero, Napoleon, Hitler, Saddam, etc. Hell, Grapes even bought a copy to give to President Estregan as a Christmas gift. LOL! Wonder how he'll take it. Don't get me wrong, I'm not angry with my grandfather. To be angry implies you care. I just feel sorry for him. Anyway, I'll be late for our bacon-cheeseburger date. You'll have to tell me the gory details of your trip home and that speech at the CCP. I'm dying of curiosity.

*

"Fittingly, my father's name was Narciso," Salvador wrote in *Auto-plagiarist*. "At one time, somewhere in the lineage before him, the name possessed the tragedy of the myth and the irony that such a name could be possessed by such a man so distinctly unnarcissistic. Upon my father, however, all such nuance had been lost: it was as if to him the name was bespoke, and the very act of christening him 'Narciso' authored a parody of a sacred sacrament, wherein one is named for his essence, for that worst characteristic by which he would be forever remembered. In fact, he is belittled further as 'Ju-

nior,' in that unabashed, and strangely Filipino, habit of giving ignominious nicknames. A self-fulfilling prophecy: try as he did, he was
damned forever to be the tiny narcissus."

—from the biography in progress, *Crispin Salvador:
Eight Lives Lived*, by Miguel Syjuco

*

"You're the most handsome of all my grandchildren," Grapes would
often tell me. I never knew how to reply, so I smiled the smile of a
shy child basking in attention. I of course didn't believe him. I was
afraid to.

"You are the most handsome because you're the one who looks
most like me," he'd say. Then: "What do you want to be when you
grow up?"

"The sergeant of the army."

Grapes laughed, amused to no end. "Not the president of the
Philippines?"

"Whichever is higher."

"I'll be president," he'd say, "and you can be the sergeant of
the army."

He would pick me up with an exaggerated grunt and carry me
to my own bed. He smelled of Old Spice and pipe tobacco, which, I
realize now, are more of those comforting clichés. But that's really
what he smelled like.

"All right, Sarge," he would say, tucking me in. It became his
pet name for me. We all had them, his private names that made us
each his unique grandchild. Jesu was "Groovy." Claire was "Reina."
Mario was "Smiley." Charlotte was "Princessa." Jerald was "The
Plum." I was Sarge. Maybe it's not "was" but "is." I don't know.

A lifetime later, Madison would call me "Beauty." She'd look at
me in bed, touch my face with her fingertips, as if afraid of breaking
it, and she'd tell me: "You are a beautiful man." I of course believed
her. I was afraid not to.

Every night, under the covers, her foot would be pressed against
mine. We always wanted to spoon but, because of my troublesome
cervical curve and my orthopedic pillow, I had to lie on my back if I
didn't want neck pain the next day. We touched feet through the

night, a gesture of reassurance that we'd stand together through the darkest.

"I love you," I'd say.

"I love you, too."

"Do you love me more than I love you?"

"Yeah."

"Good," I'd say, sliding into the edge of sleep. "See you in a minute."

"G'night," she'd say. "In our dreams then."

I never told her that I don't have dreams or can't remember whether I do.

*

From Marcel Avellaneda's blog, "The Burley Raconteur," February 14, 2002:

Happy Valentine's all! But let's get to the point: The nerve of that Salvador, no?! The biggest sin a Pinoy can commit is arrogance. Yes, dear readers, you may have already heard the latest literary scuttlebutt about our former comrade and compatriot Crispin's most recent visit to our shores. Last Friday's awards ceremony at the Cultural Center of the Philippines was marred when his acceptance speech turned into a tirade against our literature and a threat to publish something that would "lop your heads off." How we'd hoped he'd mellowed. How I'd hoped my old friend would return humbled by failures. Autoplagiarist? (He should have ripped off from someone else.) There is a time and place for everything, my dear old Crisp. Haven't you learned that by now? For those interested, literary blogger Plaridel3000 has posted a clip of Salvador's speech on his weblog here.

Some posts from the message boards below:

—Wat a twatface that Salvador is! Lets c wat his so-called *The Bridges Ablaze* has 2 say. I herd it hits at the Lupases, Changcos, Arroyos, Syjucos, Estregans, among others. (Bethloggins2010@getasia.com.ph)

—It's sooo sad a man like Salvador has lost himself to hubris. Shouldn't literature do more than just criticize? Goes to show he doesn't have the answers. (kts@ateneo.edu.ph)

—LOL! More power to you, Marcel! Lop the head off that commie. IMHO, he's in with the Muslims for sure. (Miracle@Lourdes.ph)

—Hey, kts@ateneo, I think you are correct. But in fairness, do any of us have answers? (halabira@pldt.ph)

—Love dat clip of his speech. Hilarious. Check out the yellow armpit stains in his barong! (fashionista@dlsu.edu.ph)

—How do you get rid of pit stains like that anyway? My bf has stains like that. (edith@werbel.com)

—Dilute a T-spoon vinegar in cup of water, den apply carefuly w/ basting brush. Should work gr8. Ur wlcm! (doiturself@preview.ph)

—Halabira, I hab d answr to r cuntry's probs: just kill d rich & reboot d systm. (gundamlover@hotmail.com)

—Gundamlover, that's been tried before. See: en.wikipedia.org/Khmer_Rouge. (theburleyraconteur@avellaneda.com)

*

Out of the corner of my eye, I look at my seatmate again. His head is nodding, slumping away from me. My little bottle of alcogel peeks from his breast pocket. My hand hovers to fish it out. I decide against it. Instead, I try to sleep. I try not to think of Madison.

In the month before Crispin died, it got to a point that being with Madison was like walking naked around a cactus with your eyes closed. She even began questioning my long hours spent at Crispin's apartment. She liked to alternate her homoerotic suspicions with accusations of literary mercenariness. "Why don't you like hanging out with people your age, Miguel?" she asked, in the implying, opinionated manner of beautiful women not blessed with big breasts. When I recounted to her my interest in his work, and, later, after he died, my eventual dream of writing his biography, she accused me of sounding like a young naive version of Bellow's Charlie Citrine. That was one of the lovers' things Madison and I did, our own affectation of Atlantic academia: we referenced fictional characters as if they were people to learn from. As if real-life people were too nebulous, too private and unreal for us to understand. We liked to believe there is an alternate world, a better world, populated entirely by characters created by the yearnings of humanity— governing and inspiring themselves with all the lucidity with which we rendered them. We posited such a world to be an afterlife for the monumentally great and flawed men and women of history, because Julius Caesar is as real to us as Holden Caulfield, Pol Pot is as alive as Judas Iscariot. Madison had just finished *Humboldt's Gift*. Like Citrine, Madison said, I ceaselessly rationalized my relationship with my dead writer friend, before finally admitting that "the dead owe us a living." I don't remember what happened in Bellow's book, but in Crispin's case I believe it is the living who owe the dead. The debt inside ourselves, as we Filipinos say. My biography of Crispin will be an indictment of my country, of time, of our forgetful, self-centred humanity. I can hear Madison now: "Oh, how wonderfully romantic of you. Romantics are really only in love with themselves."

*

Christened Crispin, after the patron saint of cobblers, the eight-pound two-ounce baby was brought from the hospital three days later to the family estate at Swanee, to much fanfare. Hand-painted canvas banners had been strung up at the gate. Dozens of farmworkers lined the gravel drive, straw hats pressed solemnly against their chests as they craned their necks to glimpse the child through the windows of the silver Packard. Some of them had undone their neckerchiefs and waved them like makeshift flags. As the vehicle passed, a whistle blew and on cue the workers tossed up cheers and hats that flew in the family's wake. The car pulled up to the two-story manor, and the household staff in their cream uniforms, lined up in order of importance from the mayordoma down to the stable boy, erupted in applause. Leonora stepped out from the car, reached in to take Salvador from Ursie, and proudly showed him off. Pink cheeks were touched, the bridge of his nose pinched again and again, and his already thick head of fine blond hair caressed admiringly. They marvelled at his hazel eyes. Until he reached the age of four, two years after his hair darkened to brown and into the first months of the war, Salvador's nickname among the staff would still be "Golden." When those who'd called him that had fled to their own families or had became casualties of the fighting, the name was forgotten and Salvador himself would not know of it until he was finally an adult.
—from the biography in progress, *Crispin Salvador: Eight Lives Lived*, by Miguel Syjuco

*

Here's a memento I took, out of the only frame on Crispin's desk. An old four-by-five in sepia: in front of the Salvador ancestral home outside Bacolod. From left to right (all squinting in the sun): Ursie, short and stout; reedlike Lena in her school uniform; tousled Narcisito holding his toy glider; Crispin, almost too big for his perambulator; the punctiliously attired Mortimer J. Gladstone, their Bostonian tutor; in the background, walking beside the rosebushes, his face hidden in the shade of his straw hat, Yataro, the Japanese gardener.

*

"You sure you'll remember everything we've said? Cristobal, are you listening?"

He doesn't reply. He picks up his watch from the desk and looks at it. "The train to Barcelona leaves in three-quarters of an hour," he says. He winds his watch until it can't wind anymore. He tries to attach the chain but has a hard time. After a few moments he gets it right and slips the watch into the pocket of his waistcoat.

Yciar gets up from the bed. She picks up the silk robe off the floor and pulls it around her. Cristo watches her silhouetted against the thin, bright lines of sunlight coming through the shutters. They look like gashes on her, on everything.

She walks barefoot across the room and stands on his feet. She holds him around his waist. They waltz a few steps.

"I'm sure," he says.

"Think of me when you're on the boat."

"I'll have my letters sent here when we berth at Port Said. Then when I transfer at Hong Kong. And of course the minute I land at Manila."

"You belong here. Not there."

"I know," he says.

She studies his face and seems guilty. She looks down. When she looks up again she is smiling. She straightens his cravat. "No. I know. You must rush home, to that hospital to care for your mother and sister. It's your duty now." She stretches up to kiss the bottom of his chin. "You'll arrive in time to usher in 1895. Promise not to forget me. Being remembered is all anyone can ask from a lost love. I'll remember you, *Don* Cristobal Narciso Patricio Salvador." She laughs at the length of his name. "Cristo," she says. "You look nothing like a patriarch." She pinches his nose. "Even a new one."

"I'll come back," he says.

"Before you go," she says, reaching up on tiptoes to whisper in his ear. Her voice is so gentle he can barely hear her. "Before you go, I have to tell you a secret."

—from The Enlightened (page 52), by Crispin Salvador

*

My seatmate finally asks to borrow my copy of The Philippine Gazette. He'd been eyeing it for hours. I take it from the seat pocket in front of me. He opens it and begins to leaf. Tsk-tsk, he says, shaking his head. He nudges my elbow off the armrest and points at a particular article. Two more suicide bombings, just this morning. This time down south, in Mindanao. Six dead, twelve injured by the first blast, at a Lotto outlet in front of the city hall in General Santos City. Most were municipal employees wagering just-cashed salaries. The second blast was at a children's birthday party in a McDonald's in the Lupas Landcorp's Cotabato Plaza Mall, leaving nine primary-school students dead, six others wounded. No one has asserted responsibility. The Estregan administration suspects various groups: the Abu Sayyaf of Mindanao, the Moro Islamic Liberation Front, the Indonesia-based Jemma Islamiah, the Middle East's Al Qaeda. The bombings are assumed to be retaliation for the coalition-led invasion of Afghanistan, of which President Fernando Valdez Estregan has made us a part. I look at my seatmate and shake my head at the article. Then I pretend to go to sleep.

A minute later, I hear him chuckling. I peek with one eye. He's reading the article about the "trial of the century." I recall seeing that case online. Even I was shocked by the not-guilty verdict received by the Filipino-Chinese couple, who killed their maid by forcing her to drink Clorox Spring Flowers bleach. The maid was minding their son when he drowned in the bathtub. She had been busy text-messaging. It wasn't the sensationalism of the trial that got my attention. I hate lowbrow tabloid junk. I only clicked on the link that once, because the family involved was named Changco. I thought they might have been related to Dingdong Changco, Jr., who was supposed to figure prominently in TBA. It turned out the family in the trial was of no relation. If they had been, they wouldn't be in this mess.

In fact, the trial of the century kept getting bigger until the media was calling it "the trial of the millennium." In the weeks following, articles teased out the fact that the couple offered a large sum to the presiding judge. The couple claimed he took it; the judge denied acceptance. The Changcos threatened to sue. Investigators confirmed a withdrawal of two million pesos had been made by the couple, though not a centavo surfaced in the accounts of the judge. Blogs poked fun at how Mr. Changco said at a press-con: "Now we are out two million pesos." The myopic-looking Mrs. Changco quickly followed with: "And our youngest son is dead."

But then the case turned into something almost mythical. Following the trial, the boyfriend of the murdered maid, a security guard named Wigberto Lakandula, also formerly employed by the family, vowed "violent vengeance." A day later, Mr. and Mrs. Changco returned home to find their three prizewinning Chihuahuas beheaded in the living room of their gated home. In the past couple of weeks, the love-and-retribution story has turned Lakandula into an unwitting celebrity—as soon as the media learned that he had wooed his now dead beloved by writing songs for her and playing them on his guitar, he became a national heartthrob. Photographs of him were bought by tabloids and pop magazines at exorbitant prices. My seatmate is looking at a photo of Lakandula as a construction worker in Saudi Arabia, shirtless and muscled, leaning against a front-end loader. His smile is bright, his hard hat askew on his thick shock of black hair. Lakandula is, the caption says, currently in hiding, "a fugitive from the long arm of the law."

*

Unable to sleep, I return to my notes. Among them are slips of paper filled with jokes, some in my handwriting. Crispin was obsessed with our oral traditions and doubly infatuated with translating Filipino humour into English. He called jokes "our true shared history," "our sweetly bitter commentary."

"Jokes are the hardest things to translate," he said. "There is a danger in not getting it right. For example, capturing how the deprecation is in actuality self-deprecation."

"You really think so?" I countered. "I think we're just mean."

"No. It's not divisive. The act of hearing a familiar punch line, the ensuing moan of corniness, that's all unifying. Jokes are as palliative as a proverb," he said. "Without them, we wouldn't understand ourselves."

And so it became a habit for Crispin and me to trade these well-worn classics, particularly the ones about our distinguished alma mater, writing them on slips of paper to pass like shibboleths when next we'd meet.

"Three male students loiter around Shoe Mart Megamall," one note said. "One is from the exclusive Ateneo de Manila University. One from the rival De La Salle University. The third, named Erning Isip, is from the populist AMA Computer College. The three students spot a very pretty light-skinned girl. Each of the boys takes a turn at trying to woo her. The Atenenista says: 'Why, hello there. Perhaps I should text my driver to bring my BMW around to chauffeur us to the Polo Club so we can get some gindara?' The Lasallista says: 'Wow, you're so talagang pretty, as in totally ganda gorgeous. Are you hungry at all? Let's ride my CRV and I'll make libre fried chicken skin and Cuba libres at Dencio's bar and grill.' Erning Isip, the AMA Computer College student, timidly approaches the girl. Scratching the back of his head, he says: 'Miss, please miss, give me autograph?'"

*

From the window you can now see Manila. Rain streaks sideways across the glass. Suddenly the plane dips. Our stomachs squeeze into our throats. Passengers squeal, straighten, clasp armrests tightly. Many double-check their seat belts, more than a few pull out rosaries and begin moving their fingers in time with their lips. Fuck. I hope it's not a water landing. The pilot announces: "Cabin crew, take your seats." The plane steadies. Its interior lights dim. Muzak standards are played from the PA system: a tinkling piano version of the theme from *The Godfather*. The only person unfazed is my seatmate, who pulls out my bottle of alcohol disinfectant, takes off his socks, and starts slathering his feet, holding the plastic bottle between his teeth as he gets between his toes with all the fingers of both hands. He slurps to keep his saliva in. So much for my bottle of alcogel. The plane shakes violently again.

I close my eyes. The *Godfather* tune makes me picture silk-socked mobsters skating lithely on mirrored ballroom floors. Liberace at his piano on a dais, watching expectantly for the imminent crash that would break everything into a million little pieces.

I'm pleased by the idea of not having to make small talk with the men Granma always sent to whisk me past customs, to tug my suitcases from the carousel, to drive me home. I'm overjoyed I won't have to greet my grandfather. I love the new freedom of life without Madison, not having to call to tell her I've arrived safely, my reassurances met with inordinate tears that made me feel both wanted and burdened. Independence is bliss. It really is.

I remember, though, when Madison and I decided to get our own place in Brooklyn—my first real taste of independence. It had gotten to a point where my conscience bothered me, hiding her there in my grandparents' apartment at Trump Tower without Grapes's permission. I remember when I called him in Manila to let him and Granma know my decision. "Just make sure," Grapes said, "that you scrub the floor well so we can rent it out quickly." Part of me was flabbergasted that he was so unconcerned, that he didn't just tell me to stay. But part of me was relieved that I had pulled it off so easily. Madison and I moved our stuff into our shitty little wonderful new place, and returning the U-Haul truck felt like I was navigating my new yacht to one of those all-inclusive island resorts with vacationing Pilates instructors in G-strings and a pool with a bar in the middle of it.

The next month, however, my grandparents arrived suddenly. After a couple of days of enjoying accompanying them to Broadway shows I'd have dismissed otherwise, and going to dinners with them where Madison and I ate well for a change, Madison was fairly convinced I had exaggerated all my complaints about them. Even I began to doubt myself. I thought, perhaps, my independence had earned their respect. Then they asked to see me alone on their last night in New York; they were leaving for Tel Aviv the next day to see a man about some especially fertile chickens.

Grapes stood by the table in their room at the Holiday Inn. The place made me sad, disgusted even. Ever since I was little, he liked to remind me that his wealth came from knowing how to save. My grandfather's thick silver hair was uncombed, and he was in his boxer shorts and undershirt. The shirt was inside out. When he turned around to get something from his suitcase, I saw that the maids had written "Sir" on the shirt tag with a felt pen. The same hand, the same pen, had written "Migs" on all mine. Grapes turned around and sat down at the table. He placed his seven-day pillbox in front of him, opened it to Tuesday, and began taking out tablets and capsules and arranging them on the tabletop. They looked like candies. He hadn't even glanced at me since I walked in. Granma sat in the corner, looking at her hands. Grapes sighed. It was a brutal, crushing sigh. Like Aeolus, the windwarden from Greek mythology, blowing down all too easily every wall I'd constructed within myself to contain my confidence and pride in the new life I'd just begun. "Why don't you tell us why you have been lying to us?" He sighed again. "I know you are doing it for that girl." Sigh. "Wasting your life." Sigh. "I sent you to an Ivy League school." Sigh. "What are you doing working for that magazine? You went to Columbia! They should make you editor in chief. Do you want me to go with you to talk to them?" Sigh, sigh, sigh.

"I've got a good position, Grapes."

"Do you? I looked at the masthead. Are you editor? Let's see here. Brigid Hughes, managing editor. Is your name Brigid Hughes? Ben Ryder Howe, senior editor. Is your name Ben Ryder Howe?"

"Grapes, I'm an editorial assistant. If I work hard enough, I'll make editor one day."

"Hmm, let's look at the other names. Oliver Broudy, senior editor. Is your name Oliver Broudy? George Plimpton, editor. Is your name George Plimpton? Where's your name, little Miguelito?"

"I'm still new," I said feebly. "They haven't updated the masthead."

"There you go, lying again. Always the same, huh?"

"I'm telling the truth."

"Your version of the truth. Are you the janitor?"

I looked at Granma. She sat quietly in the corner of the room, looking at her fists. My attempts to make eye contact with her, I still don't know whether they were for her or me. My own hands started to hurt and I realized I was clenching them so tightly that my nails almost broke the skin.

When I spoke up, I could feel myself shaking. "Grapes," I said, "you don't understand." How childish that sounded. I steeled my voice. "This is about my short story. Right? I knew I shouldn't have shown you the magazine. It's always this way. Why do you think the father figure is always you?"

"I've never understood why you can't just write nice stories. Stories your grandmother would like and can show off to her friends."

"Granma, is that what this is all about?"

Granma spoke up. Her voice was surprisingly angry. "Why can't you write nice things?" Her voice softened. "Why would anyone read your story and want to visit our country?"

"A writer has to talk about the things that go untalked about."

Grapes banged his pillbox on the table. "Don't argue literary aesthetics with your grandmother," he said. "She's right. You are always trying to shock. You have all this horrible stuff in your work. Not very Christian things. Not very patriotic. And you say things that are not yours to say."

"If you have to hide something, then you shouldn't have done it in the first place. Right, Grapes? If you had some integrity—"

"Don't you dare speak to me like that! You're one to talk! What do you know about owning responsibility? We helped you play mommy-daddy with that girl in university. What happened there? But of course we helped you. We'll always help you. Because we love you. But how do you repay us?"

"Love isn't based on gratitude. Respect isn't based on debt. I'm not your constituent."

"Oh, how dramatic! Listen to yourself. In what book did you read that baloney? We've all always known that you were the selfish one. Out of all of you six."

"None of us kids have stood up to you before. Well here I am. Finally. One of us six. I'm telling you who I really am." He looked like he was going to say something, but he didn't. Good. I continued: "You hate that I'm independent. That you can't control me. That I didn't go into politics, like you, like my father . . ."

"Those were suggestions," Grapes said quietly. "I paid for your writing education."

"You'd tell me, 'When you're done *playing* Hemingway, when

are you going to come home and take your role in politics?' It's all you ever talked about. But look at where it got you."

"Yes," Grapes said. "Look at where it got me!"

I held back. I wanted to hurt him, but not that way. A man's life is all he has. When you're old, it's all you'll ever have. I said instead: "Look at where it got my dad. A *hero*'s death. Don't think I don't know what really happened."

"I just want you," Grapes said quietly, "to reach farther than I did. Than your father did."

Granma piped up. "We love you."

"If I became a politician, either I'd be corrupted by the compromises I'd be forced to make, or I'd be shot for my ideals. Don't you see?"

Grapes wasn't even looking at me anymore. "You always have to have the last word," he said finally. "Don't you?"

I thought of what to say, but realized I'd only be having the last word. We stewed in the silence of a stalemate neither of us expected.

In a small voice, Granma told me: "I think you better leave now."

I couldn't believe it. I looked at my grandfather for what I knew would be the last time. He looked old. I went out into the hall. Granma followed. She started pulling wadded hundred-dollar bills from her pockets and pushing them into my hands. I kept my fists closed. "No, Granma. I don't want to take any more of his money."

"Please," she said, starting to cry. "Take it. It's mine. Please. For me." She stuffed them into the pockets of my jeans. I let her. I hugged her.

"Why don't you come home with us?" she said. "Just leave her. You don't have to be responsible for her."

"What will I do in Manila?"

"I don't know," she said weakly. "Enter politics?" Her voice was so quiet. "I'll help you," she said. "I'll take the weight for you." I hugged her and told her I loved her. Then I walked to the elevator. I pressed the call button purposefully. We stood there. Granma brought out a Kleenex packet and tried to open it. I pressed the button again. Granma hid her face in a tissue. I pressed the button again. Granma began to blow her nose. The elevator finally came. I was grateful that it was empty. I turned to look through the closing doors, but my grandmother was gone. The elevator went down and down and down until it stopped. The doors opened and I was faced with a group of guys who looked like Midwesterners in town for a wrestling competition. "Hey," one of them whispered, "that dude's crying."

The plane steadies, banks, straightens, and makes its final approach. "I'm sorry for the delay, ladies and gentlemen," the captain says over the PA. "There was a, uh, problem on the ground."

My neighbour finally asks me, in English, "You visiting?" I nod. "Me," he says, smiling, "I come home. For good." He fishes out a thick wad of U.S. dollars from his belt bag, opens it like a booklet, and flaps it proudly. "My savings. In past times, I work very hard. I remit money for a long time. I will now change everything." I nod. The money in the middle slips out of the stack and bills shower into our laps. He laughs as we pick them up. I hand over what I collected. The bills smell like sweaty hands and baking bread. I feel unspeakably happy for him. And guilty for having resented him. And sad that I've come home with less definitive intentions. "I work so far away," he says, as if I didn't understand him. "In past times. Now, for the future of my children, I come home."

I can picture his family at Arrivals, a bright stain of joy on a tapestry of disorder. The Ninoy Aquino International Airport is your apt introduction to my country. You'll be struck by the ubiquity of armed guards, enticed by the glossy luxury shops selling duty-free liquor, cigarettes, last-minute presents; you'll tumble out into a warlike fug—an overcrowded arrival area with desiccated, air-conditioned air, worn linoleum, and creaking baggage carousels; a quintet of blind musicians greets travellers with faves like "La Cucaracha" and "Let It Be"; a larger-than-life, smirking President Fernando V. Estregan welcomes you from a poster taking up the entire wall; a sign declares, "Welcome to the Philippines, the most Christian country in Asia"; beneath it, another, "Beware of pickpockets." Grasping your possessions tightly, you pass through the gauntlet of taciturn but thorough customs officials before an exit orphans you to the insidious ninety-five-degree heat and humidity and the swarming masses of other people's family members, all of them periscoping necks to stare collectively at you. Your armpits drip sweat like a tap, though the sky is almost always white, the sun almost always hidden. On the street, taxis done up like carnivals will honk straight at you, their drivers accosting your bags as if intending to hold them ransom for a twenty-cent tip. In their cabs—perfumed with three different fruit-scented air fresheners, pork cracklings, and spicy vinegar—they hospitably turn the air-con to arctic freezing and crank up the volume on their stereo just for you, so that the Bee Gees fly high-pitched and crystalline from the speakers by your ears. Soot-caked cops do their best to direct the beast that is our traffic, their ineffectual whistles exacerbating the chaos that is our order. It takes you two hours to get anywhere; and when you arrive, it's almost time to go. Let me welcome you to my first country, my Third World.

*

The country has changed so much, my childhood years before the war seem improbable. I'm not sure if I remember the events as actual or if they were stories later told to me, Salvador folklore in which I reportedly took part. Most wonderful in my mind are the caged animals on Tito Odyseo's farm. At dusk, when no other humans were afoot, Lena, Narcisito, and I would creep slowly between the cages. There was the jaguar, with his immense paws. The pair of aardvarks, named for Saints Peter and Paul. The Palawan bearcat. The ring-tailed lemurs. The buff-faced gibbons. The Philippine monkey-eating eagle named Bonifacio. And the baby giraffe, who died before he grew to his full height. I'd run with my brother and sister, around the slow-footed casso-waries that were permitted to roam freely. On those Sundays when his family would host all the others (or at least those in good grace), Tito Odyseo would sometimes release the gazelles, a fleet trio that ran without knowing the es-tate was a larger, inescapable cage, or ran because a dozen children gave chase, or ran for the opportunity and sheer love of running. I remember how we took after them, for those very same reasons. If only someone had taken a picture of that last picnic, with the animals in the background and the family all present. That was the last time we were together, the last time our ances-tral land was still ours, the last time the spirits were still present there in the shadows beneath the trees.

When the war came, the animals were quickly stolen, one by one, by hun-gry farmworkers. Tito Odyseo was severely beaten one night when he fell asleep guarding the cages.

—from *Autoplagiarist* (page 188), by Crispin Salvador

*

From the window he can see Manila. Rain streaks sideways across the glass. Suddenly the plane dips again, and his thoughts take on the tinge of desolation, as they do in such moments. He closes his eyes and tries not to pray.

*

The airplane comes down low. From above, the city is still beautiful. We pass over brown water off the coast, fish pens laid out in geometrical patterns, like a Mondrian viewed by someone color-blind. Over the bay, the sunset is starting, the famous sunset, like none anywhere else. Skeptics attribute its colours to pollution. Over there's the land, the great gray sprawl of eleven million people living on top of each other on barely more than 240 square miles—fourteen cities and three municipalities, skyscrapers and shanties, tumbling beyond Kilometer Zero and the heart of every Filipino, the city that gave the metro its name: Manila.

The megalopolis's components, when named, sound like mountain music, all drums and cymbals and gongs: Parañaque, Mandaluyong, Makati, Pasay, Navotas, San Juan, Cubao, Quezon City, Caloocan, Taguig, Malabon, Pasig, Las Piñas, Marikina, Muntinlupa. Connecting them, the grid and the superavenues—Edsa, Roxas, Aurora, Taft—countless overpasses built like Band-Aids, innumerable billboards, restaurants for every nationality and budget, huge shopping malls with Bulgari, Shoe Mart, Starbucks, Nike, you name it. You want it, you can get it in Manila, in shops and tabloids, alleyways and boardrooms. There, by the shadow of our airplane, near Rizal Park, where the statue of our hero stands as centennial testament to a stolen revolution, we're now flying low enough to see tangled lines of jeepneys and buses bringing people home from work; that crowd there, with the banners, is a small part of a million worshippers en route to the weekly, desperate, El Ohim prayer rally, where Christ is the answer to unanswerable Boolean questions. If you look closely, there's Reverend Martin onstage, in his metallic double-breasted suit and happy-coloured tie: a man of God and man of the people whose faith earned him financial security and a mansion in a gated subdivision.

Modern Manila. She who once was the Pearl of the Orient is

now a worn dowager, complete with the hump, the bunions, the memories of the Charleston stepped to the imported and flawlessly imitated melodies of King Oliver, the caked-on makeup and the lipstick smeared in thick stripes beyond the thin, pursed lips. She, the trusting daughter of East and West, lay down and was destroyed, her beauty carpet-bombed by her liberators, cautious of their own casualties, her ravishment making her kindred to Hiroshima, Stalingrad, Warsaw. And yet, from the air you think her peaceful and unflustered. On the ground is a place tangled with good intentions and a tyrannical will to live. Life works with the Lord's benevolence and a generous application of duct tape and Filipino ingenuity. Five hundred years ago Spanish conquistadors sailed their wooden ships into the world's most perfect harbour to begin their mission of, as historians say, God, gold, and guns; their walled fortress is still there, as is their religion and blood, but the gold they, and others, took with them, or apportioned among their few native deputies. Manila has changed much since. It's changed so little. If you know where to look, this is the most exciting city in the world.

The airplane's wheels touch down. The passengers clap.

*

The spectators watch the action eagerly. At the intersection, stranded cars block Antonio's way. Our hero slows. Eagle-eyes search for Dominador. There he is! He's abandoned his Jet Ski and is running up the stairs of the pedestrian overpass. "Santa Banana," Antonio mutters. "If he gets through, he'll make it into the shopping arcade, and I'll never find him in that crowd." Antonio revs his Jet Ski ferociously. It speeds across the water, between buses, between taxis, their occupants blinking at what they're witnessing. Antonio builds velocity, his black leather jacket flapping like a cape. He jerks his vehicle to the right, heading straight for a half-submerged car. The Jet Ski slides over its hood, up its windshield, and flies through the air, Antonio hunched over the handlebars. Man and machine arc higher and higher, the engine screaming like a banshee in heat. He lands on the pedestrian overpass, the Jet Ski's underside trailing sparks as it slides over the cement. The fleeing Dominador looks behind him, wide-eyed and stupid-looking. The Jet Ski closes in. Antonio leaps over his handlebars, like a gazelle through the air, and tackles Dominador. They tumble together. Antonio whispers in his ear, "If you don't mind, I really prefer being on top."

—from Manila Noir (page 57), by Crispin Salvador

*

A woman cries out from the rear of the plane, silencing the applause. Seat belts click, click, click. Passengers rush to the windows on the right. Over someone's head I can see, beyond the gleaming new terminal, rain clouds, dark and heavy. Two pillars of evil black smoke, clambering up in the distance, seem to hold the heavens up. At their feet, fire.

2

These are the broad themes: enigmas, dreams, mythologies, the tyranny of absence, the shortcomings of language, deciduous memories, endings as beginnings.

—from *Autoplagiarist* (page 188), by Crispin Salvador

*

That part about my seatmate in the plane and his wad of falling money didn't happen exactly as I recounted. That last bit about his coming home for his children, that wasn't accurate, either. If I had spoken to him, I reckon that's what he'd have said. In a way, I wrote that part for him. He became more than the guy beside me with annoying manners. What I said that he said to me, I could see that in him. But no, I didn't talk to him. When he tried to strike up a conversation, I closed my eyes and pretended to be dreaming.

From this point on, I should promise to tell the truth.

*

During Crispin's last months we became closer than I expected. I even reached the point of being able to cuss in his company. The friendship started with me doing a profile on him for my class with Lis Harris. Crispin and I would sit stiffly formal, a tape recorder like a string of barbed wire between us, always at some coffee shop or restaurant. Usually Tom's Restaurant on Broadway, the one they always used in *Seinfeld*. I finished the semester and turned in the profile. I had a feeling Crispin wanted to see it, though he didn't ask and I didn't offer. A couple of weeks after our last interview I was finally invited into his office for a cup of Lapsang souchong and some madeleines. He was visibly more at ease now that he was no longer under scrutiny. His smile, I noticed, was unexpectedly shy. We sat and nibbled and talked about stuff. I don't remember what. Books, probably. Writing. Crumbs clung to the front of his argyle sweater. When I saw him the next day they were still there.

I don't know if it was from need or whether he actually liked me, but we started to hang out often. In the beginning I felt uncomfortable, the way one does when first spending time with the obviously lonely. Crispin was a fixture on the busy campus, and his solitude was as familiar to everyone as the bronze Alma Mater statue. Every morning and afternoon he would lope up and down the steps between Butler Library and his office in Philosophy Hall—his countenance rueful, his attire that of a flaneur with tenure. He reminded me of the way a Tokyoite looks in a cowboy hat, though Crispin somehow almost succeeded with his affectation of brown tweeds and a wilting red fedora with a green feather in its band. Always a variation of that outfit, no matter what the weather; always a notebook covered in orange suede tucked under his arm. Usually he'd be staring into an open book; I watched with a mix of anxiety and guilty anticipation to see whether he'd trip or be hit on the head with a football or Frisbee.

During our interviews, however, he was lucid and confident. He held court on such subjects as the primacy of literature as "*the* art, *the* record, of the human condition"; or the "arbitrary scrim" between fiction and nonfiction; or the ailments of our national literature; or the challenges of literary bricolage as a narrative structure. I learned much from Crispin, though a lot of the things he went on about passed over my head. But he was one of those teachers who, by a kind of osmosis, helped you discover the quantity of areas in your life in which you are still so ignorant as not to have even considered forming a wrong opinion.

In his mind, the trivial shared equal prestige with the academic, and his sudden flaring intensities, set off by a word, an image, a private thought, made his conversation unpredictable. Listening, you lived vicariously within the corners of a kind of universal mind, the near and far reaches of the universe, the infinite expanses of the ages. An idle conversation could, for example, and did once, stretch elegantly from fractals to the complex etymologies of Filipino slang to the honest agonies of self-doubt in Steinbeck's diaries, then onward to the intimate but epic histories of Herodotus and the challenge of fitting reality "into the lacy corset of language," to the shortcomings of Rousseau's ideal of the noble savage, and then forward to José Rizal's reversal of the Spanish derogatory *indio* into a mark of pride as "Los Indios Bravos," and comparing such self-conscious flippings of meaning to African-Americans' exclusive appropriation of the word "nigger"; from there Crispin lingered on Australian Aboriginals and their dot paintings as "the last frontier of modern art," before growing flushed over the geologic wonders extant from prehistoric *terra australis incognita*; he proceeded to their echidnas, platypuses, and other zoological oddities, then the creative urges of the larger animal world, epitomized by the phenomenon of cats and elephants painting; then he riffed on the pinnacle of sensuality in the softness of Bernini's Baroque marbles, the impression of the rapist Pluto's fingers on Persephone's supple thighs, Daphne's gradual then startling transformation into a laurel tree as you circle her fleeing Apollo; finally, Crispin grew agitated over José Honorato Lozano's *Letras y Figuras* paintings, which, he said, ingeniously combined landscape, still life, typography, and thematic tableaux into an artistic concession to the vanities of nineteenth-century Manila socialites. All this over chipotle nachos before our cheeseburgers arrived.

Crispin's monologues attained velocity in that way. His Comp Lit lectures, with students spilling out the doorway, were legendary for their gee-whiz fervour, violent digressions, miraculous convergences. Yet he struck me as possessing the self-centredness of the calcified lonesome. During our first casual conversations, he chose his words with caution. Only after a few meetings did his focus shift away from discussing himself. That's not to say it moved to me. No. It bounded past, to another realm he found more familiar, the wondrous specifics of the great cosmologies. More than twice he jumped up to shift piles of books around, sending the topmost tumbling down, just to leaf to a spicy passage which he'd recite from memory anyway, with closed-eyed gusto. I had to strain to hear the incantations from Cid Hamete Benengeli, Julián Carax, John Shade, Randolph Henry Ash. Then he would sit in silence, soaking it up. Never did he ask how my weekend went. Rarely did he solicit my opinion, except perhaps to pass judgment on me.

When Crispin went on and on, I would sometimes tune out, watching his hands gesticulate. Each was scarred bizarrely. The tissue, the size of a dime, was raised and silky, right in the center on the front and back of each hand. Like stigmata. Such personal mysteries intrigued me.

When the conversation would inevitably lapse, we'd sit and stare at the large poster over his desk, Juan Luna's masterpiece, the *Spoliarium*—its dead Roman gladiators being dragged across the floor of a coliseum's subchamber, the faces of onlookers filled with grief, shock, disinterest, gothic fascination. At such times, I studied Crispin out of the corner of my eye, hunched, tired, in his squeaking chair in a tiny office that smelled like a goat wearing expensive aftershave, and I wondered about the road that had taken him to this point.

*

That evening, Erning Isip, the student from AMA Computer College, is still hanging out with his friends from Ateneo and La Salle. They drink and watch the Purefoods vs. Shell game in a beer garden near Padre Burgos, Makati's red-light district. The student from Ateneo regales them with his dream of being a Supreme Court judge. The student from La Salle intimates that he'd like one day to run a shipping empire. Erning Isip tells them about how he's behind in tuition payments. A particularly skanky girl passes, wearing a micro-mini denim skirt, a halter that reveals her muffin-top belly, long straight hair to the small of her back, and those precarious Plexiglas stilettos popular with dancers of the exotic discipline.

The Atenenista says: "My God! A veritable Whore of Babylon!"

The Lasallista says: "Nyeh! What a puta!"

Erning Isip stares at the woman for some time. Then he exclaims: "Uy! My classmate from Intro to HTML!"

*

"It's been nearly a year," Granma said. "Isn't it time you made peace?"

"It's only been eight months," I said.

"Why don't you come home and spend Christmas with us?"

"How's Granddud?" The line was bad and there was a lag in our sentences.

"He's still your grandfather," Granma said. I heard the honking of a horn, the clicking of a turn signal. "Not here," she said to the driver. "Enter at the Tamarind Street gate."

"New York is beautiful, Granma. Fifth Avenue is all lit up for Christmas and it's not even December yet. I wish you were here. How's life as governor?"

"Hello, can you hear me? The line's cutting out."

"Granma? Hello? I said, how's the governorship?"

"Great, actually. You would have enjoyed it. It would have made your grandfather so happy."

"Granma . . ."

"And your father would have looked down from heaven and been so proud. Because you'd be a statesman, just like he was."

"Granma, please, don't—"

"It's very fulfilling, you know. It keeps me awfully busy. Which is good. Especially in this season, when everyone wants something from you."

"I heard about the president's latest scandal."

"Which one?"

"The links to the bombings."

"Oh. That will pass."

"There are others?"

"Each one is the same. They're always trying to impeach him. Always suspecting him of being on the verge of declaring martial law. But their parliament of the streets is just mob rule."

"So the scandals aren't true?"

"What's true?"

"That he's on the verge of declaring—?"

"I meant, what's true?"

"Aw, Granma, can't you do anything? Aren't there people in government who . . . I don't know. People like you."

"Oh, sweetheart. What can anyone do? That's just the way things are. You really think you can change the world?"

"I can be part of the change."

"What would you change?"

"Everything."

"What would be different?"

"I don't know. It would just be better."

"I don't think we can really change anything. It's too difficult."

"Granma, please don't say that."

"Anyway, I'm home already. Your grandfather's home. I have to go before he sees me on the phone."

"You don't *have* to tell him it was me."

"I better go. What time is it there in New York? You better get to bed."

"Bye, Granma."

"I love you, Miguelito."

"Love you, too."

*

But Dominador is like a bull. He pushes Antonio off with his powerful arms. With a press of the button, the villain unsheathes his switchblade. "I'm going to stick this in your gut," he growls, "and turn you on like a tap." Our hero reaches to draw his trusty pistol, but doesn't. It wouldn't be fair. Dominador sneers. "Where's your big gun?" he says. Antonio smiles. "Here in my pants," he replies. "But I don't take it out for ugly pigs like you." He assumes a kung fu stance and motions Dominador closer. His opponent closes in, slicing the air between them.

–from Manila Noir (page 57), by Crispin Salvador

*

I pass the night at a cheap pension near the Manila airport. My flight to Bacolod leaves early tomorrow.

The traffic was too heavy to venture farther. I sat in the back of a taxi as it inched along a cordon of traffic cones, across the broad highway from a wall of fire swallowing blocks of shanties. Black shades of men and their hulking machines moved and shimmered against the backdrop of wrestling yellows and reds and oranges. In places, spires of brilliant blue leaped and twirled and fell and shifted colours. The taxi driver and I sat transfixed, our faces pressed to the warm windows. "Two more blasts," said the Bombo Radyo announcer, in his rapid-fire Tagalog, "at the duty-free store outside Ninoy Aquino International Airport have resulted in fires spreading to nearby residences. Let us hope, my friends, and let us pray, that the rains will aid the brave firefighters in their heroic task."

A couple of times when Crispin went on about his exile being heroic, I began to wonder. What was it really that kept him from returning to Manila? I even asked him once, and he said living abroad was harder. That it took more guts to be an international writer. But there was always a lack of conviction in his voice. A defensiveness. Could it be that he had just grown too soft for a city such as this, a place possessed by a very different balance? Here, need blurs the line between good and bad, and a constant promise of random violence sticks like humidity down your back. Wholly different from the zeitgeist lining the Western world, with its own chaos given order by multitudes of films and television shows, explained into our communal understanding by op-ed pieces and panel discussions and the neatness of stories linked infinitely to each other online. Had Crispin grown to love the mythology too much, the way Emma Bovary loved romances? Like a hermit with a credit card and a telephone, Crispin sat back and dismissed what was happening outside his door. "The beggars have changed, but the lash goes on," he said, "and armchair guerrillas have taken to the jungles of cyberspace. Everything's now so Hollywood, the world is lopsided. No wonder it revolves."

I disagreed. Maybe because I was younger and post-postcolonial, I knew that even if it rotated askew, it was still one world. When a butterfly flapped its wings in Chile, a child soldier killed for the first time in Chad, a sale was made on Amazon.com, and a book arrived in two days to divulge the urgencies outside our lives. Sure, having moved from Manila to New York, I saw that the global village had made it, ironically, easier for me and my friends to continue with our lives unhindered: tuning out on iPods made in China; heeding the urgings to revitalize the economy by shopping; attending rallies only if we didn't miss too many classes, because a competitive job market or student loans stood like chaperones beside our consciences. But we also took fervid stances on issues burning up the blogs, even if engaged from the safety of our homes, our windows wrapped in plastic and duct tape. My friends and those like us monitored Fox News constantly, trying to understand the hypocrisy of the enemy, relishing our feelings of superiority before changing the channel to search for whatever subjectivity we found most satiating. Sure, we abandoned the Philippines, inhabited Manhattan, and claimed the deserted nighttime streets, always in an incredulous state of self-congratulation for what we would one day do. Sure, we went out constantly, driven by our fear of either missing out or dying lonely or simply growing old. Sure, we sat in Alphabet City bars, amid jukebox music and cigarette smoke, sucking down PBRs and arm-wrestling each other in debates on homeland security and human rights in a country that still wouldn't give us green cards. Sure, each night we staggered home, unfired, unglazed, already broken without knowing it. But at least we were trying.

Around that time the Philippines was listed by Western governments as a terrorist hot spot, though many Filipinos scoffed. Asphyxiating a poor country's vital tourist industry because a handful of Muslim rebels are playing hide-and-seek in the southern jungles of Jolo is like warning tourists not to visit Disneyland because of the Ku Klux Klan in Alabama. Crispin not only ridiculed the warning, dismissing it with the air of having seen it all before, but he also shrugged off the ubiquitous stories of quashed coups and extralegal killings that we in the know recognize as the more pressing, if less sensational, concerns.

And I forgave him that. Even if I thought he was running away from something by living abroad. Maybe I excused him because he was a man who'd already made many a stand, perhaps one too many, and it was now the era for people like me to step up. Or maybe I admired him because he had graduated into a different role. When Crispin spoke about his writing, he wielded adroitly a life sharpened by learning, defending a ferocious belief that merely being in touch with today is limited, even juvenile—in the way that this morning's newspaper is revealed as tonight's fish-and-chips wrapping when works like *One Hundred Years of Solitude* or, indeed, *Autoplagiarist* are picked off the shelf. A man with battered hands is shown to be a craftsman only when he puts them to work.

Yes, I gave him that. Because *TBA* was supposed to reach for more than a thousand young Turks like me ever could. But when the bombings reached the cities, when our relatives at home were afraid to go to the malls, then Crispin's indifference really disappointed. We the young are necessarily impatient with our elders' patience. How are they so serene when they have so much less time than we do? I hoped Crispin would have looked in the mirror one morning and said: You obsolete old bastard. And that would have spurred him to a final assault. But that time I questioned him about the toothlessness of exile, he paused, then replied: What can one do?

The scent of fire is pleasant. It wafts into my room at the pension, through the vent of the gargling air-conditioner unit. Despite myself, I enjoy it. The odour of burned homes, chilled by Freon, is wintry, like Vancouver memories of s'mores and campfire stories. I still can't sleep. Two cockroaches climb the far wall, their antennae waving at each other. A drunk unheroic tenor belts Vita Nova love songs from the karaoke bar downstairs. I sit in bed, read my notes, and prepare tomorrow's questions for Crispin's sister, Lena. Later, the silence after closing time uncovers the cries of sirens still blazing in the distance. Thunder sunders all. Wind pelts rain on the jalousie windows with such force it sounds like a riot.

I sleep.

I'm on an island in the middle of nowhere. The tiny house is gathering dust. I watch it collect on the surfaces, on the objects. A red fedora. A gramophone. A framed photo of a little girl at First Communion with her parents. On the beach, I listen for a boat. The sea is reticent and raucous. How could I have never learned to swim in something so beautiful? Bangs of typewriter keys resound through the window. I rush back in and see an Underwood with paper in it. I search the house again, growing desperate with each successive pass. It's been four days, I know. I doze in and out, unable to sleep, but trying desperately for some sense of normalcy. It's getting hard to inhale, as if my breath is slowly evaporating. I stumble up to suck, in vain, at the faucet attached to a plastic drum in the kitchen. When I bang the drum it makes a noise like a bell underwater. I lie down again, then have to rush outside to vomit. I lie down once more, then run out to shit diarrhea. I stagger to the bed, my heart pounding, and pain a new regularity in my head. I can almost feel my kidneys ache. One imagines strange things sometimes. My blood, I somehow know, is becoming more acidic. Hypovolemic shock. I heard the term on a medical TV drama. My blood is pulling moisture from my body tissue, from my brain. Knowing what is happening doesn't mean you can do anything to stop it. The bedsheets are icy. Visions play with my mind. I'm raising an infant child in the air, tossing her up so that she'll giggle with joy. I'm leaning out a car window and looking up as fireworks bloom and wilt. I'm waiting in line outside a museum, shaking my head at the inane conversation of tourists. I'm helping Madison sew name tags on the clothes of her grandfather the night before he is put in a home. I'm holding a phone receiver against my cheek, listening to the tone, looking at the familiar numbers on the old piece of paper in my hand. When the sun rises over the island, my throat feels like it has shut. With a panic like realizing your mother has left you in the supermarket, I know I am going to die.

I wake up. It is the accepting moment of a dying night, just before dawn, just before the roosters have awakened. I can't believe I've remembered my dream. I lie in bed and try to recall it before it slips away. It must be the jet lag. Morning arrives, slowly, then noisily. The cockroaches, in their wisdom, have fled.

*

The boy had always been quickly on his way to becoming a character misled by his own good intentions and assurances of self, and perhaps interesting in that way.

And so, this is where he is declared our protagonist. The dramatic angle to his story begins with recurring images of him fidgeting in his own silence, in deserted subway stations, in classrooms surrounded by schoolmates, in a forenoon queue at MoMA. You can see in his face he is searching, hoping to dispel those things that nettle and diminish him, finding purpose in the conceit of himself as a modern-day member of the ilustrados—a potentiality owned by every expatriate today, a precedent granted by those first Enlightened Ones of the late nineteenth century. Those young Filipino bodhisattvas had returned home from abroad to dedicate their perfumed bodies, mellifluous rhetoric,

Latinate ideas, and tailored educations to the ultimate cause. Revolution. Many dying of bullets, some of inextricable exile, others subsumed and mellowed and then forgotten, more than a few later learning, with surprising facility, to live with enforced compromise. What's the difference between them and him and all the other peripatetics, except that the ancestors had already returned? His thick, furled intentions and rolled-up plans would also be shaken out to flap alongside our national flag, one day. So he waited, just as they did, collecting himself into integrity, just as they had, anticipating the final magnetism of native shores.

Now, having come home, we see him, our patriotic protagonist, sitting in bed, wondering, Where are the trumpets?

*

When Cristo isn't in his quarters, writing on the special lap desk he designed and built with springs and pads to allow him to work on any mode of transport, he sits and stares at the sea, pushing away the thoughts of his murdered father, his mutilated mother, and his abused sister. This ocean is said to pacify the deserving—he thinks, trying for the bravery of a smile—and I am hopeful.

If he looks hard enough, he can see land on the horizon. But when he blinks, it disappears. He's never as close as he hopes.

—from *The Enlightened* (page 92), by Crispin Salvador

*

Apparently I had been Crispin's only friend. Lena rang me very late one night, to my surprise. It was hours after I fought with Madison, who had stormed out dramatically. When I picked up the phone, I was expecting my girlfriend's voice, grated by tears, and I answered sternly. I startled Lena. She kept repeating herself. Her sentences were tinged with a British-school accent long blended into the blocky lilt of a life spent in Bacolod. She asked me to go through Crispin's things—sending home what was significant, taking from what was left anything that interested me, and donating or discarding the rest. What could I have said?

The task proved daunting. There was a lot of stuff. Yet I came to enjoy the work, hoping to understand his life from the artifacts left behind. I was now free to pick leisurely through his possessions, to recline and relax on his chairs, to make tea without asking permission, to open windows. There were no longer secrets hidden by drawers, darkened corners, closed books, doors. The resulting oddity left me curious and angry and exceedingly depressed. It reminded me of stretching like a starfish in the very middle of the bed those nights Madison stayed out late to spite me. But at least the morning would bring her back.

There were hundreds of books in Crispin's apartment. Shelves covered every wall. He used to call his library his *akashic*—Sanskrit, he'd said, for an unending library containing the totality of information. Included, on their own shelf, were scores of his notebooks in the orange suede covers he'd ordered specially from a workshop in an alleyway off the Arno. On the bottom shelf in the living room was his sizable record collection. I leafed through and put on Chuck Berry, to disperse the limitless silence. He sang about going down to the Club Nitty Gritty.

I walked through Crispin's study as if I were in a museum. Atop his desk: a typewriter, the letters worn off its keys; a Bohemian-crystal decanter, filled with water; a matching glass beside it, fruit flies floating dead on its surface; an ashtray holding his forlorn pipe—meerschaum, stinking of Cherry Cavendish.

That was when I searched the place for *The Bridges Ablaze*. I found nothing. I did, however, discover a receipt for a large package he had sent to a post office box near the Hundred Islands, in the Philippines. It was dated the morning before he died.

On a table in a corner was Crispin's chess set, our game still on it. I made my move: rook to king-four. Check.

*

The boy watches the scene slide past. The homes are all ruined, charred a black so deep it is as if it were always inevitable. Men and women and children sift through the wet rubble, hopelessly, their legs and arms sapped of colour. Our angry protagonist wants to go out and help, but what can he do but get in their way? In traffic ahead, the long-haired soldiers lounging on the back of the armoured personnel carrier pay no mind. Their rifles are propped between their legs. Those men already know all they need to know.

*

I forgot to mention what happened last night behind the pension where I stayed.

I was tired and lugged my suitcase, hand-carry, laptop bag, and orthopedic pillow through the rain, only to find the front door locked. I went around back to a desolate parking area. In the darkness, I heard, then saw, a young police officer in uniform, shoving two small street children against each other. The kids were in a daze. One clutched the telltale stuff: a bit of cardboard, Rugby adhesive blobbed on it, wrapped in a National Bookstore plastic bag. Both children had sampaguita leis around their necks, the evening's unsold wares. The policeman was knocking the two kids together repeatedly, like two hands clapping. When they fell, he grabbed them by the waists of their shorts and pulled them up roughly. He was growing increasingly agitated. He rifled through their pockets, looking for their day's earnings.

I put down my luggage and my pillow, already formulating what I would say. I was going to mention my surname, tell him who my grandparents are. He would stop, slack-jawed, quietly fuming, but stop nonetheless. I was going to demand his name and precinct and threaten to report him to Senator Bansamoro.

But what would have been the point? Sometimes you can't help but wonder, in the grand scheme of things, if kids like those are better off never having been born. And any cop who'd steal from street urchins is liable to shoot me in a second.

I carefully picked up my pillow and luggage, and quietly went through the back entrance of the pension. Inside, the electric fans mounted on the walls squawked.

I forgot to mention it.

*

INTERVIEWER:

What then was meant when you wrote: "Translation kills so that another may live. Manila is untranslatable." Were you able to address this, and how?

CS:

I meant you can't bring an unwritten place to life without losing something substantial. Manila is the cradle, the graveyard, the memory. The

Mecca, the Cathedral, the bordello. The shopping mall, the urinal, the disco-
theque. I'm hardly speaking in metaphor. It's the most impermeable of cities.
How does one convey all that? If one writes about its tropical logic, its familial
loyalties, its bitter aftertaste of Spanish colonialism, readers wonder: Is this a
Magical Realist? So one writes of the gilded oligarchs and the reporters with
open hands and the underpaid officers in military fatigues, the authority of
money and press badges and rifles distinguishing them as neither good nor
bad, only unsatiated and dangerous. And readers wonder: Is this Africa? How
do we fly from someone else's pigeonhole? We haven't. We must. And to do
that, we have to figure out how to properly translate ourselves. Let me tell you
how I think we can do it.

—from a 1988 interview in *The Paris Review*

*

The morning flight to Bacolod leaves in fifty-five minutes and I'm
still stuck in traffic. The taxi driver keeps looking back at the wreckage and going on about the fire. He says that before the bodies were
collected, the place smelled like roast suckling pig, a scent so delicious that he vomited until he thought he would faint. The traffic
light seems frozen on red. In the open back of an armoured personnel carrier in front of us, a dozen soldiers sit. Dressed in combat
fatigues, all but one wear their hair long around their shoulders.
They slouch lackadaisically, dark ropy arms thrown back idly, elbows
propped up behind them on the truck's railings. Automatic rifles held
between their knees look like penis sheath gourds of New Guinean
warriors.

These are different from the surreptitious-faced troops regularly
transported from bases around Metro Manila. These are special-
ops, distinguished by their ways and miens, fully armed and battle
ready. Strangely obtrusive. Patient. They smoke cigarettes and wrap
T-shirts around their necks for protection from the sun. Their
sergeant reads today's paper. The tabloid headline asks, over two
lines: "Philippines First Corp: Hero or Villain?" The photograph
below is of the company's fireworks and munitions factory on the
Pasig River, taken from the opposite bank. Large pipes above the
waterline spew viscous gray sludge lacquered in a spectrum of
colors.

A soldier spots me staring. He nudges his seatmates. They all stare back. The sergeant lowers his newspaper and looks at me. I turn my eyes to the embroidered *Playboy* symbol on the back of the taxi driver's headrest. The men laugh.

*

Erning Isip, in hand a newly minted degree from AMA Computer College, visits his cousin Bobby in Daly City, California. Silicon Valley, Erning knows, is only a bus ride away. Bobby is a male nurse at one of the hospitals and has to go to work every day. At first he leaves Erning at home with a box of cornflakes and the TV on, so that Erning has something to eat and can improve his poor English. After a week of staying home, Erning tells his cousin: "Pinsan, sawang sawa na'ko sa cornplayks" (Cousin, I'm tired of cornflakes). So Bobby shows him the local diner and instructs him to tell the waitress that he'll have an "apple pie and coffee." Erning repeats it as best he can: "Affle fie end copee." He practises it all morning: "Affle fie end copee. Affle fie end copee."

That afternoon, Erning bravely ventures to the diner. The waitress approaches his table. "Whaddya want?" she asks. Shocked and nearly lost for words, Erning stammers: "Affle fie end copee." The waitress leaves, much to his consternation and relief. A minute or so later, she brings him a slice of apple pie and a cup of coffee. Erning is flushed with accomplishment.

After a week of going to the diner, having the waitress accost him with "Whaddya want?" and eating apple pie and drinking coffee, Erning is feeling quite cosmopolitan. Before Cousin Bobby leaves for the hospital, Erning tells him: "Pinsan, sawang sawa na'ko sa affle fie end copee" (Cousin, I'm tired of apple pie and coffee). So Bobby tells him to order a "Cheeseburger, medium rare, with a large Coke, no ice." He's very specific about ordering no ice, to get more refreshing beverage for his money. Erning gamely practises his new English phrase in front of the mirror. "Chisborger, midyum rayr, end large Cok, no iys." He practises all morning: "Chisborger, midyum rayr, end large Cok, no iys." When lunchtime comes around, he makes his way to the diner. Under his breath, he turns the phrase into a jolly song. "Chisborger, midyum rayr, end large Cok, no iys."

Erning sees the waitress come toward his table. He holds his breath. "Hello again, honey," the waitress tells him, unexpectedly. "What can I get you?"

Erning blurts out: "Affle fie copee! Affle fie copee!"

*

Beside the chess set in Crispin's study stood a large metal filing cabinet. Forcing it open, nearly cutting myself in the process, I found: a photo album, cameras, binders filled with negatives and contact prints, boxes of assorted black-and-whites and oversaturated coloureds (artful nudes, scenes of markets and nightlife, traditional wood-and-stone Visayan manors, old friends from the Cinco Bravos debating and drinking in smoky bars, a series of stark duotones of the annual flagellants and crucifixions in Pampanga).

*

Nation, we must consider deeply: Isn't the President justified in his attempt to extend his tenure? He is, after all, forgoing a comfortable retirement for the good of the country. In 1998, when the Supreme Court upheld his bid to run an extra term (validating his argument that the shift from V.P. to President was thrust upon him—we can recall him as "reluctant but ready"), the public protestations were legally repudiated. And what followed were years of stability. Now is little different. And still the opposition wrap themselves in the banner of democracy. Salvos of accusations are omnipresent in any presidency (people die, policies falter, thieves will steal until they are caught) and a parliament of the streets undermines the fabric of our constitutional republic. As his motto goes: Don't change horses in midstream! Full speed ahead, often, is the bravest option, even if not the perfect one. For in democratic politics, there can be no perfection.

—from an editorial in *The Philippine Sun*, December 2, 2002

*

Salvador's father's father was the son of Capitan Cristobal Salvador de Veracruz, a Spanish garrison officer who emigrated to the Philippines from Alburquerque in the province of Badajoz, in the region of Extremadura—an area from which came many great Spanish explorers, including Hernán Cortés, Francisco Pizarro, Pedro de Alvarado, and Pedro de Valdivia. (The Capitan's own father was the famous Extremaduran matador El Narciso Splendido, mortally gored in Ronda in 1846.) A near-fatal bout with pneumonia on the journey to Las Islas Filipinas in 1860 left the twenty-five-year-old Capitan with a phobia of extended sea voyages. He would never return to his homeland.

After a brief posting at Fort Santiago in Intramuros, the walled city of Manila, the Capitan was transferred to duties on Negros Island, a position almost certainly more desirable to a soldier with agricultural roots. In 1865, after being discharged from active service following a crushed testicle inflicted during a riding mishap, the Capitan quickly married a local mestiza beauty named Severina "Stevie" Moreno, whose American mother had emigrated to the Visayas from Brookline, Massachusetts, in 1849, after marrying the globetrotting Catalan-born Visayan shipping magnate Patricio Moreno i Monzó.

The Capitan and his young bride settled easily into the privileged life of the new Spanish gentry. In 1868, they had a son, whom they named, after their respective fathers, Cristobal Narciso Patricio Salvador. They nicknamed him Cristo. In the succeeding years they also had a daughter, Paz Isabel. The frugal Capitan invested his savings and officer's pension in a textile factory and a farm for cattle, and they both yielded a modest fortune. In the 1870s, when fabric imported from Manchester flooded the market and killed the thriving Iloilo textile industry, the Capitan stubbornly held on, giving up his looms in 1874, rather too belatedly. He then devoted himself wholly to his small holdings of land across the Guimaras Strait, breeding, for stud, bulls of the highest quality.

Some years after young Cristo left for Madrid to join his peers in receiving an education, the Capitan faded into a historical footnote, hacked to death by his own drovers during an uprising in 1894; his wife and daughter succumbed to wounds and infection some weeks after. The three were buried in the nearby San Sebastian Cathedral (the coral-stone church their contributions helped build). Cristo did not arrive from Europe in time for their funeral. Their passing bequeathed him land and respect. He was then all alone in a new life, except for a dark family secret, of which everyone in good society knew.

—from the biography in progress, *Crispin Salvador: Eight Lives Lived*, by Miguel Syjuco

*

Dominador's face is fierce. His teeth, filed into points, make him look like a wolf. Antonio points and tells him: "Ay, punyeta! Look behind you!" Dominador just laughs. "The oldest trick in the book," he says. Antonio replies: "Not in this book," then jumps off the overpass and into the water. When Antonio surfaces, he sees eight policemen chasing Dominador. His nemesis, however, is surprisingly quick for a man of his bulk. "I'll get him in a following chapter," Antonio mutters before diving, lest the fuzz spot him.

—from *Manila Noir* (page 58), by Crispin Salvador

*

I guess what I miss most about Madison is our unique breed of passion.

We shared the daily papers religiously. Debated politics. Recycled. Always bought a little something—a Gray's Papaya hot dog, a hot cup of joe—for the bums panhandling on the cold sidewalks. We even boycotted China. We were among the first of everyone we knew to do so. After much debate, we'd reached the consensus not to shop at 99-cent stores; morality, Madison had said, comes at a price. We weren't going to watch the Beijing Olympics, either—a plan she'd hatched for an event still years in the future. Not even the opening or closing ceremonies, which was something that really bothered me; won't it be enough to hurt the sponsors by turning off the TV during the ads? What about the deserving athletes? I complained, on several occasions, about friends and colleagues who did business in China; Madison, quiet, let me speak, exploding only once, in the host's guest bathroom, and accusing me of referring to her ex-boyfriend, a rich Chinese-American real-estate developer now based in Shanghai. Together, however, Madison and I moaned about how CNN had stopped calling it Communist China, except during negative news stories about lost American jobs or consumer safety violations. At parties I'd hear Madison ask people: What about

Tiananmen? Falun Gong? Censorship? Endangered species decimated for quack medicine? I'd be on the other side of the room, saying: Tibet really should be freed, the IOC should use their leverage while they still can. The Panchen Lama is a tragic figure. Don't get me started on their backing the junta in Burma.

China: one of the many, perhaps arbitrary, causes that incited communal indignation in the two of us. Part of a list that included SUV drivers, unchecked capitalism, fur wearers, people who spit in public, and the plight of Palestinians. Obsessions that fused us together in our private spiral of frustrated, but very noble, negativity.

*

At the airport, two ladies in line wait to check in their golf bags:

"Oh my Lord, I heard he's so handsome," says the short woman with the big hair.

"I don't believe!" says the tall one wearing fake Gucci from head to foot.

"Oh yes, like a matinee idol. Like a young Fernando V. Estregan, but with great pecs. Why can't I have security guards who look like him?"

"They say he's like a modern-day Limahong. But more of a Robin Hood! They say he made some money as an overseas worker in Saudi, came home, and invested it, but was a victim of another one of those pyramid schemes. They say he might be the one behind all the bombings. But I don't believe. He just wants to get back at the Changco couple."

"I know! Imagine? Out of love! His love made him totally loko!"

The Gucci girl retrieves from her bag one of those glitzy local celebrity magazines. She holds it up reverently. On the cover is a hazy headshot of a dark and handsome man in a blue security guard's uniform. Something in his bearing is exceedingly dignified. Something in his epaulettes and shotgun slung over his shoulder. In his badge polished to a proud shine. In his unruly brush of black hair uncowed by the caps security guards are forced to wear. He looks authoritative. His eyes stare out as if he's been expecting all his life a chance at something larger than what he has.

"Oh my Lord," says Gucci girl. "Yum."

"And what a noble name! Wigberto Lakandula!"

*

Our curious protagonist—eyes closed as the plane takes flight for Bacolod, the thrum of the engines a gruff sedative—bows his head to the persistence of jet lag. In his dream he is typing a passage. Or maybe someone else is typing it. He can't be sure. It's only hands that he sees. The letters collect. "You must make a choice. It will be difficult. You have to take sides. You cannot sit on the side-lines. If you do, you are a deserter. No man is an island, isthmus, atoll, conti-nent, or hemisphere. Everything to the west is yours, everything to the east is theirs. Whatever they may say, your story is truly your own. You have a re-sponsibility to it, the way a father has to a child. Damn your detractors, your hurt-faced family. They can't take it away from you, just because they feature in it. They lay no rightful claim. They've already laid claim to their lives. Too late! It's been done. What's yours is yours, theirs is theirs. Nothing to be done, Pozzo. You can't wait for them to die, because the dead must be respected. Truly, what epiphany will force you to a decision? Riches and fame? Fire-works? A great flood? A riot? A river aflame? Yet another death? A choice must be made. Independence or duty. Love or freedom. Poor little rich boy. A father must take credit for his child, but never a child for his father."

*

Cristo was not alone. His father the Capitan, a devout Catholic, had sired a child outside the marriage in the early 1860s. Though no documentation exists, family mythology shamefully insists that the story is fact. The Capitan's illegitimate son—Cristo's half brother—became a Recollect friar, Fray Augustino Salvador, who, it was said, in turn impregnated, in the confessional, the fourteen-year-old Sita Reyes, daughter of Bacolod's roaming knife sharpener, Joselito, fa-mous for his baritone voice that sang out beautifully as he lugged his whetstone wheel from street to street. Sita was disowned and gave birth in a hospice. When the nuns took the baby from her arms to raise him, out of sin, in Iloilo's Orphanage of San Lazaro, Sita's fac-ulties twisted irreversibly. She was damned to wandering the streets of Bacolod, searching for her child and threatening to take any un-watched baby as her own, as if a character from the books of Rizal.

Under the tutelage of the nuns, Sita's son grew to become Respeto Reyes, the powerful Ilonggo politician who would challenge the Capitan's own grandchild, Junior, at every turn of his career. The legend is generously helped along by Reyes himself, who successfully manufactured a cult of personality as a true Visayan patriot: an orphan, of the people, against the Spanish-descended hegemony, beyond the reach of Americans. Among the Salvadors, however, the story was always avoided and, when mentioned, met with wry and condescending smiles. Junior, however, was more vehement: whenever faced with the gossip, he liked to declare, "The Salvador family would never breed a bastard."

—from the biography in progress, *Crispin Salvador: Eight Lives Lived*, by Miguel Syjuco

*

Overheard in the airplane:

". . . and of course, due to that, they're in real trouble," one man says behind me. "You can cover up your environmental sins locally. But as soon as the world media gets involved, the government gets egg on its face."

"Tell it to the marines!" says the other man. "Nothing will come of it, believe you me. Remember when they blew up their asbestos plant? Acquittal! The judge even ordered the insurance company to pay."

"But how can there be no consequences *now*? There was a front-page story in the Asian edition of *Time* magazine. And those World Warden environmentalists are stirring trouble."

"Nothing will come of it. Remember '91? PhilFirst Timber's illegal logging and the landslide in Ormoc? More than two thousand dead. What happened then? Scot-free! Changco even *made* money. As he said at the last Elite Club meeting—"

"I wasn't there. I had business in Hong Kong. You should have seen her. Almost six feet tall, Russian blondie. Pink nipples, Jake! Pink. No bigger than a peso coin—"

"At the Elite Club, Dingdong tells the audience: the Chinese character for crisis is the same one for opportunity."

"I don't read Chinese."

"Well, it's true. I told him after, 'D.D., that may be so, but in Filipino there's only one word for success: cashmoney.' We had a good laugh at that one. I mean, come on: two thousand–plus washed into the sea. What happened to D.D.? PhilFirst Funerals made a killing—"

"Haha!"

"PhilFirst Construction developed those pastel houses. PhilFirst Homes sold them. PhilFirst Holdings posted record profits that quarter. Now there's a PhilFirst SuperMall, where the bodies were piled."

"You know the company slogan. 'There's no stopping progress.'"

"Go ahead. Sell your stock. To me! D.D. has Estregan's ear."

"More like his balls. But what about when Bansamoro has Estregan's head? I'll bet PhilFirst will slump."

"Game! A weekend at Tagaytay Highlands. We'll stay in my chalet and play two rounds. Then have a Kobe steak dinner. We'll even open the Petrus."

"And if you win?"

"We take your chopper to your beach house. You bring the girls. But not that one with the bleached hair. I prefer the charming student from AMA. We'll help pay her tuition."

*

I had lunch at La Perle d'Bacolod City. Spent time at a lonely Internet café. Still no response from crispin1037@elsalvador.gob.sv. I even went through my spam in box, but found only the typical crap. Then I went and sat under a tree in the Public Plaza while studying my *Lonely Planet* guidebook.

I didn't have to look hard to recognize the city of Crispin's early stories: the groves of ancient acacias with wide branches, the grand old bishop's palace and San Sebastian Cathedral, the stone gazebo with spires and bevelled dedications to Mozart, Beethoven, and Haydn—crumbling landmarks standing valiantly among belching vehicles, spitting pedestrians in Fubu sleeveless shirts, signs hawking cell-phone credits, saccharine radio hits remixed to techno beats, the flashy lights of Lupas Landcorp's Bacolod Plaza Mall. The neoclassical Provincial Capitol building—now the Sugar Museum—was where Crispin used to play on the steps while waiting for his father, under the watchful eyes of Gorio, the equestrian-booted and capped chauffeur. It now houses an array of sugar plantation artifacts and a bequeathed toy collection.

Awaiting the hour of my appointment with Lena, I walked among the exhibits, endeared and saddened the way one is sometimes by the museums of our country: the typewritten display notes often misspelled and fastened with by-now brittle and peeling cellophane tape; old photographs and paintings succumbing to the slow but constant assault of moisture; dioramas and taxidermy specimens well on their way to manginess; the Plexiglas donation box thinly lined with the lowest denomination of coins and plastic straws and Juicy Fruit wrappers. I overheard the ancient curator giving a tour to a pair of odorous blond backpackers; his English was proper and colonial, with such a fresh earnestness it was as if he were presenting memories entirely his own. The backpackers seemed to be having a hard time following him.

Now, on the way to Swanee, the Salvadors' estate, the long roads leading to the haciendas, lined claustrophobically with tall green cane, offer glimpses of the distant sea. When passing a crossroads I turn my head and follow, briefly, until it swings away as we move on, the long green corridor ending in two swatches of different blues.

*

Cristo arrived at the New Year's party unexpectedly, inciting among his old friends quite a commotion, with several of them abandoning the dancing to come shake his hand. It had been several years—five, to be precise—though he was surprised that his peers had changed only incrementally. Only the styles of their moustaches, beards, and attire altered, keeping with the latest European vogue. After the fanfare of his welcome subsided, his friends returned to their circles, and Cristo stepped outside onto the porch.

The moon has already risen. Every night for forty nights he watched it waning then waxing over the deck of his ship, and now it is becoming whole again. Bigger, fuller, than it had ever been in Madrid. The air here is much cooler than it had been in Manila, as if the walls and streets of the capital retained the warmth of days, or imbibed the heat of the rumours of revolution he'd heard spoken in private places. Here, at home in Bacolod, the evening seems to breathe more freely. Or perhaps, he considers with a smile, I am just succumbing to the nostalgia of arriving. He lights his pipe.

Only after he has stoked it and it burns well does he realize he is not alone on the porch. In the darkness of the far corner, beside a large potted plant, he sees three figures huddled, whispering emphatically. He considers returning inside before they notice him, but the shadows abruptly adjourn their furtive congress and face him. One, then two, then all three of them call out his name, joyfully. The conspirators emerge from the gloom, large smiles on their faces, and grab and shake his arms and slap him across the back, welcoming him home and wishing him a prosperous 1895. They are his old, dear friends, Aniceto Lacson, Juan Araneta, and Martin Claparols, the three laughing out loud, the way one does when embarrassed suddenly, as if hiding something ignominious.

—from *The Enlightened* (page 122), by Crispin Salvador

*

In any of the predestinations of Fate there exists complex, unexplored dramas. Each of us is born into trouble . . . even freedom resulting from material security creates a vacuum, a Fourth Hunger, that must be filled, by either opportunities taken or ennui, or any combination of distraction, faith, success, neuroses, or social/familial dysfunction. Pity not the elite, but do not condemn them all. It is not in the interest of any progressive-minded citizen . . . Vilification, by its definition, creates an antagonistic struggle, an us-versus-them mentality, that throws us all into a senseless battle-royale. The slaves of today will become the tyrants of tomorrow—the proletariat overthrows the hegemon to become the hegemon itself, only to be eventually overthrown by a proto-hegemon that will in turn lose its position. It is this dizzying cycle that keeps humanity chasing the tail it lost millennia ago . . . The Alienation of the Elite is the unpolitical effect of the political. It concerns the plutocracy's own legitimate, and sympathetically human, frustration with this downward-spiralling human condition, and not just the malaise of having.

—from the 1976 essay "Socrates Dissatisfied," by Crispin Salvador

*

The estate, dubbed Swanee by Salvador's grandparents, Cristo Patricio Salvador and Maria Clara Lupas, lies seven and a half miles from Bacolod, the major city on the island split by the provinces of Negros Occidental on the northwest and Negros Oriental on the southeast. The plantation fits snugly between Talisay and Silay and sits at the very beginning of the very first foothill that precedes Mount Mandalagan. For three generations, due to the intermittent reliability of the unsealed roads and the heavy traffic of carts drawn by water buffalo and the cane-laden trucks, the estate seemed more isolated than it does today. The beach, however, not far by horseback or bicycle on a path that leads straight from their front door, presented another world for the Salvador children—a rocky curve of white sand giving on to susurrating waves. In the summer, the water was so clear the aquatic life seemed suspended in air—galaxies of sea urchins, rainbows of anemones, clouds of fish. During the rainy season, due to runoff from the denuded mountains and foothills, the water became murky enough to present a mystery and a sense of foreboding. On every corner of Swanee, on months with the blustery Habagat, the air would smell of sea; and when the Amihan blew, the wind carried the scent of syrup from the Horno Mejor sugar mill.

Swanee is the centre of five sugar plantations carved out by the clan after the land was sold to the elder Salvador at a rock-bottom price by Gobernadorcillo Bernardino de los Santos in January of 1890. Each of the five plots—on New Year's Day 1905 named Swanee, Kissimmee, Mamie, Clementine, and Susanna—was given to one of the five Salvador sons, though by the time Crispin was an adult two had been sold to in-laws from the Lupas clan. Atop the hill overlooking the five estates is the manor Salvador's grandfather Cristo had built entirely of coconut timber. In its courtyard is an old Spanish-era tower that served, in turn, as a lighthouse, parish belfry, hermitage, and sniper lookout. During Salvador's childhood, it was the private perch of the white-crowned patriarch, who had filled it with books, celestial charts, rifles, bird cages, and shiny brass telescopes. From there, the elder Salvador, a widower since 1925, would observe the operations of his sugar mill and his children's plantations, spending hours squinting through the eyepiece of his big reflecting scope to watch each family's comings, goings, and odd hobbies, sending unheeded instructions and baseless remonstrations by carrier pigeon. Even approaching his deathbed, Cristo insisted on managing affairs, having a quartet of burly maids (he called them "pallbearers") carry him on a cot to the mill each Monday.

—from the biography in progress, *Crispin Salvador: Eight Lives Lived*, by Miguel Syjuco

*

Come to think of it, I was not surprised when Crispin asked me to be his research assistant. There'd been a shift along the way. He began to address me with the Filipino familiarity "pare," the way we do old compatriots. Sometimes he was even playful with it, perverting the soft "pah-reh" by pronouncing it as would an American GI on shore leave, with the hard consonants and overly elongated final syllable—"pair-ree." This sudden casualness made all the difference.

Around that time, Madison and I were speaking seriously about moving to Africa—to help build houses for Jimmy Carter's Habitat for Humanity, or work with the Peace Corps in Swaziland. It was her grand plan. She was convinced it would be to her benefit in her eventual application for a master's at the School of International and Public Affairs at Columbia University. She thought it would also serve my writing well for me to witness some, as she said, "real suffering." As if I'd not grown up in the Philippines. As if I'd not been through the slums and dying farmland on my grandparents' campaign trails. Africa, however, was a really big commitment. I didn't want to give up everything I had in New York to find myself dumped in the middle of the sub-Saharan continent after she left me for some Wagner-singing German archaeologist with a big shovel.

I knew Crispin was working on *TBA* and I wanted to help. I gently hinted to him that I either needed a job or would have to leave New York. I of course made it clear that I much preferred to work for my country (which is what Crispin always considered writing about the Philippines to be). With a show of benevolence, he made me an offer. I accepted, even though sudden apprehension rose up inside me regarding our developing relationship—a dandy with few friends, estranged from his family, solicitous toward me, never had children. It wasn't anything overt. But why his interest? I suppose it spoke as much of my own insecurities about my abilities and personality as it did my perception of his liberal, meticulous ways. I was disappointed when he didn't let me work on *TBA* at all, instead relegating me to assisting in his class work.

To make Crispin aware of the boundaries of our friendship, I often spoke of Madison. About, for example, how upset she was that we weren't leaving, about her behaviour after she wrote her e-mails declining the African opportunities. The hour of our planned departure to the heart of darkness had come and gone. To make it up to her I'd cooked a romantic tofurkey dinner. We ate in silence. Then, after watching the season finale of *Survivor*, which I'd thoughtfully taped for her on our old VHS recorder, Madison blew up. Crispin listened kindly to such stories, though he declined to offer any advice.

I eventually decided he was more avuncular than pederastic. At times he was even fatherly, which made me officially feel sorry for him. He would have been a good father. At least I think so. He seemed to understand my thirst for those obscure things that I didn't yet possess as part of me. The things that mattered in the grand scheme. You see, Grapes had always been all about the details, results, recognition. I was surprised to discover that Crispin possessed a gentle tolerance, though only after he convinced himself of his faith in you. He was kind in the way only the ungenerous can be. As we became closer, my opinion, while not usually accepted as correct, was increasingly solicited. And dogsbodying for him wasn't difficult, even if he often asked me to do tasks like shine his wingtips or trim his bonsai trees.

*

As the cane fields blur along the road to Swanee, my mind goes to my mother. She was born near here, and so was I. In a way, I'm like a salmon coming home to spawn, at a point of origin so alien it feels like my birth certificate was false. But with very little imagination, I can see the sort of life she had, for Bacolod is a place of constancies. That must be reassuring to those who live and die here.

My life's own only constant has been the secondhand memories of her and Dad, filed inside me like vintage postcards in a curio shop. Wish we were with you, the messages on the back would have said, scrawled in an obsolete style of longhand. What passes for my roots are old moments I did not witness, memorialized in mirrored frames on my grandmother's baby grand piano. Mom in Venice, smoking a cigarette while leaning on the rail of a vaporetto; on that trip she'd spent too much on antique masks and she and Dad had fought—he knew he'd been vicious, and went secretly back to the shop to buy her the most expensive one. My father at a massive rally, standing on one of those dilapidated tractors donated by U.S. aid agencies, his head back and arms spread wide like the *Oblation* statue at the University of the Philippines—the eve of his first election victory, a young man at the cusp of his dreams. Both my parents dancing a waltz at a wedding in the garden of an ancestral home somewhere on this island, Dad whispering something in her ear, Mom pulling him close and laughing as the crowd behind them watched—this is how I best like to remember my parents.

This place, too, is where two of Crispin's lives began. The first, his birth. The second, his independence. It was 1975, a year made for those romantic tragedies distrusted by the moneyed, loved honestly by the poor, and watched guiltily by the middle class when seen in soap-opera melodramas: Bacolod families tottering on the brink, squabbling like dogs over a carcass, suddenly renewing their faith in God, waiting for the market to right as if they were dancers looking to the sky for rain.

It's an intriguing scene: Sugar, like mountains of gold dust, filling bathtubs, ballrooms, garages, pelota courts. Junior standing at the front door, screaming that any discussion of his marital indiscretions only hurts Leonora more. Crispin turning his back, hefting his suitcase onto his shoulder and setting out toward the dusty road away from Swanee, his father having refused to let anyone drive his son to town. The windowpanes trimmed with plastic holly, a painted plywood Santa and Rudolph on the roof. Narcisito and Lena peeking like children from an upstairs window, faces twisted and wetted by their impotence. Crispin's receding figure wrinkling in the yellow heat, pausing to look one last time at his siblings, his childhood paradise, the swimming pool brimmed with sugar, the now empty doorway where nobody else had stood to see him off.

That's when the family started to fall to pieces.

3

From Marcel Avellaneda's blog, "The Burley Raconteur," December 2, 2002:

And the latest scuttlebutt. The President's speech yesterday to members of the Combined Military Forces at Fort Bonifacio was disrupted when twenty-six hecklers were arrested and charged with "scandal" and "alarm." They were mauled by crowds as they were brought into the precinct office, though none suffered significant injuries. Read the full story in Ricardo Roxas IV's blog, My Daily Vitamins, <u>here</u>.

In other news, the President's Unanimity walk was again nixed this morning due to the unseasonal typhoon conditions. Politicians and dignitaries waited for rain to subside while photographers snapped them yawning, texting, picking their teeth, and looking at the sky. This is the twelfth Unanimity procession cancelled. It has tongues wagging that while the President's national Unanimity party does include powerful lackeys and cronies, even God and Mother Nature have cast their lot with members of GLOO.

Speaking of GLOO, there has been much comment from members of the GLorious OppOsition party, particularly from Senator Nuredin Bansamoro, admonishing the wagging tongues for hyping up threats of an imminent coup. Bansamoro, looking self-assured and presidentiable, said "a coup is only likely if launched by the government as a diversionary tactic." He also said that "a house divided upon itself is like a mental patient" and "any armed conflict would further discourage Ikea from opening shop." This from a man who is alleged to have made his fortune as the mastermind behind the kidnapping fad of the last decade. Read the full insider's story in Cece Cebu's Syutukil <u>blog</u>. Also catch the funny, unauthorized photographs of pols milling about looking at rain clouds in Bayani-ako's <u>Bayan Bayani</u>.

Some posts from the message boards below:

—That's 2 funny! (derridalover@skycable.ph)

—Buy cellphones at CellShocked.com.ph! All unlocked. Authentic Louis Vuitton reprod belt case free with every purchase. (Paulojavier@cellshocked.com.ph)

—I think Estregan's smarter than he looks. (radiohead@destiny.ph)

—Does anyone know what the 26 hecklers said? Wld luv to hear it. (joey@excite.com)

—Nuredin Bansamoro scares me. Could his Muslim faith link him to the bombings in Mindanao? (Miracle@Lourdes.ph)

—Miracle, don't you know that Bansamoro is famous for not allowing his faith to enter politics? As he's famously said: "My religion and government are forever separate. Neither will they be in opposition nor in complicity." And his track record has proven it so. (theburleyraconteur@avellaneda.com)

—Who cares about all this shet anyway? You guys are wasting ur time posting on these blogs. (cutiepie.gomez@philfirstcorp.ph)

—Buy cellphones at CellShocked.com.ph! All unlocked. Authentic Louis Vuitton reprod belt case free with every purchase. (Paulojavier@cellshocked.com)

—Buy cellphones at CellShocked.com.ph! All unlocked. Authentic Louis Vuitton reprod belt case free with every purchase. (Paulojavier@cellshocked.com.ph)

—Hey, what's going on with your blog, Marcel? Backchannel me and I'll tell you how to fix the spammers. (Linuxlover@me.com.ph)

—Thanks Linuxlover. I've fixed it. It should be okay now. (theburley raconteur@avellaneda.com)

—OMG, dont by from CellShocked. Its a total rip! Da LV belt carrier s like plastic & it peels rly easy. Caveat emptor! Thats empty cave, 2 u idiots. (gundamlover@hotmail.com)

—Has anyone heard about what that starlet Vita Nova is saying? I got a text message on my cell this a.m. about how she's got dirt on Estregan. Something about a sex tape. (chis-miss@pldt.ph)

*

Confidently ascertaining the facts of Salvador's childhood is impossible. His own autobiography is famously at odds with his father's much-read reminiscences, which were serialized in 1993 in *The Philippine Gazette* and later made into the PhilFirstTV Channel miniseries, *Confessions of a Statesman: The True-to-Life Story of Narciso "Junior" Salvador.*

According to *Autoplagiarist* and other sources, Crispin Salvador's childhood was almost entirely devoid of his father's affection, yet absolutely filled with his father's politics. He was, after all, the golden child of Junior Salvador, and before young Crispin could speak or toddle he was already branded "the future president for a future nation." In the era between the Philippine-American War and the Second World War, such effusive patriotism was not uncommon; in addition to the timeless jockeying for position and influence, there abounded, in many circles, a persistent preoccupation with independence. In those years, the young Salvador children rarely saw their father, whose position in the Philippine Legislature required his presence in Manila; his burgeoning rivalry with the fiery nationalist Respeto Reyes took all his attention.

For Junior, the life away from his family suited his wayward nature—Manila in the 1930s, after all, was a place of energy and intrigue, a spicy stew of global influences, in which those who lobbied for independence were considered by certain cognoscenti to be fighting the noble and ever loyal fight, even as they were engaged in necessary compromise.

It was a fine time in one of the finest cities of the world. On the streets, enterprise and history vibrated together, and perspiring archetypes—businessmen, charlatans, refugees, fortune hunters—came from around the globe and thrived: Jews fleeing Europe, Germans operating a glassworks, Portuguese gamblers from Macau, Chinese coolies from Fujian province, Japanese labourers, Indian moneylenders, Moro imams with scraggly beards, Latin American industrialists in fine linen suits, Spanish insulares born on the islands and peninsulares born in the mother country, Dutch merchants, even the descendants of Sepoy mutineers from the two years Britain ruled our archipelago. Most brash among the immigrants were the Americans, some outrightly imperious, many well-meaning, all inspired by William McKinley's "benevolent assimilation"—civil servants, missionaries, teachers, soldiers, entrepreneurs, wives. Imported from the far corners of the planet were the latest practices and fashions, each unerringly seized by the locals and turned into a virtual parody by overly vigorous execution. Junior, with his talent for languages, thrived in this city. He was often spotted at the Polo or the Army and Navy clubs sporting a new hat, or photographed hobnobbing with such imposing figures as General MacArthur, whom he visited often in the Manila Hotel, bearing gifts.

But when she was pregnant with Crispin, Leonora gave Junior an ultimatum: Leave his Manila mistress, a beautiful minor actress in the fledgling Philippine film industry, and spend more time in Bacolod. Otherwise Leonora would leave with the children. Whether from the impetus of love or an aversion to scandal, Junior dedicated more attention to his family in the province, and Leonora, at the start of her third trimester, took to accompanying him on his trips to Manila. As a result, after Crispin was born, his position as a "reconciliation child" forced on him intermittent bouts of—when his parents were home—suffocating attention, overstarched hand-me-down sailor suits, mollycoddling, and—when his parents were absent—liberating stretches in which to play with his siblings and spend time with his tutor and beloved gardener. Even Junior's distant attitude toward his children was influenced by Leonora, who made up for her general lack of maternal warmth by hogging the kids whenever her husband was present, doting on them so sporadically it left them bewildered and forever cynical of her intentions. Indeed, Crispin's first memories were of being "a performing monkey." In *Autoplagiarist*, he describes being made to "sit up as straight as a stone saint and recite the infernal ABC's for my father, then the prayer to Saint Crispin for Mama. More often than not, errors resulted in their disappointment in me and, of course, scoldings for my tutor and nanny and siblings—for their supposed neglect of my education."

It was the first of many incidents, however, that cracked the struggling idyll. One dry-season evening during the hottest week in memory, as the Salvador children slept, Crispin's sister, Lena, was awakened by the opening of their bedroom door. She saw the shape of her father's form outlined against the light in the hallway, and, according to her brother's account of the event, she "could hear the sobbing screams from our mother's bedroom, her doorknob rattling desperately against its lock." Lena, Salvador wrote, heard her father's breathing—"an unforgettable, savage sound"—and smelled the gin. Salvador described her as watching in both fear and relief as their father bypassed her to stand over the sleeping Narcisito. Distant down the hall, their mother banged and screamed. Then Lena saw her father "brandishing his rattan riding crop, saw it held high above his head, heard it come down repeatedly until poor Narcisito cried out for mercy, witnessed it strike again and again until our brother fell into whimpering silence."

—from the biography in progress, Crispin Salvador:
Eight Lives Lived, by Miguel Syjuco

*

After my parents died, we kids were flown from a Manila polluted by tragedy to the happy, fresh air of the Vancouver airport, the grandparents we hardly knew waiting for us in Arrivals. I remember, slightly, the terror we kids had faced getting on that airplane, our awareness of its heavy fallibility all too fresh in our minds. I recall, vaguely, the grief I held on to during that seventeen-hour flight—though sometimes I feel that, in honour of my parents, its memory should be sharper. Instead, it is the happiness that followed that fills my recollections: the glow of fresh paint in the brand-new house my grandparents bought to fit us all; the breakfasts in the kitchen by the big window from where we'd watch crows gather on the telephone lines; our first exuberant encounter with snow; Granma's bedtime stories of Grapes's vast political dreams, the excitement of the rallies, his long campaigns, the glory that would one day come again; Grapes sleeping the days away to spend wakeful nights that were days somewhere else—a parallel unseen dimension we were told was still our home, though we slowly disbelieved it.

To catch up on having missed our childhoods, Grapes and Granma let us camp on the floor of their bedroom, let us skip more school than they should have. I knew my way through the darkness of their room, blacked out completely from the sun, guided by Grapes's snores or the lingering scent Granma left in bed—Oil of Olay and cigarettes. When Grapes awoke, I'd climb into bed happily, to walk on his back, or hide with him beneath the covers—soldiers in a foxhole evading the Vietcong. At night, we made bullets in the garage: still with me is the tinkle of the machine that tumbled the copper casings, the smell of lead bars and the mystery of bullet moulds, the satisfaction of pressing a lead slug in place. With Granma, I read aloud till it was she who fell asleep beside me. I broke her cigarettes so that she'd quit. I imagined throwing tantrums each time I heard her fighting with Grapes; my wails would have outdone her screams and accusations of broken promises, of contrary dreams fueled both by her hunger for peace and by his frustration that he would likely die, unfulfilled, in exile. But I never had the guts to create a diversion. I didn't know yet the collateral damage of one vitality succumbing to another; even if I knew that nobody should see their grandmother cry.

Then we kids were driven from our warm house to the sad, damp air of the Vancouver airport as our grandparents checked in their hoard of bags—enough to last them the months they'd be gone. Their subsequent trips were longer than the first: to see what it was like post-Marcos, to see if Grapes could return to politics, to see to the zipper business, to run in the gubernatorial election. It was always the same: from the huge, cold windows we'd wave at the airplane being towed slowly backward, wondering if Grapes and Granma could still see us from their seats. We'd wave until it took off, until it was a speck in the sky, and wave some more, just in case.

We'd return to our house on The Square, the one tour buses stopped in front of; to the home filled with gold reclining Buddhas and dark wooden furniture that smelled of polish, with a Xerox and a telex, with a room just for Grapes's suits, with a treadmill and a massage chair and one of those contraptions that inverted Grapes for circulation and posture. His presence was more ubiquitous because of his absence. We were too busy missing him to miss our father.

My older siblings became my parents.

My eldest brother, Jesu, with his Inuit moccasins and electric guitars, taught by example the concept of cool. With him, I discovered the world beyond books. We camped in the backyard, hiked mountains, assembled a remote-control plane. It was he who held the back of my bike seat the afternoon my training wheels were removed, his arm holding me straight so that I could shoot off free for the first time.

My eldest sister, Claire, the natural mother, was used to, and therefore intent on, being everyone's favourite. I would sit with her at her dresser, watch her put on makeup, pleased when she made up my face with a fake shiner. When she giggled to her boyfriend quietly on the kitchen telephone, she made us younger ones look forward to finally being in love.

My next older brother, Mario, who wrestled with me and Jerald, was never too grown up to make believe with us at being André the Giant and the Iron Sheik. He'd ring me from our second phone line, pretending to be Irene Cara, making me blush until I cried. Many a morning I'd tiptoe into his room, dodging socks and tissues and tennis balls, to wake him to bring me to school, knowing that later his fingers around the back of my neck would half guide me, half carry me to the bus.

My next older sister, Charlotte, the handful, impressed me with her notorious hairstyles and varsity volleyball jacket. She'd bring Jerald and me to Baskin-Robbins for pineapple sundaes, picking up her forbidden sweetheart on the way, to see him for just ten minutes. From her I learned that my life could be my own.

And of course, my baby brother, Jerald, who had me just as I had him, until I became a preteen and he was still a kid—when he saved for me the cookies he got in class, I refused to eat them, because they were iced with clown faces and were for immature babies. Even then, we stayed best friends.

And always, the parents of us all, the succession of yayas my grandparents imported from home, who'd arrived as Pinay provincials, learned the ways of the West, then left to start the sorts of lives they'd never dared dream of: Sula, who raised each of us, who ran barefoot in the snow to carry me to the emergency room to stop my convulsions, who broke my heart by getting married; Estellita, skinny, severe, and elegant, she cared for us without knowing how to play; Juanita, who shared with us the games and songs of her still-recent childhood, whom we mocked for her accent and her foreign rhymes; the sisters Bing and Ning, equally patient, equally loving, equally underappreciated.

These were my days: grey rain; rides over Lion's Gate Bridge; sitting in the backseat, windows down, Level 42, Huey Lewis, Steve Winwood coming to us from CFOX; O-Pee-Chee hockey cards; knees burning on the Last Sorrowful Mystery of one Glory Be and Ten Hail Marys; my purple school sweater and tie; rumours of the Brothers who taught other grades molesting boys in New Brunswick or Ontario residential schools; pissing myself at a pep rally because I was too shy to ask to go to the restroom, then claiming I'd sat on something spilled; the ice on my back and my heart in my ears and the sky in my eyes as I tried to ignore the skating teacher calling my name. Then, puberty: the first odd hair; the unfathomable urges; the relentless turgidity; the desperate experiments against the wall or within cardboard toilet paper rolls; stealing Mario's lemon-fresh Right Guard deodorant to slick down the new fuzz in my armpits; breathlessly molesting with my eyes the perfectly drawn European girls in the *Heavy Metal* comics Jesu kept beneath his bed; then, the discovery of release thanks to the back massager Grapes kept plugged in beside his La-Z-Boy armchair—the glorious synchronicity of a Hitachi Magic Wand strategically applied during Madonna or Alannah Myles videos on MuchMusic. I heard my voice deepening, I saw contact lenses fitted into place, I watched Arsenio Hall each night, called the New Kids on the Block rad, wore mock turtlenecks and pinned the hem of my baggy trousers, hairsprayed my hair as high as it could go, danced the Running Man and Roger Rabbit, hung out in the mall with my friends, called the New Kids on the Block hosers, went to school dances, during "Stairway to Heaven" had a chick move my hands up from her ass until Page, Plant, Jones, and Bonham started rocking and she and I were forced to part and look at each other one last time before they turned on the lights.

Just when things were getting good, Grapes and Granma sat us six kids down and spoke seriously. "It's time," Grapes said, "for us all to return to the Philippines."

*

From Crispin's 1990 short story "Noblesse Oblige": "Efren Del Pais is a gentleman farmer with good intentions." He willingly, if not eagerly, submits to the CARP laws, the controversial agrarian reform legislation that appropriates plots of private land to distribute among the tenants who tend them. Most landowners resist the reforms—often violently, with militias intimidating the poor farmers and local officials. The smarter landowners take to exploiting a loophole, buying back the land from tenants who can't afford its upkeep. Del Pais, however, hopes to serve as a good example. The aging haciendero, educated by Jesuits, informed by the likes of John Locke and Thomas More, sacrifices his sprawling farm, keeping for himself only the ancestral home in which he and his children were born. His wife is dead, his son moved to England, his daughters well married, and Del Pais finds fulfillment in giving "sound advice and loans with pious terms" to the tenants who have taken over his land. After all, he's known many of them most of his life. "Del Pais, in his fading years and with an eye toward his soul, puts his trust in God and man's laws."

I remember the story for two reasons. First, in the story, Crispin gives the best account of Swanee (the two balete trees by the garden, the house's narra floors "polished as if to intimidate women in skirts," the carved relief-work ceiling in the dining room, the Persian carpets "musked by the mold thriving in the humidity," the card table with "ridges worn into its surface by elbows, worry, hope, luck," where his mother hosted games of mahjong and tsikitsa). Second, the story presents a moral conundrum regarding changing codes of conduct and the hard realities of the neofeudal society. It ends with the land Del Pais had passed on, so willingly, being bought up by neighbouring landlords, who themselves have just repurchased their own estates. Del Pais is left with only his home and the interest from his limited fortune, "his father's father's land lost and he surrounded on all sides by a siege of greed by men who were to him once his equals, though now suddenly in one way more and in many ways less." The last scene describes the old man standing in his garden, staring at his house "as if it is on fire."

*

*Our vernal protagonist is surprised by Lena's appearance—"Crispin in drag,"
he will later write, "an unsuccessful scarecrow, in a chintz muumuu"—and disappointed by Swanee's. Yes, it remains verdant—the balete trees monstrous,
the lawn still manicured like a putting green. The tall stone tower, long ruined
by artillery, now refurbished as a cellular site for telecom companies. But the
house itself is dour, flaking, patched—the air-con units rusting and dripping,
the capiz shell panes in the wooden window screens cracked or missing, the
lost roof tiles replaced with swatches of metal GI sheets. Interviewer and inter-
viewee sit outside. He is vaguely disappointed, too, in the sister herself. She
fiddles nervously with her walking stick. Reading Walt Whitman, she says,
was perfect for her brother's funeral, a good choice for a dead atheist who believed in the divinity of all things.*

*

"Where?" Dulcé asked.

"That one," Gardener told the girl, "over there, the one with roots for
branches. If we're not careful, we'll return there before our time."

Thick branches drooped sinewy tendrils around its trunk and deep into
the ground. Its hanging limbs reminded Dulcé of curtains, its roots like Gardener's knotty toes. A teacher at school had taught Dulcé the native names for
the trees in their region—narra, bakawan, almaciga, kamagong, molave—as
well as their foreign names. This tree was the balete, or moraceae, also known
as the strangler tree. The name alone sent shivers down Dulcé's spine.

"If you sleep at its base," Gardener said, "you will awaken trapped inside
it. Nobody will find you. Once, at night, I saw the branches part to reveal a
glowing door."

"What's in the door?" Dulcé said, suspiciously.

"Where we came from and where we're going."

Dulcé was skeptical. "My stepdad told me we originally came from
Spain," she said.

Gardener spat dismissively on the soil. "All I know," he said, "is that tree
is where we're all headed."

—from *Kapatid*, Book One of Crispin Salvador's *Kaputol* trilogy

*

My regard for my grandfather first started to dismantle in a church, years after we moved back to Manila. It was the day of my uncle Marcelo's funeral. Or maybe it was long before. Who knows? Maybe Tito Marcelo's funeral was merely a day of formal finality. Or the last slope before the bottom of my relationship with my grandfather.

Grapes had me write the eulogy he would read. It was not something I felt right doing, as if I were being drawn into a private argument in which I did not belong. I still don't understand it. Sure, we'd grown up with Grapes's stories of how Marcelo was given the best of educations only to become a struggling artist who chose to be, of all things, a security guard—one of the lowest rungs in our society—because it allowed him to write and sketch while on duty. (Granma said he shamed the good name of our family.) Or how Marcelo would secretly take Granma's paintings by National Artists, canvases worth a mint, and substitute copies he had made himself, selling the originals for far less than they were worth. (Granma said that as a boy he'd often come home from boarding school with items stolen from residence mates.) Or how Marcelo had written an unflattering novel about Grapes and Granma, even though the book was set at the 1904 World's Fair in St. Louis, Missouri, and was about an Igorot native whom the Americans had exhibited like an animal. (Granma was convinced the characters of the exhibit organizers were based on her and Grapes.) Or how Marcelo had made amends with my grandparents just five years earlier, coming to them with news he had rectal cancer and needed money for chemotherapy, but had really just spent the money they gave him on gambling and whores. (Of the alleged fraud, Grapes said my uncle would "get it in the end.") Though Tito Marcelo really did end up dying of rectal cancer, all those stories only made us love our grandparents more, and love even less the aunts and uncles we did not grow up with and would not get to know. And now I had to summon elegiac phrases to describe what I could only imagine of perfect paternal love.

Grapes stood at the altar and read what I had written, orating as if to a crowd of hungry voters made captive by a meal promised afterward. The words were my best estimate of what Grapes should have been feeling at his own son's death. Perhaps, unknown to me, his sense of loss had been so profound he'd been rendered speechless. Perhaps, after having to bury my father, the favoured, and then my uncle, the intractable, perhaps it was too much for Grapes to lose his two boys. Who knows? So I tried my best to write a good speech. For gravitas, I'd put in a couple of quotes from *King Lear.* Something about how it is the stars, the stars that govern our conditions. And how when we are born we cry that we are come to this great stage of fools. It wasn't because I thought Grapes anything like Lear. Maybe, in retrospect, his tragic relationship with rage did resonate. Anyway, I'd got the lines from a book of quotes, because I didn't know what else to add to a eulogy that deserved to contain more. After, my cousin sang a beautiful song she'd written for her father; when she was done we started to clap, but Granma grabbed my and my brother's hands sternly.

The honour guard from the national security guards' union, who'd shown up suddenly at my uncle's wake to stand sleepless vigil beside his casket—despite his having fallen out with them years ago over money—now took their places by his coffin, pallbearers to their longtime treasurer. "Go!" Granma urged us brothers. We went and took the handles from the guards, elbowing them roughly aside. The coffin dipped and almost fell.

At the gravesite, the lid was opened for one last time. My Tita Natty, Tito Marcelo's third wife, held his hand and wailed at the sky. I took his other hand, hoping to find a connection I'd not known in life. I had never touched a dead person before. I've never since.

I skipped the reception after. I was afraid Grapes would clap me on the shoulder proudly and tell everyone that I'd written the eulogy.

When I got home, I could hear Granma weeping in her room.

*

Erning has trouble getting a good tech job because the Americans are wary of accepting his foreign qualifications. So he hits the job listings in the classified ads and finds this: "Wanted—Porch Painter." Erning, excited, says to himself: Wow. This is great! In the Philippines, I've painted many things. The walls of our old house. My uncle's chicken coop. My niece's bicycle. I'm very qualified!

So Erning applies and shows up bright and early at the employer's house. The burly blond fellow explains to him, speaking slowly and loudly: "Okay, buddy. I don't know how you folks do it where you come from, but I want you to paint my porch in one day. First, scrape all the paint off to the bare surface. Then apply a coat of primer. When that dries, I want you to do two coats of this pink paint. Can you do that?"

Erning thinks it a strange request. Pink doesn't seem like a good colour at all. But Erning figures this is California. Besides, it's no use understanding Americans. Especially rich ones. "Yes, sir," Erning says eagerly. "I can remove paint and apply paint very well thank you very much!"

"Okay, buddy," the American says. "You've got the job. All the material's already been unloaded from the trunk of the car."

Only two hours later, the American hears a knock on his front door. When he opens it, Erning's there, standing proudly, flecked with pink paint. "Sir, the job is finished!"

"Far out, bro," says the American. "Only took you two hours! Are you sure you scraped the paint to the bare surface?"

"Yes, sir. I'm positively!"

"And you let the primer dry first?"

Erning nods.

"And then you put on two coats of pink?"

"You betcha by golly wow," Erning says. He's thrilled at being impressive. He thinks: If Americans are this taken by our work ethic, I'll have a high-paying tech job in no time.

The American is indeed impressed. "Wow, you Mexicans sure work well. Okay, buddy. You deserve a bonus. Here's another ten bucks!"

Erning is delighted. "Sir, thank you, sir!" Relishing this feeling of being a star employee, Erning adds: "But I have to tell you, sir, 'cause maybe you don't know much about these things. You don't own a Porch. Your car's a Ferrari."

*

In addition to Latin, Spanish, Ancient Greek, and French, young Salvador also learned basic Nippongo, though from Yataro, the family's Japanese gardener, who, Salvador recalled, "had a phobic aversion to having his photograph taken." The phrases the boy learned would later prove vital during the war. But for many years prior, "the funny little Yataro" oversaw the cosmetic upkeep of the estates. Yataro was remembered as "very learned" and introduced Salvador to bonsai by allowing him to "watch him at work, while impatiently explaining the virtue of patience." Yataro also had him repeat haiku verses by Basho, Buson, and Issa, "laughing with delight" at the boy's eventual success. Yataro, with his "military bearing and plodding reliability," was very respected by the family and was given responsibility over three Visayan gardeners. As a result, following completion of various improvement projects, his requests for vacations were usually granted and he travelled widely around the Philippines, "trusty Leica III hanging from his neck," always bringing back for the Salvador children small souvenirs and delicacies from distant provinces—a mortar and pestle of Romblon marble, "gooey sweet rice paste in sealed coconut husks" from Bohol, a kris from Mindanao with a sinuously curved blade, a conch from Leyte, a carved wooden fertility god from Ilocos Norte. It was because of Yataro that Salvador "first learned how vast and varied are the cultures of our islands. Little did I know, in addition to changing my life, Yataro would also save it."

> —from the biography in progress, *Crispin Salvador: Eight Lives Lived*, by Miguel Syjuco

*

Lena looked to me like Crispin in drag, like an unsuccessful scarecrow. Her voice wispy, but without the tremolo of the aged. Her handshake surprisingly firm. A surfeit of talcum and Provençal lavender was like an invisible aura around her. Her hair, dyed such a bad brown it was orange, was pulled severely into a bun on her head like a tangerine. She wore a rainbow chintz muumuu, leather clogs, sunglasses with diamantes, and many jingling bangles.

We sat outside on the shady veranda. Tea and plates of sliced guava and papaya had been laid out. A maid in a mint-green uniform materialized to cool us with a large straw fan, like something out of a Rudolph Valentino film. From the house came the reedy serenade of "Misty," the volume much too loud. When Lena saw me look inside, she sent the maid to fetch the CD cover. "Superlative, no? I *so* love it. Much more preferable to Richard Clayderman." The maid returned and Lena gestured her toward me with a movement like throwing a Frisbee. I studied the cover appreciatively: *Romance of the Oboe.*

When Lena recited Whitman, she closed her eyes, as her brother had been wont to do. "'And what do you think has become of the women and children? They are alive and well somewhere, the smallest sprout shows there is really no death, and if ever there was it led forward life, and does not wait at the end to arrest it. And ceas'd the moment life appear'd. All goes onward and outward, nothing collapses, and to die is different from what any one supposed, and luckier.'"

I take out my pad and my pen and start the interview by asking about Crispin's death.

"I know nothing about his vest," she says.

"No, I meant how do you think he died?"

"Do I think he'd mind what?"

"I'm sorry, um—let me get my list—er, did you two keep up correspondence when he was in New York?"

"No. I never did get to visit him in New York. I wanted to, but I never had the chance."

"Did you write him letters there?"

"I'm sorry. Would you mind speaking up?"

"I said, did you write him letters often?"

"Yes. Every week. We'd done it since the fifties, when I was sent to receive my schooling at King George V, in Hong Kong. About ten years ago, we stopped writing. It was like quitting smoking, not receiving a weekly dispatch from him. But I was far too peeved by him."

"For what?"

"I'm sorry?"

"I said, for what?"

"His memoirs."

"What do you mean?"

"Indeed! They were mean! Mercenary, in fact. He may have waited for Mama to die, but what of the rest of us? My brother's response was: 'But it's art! It's the truth!' As if that made it acceptable. You think these people in this country understand art? Half can't write their names. Still we let them vote. The other half, they can read about us in his book. No good can come from that. I used to blame that book for our brother Narcisito's mental troubles. I'd even given Crispy my childhood diaries beforehand, hoping they'd help him write honestly."

"What particularly bothered you?"

"Oh, you know."

The maid beside us transfers the fan from one arm to the other and resumes waving it. She shakes out the tired arm.

"Were you upset about what he said about Narcisito and your father?"

"Things he said about the holy Church."

"What did that have to do with Narcisito?"

"Crispin also wrote ghastly things about the family connection with that fascist Respeto Reyes. Or insinuations about my father bodily abusing us, when really it was just the zeitgeist. Same with those stories about the women my father turned to when Mama was sick. Papa was a *man*. Where else was he to find solace? And Crispy made public personal matters about my father's politics."

"Were the things he said untrue, or . . ."

"The things he said were untrue. My father was . . . Papa was a man who tried to help as many people as he could. But by Crispy's recollection, my father didn't have scruples. What a hypocrite. My father did have scruples, many, but he didn't let politics get in the way. You can't govern well if you have scruples. Everyone knows that."

"What about your mother?"

"Narcisito tried his level best to live up to Papa's expectations."

"No, I said, what about your mother?"

"Oh. I'm certain Mama turned in her grave until she was dizzy. Angels keep her. Crispy painted her as pitiful."

"So they were lies?"

"Of course there were no other guys!" Lena glared at me. "My mother was the definition of fidelity."

"No, I said, was what Crispin said lies?"

"I see. You have such a soft voice. Are you a seminarian? Well, I guess they weren't lies. They weren't how *we* would have put them. Were my mother alive, Crispin would have been more respectful."

"Do you think, in a way, Crispin meant the book to be a tribute? A chronicle of the truths that the family would otherwise lose?"

"That's a bit rich. Don't give my brother too much credit. He was in a purgatory of insignificance and wanted to resurrect himself. How does he do it? Shirks his duties, as usual, and steps on those who love him. For a long time I blamed that silly girl, Sadie Baxter. The graduate student from Topeka, Kansas. She was less than half his age. Everyone was in absolute horror at how *he* would corrupt *her*. Because, oh my, she was so curious. Oh my, so blond. Oh my, so pristine. But *she* corrupted *him*! It's not age that corrupts, it's youth. Plus, I think she was Jewish. It worried Papa, the idea that she was after our money. Her family had changed their name from Bachman or Bachstein or something like that. Why change your name if you have nothing to hide? Well, Crispy was mad for her. I hadn't seen him so smitten since that love affair with Mutya Dimatahimik."

"When was that? I'd never read about that."

"In the late sixties. The long love affair that would live in infamy. It affected him profoundly. It eventually broke up the Cinco Bravos. That's why he didn't write about it. He was culpable. Also, Sadie was the reason Crispy didn't do anything with his beloved Dulcinea, and why that relationship would be his most tragic failure . . ."

"What do you mean? That name is on my list of people to . . ."

"That tiny Sadie Baxter stirred inside my brother adolescent delusions, made him selfish and reckless. Perhaps because she was constantly photographing him, with that camera she always carried. Suddenly, each morning he's taking ginseng and ma huang and rhino horn. Ridiculous! I laugh, but it comes from a place of love. My brother was silly. I know now that I despised Sadie so that I could preserve my love for Crispin. But it was my hate for her that made him resent me. What can you do? Don't we all need to blame somebody?"

"Can you tell me about Dulcinea—"

"Is that my brother's fountain pen?"

"Um. Yes. You said I could take—"

"Keep it. That's fine."

"It means a lot to me. I'm using it to write his biography. I thought it was actually fitting . . ."

"It's fine. Really. It was just odd to see it in someone else's hands. It was our father's before Crispin had it. I'm sorry, what were we discussing prior? Ah, yes. After his memoir proved a failure, it was Sadie Baxter who left him."

"But I heard that he—"

"That's how it happened."

The maid with the fan shifts her weight onto her other hip and sighs.

"But your brother even dedicated *Autoplagiarist* to her."

"I know. But in fairness to that hotsipatootsie, I can quite imagine how difficult it was being around my brother during that time. He never came to terms with failing. No, it wasn't Sadie's fault. She was young. She had hopes. Plus she was *different*. Not so much Jewish, but Western. She couldn't be expected to understand how sacred family is to us. They cut their offspring loose right when they turn eighteen. The poor girl later died while bicycling in Monaco. I'm convinced her hard life was because she was never baptized."

"I'm sorry, but I have to ask again. Pardon my frankness. But do you think Crispin killed himself?"

Lena sighs and frowns. She thinks for a moment. "My short answer: No. Not directly. First, because it's a mortal sin, and Crispin, I have to believe, saw the light before the end. Second, he didn't have it in him. I mean, okay, fine, he wasn't quite sane. But suicidal?"

"What do you mean, 'not quite sane'?"

"When my mother was on her deathbed, that's when it all started. The corruption in Crispin's heart. I told him, it's a test, be like Abraham. Remember how the Lord tested Abraham by asking him to sacrifice his child Isaac? But after Mama died, Crispin was inconsolable. He'd flown from New York to see her and arrived the day of the night she left us for the Lord. He rushed to the hospital, but Papa wouldn't allow him into her room to say goodbye. It was for my mother's good. My father, you know, he loved her very much. He still had hope that, with prayers, her cancer could be defeated. He went all the way to the Vatican and donated a fortune. Papa got on his knees and begged the Pope to ask the Lord for His intercession. But Mama was in such pain. *Such* pain! Crispin had for weeks been saying maybe it was time to let her go. Easy to say while drinking martinis in Manhattan. So when Crispy arrived, Papa didn't allow him to see our mother. He told my brother it was Mama who refused to see him. I think maybe that was unfair. After, Crispin went back to New York and wrote his memoir. He refused to stay for the wake and didn't come to the funeral. When *Autoplagiarist* came out, my father felt betrayed. It was he who gave Crispin the money to publish it. Papa was always giving Crispin money, as an olive branch. So my father was very angry. As usual, he took it out on poor Narcisito. He treated him worse than the neighbour's dog. Narcisito gave Papa his whole life. But because he did, he could never get Papa's approval. I saw Narcisito in his room at the Fresh Starts Rehabilitation Retreat Home, and after I left, he hanged himself. I often wonder . . . had I stayed . . . or not visited that day . . ."

Lena sits silently, gazing away as if having her portrait painted. I watch and wait. Finally, she dabs at her eyes. Her face jells slowly into its former composure, then breaks into a little smile.

"Well," she says. "Just your typical rich family, I guess."

The maid with the fan looks toward the house. She sticks her tongue out at someone inside, scrunches up her nose, and blinks repeatedly in an odd way.

"What happened to Crispin?"

"One thing you'll learn when you get older is that when you hate someone so much, a part of you wants desperately to forgive them. But you can't decide if it's because you really want to, or if you just want to stop hating. I still don't know if forgiveness is generous or selfish. Maybe both. Crispin was such a talent as a young man. So mischievous. But he grew so angry. There's expedience in anger. Simplicity, too."

The final strains of oboes playing "Smoke Gets in Your Eyes" fade away. The CD loops to the start and "Misty" fills the air.

"Did you ever get to make amends with Crispin before he died?"

"Before he died, that last time he was in Manila—you know, in February, for his infamous fiasco at the Cultural Center—well, Crispy visited me before that. Just appeared. The maids said I had a visitor and I came down and there he was, suitcase beside him, fanning himself with his panama hat. I was convinced I was seeing a ghost. I even did the sign of the cross. When he looked up and smiled that irritating smile of his, I told him: 'What makes you think you're welcome here?' But even I was surprised that I didn't mean that."

"He came here? Did he mention writing *The Bridges Ablaze*?"

"We didn't talk about his work."

"For how long was he here?"

"I had nothing at all to fear. He was my baby brother."

"No, I said, how long was he here?"

"I'm sorry?"

"How long was he queer?" I couldn't resist.

"I see. Less than a week."

"That long?" I'm trying to keep a straight face.

"Weren't you his friend?"

"I was. I'm sorry, I am." I feel guilty. "But I was out of town, too. My girlfriend and I were in Costa Rica, helping build wells. My girlfriend at the time."

"Why not the Philippines? Isn't Costa Rica relatively well off?"

"Um, we didn't know that till we got there. What I want to ask is, did Crispin do any research? Like, take notes? Or . . ."

"No. Nothing. Really, it was divine. I admit, I didn't dare ask about his writing. It was just wonderful to see him. I didn't want to ruin it. He'd aged so. During his stay, he strolled barefoot around the garden. Ate very well. We took walks to the beach where we used to swim as children. Talking only about wonderful things. He read to me every night. That was something we did as kids, read to each other, especially during the war. He always did the best voices. He recited 'The Raven' with all sorts of trilled *r*'s and all. I should have known it was too superlative *not* to be the last time." Lena pauses. She wipes the sides of her eyes again.

"I'm sorry. It's just . . . Growing up, it was just us three children. Papa was always away. Mama, well, she wasn't really present. Despite what you read in Crispin's memoir. Mama didn't have a good relationship with her affections. Because of my father, Mama retreated into her painting, her botany. I rarely saw her laugh. Except with her best friend, Miss Florentina. Whom I assume you are interviewing. No? You must. Amazing woman. Still she lives alone. The archangels are protecting her. Other than them, she refuses to have household help. She was a legendary beauty. Not at all like me."

"No," I say, "um, I'm sure that wasn't true."

The maid with the fan rolls her eyes. She fingers the hem of her skirt, playing with a spot where the mint-green fabric has become frayed.

"Miss Florentina's name was *whispered* in the Spanish royal court. Ask her about her many suitors. It will make her happy. They were mad for her. She could have chosen from dozens. But she was never to be tied down. Even in conversation. Beware: you think you're fooling her when all along she's fooling you."

"What was the family connection?"

"She was the *dearest* of all our titas, though we weren't related. She was first a friend of our tito, Herculeo. You know, my father didn't even attend his funeral? His own brother. Tito Herculeo was, you know. A confirmed bachelor. At that time, it wasn't something you could be. Tito Herculeo always had the most beautiful clothes, and made gazpacho that was famous from here to Shanghai. Sorry, what was I discussing?"

"You were talking about Crispin's last visit. Was there anything strange?"

"Come to think of it, there *was* something surprising. I've had a long involvement with this group of children. My old classmate from the Assumption, Shirley Nuñes, a nun, a living saint, she educates the children of two towns in Antique province. I told Crispin, you know, your trip isn't so well timed, because I'm going up to visit. I go each February, before the season becomes hot. I've always loved children. So anyway, Crispy, he tells me, I'll go with you. I said, Ha! You won't last the day. But he came. We spent two days and one night. We looked at the cottage-industry projects I fund. Weaving, that's what they do. Remind me to give you one of the loincloths they make. They're wonderful as table runners. Anyway, all the children were so happy to see us. You see, many of their parents are gone. Then the kids get to a certain age and the light dulls in their eyes. Sorry? Oh, their parents go to the fish farms in the estuaries by the coast. Milkfish. Or many become domestic helpers or contract workers in Manila. Maybe Brunei or Saudi. It's hard. My friend Shirley is aging, and these people keep having children. I remember when Shirley wanted to introduce condoms to the people there and I had to stop her. Imagine?! I told her: 'Don't you dare! I'll cease my funding! I'll tell you to the diocese.' I don't know why those men and women just can't control themselves. I did. I think it's like animals. Bless them all, but still. Shirley says many children ensure a family of helping hands. I don't know about that. Don't get me wrong, you should see these children. Miracles, each one.

"This is the strange part. On the day we leave for home, Shirley and two kids are coming with us in the car to drop us at the town where we catch the ferry. As we enter the car, Crispy notices the other children are crying. A few are being unpleasant to the two dears accompanying us. What's wrong? he asks Shirley. She explains: Every year, the two with the best grades make a trip to see the sea. Only two, because she can't afford to bring them all. Most of the children had never seen the sea, even if it's only three hours away. Bear in mind, they're very remote. They don't even have television, so how will they know what an ocean looks like? Shirley explains: 'You should hear them trying to describe it to their friends. They simply cannot. I try to help, then I realize how impossible it is.' Well, Crispy, he's upset. Angry. The way he gets. He pulls out his wallet and sends Shirley with our car to contract jeepneys from the nearest town. Crispy just sat and waited, like a mule chewing grass. Nearly two hours in silence. I think he felt ashamed. He'd famously *hated* children. He thought I'd criticize him. The school motto we had at KGV is *Honestas ante Honores*. Honesty before glory. Not the sort of rot the Salvador men believed. I dare say, on that last trip, Crispy came round. Just like Saint Augustine."

A clock inside the house makes electronic cuckoo sounds, four times. A maid in a pink uniform comes out. She takes the place of the maid in the mint-green, hoisting the fan and moving it gently above us. The off-duty maid walks to the house, slowing a few yards from the door, waving, gesticulating, and acting all goofy to someone in the shadows of the sala.

"And that is how we took *all* the children to see the sea. Thirty-seven of them. I'll never forget it. Many children, mostly the older ones, were afraid of the water. But a few brave ones jumped right in.

The younger ones, would you believe? A few who thought they were courageous came running back each time a wave came. Eventually, they were all in the water, splashing and tumbling. I've never heard so much laughter. And Crispy just stood there, among all the excitement, hands in pockets, trousers rolled up and the water coming and going around his knees. He's always had that smug way of whistling his own tune, all my life, like he's ignoring you. Or as if he knows better than you. Narcisito and I hated that. But that afternoon, when Crispy whistled like that, it was more than okay.

"Afterward I made a mistake. On the ferry, I guess I was feeling sentimental leaning on the railing with him, watching our island on the horizon. I asked if he ever thought about what he'd leave behind. Those children had affected me. Crispin grew irate and stormed off. He didn't talk on the car ride home. Then he went straight to bed. The next morning, he was gone."

*

I don't really miss Madison. I don't have any regrets. I know everything ends, eventually. Another obvious statement is that, usually, when things are done and dusted, you can make sense of them. She was the love of my life until suddenly she wasn't.

The unfathomable Madison Liebling. The girl whose laughable name I fell in love with first. Environmental science student and minor-celebutante daughter of the Lincolnshire Lieblings' "ball bearings baron," the unexpressive father who had controversially, and uncharacteristically, married and claimed his Filipina "lady friend" after a stint in the U.S. Embassy in Manila during the David W. Newson tenure. Madison, equestrian prim and Miss Manners proper, with her improbably narrow waist, with her one blue eye and the other one brown (freckles in between spangling the perfect nose). We were made for each other. Except for, of course, the differences. How did we become so prejudiced by our idiosyncrasies? Despite her Puritan ancestors, her own half-breed background, the childhood that coincided with her parents' midlife study of Eastern philosophies and the healing powers of crystals, her extensive teenage travel, her Upper East Side and Seven Sisters refinements, she still could neither decode nor understand the nuances of our shared background.

Identity was never a quest for her. We shared the same languages, but spoke of worlds so subtly different that language was not enough. Over time the big things were left unsaid; they gave way to the little things, those once-endearing imperfections that had somewhere become deal breakers. Like how—despite her senior thesis on the environmental impact of public bathroom air hand-dryers versus recycled paper towels—she persisted in leaving on all the lights in our apartment when she went out. Or how she liked to watch her favourite show, *The Golden Girls*, with the volume too loud, even when I was working in the next room. And especially how she had, despite my well-voiced aesthetic preference, enlarged and framed a photo to affix over the mantel of our Williamsburg flat: the blue Earth rising over the horizon of the moon. Astronaut James Lovell had taken it during the Apollo 8 mission. Madison and I would sit on the couch, passing the bong, staring at the picture. She loved that photo. She said that it made everything look peaceful. No people, no countries, no borders. I found the sentiment cheesy. I liked to say I could see the hole in the ozone. This would upset her. Usually, we sat in silence, exhaling smoke.

*

Despite it being agreed, by one and all, that married life and fatherhood suit him well, Cristo cannot evade his fears. What of the rumours? And the connections? It is no better than the Inquisition, and guilt is often assumed before innocence can be proven.

Late that evening, long after the guests have left and his wife and children have gone to sleep, he writes in his diary: "The developments in the provinces around Manila make me both fear and long for trouble here. This is what we've been working for so long! It is close and I'm strangled by fear. I awaken weeping, alone in my room. Suddenly it is bigger, as if I'm in a strange field. The shadows are friars, soldiers, traitors, streaking through underbrush just beyond my seeing. If I suffer such nights, what must that final one have been like for my poor old friend José [Rizal]? Only upon entering Maria Clara's room, to hear her and the children's breathing, do I find the bravery to shirk my ideas of independence. Listening to them renews my faith in the reform movement, my conviction that soon will come concessions from Mother Spain—perhaps even representation in the Cortes. And yet, hardly a year has passed since these reasonable requests brought José before a firing squad. It seems only yesterday he and I were together in Madrid, young men in love with our own promise. Dawn arrives. Poor Maria Clara mistakes my fatigue for melancholy, something of her doing. Her tears devour me. But it must be my own cross. For my sons. My pride! Narciso Junior, the running terror. Little Achillo, only now beginning to hold his neck up. My third still in Maria Clara's womb. When I'm greeted by them in the morning, I wipe my heroic thoughts from my mind. Then an evening like tonight's entangles me. Aniceto, Juan, and Martin come for supper. Our ideas and the possibilities for change, our impatience, are as thick in the air as the smoke from our tobacco. These ignite again the fire that burns in my head through yet another sleepless night. Until the infernal process renews itself yet again come morning."

Cristo puts down his pen and rubs his eyes. Pondering the decisions, crushed by their opacity, he cries out: "Blessed Mary, Ever Virgin, assist me!"

–from *The Enlightened* (page 165), by Crispin Salvador

*

It was raining heavily the morning my sister Charlotte left. At least I think it was. I was only thirteen, yet she'd intimated her decision only to me. Our rooms in the house in Iligan, which our family rented after moving from Vancouver, were connected by a bathroom. Or maybe Charlotte and I had been close. I'm not sure. When she told me—her bags already packed—I wanted to stop her, but I wanted her to be happy. So I swallowed the heavy secret. I think it was the only one I've ever properly kept.

My grandparents were five hundred miles away, in Manila. Only three hours by plane, but absent again. Grapes and Granma had lately been fighting badly, taking it out on Charlotte, on me, on all of us grandkids. Granma was sure Grapes had another woman and she therefore refused to leave his side. She was convinced politics was either an excuse or an aid for his trespasses. And so, when he went to the capital for the national conference of governors—the final one for his term of office—Granma went with him.

Charlotte was gone when they returned.

Before anyone discovered that her bedroom was empty, I sat there among her orphaned possessions. The room still smelled of her, this fresh smell that I do not remember enough to describe, though I remember it sufficiently to know it was only hers. I went through her *Elle* magazines, cutting out all the photographs of girls in swimsuits, keeping them under my shirt to later hide away between the pages of my Bible.

I was young, but I understood. I couldn't blame my sister. She'd been wrested from her high school sweetheart and brought a world away to this paradise of hackneyed exoticism—golden mangoes, sun-drenched white-sand beaches, reef diving, and a language still so foreign to us our trying to speak it made the locals smile. We kids had been assigned bodyguards, drivers, maids to iron even our socks. Luxuries that improved then dissolved the sense of freedom we grandchildren knew in Canada. I hated hearing Charlotte downstairs in the corner of the playroom, crying long distance over the phone. I hated my grandparents—for bringing me here, to a new school; for screaming at Charlotte; for relocating us to a home from which they were still so often away.

In Charlotte's room, her bed was still unmade. I sat at its foot and went through the CDs she didn't take. On the new boombox Granma gave her for her birthday, I played Whitney Houston's "The Greatest Love of All." It was one of Charlotte's favourite songs, which she used to belt out beautifully as she accompanied herself on the baby grand that Grapes bought her. Whitney sang: "I believe the children are the future, teach them well and let them lead the way." By the time she reached the chorus—about making the choice not to follow in another person's shadow, and then that powerful bit about winning or losing but at least living a life that she believed in—by the time Whitney got to that part about keeping our dignity, I could hold back no longer: I crumpled and cried, once again, as I have many times when faced with no other options. In my shirt, the pages with the swimsuit girls crinkled and bent.

The weeks and months and, finally, the year after her departure were like a bad movie. Grapes disowned her, had us sign new articles of incorporation in which her name was excised from ownership of his assets, the material proof of his love for his family. He told people he had one fewer grandchild. I don't remember much of Granma during that time, which meant she was in her room too often. What must it have done to them to have lost, this time, a grandchild?

Mario told me that he hadn't seen Granma like this since I was too young to remember, since when my parents died. He told me that even through the rough time when our grandmother found out about Grapes's other woman—when Granma left him and brought us children to the country's nicest hotel for over a month, on Grapes's credit—Granma had held strong, for us. My brother made as if he were reassuring me that our grandmother would be okay, but by the act of sharing that weight with his thirteen-year-old brother, he ended up revealing how he, too, felt alone, jostled precipitously by my sister's departure. So close were Mario and Charlotte in age that they'd constantly fought, in the manner of those who share so much. He began to have trouble at university. He never went to class. Who would want to go to a university where everyone spoke in the local dialect that you couldn't understand, some even mocking him for being wealthy and only speaking English? One evening, my grandparents were berating Mario in the playroom. He sat between them, Grapes against the far wall, Granma leaning against the pool table. My brother's reticence likely infuriated my grandparents as much as Charlotte's insolence had. Granma grasped a billiard ball in frustration. Threw it at the floor. It bounced and hit Grapes smack-dab on the forehead. To this day, we kids laugh at this, though my grandparents cannot yet.

The one who seemed to weather the changes well was my eldest brother, Jesu. Somehow he appeared to thrive, taking up scuba diving, wearing his hair long, sporting a shark's tooth around his neck. He worked with Grapes at the main zipper factory, as his protégé and right-hand man, sacrificing the last years of his youth to our grandfather, a man who could never be sufficiently pleased—though perhaps it was only that Grapes's devotion to us was so deep, so fragile in its honesty, so ideal in its wholeness, that he expected perfect love in return. From Jesu, he demanded everything. All those years I mistook my brother as thriving later became etched as fading contradictions into his assumed seriousness. Jesu worked to rally us kids together, tried so relentlessly to save Granma from her own choice of her old woman's grief, that my eldest brother's manner turned steely. I wanted to shake it out of him to find the person I once knew.

Claire, by then, had escaped, married to a charming man with a moustache and living in California. Once in a while she'd call, and she'd cry, and we'd each match her tears. You could hear the guilt in her voice that she wasn't with us.

As only the young can do, Jerald and I grew, happily, despite the cracks in the family's foundation. We learned the rough local dialect. Joined the same basketball team. We gave each other flat-top haircuts. Wore matching gold chains. Slam-dunked the minibasketball in the low rim Grapes had his men install for us. Jerald and I took pictures of each other in midflight: I was Manute Bol, Jerald was Mugsy Bogues. We went often with Granma to Ingo's—a deli opened by a lumbering German who'd married a spritely local—the only place in hundreds of miles where one could find brie, bratwurst, smoked salmon, paté; we enjoyed imported steaks that weren't leathery like the ones from local cows. Granma made us promise not to tell our grandfather.

Two years after Charlotte left, construction on my grandparents' mansion was finally completed. The house clung to the side of an ancient windswept ravine, high in the hills overlooking Iligan City. Seven stories tall, the structure's four lower levels were left undeveloped, reserved for when each of us grandchildren would start our own families. For the interiors, Grapes and Granma pored over books on Frank Lloyd Wright and Japanese Zen and through piles of *Architectural Digest*. This, you see, was to be their dream house, a place where they could fade away and die satisfied—our modern, ancestral *home*. They named the house and had a sign engraved with Grapes's arabesque script: Ourtopia.

From their room on the top floor you could see, between two hills, the deep blue of the sea during the day or the winking sparkles of the conurbation at night. Grapes had built a basketball court for Jerald and me, a tatami-covered prayer room for Granma, a Japanese tea garden with a Korean barbecue grill for family dinners. He made the place his castle, replete with a shooting range, a painting studio, even a pool only four feet deep (such was Grapes's fear that one of us would drown that he refused the risk of anything deeper). Each grandchild had a room with a view. Claire's, while she was away with her husband, became a temporary storeroom for old clothes. Into Charlotte's, when it became clear she would not be returning, Grapes moved his computer and gigantic printer to spend wakeful nights creating digital art, habituated as he was by years of sleeplessness on the other side of the world. He was seeking distraction from the politics he was missing, for shortly after we moved into Ourtopia, Granma succumbed to a dark depression, refusing to leave her bed until Grapes had sworn off the consumptiveness of political life.

Being around Grapes during those times was not easy. He was quick to anger and, somewhere in the rifts grown between us, he had developed his own views of who each grandchild was—inaccurate perceptions based on whether we listened to him or on whatever personal flaw we kids were working through. Family dinners were hell and I learned to use as my escape the excuse of testy bowels. I spent my time on tiptoes when Grapes was around, or sequestered myself in my bedroom. There—in my sanctuary filled with books, exercise gizmos, stolen *Playboys* from the seventies—I'd often watch, vertiginous above the trees of the ravine, small geckos climbing the window screens, attracted to those bugs lured by our lights. Ours was the only illumination for a mile, except for the unfamiliar stars and city in the distance. The lizards would be there the next morning, weighed down by full bellies. When the sun was strong, you could see, in their translucent bodies, their reptilian hearts, like beans in their chests. I'd flick my finger off my thumb to hit those tiny creatures through my side of the screen, to watch them hurtle, like shuriken, to the fathomless green below. Lizard by lizard, I'd flick them off, fascinated by killing, forgetting for a moment the slow rot outside my bedroom door.

My high school years were passed in Iligan, a city that didn't even aspire to pretensions. The things I learned to love founded what I enjoy until this day. I hiked the miles of dry rice paddies behind the houses of my classmates. I explored, astride my 50cc Honda, the squared-off hilltops in our newly developed subdivision. I took long walks on the beach, finding myself enamoured with and frightened by the sea. All those, simple acts pertaining to movement, to locating myself in the world.

I remember, too, many evenings in the untrimmed, unlit streets of Santo Niño Village, at the home of my classmates, Ping-J and JP, sons of Filipino missionaries. There I learned friendship, proclaiming them my best friends, regardless of whether or not they did the same. We excruciated over pictures of the latest Air Jordan sneakers. Rode jeepneys to town during lunch break, to watch the girls in their blue-and-white uniforms. We lined up for hours when the first McDonald's in the province opened. In the evenings we ventured beyond permission, three of us boys pressed together on my tiny motorcycle, our heads unhelmeted, our legs bent, our feet held an inch off the ground—to visit girls we planned to admire, to half dance, half pose at the open-air discos, to marvel and pity and squirm at the freak shows in the fiestas with their naked bulbs and the sounds of gambling and the scent of fallow fields. We courted our crushes. Brought them to movie houses that screened films without show times, coming in halfway through and watching the end, then the beginning, then the end again. I eventually had a pretty girlfriend with hideous teeth, Darlene, whom I never had the guts to kiss, though I did tell her I'd belonged to a Filipino gang back in Vancouver and had stabbed a man to see what it felt like. She asked me if he died, and I said I didn't know and that not knowing would haunt me forever. When Darlene dumped me, by mailing me a note with lyrics from the girl group Wilson Phillips's hit "Hold On," I wanted to give up on life competely. If that was love, I didn't want it. How could a feeling that leaves you so hollow be a pain that is so sharp? I tried to win her back, wrote her a poem, went shyly to Jesu with the lyrics and asked him to compose a song for me to sing to her. He informed me, gently, that music, and other things, don't work that way.

I recovered. Eventually I fell for a girl named Leanne, a real love which betrayed all the earlier ones as insignificant, untrue. I later found out what it was like to hurt someone I'd promised not to. And what it was to really regret one's actions.

In short, I made the mistakes of youth. I learned. I earned a diploma. I threw my cap into the air during my high school graduation.

In 1993, my family moved to Manila. For my college. For Granma's treatment at Fresh Starts Rehabilitation Retreat Home. For the new family enterprise Grapes set up for Jesu and Mario, as pioneers in the scented candle export trade. And, though it was never mentioned, we also returned to the capital for Grapes's revoked promise and his renewed pursuit of politics—a plum spot in the administration of the newly elected President Estregan.

There, in the nation's capital, our fractured family rejoined the world that always seemed to overlook Iligan. Ourtopia stood empty, the caretaker and her husband going room to room to turn on lights once a day, run the taps, open and close the windows so that they wouldn't rust shut. Grapes tried to sell the house, but nobody would buy it. Dreams are always patently personal. The house is now rented by a Japanese-owned school for instruction in English as a second language.

*

In the diary of Lena Salvador, found in the old overnight suitcase in the locked chest in Crispin's bedroom, there is an entry, written in the universal penmanship of an Assumption girl, dated December 25, 1941: "The family celebrated Christmas mass at Malate church today. Many families we knew failed to attend. For the past days all American soldiers are leaving the city and we're frightened. Mama says they are abandoning us to the Japs, but Papa says we are safer this way, in an open city. 'Don't let's frighten the children,' he said. When will he realize I'm no longer a child? At church we prayed for those who were not with us. I prayed an extra Apostles' Creed for Tito Jason, who has stayed in the city to protect us. After mass, Father O'Connor dressed up like Santa Claus, even if he is too thin to fool the kids and they recognized him right away. Indeed, he made a poor, sad Father Christmas. While we walked home, Crispin took me by the hand and told me he no longer believed in Santa Claus."
—from the biography in progress, *Crispin Salvador: Eight Lives Lived*, by Miguel Syjuco

*

Dulcé and Jacob looked behind them as they sprinted. "I told you," Jacob said, huffing and puffing, "They're going to eat us alive! We should've only gone there while it was still light. We should've listened to old Gardener."

At the end of the fence, they crouched down and hid. In the alley, in the full moon's blue cast, the dwendes came skipping along. Six of them. Their eyes glowed like insane fireflies, and their flowing silver beards fluttered like smoke. They stopped and sniffed the air. They were tiny, cute even, but possessed an air of vicious territoriality.

"We can't go home," Dulcé whispered, "they'll find out where we live. They'll hurt my family."

"I told you," was all Jacob could reply. "I told you. We shouldn't have disturbed their tree. I told you."

Dulcé had a sudden idea. "Follow me," she whispered, before jumping into the alley, in full view of the dwendes. Jacob crouched, shocked, frozen. He was used to following Dulcé's craziness, but this was too much. The dwendes smiled, clapped their hands happily, bared their razor-sharp teeth, and skipped forward at full speed toward the kids. "Come on!" Dulcé said, pulling Jacob by the shirt. The two ran toward Dulcé's backyard, their breaths and hearts and the cracking of underbrush the only things they could hear.

—from *QC Nights*, Book Two of Crispin Salvador's *Kaputol* trilogy

*

The rest of the afternoon is spent with Lena. When our inquisitive protagonist presses her about Crispin's death, she doesn't hear and instead asks him who his parents are. He tells her. Taken aback, and looking chastised, she replies, "I knew of your parents. They were very good people. Your father shouldn't have run back in. There was no saving Bobby Pimplicio. No, I'm sorry. Your father was a hero. A true patriot. If Pimplicio had survived, he would have won the presidency and the country wouldn't be as it is now." A familiar comment that always splits our protagonist in two—proud and indescribably sad. Lena rings a small brass bell. A maid in a baby-blue uniform appears, embracing a tray to her chest. She begins to clear the dishes. From the shadows of the house, the maid in the mint-green uniform appears, carrying a child of about two years. A dark boy, both in skin and apparent disposition, dressed in red overalls. He keeps repeating the word "doughnut." The way he says it, it sounds like a warning. Lena's eyes light when the child is passed to her. She straightens, becomes more animated, as if recharged by the sudden proximate youth.

"This is my son," Lena says. "Moses, the child of my laundrywoman. She died a few months ago, hardly more than a girl herself. Didn't wake up one morning. We never knew the father. Probably one of the farmhands. The boy is mine now. His mother gave him another name, a particularly silly one, and I changed it. Moses is rather fitting, isn't it?"

The maid stands behind them, nodding at Moses. "Tell Mama," the maid says. "Come on. Tell her."

"I love you," Moses mumbles.

"What silly things did they teach you? I didn't hear. Again."

"I love you," Moses says.

"What?" Lena says. "Island view? What a stupid thing for you to learn." The maid looks disappointed. "Oof! I think you need to be changed. Go back to yaya." Lena passes Moses to the maid, who takes him back into the house.

"That boy brings me a joy I never thought possible. All my life I was too busy taking care of Papa, pushing him in his wheelchair. Though there isn't anything wrong with taking pride in having your father be proud of you. Papa died five years ago, Mama . . . what's it been? The cancer took her nearly a decade already. Narcisito's been gone three years this Christmas. And Crispin, well, you know when that happened. So why can't I have my own time now? Moses is my baby boy. All that we have left here in Swanee will be his. Who'll contest it? Crispin's daughter probably won't. Dulcinea has her own life. Sometimes I wonder if she even remembers that the man who raised her isn't her real father. Well, I suppose he actually is. The year her mother was stabbed, I thought of attending the wake. But I had to respect my brother's decisions . . ."

Lena stops, surprised, only now noticing our tender protagonist's expression. "What?" she says. "Didn't you know? I thought it was the worst-kept secret."

*

I graduated from being a provincial high school kid into the heady lifestyle of a college student in cosmopolitan Manila. I lived from weekend to weekend, party to party, a time in my life now gathered in my head like a highlight reel. At my first party: San Miguel Beer, the frustrated lullabies of Kurt Cobain, a cool night sky over Quezon City, and everyone later raising their bottles to shout along to the lyrics of The Dawn's "Iisang Bangka Tayo." I met my first big-city girl worth falling head over heels for: bright-eyed Anais, flirting with me all night, debating José Cuervo Gold versus Silver, then asking for a ride home. I drove slowly and we spoke about graphic novels, about which teachers we'd gotten for Theology 101, about the Impressionists. She seemed thoroughly impressed that I knew my Manet from my Monet. After dropping her off, I'd sped down

Edsa in my lowered Corolla, windows down, stereo blasting, drunk on life as only a teen can be, screaming and almost crying for unaccountable, unforgettable joy. I'd fallen down the precipice of love. Three months later: the breakup by phone. You're too clingy, she said. I want to be free, she said. I don't want to "mollycoddle" you, she said. I didn't know what the word meant, but had stalled as I brought the cordless phone to the study to look it up. Then I cried and made it worse. Dumped, I moped through days, then weeks, then finally two months passed. Resilient and young, I had gotten over her.

Then came her quiet, quivering phone call. I wish I could remember—for the sake of writing honestly, for the sake of understanding our humanity—the words she told me. *I'm pregnant*, I assume now, is what they were. I'd like to think I immediately gave her the right response. I'd like to think that even at that young age, I was heroic.

I guess I asked Anais what she wanted to do. I imagine she said, incredulous at my question, that she would see things through. Of these, my words, I'm almost certain: *I want to do the right thing*. Of these, her words, I'm sure: *We'll see*.

4

In the taxi on the way to the Bacolod airport, I take from my hand-carry Crispin's photo album. The covers wrapped in vinyl crinkle and smell of old plastic. I leaf through it: a hand-tinted print of a toddler Crispin beside his father, both saluting while wearing identical military dress uniforms; an overexposed snapshot of Crispin as a bearded young man, in fatigues and holding a Kalashnikov as if it were a guitar, behind him a mountain furred in green; a Polaroid of a Cinco Bravos "Occurrence," Miggy Jones-Matute and Danilo de Borja dressed in loincloths in the foreground, Crispin in a tiki shirt between the spectacled Marcel Avellaneda and the tiny Mutya Dimatahimik, his arms draped around both their shoulders. There are more family photos: fourteen-year-old Lena doing a cartwheel, her long red skirt blooming toward the sky; nine-year-old Narcisito dressed like Sherlock Holmes, blowing bubbles in a pipe; Junior and Leonora on the campaign trail, farmer hats in bright violet, arms around each other in front of an old Baldwin locomotive engine; Crispin among his Lupas cousins at some reunion in a seaside resort (one cousin wears a T-shirt with Junior's face above a slogan: I RE-ELECT MY SALVADOR). There is also a colour photo of a pretty girl, probably three years old, with hazel eyes and amber hair. It is un-dated, but already fading.

*

Dulcé and Jacob circled, full tilt, around the pool. Jacob ran like his pants were on fire. Dulcé was a blur of gangly limbs and golden locks. She pointed to the shed where Gardener kept his tools. "In there," she whispered, "but make sure they see us."

Jacob couldn't believe what he was hearing. "Are you serious?"

Dulcé nodded. "I have a plan."

The pair went inside the dark shed. Dulcé found some rope and tied it to the doorknob. She unravelled the rope to the far end of the room, where she sat in the corner.

"Okay," Dulcé said. "I'll stay in here with this. You step out and let them see you."

"Wha—? *Me?* You're crazy, Dul!"

"I'm older than you by a month, so it should be you. Besides, like you said the other day: I'm just a girl."

"But—but—but," Jacob stammered, "I didn't mean it. And we'll be trapped in here with them."

Dulcé looked him in the eye. "Trust me," she said.

Jacob stepped out just as the dwendes were arriving in the garden. They were looking around, a couple of them even admiring the flowers. Jacob thought: This is a bad idea! But Dulcé had gotten them out of so many scrapes before, Jacob couldn't help but trust her. "Hey!" Jacob shouted. "Hey you silly dwarves! Here we are!"

The dwendes turned, clapped happily again, bared their ice pick–like teeth, and skipped toward the shed. Jacob ran inside and crouched beside Dulcé.

"Ready?" Dulcé whispered. They waited for what seemed like an eternity. Finally six pairs of orange eyes entered the darkness of the shed. They floated, sliding sideways, tilting up, glancing down. Finally, one pair zeroed in on the kids. A ghastly chuckle cut through the air. All six pairs of orange eyes turned red and were suddenly looking straight at them.

—from *QC Nights*, Book Two of Crispin Salvador's *Kaputol* trilogy

*

"Say it's not yours," Grapes said. "How do you know it's yours?"

"I know."

"How can you know? Maybe she has a guapo driver or houseboy?"

"Grapes. Please. I just know."

"You know because she's your all-all-all right now. What happens when she's not your all-all-all anymore?"

"You and Granma taught me right from wrong."

Grapes sat slouched at the desk he kept in his inner sanctum, their cavernous walk-in closet. One cabinet was wide open and the shirts and pants were pushed aside to reveal a wall rack of pistols. Grapes's quiet force was more searing than Granma's angry shouts. She sat now, hoarse, outside in the bedroom.

"You're upsetting your grandmother. She's had a brandy. You know that's not good."

"What am I supposed to do?"

"Trust us. Don't sacrifice your youth."

"I do trust you. That's the thing. But if I have to leave home and get a job, I will."

"Why must you always be the selfish one?"

"What's your definition of selfish? I'm willing to give up every-thing. So that child can have a proper life."

Grapes just shook his head and sighed again. "You're a fresh-man," he said.

"I'll leave if I have to."

"You're seventeen years old."

"If I'm man enough to make a baby, then I should be man enough to raise a baby." I'd heard that in the movie *Boyz n the Hood*.

"Why don't you go to your room and think it through?"

"I have."

"Think it through some more."

*

I still remember my first contact with Crispin Salvador. "One Stone for Two Birds" was assigned to me by the passionately stolid Mrs. Lumbera during my junior year at Ateneo. Crispin's words came as faded blue ink on pulpy mimeographed paper. We'd read works like Nick Joaquin's *Mayday Eve*, Gregorio Brillantes's *Flood in Tarlac*, and Paz Marquez Benitez's seminal *Dead Stars*. But Crispin's short story impressed me more than any other.

In it, the young well-to-do protagonist named, coincidentally, Miguel, stumbles upon a stranger brutally stabbed in a dark alley. Miguel comforts the dying man, "who cradles his entrails as if they were the entirety of his life lived previous to this scene in chiaroscuro." The man wears a fedora in a "puta red" felt and has carefully taken it off and placed it on an empty cardboard box, so that it won't be "soiled with blood's darker shades."

"These men," Crispin writes, "were a pair wrought together by the mischief of circumstance, both equally unfortunate in a cold alley in Tondo on a dark evening in February, their embrace possessing the urgency of an unconsummated love instantly made possible in a final night fading to light." The true drama of this story comes later, however, when the victim draws his last breath just as the police arrive to mistake Miguel for the murderer. "Would this fledgling man take on the responsibility thrust suddenly into his hands? Or would he flee?"

*

Lena refused to tell him anything more and immediately asked him to leave. Our discombobulated protagonist caught the last flight to Manila from Bacolod.

He looks out the window. The Airbus escapes the earth and flies over the intensifying blue. The plane's shadow is like a water-skier on the meniscus of the unknown. Our protagonist tightens his grip on his armrests. He pulls down the window shade and his body soon relaxes.

He is swimming to the sidewalk and swallows a mouthful of water. It is warm, like phlegm. Terror caresses his insides. He can see the distant sidewalk, the Lexus's headlights crossing the water and touching it, as if taunting him. He can see the night sky glow red, then blue, then yellow. Stars are falling. His body, vertical, his legs, flailing for the ground that should be there. He thrashes his arms above him, as if having just walked through a spider's web. His fingers reach through the surface. For an instant he feels air. But his body won't let him breathe. His epiglottis has seized. Life is being strangled by its very vessel. He loses consciousness and sees himself floating, his posture peaceful, curved like a closing hand. His expression, however, resembles that of a man who has just been cheated.

He awakens, falling into panic, when he feels the plane pitching gently forward on its descent. I never—he thinks—remember my dreams.

At the domestic terminal the sky is dimming. Outside the airport, he feels strange. Naked. He is conscious of his movements. They do not seem to be his own. He takes a taxi to Makati. Sits in gridlock like a patient waiting his turn for the dentist. The skyscrapers approach slowly from the darkening horizon, the white windows flickering on one by one, here then there. On the sidewalk, commuters wave at jeepneys, construction workers kid with children they've enlisted for help. Between the convoluted lines of cars, vendors hawk newspapers or cigarettes or candy, urchins sell sampaguita flowers strung on dental floss. The diorama always saddens him, the way a habitually empty restaurant does as you walk by and peer in to see the family proprietors sitting expectantly in their uniforms.

Turn there, he tells the driver suddenly. They make a hairpin turn and go down a quiet street lined with high barbed-wired walls. *Stop here,* he tells the driver gently. Then he hands him fifty pesos. The driver smiles, almost apologetically, and exits the taxi. Our pensive protagonist sits in the backseat and studies the whitewashed property wall. He watches the big metal gate as if he has X-ray vision and can see the house beyond. *Did they make the wall higher?* He can just see the top of the tree where she used to climb when she was four years old, with him reaching up to hover his hands around her in case her grip slipped. *When did they paint the gate orange? I think they did make the wall higher. Do they even still live here?*

The boy thinks of Grapes. Everything to do with fatherhood he learned from him. The boy thinks of Crispin. *Did he ever even mention his daughter?*

He watches the wall as if old home movies are being projected on it. He hopes the gate will swing open suddenly. *What if it actually does? What would he do?*

The taxi driver walks to the wall and puts his face to it. He looks like a man waiting for the firing squad. A dark stain spreads onto the ground between his feet. It's as if his shadow were melting. The driver looks up to the sky in gratitude. The gate of the property opens. The guard peeps out. The boy remembers him. The taxi driver, skipping as he zips up his pants, runs back to the car. They zoom away.

*

As soon as I leave the plane and walk out of the airport, I get this feeling like I'm being watched. There are only faces in the crowd, like a field of flowers, if flowers could frown and spit and look at their watches.

I gesture at cabs. The feeling persists. I rush into the first taxi that stops. Out the back window, I see cars lining up slowly then peeling quickly away from the curb to follow us down the street.

On the way to my hotel in Makati, gridlock gnarls us to snail-mail pace. It's like waiting for your turn at the dentist. Across the street, a bee mascot paces and waves in front of the Jollibee hamburger outlet. Commuters flap their hands at unslowing jeepneys. On the sidewalk, a pair of boys crack the top pavement with chisels and hammers. Nearby, a sign says SLOW MEN AT WORK. Workers, in hard hats and flip-flops worn paper-thin, gossip by the cart of a fish-ball vendor, smoking cigarettes in a circle. A dusty jackhammer waits beside a gaping pit. One worker, a fat one in a holey Armani Exchange T-shirt, shouts to the children and points to a fresh spot on the pavement. The boys waggle their eyebrows. One boy smiles and gives a thumbs-up. The construction worker waddles over and places his yellow hard hat on the kid's head. To the other child, he holds out his palm, soliciting a high five, unsuccessfully.

Vendors thread through the long parade of entrafficked vehicles. They carry boxes of loose cigarettes and candy. A couple of them carry newspapers, like waiters with armloads of dishes. There is news for every taste: the *Sun, Times, Gazette, TeenBeat, Abante, Bulgar.*

One paper declares: "Exclusive pics! Changcos' victory party. Maid-killers celebrate!"

Another offers: "Sucked up by the Pasig!" I can just read the print of the lede: "Young Mariano Bakakon, 28, expert swimmer from Barangay Ilog, met his death in the Pasig River yesterday after floods in surrounding areas concealed open manholes, one of which he fell into. Bakakon saved himself but later succumbed to exposure to pollutants." Included is a small picture of a corpse on a hospital bed. Beside it, a photo of an uncovered manhole—a common sight in a city where the covers are stolen and sold for scrap.

My eyes alight on the garish cover of *Bulgar*: the compulsory image of a half-naked buxom girl. It's the latest artista to be seen everywhere: Vita Nova. She throbs on the page. The holes of her tiny torn T-shirt strategically display her heaving cleavage and sucked-in stomach—she's dressed like a rape victim, though her coquettishness is unflappable, as if her sole means of power. She has struck the pose of the latest dance craze, the Mr. Sexy Sexy: back arched to thrust out her rump, hands on springy knees, face held up to smile and blow kisses. A large crucifix pendant hangs around her neck. Nestled blissfully in her rolling valley, Christ holds out his arms to skim his fingertips on her breasts and lolls his head in rapture.

The taxi driver makes a hairpin left turn off the main road. I get nervous. We drive to a quiet place and the car stops. The driver smiles, almost apologetically, and exits the car without a word. He dallies around the street. He stands at a whitewashed wall, as if before a firing squad. A dark stain appears on the wall in front of him. It spreads onto the ground between his feet. It's as if his shadow were melting in the heat. The driver looks at the sky. The orange gate of the property opens and a guard peeps out. The taxi driver runs to the car, zipping up his fly. We drive off. He turns around to look at me.

"Is something wrong?" he says.

"Of course not."

"But you are . . . um . . . you want tissue?" he says, kindly. "How 'bout radio?" He turns up the volume.

The announcer asks Bobby for a few statements and an American voice replies, barely able to speak from excitement.

". . . all wonderful! . . . time that the fucking U.S. got their heads kicked in . . ." He has an aging Brooklyn accent. ". . . time to finish off the U.S. once and for all . . ."

Then I feel it again. That sensation of being watched. Like when you sit through a horror film then come home to an empty apartment. I gaze through the dark tint of the taxi and into the cars beside us. In one, a woman is at the wheel, singing her heart out, her hairbrush as a microphone. In another, a driver is gazing ahead as if willing the traffic forward with his mind; his employer in the backseat picks his nose then examines what he's found.

The radio blares laser sounds, then the breakneck reporting in Tagalog: "My compatriots, this just in. It is reported that Wigberto Lakandula has taken the Changco family hostage in their Binondo home. My compatriots, it is believed that upon entering the domicile, Lakandula shot and slew two men in the employ of the family, a bodyguard and a driver. He immediately took the couple, their six-year-old son, and two maids captive. A police cordon has been established around the area and SWAT team members have been deployed to the scene. Already a crowd of girls has gathered at the site, screaming for a glimpse of their hero. Police psychologists say Lakandula is acting out his lifelong frustrations against society, and will therefore be violent and unpredictable. Authorities ask all members of the public to stay away to avoid getting hurt."

*

Eventually, the American dream comes true for Erning Isip. He returns victoriously to his hometown for his first vacation, proudly wielding the greenbacks he earned from his new job working tech support at Lehman Brothers. Upon arriving, however, he contracts a stomach virus from drinking Philippine water, which he is no longer used to. He goes to see a doctor at the Makati Medical Center. The doctor examines him. "I have bad news," the doctor says, "and good news." Erning asks for the bad news first. "The bad news," the doctor says, "is you require a small procedure." Erning asks for the good news. "The good news is it only requires a local anesthetic."

Alarmed, Erning replies: "Local?! Can't I have imported instead?"

*

When they reach Makati, the taxi driver asks, "Hotel Happy International Inn, is that right, sir?" He's asked it four times now. "Yes," our exasperated protagonist says, before turning to the window. He can't wait to get out of the car.

Familiar sites grind by as pedestrians blur past, faster than his stranded cab. The gleaming, splendiferous malls. The guarded gates of Forbes Park, where our prodigal protagonist grew up. The Manila Polo Club, where he and Jerald learned to play tennis, always swinging for over the back fence to see the ball boys climb like monkeys after the balls. The large home of the U.S. Ambassador, with its cameras and high walls. The larger home of the Sultan of Brunei's brother's Filipina mistress. Santuario de San Antonio Church, where all his relatives and friends are, and always will be, baptized, communioned, wedded, waked, interred. The brawny ten-lane Edsa Boulevard, host to four peaceful revolutions. All who return to Manila love to say nothing changes, but that's not true. More soaring overpasses are stacked atop each other. More rows of billboards stand like upright dominoes, sporting pretty Brobdingnagian mestizas in low-cut jeans or lingerie. There is now a Starbucks across from Santuario (you can wash down the host with a grande Mocha Frappuccino). From where he sits, he counts six towering cranes, pirouetting, and four new skyscrapers, each striving higher than the other and those that were there before. The pace of Asian progress is ostentatious. Here in Makati, this is not a poor country.

The Shell station outside Forbes Park, where he used to get gas, the flashing lights of police cars and fire trucks—blue, then red, then black, then blue, then red—urge spectators beyond a cordon. Commuters at a safe distance stare at something beside the gas pumps. A duffel bag. Two policemen approach it sheepishly. They edge sideways like adolescent boys along the wall at a school dance. Their brown uniforms and caps make them look cruelly vulnerable. One cop crouches beside the bag, unzips it tentatively, holding himself at arm's length, face turned away. "Oh my God!" says the taxi driver, "Don't do it, don't do it!" The other cop cranes his neck and peeks in. The taxi driver makes the sign of the cross. Both cops jump back. Everyone stares at the bag. Nothing happens. The two cops approach again slowly. Drag it carefully away from the pumps. They are near the wall of Forbes Park. A sudden flash of light, smoke, the rattling of the taxi windows, a thunderclap, and the two men are no more. Car alarms scream. Nobody moves. Suddenly everyone is moving. The cabbie leans on his horn, cursing at the cars in front, who do the same to those in front of them. Now that it's done, nobody wants to be involved. The boy bends over, breathing gingerly, trying not to vomit into the taxi's Power Rangers tissue-box holder.

*

I look out the window from the sixth floor of the Hotel Happy International Inn, revelling in the anonymity of my room hidden safely among the others. This is a space for faceless businessmen and other itinerants with credit cards. The thin white sheets, the bouquet of Tetley teas, the plastic electric kettle with calcified coil make me feel, strangely, at home.

Outside, the night is neon. Signs flash like a row of pantyless chorus girls: Pussycat's Karaoke and Grill, 7-Eleven, Bacchus Hydro-Massage, 8-Twelve, Tapa King, Ichiban Singalong Bar. The sostenuto whine of 150cc passenger trikes is accompanied by the ostinato bass from discotheques. Already, the loping Americans and Europeans go up and down the street, in and out of bars. They ogle and hold the teeny-tiny bodies of the GROs—an easy acronym for a clever euphemism: "Guest Relations Officer." One looks like a little girl who got into her mother's makeup. I wonder what her parents could have done differently.

The laminated room-service menu offers "happy international delicacies *inn* the comfort of your *hotel* room." I call for a bacon cheeseburger. A bellboy brings it up and lingers, bowing to me as if I were Japanese. I tip him in pesos, he frowns at the money, turns on his heel, and almost runs down the hall.

Mechanically, thinking about the news I've discovered about Crispin's child, I raise to my lips the bacon cheeseburger. No sooner does the gooey cheese and medium-rare beef touch my palate than a shudder runs through me and I stop midchew.

Crispin and I shared a passion for hamburgers. His apartment was above the famous Corner Bistro, and he said it was like living upstairs from your favorite brothel. More than a few times, while working together in his study, the eroticism of grilling meat would waft through his open window, and we would grab our coats to go cross off yet another from our list of the great purveyors in New York City—Soup Burg, Peter Luger, JG Melon. It was as if we thought they could offer us some explanation of what we were looking for in America.

One warm autumn day, we left our work to fetch takeout from the Burger Joint on West Fifty-seventh and walked to Central Park to continue our game. The last time we played, we'd adjourned with my rook and knight harassing his king, while my pawn was making a final sprint to queenhood. Crispin was almost as delighted as I was at the prospect of my beating him for the first time. "You're quite the Bobby Fischer," he'd teased. "We all need idols," I'd countered.

It started to rain, and he and I ran, like lovers in a romantic comedy, to the Chess and Checkers House. The place was empty, except for three children huddled in a doorway, impatiently looking at the sky. As soon as we set up our board, the rain stopped. The kids began jumping over the puddles, the eldest, about eleven, laughing like a seagull.

We unwrapped our burgers. I moved my knight to queen-eight and waited for Crispin. I remember he took a long time, and I looked up from the board. He was watching the children play. He noticed me and smiled. "From time to time," he said, "I wonder at the value of things such as those. Maybe I should have mustered the courage to raise one."

I studied the board. "I think you made the right choice," I finally said. "The world's overpopulated. Don't you think we all have our roles? Your books will have a greater effect." I bit into my burger.

Crispin gestured with his thumb at the children. "If I'm not writing *TBA* for our offspring, then who for?" He watched them for a moment. "One day, you'll understand."

"I get it now. It doesn't mean I agree."

"I think you'll find even literature has limitations. That will be a good thing, if you discover that."

"Limitations keep us striving."

"After the *Tractatus*, Wittgenstein became"—Crispin picked up his king, then put it back. I let it pass—"a primary school teacher. Rimbaud grew bored with poetry and left for Africa. Duchamp gave up art for this very game we're playing." Crispin moved his king next to my knight. "With every year come new regrets, Miguel. You'll have your collection of them."

"That's condescending," I said, surprised by the acid in my voice. "I have my own."

"I'm sorry that you didn't know your parents. But there's more to life than that."

"You wouldn't understand." I couldn't look at him. I wish I had. Maybe I would have seen. But I went on. "That's why with literature, at least I can control what happens. We can create, revise. Try better next time. If we fail, we only screw ourselves . . ."

"That last part's not necessarily precise."

"But if we succeed, we can change the world." I moved my knight. "Check." I looked up at him.

Crispin's face was like how I imagine my father's to have been, magnanimous and amused. "Changing the world," he said, "is good work if you can get it. But isn't having a child a gesture of optimism in that world?"

"Ugh. That's a little twee for my taste."

"Seriously, intellectually speaking. Consider it a moment."

"Sometimes we just aren't given a choice in the matter." I heard myself. I'm ashamed of how I sounded.

"We always are." Crispin moved his king. "Checkmate," he said. Sure enough, there was nowhere I could go. Crispin got up and looked at me with either naked disappointment or brutal pity. He put his hands in his pockets and went and watched the children splashing. I still remember the tune he started to whistle.

*

On one of the last few days before the city fell to the Japs, we lined Dewey Boulevard, scores of us along the broad avenue, the breeze off the bay just cool enough for goose bumps. I was perched on Tito Jason's shoulders and I remember watching birds duelling recklessly in the blue sky above the long curve of water. They fled into the endless expanse when a bugle called. The sky then was still trying to retain its innocence.

Then I saw the men on their mounts, arriving for their dramatic departure. Dividing the crowd, splendid, tall, like centaurs passing through wheat, they came, the Twenty-sixth Cavalry Regiment of the Philippine Scouts—Americans and Filipinos side by side in formation in two long columns. I still hear their equipment jangle, the slow clop of hooves, still see the sun reflecting on their horses' polished martingales, on their own breast buckles and the insignia with the charging horse head and the saber raised above it. The metal on their bodies glowed like our hearts. The Japanese were to land at Lingayen and the cavalry began their journey to be among the first of the USAFFE to meet them. We, the people, were silent, then we cheered, women reaching hands to caress the soldiers' boots and legs, to stroke the horses' manes and flanks—the way hopeful believers hold their hands out to rub the feet of cathedral saints.

I remember, and regret, I covered my ears from the cheers. I've never heard its equal since. Tito Jason handed me to one of the riders, his brother, my uncle, Tito Odyseo, who let me ride in front of him for some way. To this day the scent of leather and horse and male perspiration reminds me of that singular moment when I rode as one of them.

When I was finally passed back from uncle to uncle, I struggled, not wanting to be left behind. I cried. The lines of cavalry took an eternal instant to pass among us. When the spectators closed the gap behind them, those around us shook their heads and made the sign of the cross. Many wept. I could feel Tito Jason shudder convulsively as he lost sight of his brother. All the nights Tito Jason had spent painfully rolling his ridiculously flat feet on Coca-Cola bottles had proved for naught when my father begged him to stay to help protect our family. I held on to my uncle as we all listened to the sound of hooves fading.

My young boy's memory may have inflated these details, but this is how I remember that day.

Outside the town of Morong, on January 16, 1942, that group of brave men and strong steeds later made the final horseback cavalry charge in the history of the U.S. military. These were the last of an ancient tradition, many felled by the cowardly hail of anonymous lead and mortars from Japanese positions. Those of the Twenty-sixth who survived the charge fought on as infantry. Eventually, attrition forced General Wainwright, a cavalry man himself, to give the order to butcher the horses for food. How cruel that meat must have tasted. Since then, the U.S. and Philippine cavalry have been tanks and helicopters, machines that know not the sacrifices of courage and duty.

—from *Autoplagiarist* (page 865), by Crispin Salvador

*

His Nokia tring-trings. Our forlorn protagonist sits up in bed and fumbles in the darkness. He looks at the bright screen of the cell phone. It's a text message from his old pal Markus: Welcm bak, bro! Old skool tunes all week @ Club Coup d'Etat. Our crew will be there, with Charlie. My treat. DJ Super-modeldiva spinning phat beats. *When the screen dims, the hotel room seems to get smaller.*

It would be fucking awesome—he says to himself—to go out, to see the old crew. I'll just play it cool, be grateful but firm, gracious but not dorky, when they press the baggie into my hand. He knows he can't use the self-righteous pose, that artificial form of fortitude, of the recovering user. They know him too well. Anyway, he says, I can have fun on just alcohol. I'll buy a few rounds. Thank God for the mighty dollar. I should continue my nap before going out so I can keep up with everyone. Anyway, I don't want it to be a late night.

*

The pain makes him dizzy. He fights to stay conscious. "That son of a gun," Antonio growls. "He's dead meat." He leans against a tree and looks at the switchblade in his thigh. He starts to pull it out but it's stuck. He fights not to cry aloud and give away his location. He's lucky the blade didn't hit his bone and he knows it. From atop the hill, two of Dominador's lackeys appear. Uh-oh! They spot Antonio, point at him, and come running down the hill. One brandishes nunchuks, the other has drawn a jungle bolo. Antonio checks his gun to see how many bullets he has left. "Santa Banana," he says, "only one." The two men are getting closer, screaming all the way. Antonio's reflection gets larger in their aviator sunglasses. The nunchuks blur around one goon. The razor-sharp jungle machete is held aloft by the other. Antonio takes Dominador's knife, grits his teeth, and pulls it out of his leg. Pain sears up the right side of his body. Gasping to stay awake, Antonio holds the blade in front of the barrel of his gun. He pulls the trigger. The two attackers clutch their chests, cry out in pain, then tumble head over heels down the hill. Their lifeless bodies roll up to Antonio's feet. "Not today, boys," he says. "I've got a headache." He retracts the knife then limps quickly away before more goons arrive. At the treeline, he searches for a place to bandage himself. He knows he can't take too long, or he'll never save his beloved Mutya from the slimy clutches of Dominador.

—from *Manila Noir* (page 102), by Crispin Salvador

*

From Marcel Avellaneda's blog, "The Burley Raconteur," December 3, 2002:
I don't know what the media's smoking, but let's not get carried away by the kickback scandal from the proceeds of the popular Mr. Sexy Sexy Dance ringtones, and the alleged guilt of Vita Nova and her uber-agent Boy Balagtas. Let's not even posit President Estregan's hand in preempting her culpability before Nova could release the rumoured sex tape linking el commandante-in-chief to the bombings. I, for one, cannot believe he'd be so stupid as to let the tape run while he takes a call from the Minister of the Interior.

Let's instead look at the certainty of things divine. Today we examine the impact of Reverend Martin's allegiance in two reports: In Pearls Before Swine, Felix Resureccion describes the ill effects of the El Ohim's meddling—as a kingmaker, Reverend Martin may well be the most powerful man in the country. Resureccion goes as far as calling him "Our father, who art in a lucrative position." In My Daily Vitamins Ricardo Roxas IV examines the church leader's moral accountability—Reverend Martin has a present-world responsibility to all those hopes and aspirations he foments in his followers.

Some posts from the message boards below:
—I wanna lick Vita's ass-crack. (gundamlover@hotmail.com)
—What's that got to do with the price of rice, anyway? (edith@werbel.com)
—reverend martin is a saint! let him have his mansion. he's inspired the nation and brought together people who are all too often alienated. problem with our country is we can't stand to see people succeed. there's perpetually some fault to find in others. it's quite sad. it's not just jealousy either. it's more like a way of explaining to ourselves why we're having such difficulty whilst others are attaining success. how petty is that rubbish? (ningning.baltazar@britishairways.com)
—Defence mechanisms may be justified, Ning. But we can't just leave it at that. Symptoms indicate a disease beneath it all. Reverend Mart is preying—Ha! No pun intended—on the needs of the most vulnerable. There's no justification for that. (Ricardoroxas4@yahoo.com)

*

Cristo keeps silent as Maria Clara bids the guests farewell. When he and Aniceto shake hands, the latter looks at him meaningfully, clasps his hand in both of his. Juan tilts his hat and strides down the steps with such pride Cristo can't help but smile. Only Martin is also pensive and doesn't say a word or offer a gesture as he steps into his carriage. His wife reaches over him to wave a final farewell, but Martin is oblivious.

Maria Clara touches Cristo's shoulder, then goes inside. He stands in front of the house until the clatter of the horses and the hiss of the carriages on the gravel fade completely. Then he goes to his room to consider his decision.

Only a few days later, on November 6, does Cristo find out what transpired without him. While merienda is being served, a man from the Claparol estate comes running breathlessly to Swanee, asking the servants to summon their master. "Don Cristo," he says, "Don Martin has tasked me with this message. The Spaniards have signed an Act of Capitulation. There was no blood lost."

Cristo presses the man, who tells him the details of the story, complete with embellishments. Yesterday, fortified by the successes in nearby towns, Aniceto and Juan joined the others to lead their men on Bacolod. Poorly armed against the enemy, the men prepared whatever weapons they could—bolos, knives, a few guns. Their arsenal had been smaller than they'd hoped, and they'd taken black paint to carved nipa sticks and rolled bamboo mats. These they piled conspicuously on open carts. From a distance, they did look like rifles and canons. The two groups of revolucionarios took positions on the Lupit and Mandalagan rivers, in a pincerlike maneuver on the city. The Spanish commandant, Coronel de Castro y Cisneros, whose scouts reported the Filipinos comprised a large, well-armed force, surrendered with little delay.

Stuttering, Cristo thanks the messenger. When the visitor closes the door behind him, Cristo sways, then stumbles into his chair. Spanish rule is ended! The revolution is a success! Three hundred seventy-seven years of occupation are finished. Cristo locks the door and pours himself a brandy. He dispatches this quickly, then pours one more. He takes the bottle with him to his seat.

That evening, when Maria Clara has the door forced open, she finds her husband drunk, shirtless, weeping. "I am not a man," he says to her. "How could I have done nothing?"

"Cristo," she says, holding his face to look him square in the eye. Her voice is urgent and strong. "Cristo. Listen. Cristo. Let me dress you. You and I must go to the Claparol estate. Martin has tried to take his own life."

—from *The Enlightened* (page 198), by Crispin Salvador

*

Our nostalgic protagonist sits on the bed and leafs one more time through the photo album of his dead mentor. His spirits fall with every page he turns.

Where did my own life go? he thinks. What became of all the friends I had, the jobs I was offered, the little family I was starting? What happened to the promising young phenom to whom words came so willingly? My plans to be the youngest, the best, snorted away in some Lower East Side bathroom cubicle with a sticky floor. My confidence flowing and ebbing with the high and the comedown. What about my grandparents' stacks of millions of pesos converted, at great loss, into a piddling wad of greenbacks, for my foreign, sentimental, "superior" education? What did those dollars buy? So many un-

finished story collections. Epic novels that reached chapter two. And those damn confusing experiments with style. The thing is to write a straight narrative. That's the trick: no trickery. Go back to basics. Emulate A Passage to India. *Write Crispin's biography. Spin the yarn, follow it home. You'll never be the youngest, but we'll see about the rest. He closes the album.*

Maybe maturity—he thinks—is merely accepting the tally of all the disappearing options of life.

But who says he's accepted anything?

*

INTERVIEWER:

And how do you feel about it now, after the fall of the Soviet Union?

CS:

The Soviet Union sold out the working class. Tyrants hide behind the noblest ideals. "Je ne suis pas marxiste," said Marx. That's exactly how I feel. If anything, je suis un Groucho Marxist. But listen, just because an ideology dies doesn't mean the value of its ideas is nullified. I felt at the time that communism was the way because it was the only viable means to real progress in my country. I no longer believe it can work. We're simply not that noble. I still believe revolutionary change is the only remedy, but it will be through something far more primitive. A populist coup d'état, perhaps. A military strongman with his roots in the dirt and the decency of knowing how much is enough. The ideology of communism was an enticing potentiality in a society whose continuous attempts at renewal merely overlaid the old structure with fresh inequalities. Call communism my youthful reaction to the garish conservatism of an entrenched elite. What repressed young man, absolutely priapic with patriotism, wouldn't follow a bare-breasted Liberty leading the people? I was a fool. All revolutionaries are. Thank goodness for that.

—from a 1991 interview in *The Paris Review*

*

The most difficult moment of the war for us was neither the occupation nor the liberation, though the nightmare of the latter, with its destruction of Manila, was in many ways harder to take than the heartbreak of the former. The most difficult moment for our family was the conquest.

After waiting hours in the hot crowded plaza where we queued to register, like common criminals, my father lost his infamous temper and marched my mother and us three children to the front. He wanted us to watch him berate the little Japanese clerk recording names at a desk, typing slowly with two fingers and peering over his thick spectacles, like some caricature in a postwar Hollywood film. One of the guards, swollen with the arrogance characteristic of the invaders during the first year, put his hand on his samurai sword and came forward with the intention of slicing my father in half. I knew we would be next. As he drew the blade—what a sound it made, like metal being torn—a shout rang out. The soldier froze, his weapon held high above his shoulder. Through the crowd pushed a Japanese officer, sinewy and straight. It was Yataro, our ingenious gardener. It turns out he was, and had been all along, a Kempeitai intelligence officer. In this way, he came to repay my family for the kindnesses we had showed him. His friendship would prove invaluable.

—from Autoplagiarist (page 992), by Crispin Salvador

*

Erning returns from his vacation in the Philippines and meets a pretty girl at a friend's pool party in San Jose. Her name is Rocky Bastos and she hails from the same province he's from back home. Unlike the other Filipina girls at the party, she wears a two-piece swimsuit. The men gather at the barbecue and talk about her flat stomach. To get her attention, Erning continuously does the "cannonball" dive into the pool. She looks over at him each time he does it. He takes that as promising. Rubbing a towel suggestively over his chest, he sidles up to her and asks her out. To his joy, she accepts.

They go to dinner at Red Lobster, because Erning has been saving coupons for such an occasion. Afterward, she asks him up to her place for some Red Passion Alizé. It's become a red-themed evening, and they blush simultaneously when they eye each other in the elevator. Erning is sure he could be with her forever. Upstairs, they sit shyly on the couch, as if waiting for the same bus. The cognac–passion fruit cocktail clouds their heads. Rocky, however, has lived in America for some time, and has already taken to American values.

Rocky: "Let's play hide-and-seek. If you find me, I'll let you have sex with me."

Erning: "Eh, and what if I don't find you?"
Rocky: "I'll only be upstairs, behind the bathroom door!"

*

In the last months of the relationship, Madison kept asking me what I was still hiding. What was I doing when I locked the door of the room where I wrote? She didn't believe I was working. "You sound like you're crying in there," she said. "Why can't you let me get close to you?" So I told her.

I told her that I was watching pornography. But I made it sound fun. I tried to show her, tried to share, what I found stimulating. Madison had, after all, come to like the other predilections I'd shared with her earlier in the relationship. She took easily to sneaking tokes with me beside the reflecting pool at Lincoln Center, then slipping in at intermission to find vacant seats as the Philharmonic played Schumann's *Kreisleriana* or Vinteuil's Septet; though at first she cringed at the possibility of getting caught. She grew to love discovering, despite having initially mocked me as "nerdly," the crown-crested and colour-breasted birds in the Ramble in Central Park; though she refused to be seen carrying the folding chairs and binoculars on the street. Pornography, I'd hoped, would be one more of these quirky delectations.

Madison smiled an unsure smile. She was trying to be game. Like a connoisseur pointing out the levers, gears, and jewels that fascinate within clockworks, I showed her the top-shelf videos on my hard drive. I introduced her to my favourite strumpets: Jenna Haze, Belladonna, and the Filipina-American Charmane Star. I told her my dream of writing about them in a book that would get published by a major literary house. She nodded from time to time, conceding, grudgingly, Yeah, Jenna's hot. Yeah, Bella's got skills. Then Madison turned to me and asked why she wasn't enough.

In fairness, in the following weeks, she tried, with her feather ticklers, her riding crop, her latex French maid's uniform. In the end, though, she grew disgusted, accusatory. Then came her paranoia: whenever I locked the door (even if I'd actually been working), whenever she went to bed before me and I didn't follow right away (even if I often suffer from insomnia).

The few times after that when we tried to make love, she looked at me strangely. Like I was somebody she loved less.

It's foolish to believe that we should be entirely honest.

*

"Ready?" Dulcé whispered.

Jacob whispered back: "Uh, yeah. Hours ago."

The dwendes' eyes came closer and closer. Their teeth were so sharp they glinted even in the half-darkness.

"Now!" shouted Dulcé, pulling the rope, slamming the door of the shed shut so that the interior was as black as black could be. The red eyes gazed around, looked up maniacally. Six little voices gave off strange, strangulated cries, and the eyes went from red to orange to yellow until they finally faded and disappeared.

"What did you do?" Jacob asked, obviously relieved. He flicked on the light. Except for its hum and the tapping of moths on the fluorescent bulb, the kids were completely alone. On the ground were six tiny hats, which disappeared into thin air right before the pair's eyes.

"When I was a kid," Dulcé said, "my stepdad told me all about dwendes. Remember, he researches folklore at the university."

"Yeah, I remember."

"A long time ago, when I was really young, he told me that dwendes are so dumb that if they find themselves in complete darkness, without even the light of the stars, they'll just fade away. They'll stop existing. They mistake darkness for death."

"Your stepdad told you that? Then why didn't he believe us earlier when we told him about the magic tree?"

"I don't know," Dulcé said, looking visibly perplexed. "I really don't know."

—from *QC Nights*, Book Two of Crispin Salvador's *Kaputol* trilogy

*

I put Crispin's photo album aside and get up to flop into the vinyl couch. It squeals with my weight. Opening a can of San Miguel beer from the minibar, I switch on the television. They have cable! I channel surf.

A basketball game is on, between the San Miguel Beermen and the Lupas Land Mallers. Two African-American imports post up against each other beneath the ring, the clock in final digits. The diminutive Filipino point guard tries for three points. I change the channel.

A commercial. An orchestral rendition of "Joy to the World" plays while images of mutilated hands, missing fingers, amputated limbs flash on the screen. "This holiday season," a man's voice says soberly, "please be safe when using firecrackers and fireworks. This has been a public service announcement from the Philippines First Corporation." I change the channel.

News headline emblazons the screen: JELLYFISH ATTACK!!! The reporter says an underwater earthquake in the Celebes Sea caused a massive movement of jellyfish upriver, which clogged a Mindanao hydroelectric plant and plunged the island group into a sudden blackout. Camera cuts to the scene. A colonel on location at the Rajah Tuwaang power plant explains, in broken but adamant English, that the blackout had nothing to do with Moro rebels. Behind him, soldiers shovel jellyfish into dump trucks. One heap towers at least eight feet. I change the channel.

A crowd surrounds the besieged Changco home. Some look up at the news helicopter and shout unheard. A male voice-over reports that more than a thousand people with candles and sampaguita leis are singing songs and waving signs proclaiming their support for Wigberto Lakandula. One banner says: PYRAMID-SCHEME VICTIMS 4 LAKANDULA. Another: WIGGY, WE ♥ YOU, MARRY US!— ASSUMPTION H.S. CLASS OF 2004. Riot police have been called in to keep order. I change the channel.

An infomercial touts the Ped-Egg. A hand rubs it against a foot while a voice says, "It's perfect for boyfriend, for girlfriend, for mother, for father, for grandmum and grandpa, for sister, for brother . . ." I change the channel.

Camera pans slowly over rice terraces of a mountain province. The slopes reach like a glassy ziggurat into the cloudless sky. A zoom onto a cluster of huts gives a perspective of how extensive the constructions are. Fade to an old Ifugao man, leathery-dark and toothless, speaking from inside the hut. He prepares betel nut while speaking, taking ingredients from a carved box. Subtitles on the bottom of the screen: "An American once came and told me our terraces are the eighth wonder of the world. I only know this is how we cultivate rice. Our way, for four thousand years . . ." I change the channel.

More news. Familiar image of Reverend Martin, preaching in a Burberry-plaid suit, cuts to an image of him being led from his mansion, surrounded by police, head down, facing away from the TV-camera lights and reporters with foamy microphones. He wears red silk pajamas. The voice-over says something in rapid Tagalog, which I hardly catch. Something about embezzlement in the El Ohim. The scroll across the bottom of the screen says the Phisix is down two points at closing today. I change the channel.

A concert at Araneta Coliseum of the country's "top fifty Elvis impersonators." All in identical bouffants, sunglasses, and sequined jumpsuits, though comically varying in size and weight. Two are drag queens, bedecked in fishnets and blue suede high-heel shoes. I change the channel.

Chinese news. Something about Shanghai, static shots of the skyline, workmen and material being hoisted up on cranes. I change the channel.

Chief Justice Santos is speaking at a symposium. "At the heart of law is morality," he says. "But at the heart of morality is spirituality. Our faith in the Almighty is our best guide in interpreting the laws of man." I change the channel.

F1 racing, Montoya leading at Monza, Schumacher a close second on the penultimate lap. I change the channel.

News report about another bombing, in Mindanao. General Santos City. A reporter stands in the glare of camera lights, a twisted chunk of metal behind her. The wreckage was once a bus, she says. Twelve were killed and another twenty-two have been brought to a hospital. Scene cuts to Manila, to Senator Nuredin Bansamoro (unassuming, bespectacled, pomaded), surrounded by scowling subordinates. "This is the, ah, sixth bombing in a month. It is, ah, believed . . . ," he says in very deliberate English, spitting out certain words with emphasis, ". . . believed to, uh, be, ah, perpetrated by, ah, the same cadre of dastardly scoundrels responsible for the, uh, Lotto and McDonald's bombings last week. To be sure, there are extremist members of the, ah, Abu Sayyaf network operating in these, ah, bicinities. Though we cannot, ah, be sure if there is a connection to the blasts in Metro Manila. I denounce reports that this is a precursor to, uh, a coup attempt. I have no comment on the rumours our, uh, dear president will institute martial law. If I had to comment, I would say it is a bery bad idea because, uh, I for one will stand against—" I change the channel.

A pretty mestiza is rubbing Block & White deodorant into her underarms after she showers. Scene cuts to her in a sleeveless blouse, raising her hand confidently at a university lecture. Her darker-skinned seatmate looks envious before crossing her arms to hide her own armpits. Next scene shows the dark-skinned classmate applying the deodorant, followed by before and after photos. Her armpits are clearly lightened after "just a few weeks of regular application." I change the channel.

CNN: a program about last month's antiwar protests in Toronto, Montreal, Vancouver, and Halifax. In Queen's Park, cops on horseback watch the crowd. A young man climbs on top of a *Globe and Mail* newspaper box and takes off his ski jacket to reveal a shirt that says WEAPON OF MASS DESTRUCTION. A mounted officer waves him down. The crowd shouts: "Get those animals off those horses!" The news ticker at the bottom of the screen says the Nasdaq and Dow Industrial are up. I change the channel.

A Portuguese nun discusses the beatitudes, quoting from the Gospel of St. John. Blessed are the meek, she says. I change the channel.

A female presenter on the Weather Channel says the coming storm is very strange. I change the channel.

Taiwanese news. Guangdong province, People's Republic of China. A reporter wears a surgical mask in front of a hospital. Inside, two sallow patients lie in bed, gazing at the camera as if it could save them. I change the channel.

A live pan across a massive crowd in Rizal Park, every person holding a candle and raising a hand in the gesture of born-again praise. It looks like a lazy fascist salute, or people at a karaoke party singing "Stop in the Name of Love." The commentator says a hundred thousand people have arrived in the two hours since Reverend Martin's arrest. Some hold banners that say PEACE or HOPE. A reporter does a vox pop with a lady in the crowd. What brings you here? "My love for Reverend Martin, of course. The Apostle of the People." Why do you love him so? "He gives me strength to make it through each week. I used to be a drug addict and—" A man with big muscles leans over her shoulder to shout: "Me, I used to be gay!" Thunder crackles in the sky. Some in the crowd open umbrellas. Chanting is picked up in waves by the microphones and fills my hotel room. I change the channel.

A bulletin of tonight's top stories: "The *Paul Watson*, the flagship of the North American environmental group the World Wardens, remained docked today in Manila despite protests from the Japanese embassy after last week's collision with the whaling vessel *Nisshin Maru*. The Soldiers for Military Reform have been granted amnesty by President Estregan, though a spokesperson for the Lupas Landcorp's Gloriolla Mall—which SMR troops overran last year and threatened to blow up if their demands for bureaucratic transparency weren't met—says the corporation will pursue civil charges. The Chinese-Filipino community inaugurated a memorial in Binondo, a multitiered pagoda in remembrance of all the kidnap-for-ransom victims killed or never found. And in tonight's edition of *In-Sight*, don't miss a special report on life in Olongapo and Angeles City, eleven years after the eruption of Mount Pinatubo and the closing of Clark and Subic bases. No longer home to the two largest American military installations outside the continental U.S., are we better off without them? Find out in 'From Dollars to Desert.'" I change the channel.

Lakbay-TV travel channel, opening credits: *Ancient Cultures of Mindanao*. A couple in intricate fabrics and headpieces. A sword brandished by the groom-prince, its blade voluptuously serrated. The bride, concealing her face with a fan, dances between two pairs of crossed bamboo poles clapped crisply together by attendants kneeling at her feet. The prince, his sword leaned on one shoulder and shield wielded firmly in the other hand, follows his bride, stepping in and out of the intermittent traps, the pace quickening rapidly. The bride steps back to watch her groom, his feet a blur among the wood cracking dangerously together. The hastening rhythm of the clack-clacking bamboo upon bamboo becomes hypnotic, like the rise to crescendo of Ravel's *Bolero*. I change the channel.

BBC World News: Chief UN Weapons Inspector Hans Blix is being interviewed, shaking his head, frustrated at what is being said about Saddam Hussein's Iraq. I change the channel.

One of those strange digital channels: in one corner of the screen, a music video from the Eraserheads, who sing about the unrequited love of a young girl from an exclusive college. On the rest of the screen are blinking text messages, updating in real time. Prettypinay89 writes: Hi 2 tropang Marikina! Gdluck 2 chem17 studnts of Phil Womns Schl with ur exams 2mrw. Gothgrrrrl3000 writes: Any1 here in2 deathmetal? Greyhounds rock! Eraserheads suck! And AnAk_ Ng_KidlAt writes: Is any1 out there 2 hear me?

I turn the television off.

*

"One more thing," Crispin said. "One last story." He stared at the typewriter in front of him. "When you get to my age, the most insignificant memories take on significance. Unrationalized blame, casual kindnesses, random gestures—one day you just need to tell someone about them. There was this time, when I was a boy, when my father was consumed by jealousy." I already had on my parka and backpack. I was cradling the bundle of outgoing mail in one arm. "Papa had always coveted the zoo my uncle had on his farm. So he decided to get an animal of his own, but for our house in Manila. He wanted to impress my mother, as well as coax her into spending more time with him there than in Bacolod." I poured Crispin a glass of sherry; he looked up at me, nodded. "Of course, my father didn't know anything about animals. He just liked having them. He must have thought he could hire people. As one does. He wanted a tiger and somehow he got one. I don't know how, I was too young. I remember he kept it in a cage by the swimming pool, near the lanai where we had our meals when we ate outdoors. Actually, I think the tiger was there in Forbes Park because it was being transported to the farm at Swanee. I'm not sure anymore."

Crispin sipped his sherry. He still hadn't changed out of his ruined barong. Two black manuscript boxes were on the floor beside him. I leaned on the doorjamb and looked at my watch. Madison would be waiting at home with Valentine's Day dinner. This morning, to my dismay, she'd told me about finding a recipe for tofu Peking duck, and I still had to somehow find some gluten-free hoisin sauce. It had come to feel like our relationship counted on the successful fulfillment of such errands. I undid my scarf and unzipped my coat.

"Anyhow. At that time it was a big tiger to me. Huge. I think it must have been an adolescent, because the space by the swimming pool and the lanai wasn't that big. Doesn't everything seem bigger when looking back? Well, I can only imagine what the neighbours thought. What arrogance, a tiger in your garden. Ha! Truly. Thing is, the damn thing wouldn't eat. It was traumatized by the flight or the truck or however it had been transported. It was a mess. I'm not sure whether it was a he or a she, or what became of it. It lay against whichever corner of the cage didn't have sun. The cage was barely large enough for it to pace and turn."

Crispin looked at the manuscript piled in its open box beside his typewriter. "One time my father had us eating breakfast outside, to appreciate the tiger. This part I remember well. We didn't want to because it smelled bad. Sour and musky. But we had no choice. We sat there, pushing the food around our plates. Mama was reading her pocketbook mystery. My father was in a good mood and he picked up a few bacon strips and approached the animal. How macho, he wanted to feed it by hand. But the poor animal was afraid. It cowered in the corner. Papa got angry and started shouting at it. I'll never forget what he said. He yelled, 'What kind of king of the jungle are you?!'"

Crispin laughed heartily, then sighed. "Yes, it's funny now. But at the time my brother and sister and I were terrified by the whole thing. The sadness was only felt later. You know how it is. My father threw the bacon at the tiger and hit it in the face. This puddle of piss formed under the animal, like some fluorescent toxic spill. I can see it like it was yesterday. The tiger cowering in its urine. Papa standing over it screaming. Mama still reading. We children averting our eyes, watching flies land on sliced mango on the fine china in front of us."

Crispin rearranged his ashtray and meerschaum pipe, moved the decanter to the left, placed the matching glass beside it. He stared at what his hands were doing, watching with absolute disinterest in their tasks. "I remember telling this story, years later, to my girlfriend, Gigi. It was odd, I hadn't remembered it for twenty years until I recounted it to her. I wept after. The first time since childhood. Gigi told me our country needs a revolution. Of course she'd say that, she was French. It took even me a long time to understand that in our country revolution isn't just parricide. It's deicide. I finally think our redemption will have to be more noble than that. Anyway, I always wanted to use my memory of that tiger for a short story, or a scene in a novel. But some things are better kept in the past." He pulled the paper from his typewriter, added it to the manuscript, and closed the box. He put the box on top of the other two. "After I wept, I remember how clear my eyes were."

Crispin looked at me. I'll never forget how he looked at me. As if I was a holy ghost. As if he realized what had to happen.

"So long," he said, with his shy smile. "Keep it bouncing."

I went home to Madison, the screaming of the living room smoke alarm, windows wide open, and an apartment as cold as the winter outside.

That was the last time I spoke with Crispin.

5

Cristo rears his new dappled charger at the crest of the hill, the sound of his men following like the drums of war. The horse whinnies nervously. Already Cristo is missing Paloma, swearing the Americans will pay for shooting his beloved mount.

There, at the bend of the river in the distance, is the infantry of Captain Peter Murray. His old nemesis. The campfires are intermittent like distant lighthouses as soldiers pass in front of them, pitching tents, fetching water, preparing dinner. Sergeant Lupas stops his own horse beside Cristo's.

"They have no idea," Cristo says.

"Yes, sir. But what of the women and children in the village?"

Cristo is silent.

"Capitan, the men are worried. They are wondering if it would be better to surrender."

At this, Cristo lowers his voice to a rare sharpness. "You mean *you* are wondering. Not them."

"I don't need to prove my loyalty to you, Cristo."

"Don't you see, Ricardo? *This* is what those Amerikanos want. They think they can create a cordon, to cow the villagers into giving us up."

"Our food is dwindling rapidly. Our supply lines are nonexistent. And the toll their cordon is taking . . . Cristo, the villagers . . . the women and children, they are starving."

"After three years, we will give up? Does any man think I don't worry for my own family? No, Ricardo. We won't play into the enemy's hands. Not after so long. Bear in mind, old friend, when we win, such worries will be over."

"They'll only send more troops, Capitan. And more after that. America is a big place."

"In your mind, Sergeant Lupas, we've already lost. Haven't we?"

"Of course not."

"Tell me. Who do you think is being hunted? Us or them?"

Lupas does not say anything. He only nods.

"Prepare the men for our charge," Cristo says, his voice low and careful. "Tell them it will be victorious or it will be our last."

–from *The Enlightened* (page 223), by Crispin Salvador

*

I entered into fatherhood with only the best intentions. I think that in the beginning I did things right. As best a boy of seventeen could. Every teenager is both a hero and a failure. When we become adults we have to choose where in the middle we'll be. I guess I've chosen.

It wasn't always that way. I remember what made it easy to choose otherwise. Anais. Fetching her from painting class, her belly growing beneath the smock, her clothes scented by linseed oil. Listening to her dreams of moving away to raise our child in Prague, Buenos Aires, Antananarivo. Her empathy for Vincent van Gogh, of E. E. Cummings and that poem about love being gentler than rain with small hands. Together, we did the ultrasounds, the Lamaze classes. Together, we looked through baby-name books, leafing through the pages of all the possibilities of our shared future. Together, we made love, the baby inside her every hope held firmly between us. I received the call in the middle of the night from her maid: the water was broken, Anais was being rushed to the hospital. I was there through the prolonged delivery: my hand feeding her ice chips, my little voice saying, breathe, breathe, Anais turning to me to say, finally, I love you. Just like in the movies. Then came the doctor, telling us the baby was in trouble. Then came the emergency C-section and my long paces in the waiting room. The first time I held my daughter and realized my childhood was over, I was ecstatic about it. She was worth every sacrifice. Then, the changing of the diapers, the burping, the first steps and the first words. Bringing the tiny, tiny girl to visit my grandparents—how they cooed and fawned, had their pictures taken with her in their arms. Then, after, in private, Granma, tearful, telling me: "You looked like you were playing house." Later, the struggle to keep my grade point average high enough to stay in school. And of course, the month that I wasn't there—when my grandparents sent me "to see the forest from the trees" by visiting my brother Jesu in London, where he was completing his MBA. Anais felt abandoned, or maybe she felt scared, or maybe she was just as lost as I was, and she threatened to cheat if I didn't come home. Later that summer, my too-late return home to Manila, Anais's threat made good—she'd kissed another boy.

At least, that's how I recall it. It was so long ago.

For our little family, for our daughter, for myself, I tried to win Anais back. But the betrayal had wound its way between us like barbed wire. I'd left her, and she'd left me, and we wanted to make each other regretful. She, like me, was a kid raising a child. Anais said she was sorry, and I know she meant it. What I don't know is why I couldn't forgive. I thought of which places in the house the other guy could have kissed her, and I learned to avoid those spots. I twisted inside at the thought of him holding my child. I could not force from my mind the look Anais must have given him as they embraced outside, beneath the orchids her mom grew on posts, where we had always embraced, where we were trying so hard to embrace now. What plans had been made? What promises were exchanged? But what more could Anais do but say sorry, kiss me again, reassure me?

I'm making this confession without hope for absolution.

One morning, I pretended to go crazy. Perhaps in pretending, I proved myself so. I looked into the middle distance, whispering to Anais: "Jacques Chirac is after me. Listen, can you hear him? We have to hide." I crouched behind the couch. Anais held me. She believed me. I was intoxicated by a cocktail of success and anger and disbelief. She believed me? She wordlessly tightened her arms around me. "Beware of Jacques Chirac!" I exclaimed.

Anais grasped my face, looked me in the eye, and said calmly: "Jacques Chirac's in France." She began to cry. I did, too, for all manner of reasons.

After, my absence was gradual, until one day it was complete.

*

On the second New Year's Eve during the war, minutes after raising his glass of sake and pledging undying love and protection for his brother, sister-in-law, and their children, Salvador's uncle Jason disappeared. "He was there," Salvador recalled in *Autoplagiarist*, "and when we turned around from hugging each other in hopeful, even desperate, celebration of the new year, Tito Jason was gone. I was devastated. For a long time we were all mystified. Only after the war ended did we discover what had happened to him. What he experienced, and the stories he later told me, would ultimately push me to make the decisions I made as a young man."

—from the biography in progress, *Crispin Salvador: Eight Lives Lived*, by Miguel Syjuco

*

People are spilling out of establishments, watching the rain, enjoying the breeze in the open sections of the Greenbelt Mall. The hustle of the cafés and the bustle of the shops are almost too much to bear. Christmas carols play like torture devices. It's like I'm in one of those dreams where you go to school and everyone stares, horrified. I check my fly. I quicken my step. Some faces turn away, into their coffees, up at the light fixtures.

In the Club Coup d'Etat, it's hot and murky. The soaring hall is dark and foggy and dense with techno. The bass penetrates, charging the bones. The melodies are anthemic and ineffable. On the dance floor, light flashes red, then green, then blue, then yellow, then red all over again. Tonight is billed as Old-School Trance Night. When did trance music become old-school? The place hasn't changed, except I don't know anyone. They're all so young. They dance self-consciously, humid with movement. In the sapphire neon near the entrance a camera flashes like lightning—the spherical Albon Alcantara waddles through his rounds for his *Gazette* column, "Albonanza," his subjects posing like big fish just caught. In dim corners, figures do their best to melt into plush pleather couches. One couple is trying to dry-hump unnoticed, like modest dogs, in the darkness near an air-conditioning vent. A boy-faced dancer plays with glow sticks, makes simple circles in the air. I'm tempted to borrow them and show him a thing or two. How strange it is to be old enough to have fantasies that are no longer only concerned with the future.

My cell phone vibrates in my pocket. A text from my old friend Gabby. How'd he know I was back? Edsa 5 brewing while you read your text messages. Protests planned this weekend against the Estregan Administration! Stay tuned. Every body will count.

Bouncers block my entrance into the VIP area. From within, an acquaintance spots me and almost leaps in place. I don't remember his name. He was much younger, from the International School while I was in college. I remember not liking him. He tells the bouncers I'm "cool." They eye me uncertainly. Inside, old friends pick me up with their hugs, slap me hard on the back, shake my hand as if I'd won something. "When did you arrive?" Mico asks, shouting over the noise. He tries to slip a pill into my mouth. I keep my lips shut tightly. I smile and shake my head and hug him in deep gratitude. The gang's all here.

Tals (warmly): "Hey, cuz!?"

Mitch (looking over my shoulder at a bevy of college girls): "Pare, check out those biatches."

Edward: "Where you been hiding, nigga? You were abroad? Since when?"

Angela: "Can I bum a cig?"

E.V.: "So you've returned to the decline of the Roman Empire."

Pip: "O! Wassup?"

Ria: "I haven't seen you since you stopped updating your Friendster profile."

Chucho (shaking my hand vigorously): "What a guy what a guy what a guy!"

Rob (not really meaning it): "Dude, we're leaving for another party, wanna join?"

Tricia: "Fucking trance, man, fucking trance."

Markus is also happy. "You came!"

"No," I shout back. "I always walk this way."

We exchange effusiveness. He puts a baggie into my pocket. I push it back in his hand, but it's already closed into a fist. "Homecoming present," he shouts. I joke that he's an addict. He replies: "Dude, you're only an addict when your supply runs out."

It's nine months since I stopped having my own supply. Five months since I last touched that bullshit. I really don't want to go back to that vibrating wakefulness, that bubble of abrasive beauty and precarious self-confidence that should come from inside me but doesn't. How sexy it was: Madison waking up on the weekend, rolling over naked, shrewdly wrapped in the thin white sheet, saying, "Hey, let's get high." How easy it was: wadding up a couple of hundred bucks and picking up the phone and calling the "car service," telling the operator that I needed a "Cadillac" for coke, a "Mercedes" for marijuana, a "Lexus" for ludes, or for the driver to bring "umbrellas," because it looks like rain, when what we really wanted were shrooms to trip on at the natural history museum. It was simpler than ordering a Domino's pizza. And we didn't have to tip.

Cocaine made life uncomplicated. We never had to cook, never got tired, never worried about personal insufficiencies. It fuelled electrified sessions when I'd write twenty-page short stories in a night, overflowing with confidence that would eventually fall, but easily rise again an instant after I lifted my head from the mirror on the coffee table and wiped my nose. I was the best writer at Columbia. The best writer in New York. The best writer in the world. The best-kept secret, waiting for his time. I had a mission from God, to act on behalf of my people. Madison would joke that we use mirrors for our lines so we can watch ourselves being stupid. Then we'd do a few more hits and have excellent sex that we mistook for love. When the anxieties came, as they did, with the comedown, it was as simple as pouring another drink, or popping a pill to pass out. My sleep, those times, was always deep and restorative.

I pocket Markus's baggie. I can hear Dr. Goldman, my therapist in New York, speaking from her armchair: This is the first step to failure. But such an expensive gift would be rude not to accept. I don't have to do any of it. Anyway, it's been so long. I'll just have a bump. Or two. Maybe a line. Or a couple of small ones. Maybe just half the baggie, and share the rest with my friends. If I consume it all myself, nobody will care. I'm home and safe and filled with the comfort of being somewhere I've already been. The ruckus of homecoming is brutally enjoyable and everyone makes me feel like I'm a champion. And all I had to do was stay away long enough.

*

Poor Cousin Bobby is a casualty of the slumping economy. He loses his hospital job and falls in with a gang of Pinoys with pimped Subarus. One day, Bobby is arrested and brought to court, accused of raping his date after they watched *Eyes Wide Shut*. Erning, of course, sits right behind him, to lend moral support. With his new cell phone, Erning takes surreptitious photos of his cousin, to send to family back home, but he can only capture the back of Bobby's head. The bailiff comes by and threatens to confiscate it.

When the trial gets under way, the rape victim is asked by the prosecuting attorney: "Jhanelle, would you please describe here for the court the person who assaulted you sexually."

The rape victim, on the verge of tears, says: "Very dark-skinned. Short. Wiry black hair. Narrow eyes. Thick ears. With a broad nose with a flat bridge."

Erning jumps to his feet, shouting angrily: "Stop making fun of my cousin!"

*

"Don't use that tone with me," Madison had said.

"What tone?"

"That tone."

"Madison, I'm just talking."

"But why that way?"

"Sweetheart. Liebling. Madison. What way?"

"Is it the new toothpaste?"

Madison and I had been needing quality time and I'd brought her out for lunch. We had steak-of-the-forest burgers at her favourite vegan place, in Chelsea. Run by a couple of forgetful hippies, it wasn't very good, but Madison had a soft spot for failing restaurants. She said she couldn't stand to let people lose hold of their dreams. For dessert, we shared a carob brownie and held hands while walking to the museum. When we went into a bank's ATM enclosure to get cash, Madison looked up at the wall of curling flyers about people still missing. She gathered off the floor the sheets that had fallen like leaves and she blue-tacked them up again. Madison went and waited outside. She was really moody when we got to MoMA.

I told her: "It wasn't the toothpaste."

"If not, why throw a hissy fit when I didn't change the channel?"

"Liebling, please don't raise your voice here."

"Was it because of that show on princes William and Harry?"

"Why would it be?"

"I shouldn't have told you."

"Told me what?"

"That I used to have a crush on them."

"Please. What do I care? I used to have a crush on Phoebe Cates. I don't know what you see in them anyway. They're just princes."

"Who lost their mother tragically."

"So did I."

"You only talk about your parents when you need the advantage. I *knew* that this was about William and Harry. Or is it *also* the toothpaste? What's with your hate for organic? I thought you cared about Mother Earth."

"I do. I just don't know why she's so self-important. Come on, give me a smile. That argument was so this morning. I asked why you bought that toothpaste. And you said—"

"No. First, I was like, Surprise! Look at this. And then, you said . . . What did you say?"

"No. That's not true. I said, Sugarbabe, if you're making tea, could you make me a cup of rooibos. And you said—"

"No, you've got it all wrong. First you were like—"

"Madison. I know what I said."

"So what's wrong with the toothpaste?"

"You know we have huge credit card debt."

"And you blame me? If you had quit scoring to party every weekend, we'd have savings for our future."

"I thought you supported my writing."

"I do."

"I've got to make this dream work. You keep talking about feeding kids in Tasmania."

"That's Tanzania. See? You're in your own little world. I just want us to do something good. Besides, I don't get your Crispin obsession."

"Look, this fight's about the toothpaste. This morning, I was just saying . . . Aw, forget it."

"Fine. It's easy to forget. A joy, even, to forget you. All that time you spend in the library. With the memory of your dead friend."

"It's work. Finding *TBA* will jump-start my career. Don't you get it? It's art. Art is important."

"Art with a capital *F*."

"Dead Crispin's better than a living you."

"Quit with the drama," Madison said. She inhaled slowly, digging deep for patience. "Miguel, I love you. Why do you always seem to feel so incomplete? I'm trying my best to be . . ." Her voice cracked and she shook her head in disgust. "You're not even listening. Screw this sucky shit." She left me and went to look at the huge Pollock. She always hated Pollock. I loved him, particularly this one. It was like someone had set off all the fireworks at the same time. Madison looked like a little girl gazing at the sky on the Fourth of July. I considered going to her and taking her hand. Maybe I should have. But I didn't know what to believe. You can't trust a whiner. You can hear in their voices their hidden motives.

Everyone else in the room was walking the way people do in the presence of inexorable art. Like zombies. I should have gone to Madison. Instead, I stood before Yves Klein's blue painting, hoping its oceanic electricity would embalm what was expanding in me.

Nearby, a tourist, her thickened ankles almost trembling with the load of years and bags of I ♥ NY souvenirs, spoke Russian to her younger companion. They zombied closer, to stand beside me. The old lady studied the painting, seemingly entranced by its intense beauty. Turning to her companion, she pointed at the canvas and declared in her thick accent: "Blue Man Group."

They went and joined Madison in front of the Pollock.

*

From Marcel Avellaneda's blog, "The Burley Raconteur," December 4, 2002:

Today's bruit around watercoolers: the Administration reports that Israeli, American, and Australian explosives and ballistics experts agree that the November 19 bombings at the McKinley Plaza Mall were *not* accidents. This is the latest in the battle between the Administration, which wants to retain the status quo ("The economy is falling! Bombs are exploding!" they shout. "Don't change horses in midstream!"), and the Lupas Landcorp ("Faulty LPG canisters from PhilFirst Gas Corp were the culprits," Arturo Lupas said in a statement. "Our security is fine, and we're not bombing ourselves. We don't need to claim insurance—we're Lupases, not Changcos. We won't be part of Estregan's smoke screen").

True Believers, what could it all *really* be about? Is the Estregan Administration covering up real problems, to maintain its hold on power? Or is the Administration merely *pretending* to cover up real problems, to seem in control and justify ramping up its hold on power? Or is the Honorable Fat Cat himself *pretending* to cover up problems that *ARE NOT* there? Or, perhaps most sinisterly, are Estregan and his litter of Chubby Kitties *actively* manufacturing problems, to allow them to justify an increase in their power? Hors d'oeuvres before martial law, anyone? Hmm. Isn't that too much a trick out of Marcos's playbook? Or is its obviousness its very smoke screen? My friends, with the election less than two years away, of all the lies, half lies, half truths, and hidden truths, perhaps what is real is merely all of the above.

Nevertheless, hot on the case is our network of tireless bloggers, working to wrest reality from the jaws of misinformation. Monkey See pokes holes in the Theory of the Faulty Propane Gas Canister, which the government denies is the cause of the Lupas McKinley Plaza Mall blasts. The inimitable Ricardo Roxas IV's My Daily Vitamins questions why the aforementioned Western experts weren't allowed to be interviewed by local media. And Wasak asks the impertinent but very pertinent question of whether any of this is relevant to anyone: "No matter who is in power," he writes, "our lives go on with their usual troubles."

In this kaleidoscope of shifting vested interests—and assuming the blasts in the south *were* put together by Islamist militants—one incident remains unaddressed: What about the one at the Shell station near Forbes Park? Hmmm. No shit, Sherlock. Dig deeper, Watson.

Last but not least in today's edition, we look at the transcripts of speeches for and against former security guard Wigberto Lakandula's defiant stand: against, by Senator Nuredin Bansamoro, can be found here; and for, by the elder but still eloquent solon Congressman Respeto Reyes, is available here.

Nuff said! Until next time, True Believers.

Some posts from the message boards below:

—This rivalry between the Lupases and Changcos is going overboard and we're all getting stuck in between. (bernice@localvibe.com)

—No honour amongst thieves! (ningning.baltazar@britishairways.com)

—Wow, u rly br0ke it down 4 us, Marcel. All-Of-The-Above is my gess.

BTW, Estregan dsnt kno wat he s doing, bt he s certnly doing sumthn. IMHO, he s tryng 2 cnvince us he s in control. Der4, dat shows he isnt. (gundamlover@hotmail.com)
—Why do they have to import experts from abroad, when our experts here are as good, if not better? (bayani.reyes@up.edu.ph)
—Could it be that Bansamoro is trying to get power by playing both sides? I'm just saying! (pel234@yehey.com)
—Bayani, I think the foreign experts were brought in to lend the report objectivity and credibility. (theburleyraconteur@avellaneda.com)
—Doesnt it make sense that if Estregans gone, all his programs that are working will stop? Hes just as bad as the rest, so why not just stick with him? We need a benevolent dictator if this country is to succeed. Look at Singapore! (mano.s@thehandsoffate.com)
—I know the bomb at the Shell station was done by the Islamists. Who can be sure if the Muslim senator didn't have a hand in it? Innocent until proven guilty, but isn't it better to be safe than sorry? May the Holy Spirit protect us! (Miracle@Lourdes.ph)

*

During the Japanese-sponsored Second Philippine Republic, Junior's career thrived, though the ubiquity of random acts of violence made him nervous. He insisted that Leonora and the children travel with him whenever he went from Bacolod to the capital. "He felt we were safer with him," Salvador wrote in his memoir. "Perhaps he was wrong and put us at risk, but he preferred to err with us in his presence than have something transpire in his absence. This is the perfect flaw of all fathers."

As the occupation set like cement drying, a new social order fell into place, though in many ways it looked very much like the old one. In those years, young Salvador witnessed the benefits that his father's position in the collaborationist government provided their family, and he experienced and swallowed, for the first time in his life, the alluring palatability of necessary hypocrisies.

The Salvador residence near Malate Church seemed to the three children to be a safe haven from what was happening just outside their gate. It was in that home, sometime in 1943, where the young Salvador met a man whose life would confuse his conception of patriotism. The aged Artemio Ricarte visited Junior on several occasions. On the third of these, when the two men withdrew to speak in the study, Narcisito ran upstairs to whisper in his little brother's ear: "He's here again, the serpent is here!" The pair tiptoed downstairs to wait outside the study door to catch a glimpse of the old warrior.

Ricarte, whose revolutionary name was "El Vibora," Spanish for "The Viper," was famous for being the general who fought against the Spanish, against the Americans, and was the only one among the defeated revolucionarios to refuse to swear an oath of fidelity to the United States. His dissent had him banned from his country forever, and he was forced to smuggle himself home from Hong Kong in 1903, intent on continuing the war. Ricarte was later betrayed by his comrade General Pio del Pilar—known as "The Boy General"—and imprisoned, though his legendary stature earned him visits from high-ranking U.S. officials, including President Theodore Roosevelt's vice president, Charles Fairbanks. In 1910, Ricarte was released. Refusing a second time to pledge himself to the United States, he was again deported to Hong Kong. He ended up in Yokohama, Japan, with his wife. There he lived in exile until the Second World War, when the Japanese government brought him back to the Philippines. The old general returned in triumph, though he was surprised to discover the extent to which his countrymen had become allied with the Americans. Ricarte's task was to convince the Filipinos that their fellow-Asian occupiers were preferable to Western imperialists. After the president of the occupied Philippines, José P. Laurel, refused to allow the Japanese to conscript Filipinos into the army, Ricarte colluded with Junior Salvador to create a pro-Japan, antiguerrilla movement called the Makapili.

Junior and Ricarte's conferences would last long into the night. Narcisito and Crispin sat outside the study door until they fell asleep. In *Autoplagiarist*, Salvador remembers: "I was startled awake by The Viper himself! The kindly man of seventy-seven years was bent stiffly toward me and my brother, a hand on each of our heads, tousling our hair. 'As lookouts, you two would be court-martialled,' he said. With a sigh, he nodded and shuffled to the sofa in the sala, where we clambered up beside him to listen to stories of the wars he

had fought alongside heroes we had grown up idolizing. What I remember most vividly, however, was my father seated in his armchair
facing the sofa, looking at us, his two sons, with naked pride."
                        —from the biography in progress, *Crispin Salvador:*
                                Eight Lives Lived, by Miguel Syjuco

                                        *

"Dude, you should have seen it," Mitch says. He's tweaked, pacing
back and forth in front of a group of us guys outside the club's bathroom. It's Markus, E.V., Edward, Mitch, and me. Bubbles of saliva
froth at the edges of Mitch's mouth. "Like my house, right, it's like
at the end of Forbes, as in, right over the wall of our backyard is the
Shell station. Yes, *yes*, exactly! I know! *That* Shell station. I wasn't
home, but the maids said it made my mom and dad's fucking antique celadons slide off their stands in the cabinets. But dude, *dude*,
get this. Dude, me and my bro, we get home early the next morning, after partying. We could still feel the flavours of the E and K
and shit in us. We're smoking one of Melvin's joints in the yard. So
we can sleep, right? 'Cause like our mom can always smell it when
we smoke in the house. Yeah, right? Proof she's partaken in her
youth. *So*, Melvin and I are like sitting on the bench near my mom's
fountain—that's right, that plaster boy pissing. We're looking up,
enjoying, you know, those last fucking fingers of darkness finally
disappearing in the sky . . ."
    "You're a fricking poet," E.V. says.
    "Yeah, fuck you very much," Mitch says. "So, Mel, he gets it in
his head that he wants to swim. But our houseboy told us when he
opened the gate that they'd put in chemicals and the pool was off-
limits for the day. And I'm like, Mel, you think he's lying to us? And
Mel looks at me and is like, You think? And I'm like, Why would he
be lying to us? Mel's like, I don't know, but maybe he might be. So
we look at the houseboy, off at the far corner of the yard, pruning
the hedges with his big-ass shears. And he *does* look like he's lying to
us. Like he's pretending he doesn't see us suspecting him of lying.
And I'm like, Yeah, I *def*initely think he's lying. And Mel's like, But
why would he do that? And I'm like, Dude, just look at him. And
Mel looks at him, then is like, So you think we should just say fuck

it and swim? And I'm like, Yeah. And Mel's already taking his shirt off and is down to his boxers. Then he goes to me, What about you? And I'm like: Nah, I don't feel like swimming just yet. And Mel's halfway from the fountain to the pool, which probably had all these nasty fucking chemicals, running in his boxers with pictures of condoms on them, when he trips on something on the lawn. He tumbles and rolls like Flash fucking Gordon. And we're both like shitting ourselves laughing. But when I go to help him up, I *see* what he slipped on. Dude, it's a fuck*ing* head. It's an actual *head*. Yeah, of one of the cops. A cop's fucking head. Get this, the strange thing is, because we're all fucked on E and acid and shit, we're of course hella surprised, but *not* grossed out. Mel and I just look at it. It's like sort of beautiful. The bloody neck part's covered by the grass, so it looked like that's what our lawn would've looked like if our lawn had a face and was sleeping. We knew it was weird. But it wasn't gross. It was just, you know, the circle of life."

We're all listening so intently we don't notice that the bathroom is free. Some guy behind us says something. The group of us go in, like teenage boys slipping into the adult section of a video rental shop. As I close the door, the guy behind us looks at us funny. For a second, I'm a bit uncomfortable. For a second. Then I remember. This is Manila. It's nice being home.

In the bathroom, a couple of baggies are passed around, and we do bumps off the ends of our keys. I hide my own baggie in my pocket. A bag reaches me, I bump, then pass it to Mitch. He uses the nail of his pinky finger, which he's grown for this purpose.

"It's that fucking Nuredin Bansamoro," E.V. says, tapping his baggie to gauge how much he's got left. "I'm telling you. He's messing with the government. It's all smoke and mirrors with him. It's like we learned in lit class: 'The prince of darkness is a gentleman.'"

"Fligga, no fucking way," Markus says. "It's the Muslims. The Abu Sayyaf."

"Bansamoro and the Abu Sayyaf," E.V. says, "aren't they like fuck-buddies?"

"Dude, that's knee-jerk bigotry," Markus says. "Just 'cause they worship Allah doesn't mean they're in cahoots."

"They say," Edward offers, "it's got something to do with a

love triangle with fricking President Estrogen and that Vita Nova chick."

"Fucking funny, dude. President *Estrogen*!" says Mitch, cracking up.

"At the heart of every story," I say, "is a love triangle."

"It's Estrogen's man-boobs, pare." Edward says. "A fear of man-boobs is at the heart of what drives every man."

"Vita Nova," Mitch says, gyrating his hips. "Aw yeah! I hope that sex tape gets released. This soldier dude I play B-ball with, Marine Sergeant Joey Smith, he likes to say: Well corn my porn, that's one mighty fine LBFM. Dude, Vita's gots the launch codes for *my* intercontinental ballistic missile."

"What's an LBFM?" I say.

"Little brown fuck machine," E.V. explains.

"Fligga, please," Markus insists. "It's totally the Abu Sayyaf. Can I get another bump?"

"What's a fligga anyway?" I say.

"Filipino nigga," E.V. says.

"So what happened?" Markus says.

"To what?" says E.V.

"To the guy's head," I say.

"*So*, what happened is," Mitch continues, "we call the houseboy over. Now *that* dude's surprised. The fucking guy steps back, turns around, and hurls his breakfast. Like fucking five yards away. An *Exorcist*-worthy blow-by. But Mel and I are weirded out by him, right? 'cause we thought he was fucking with our heads about the pool. We're convinced he left the head there for us to find. So we tell him to clean it up. He just *looks* at us. Then he goes away and comes back with our driver. The houseboy's carrying a pool net, the driver has a shoebox. They try to get the head into the shoebox, but the fucking thing won't fit. They're just like rolling it around, and it's like staring up at them like what the fuck? So they go back into the house. When they come back, a group of maids follows, but they like wait on the steps, not wanting to get closer. The houseboy's carrying one of my mom's hatboxes. They use the pool net to push the head into it. And fucking-A, it's a perfect fit. Then Mel and I go to our room and crash. Dude, the funniest thing . . . later that afternoon, my ma comes into our room to wake us up for church. Mel told me later he was like totally giving it to Palmela Handerson and was about nut when our mom walked in. Anyway, Ma's all pissed and shit, going off on us in the dark. She's like: Why didn't you use a plastic bag or something? That hatbox was from Bergdorf's! Me and Mel just like hid under our blankets, giggling. My mom switches on the lights and just splits, leaving the door wide open so that the air-con could escape. Fucking bitch."

*

In the music and darkness and lights, our long-faced protagonist stands flanked by familiar voices. When his friends smile or laugh, he does the same, even if he didn't hear the joke. He raises his glass at their every exhortation. He finishes his drink quickly, to create an excuse to leave the group. That habitual tactic always makes him the first to get drunk. Tonight, it works even faster. He goes again to the bar.

The bartender brings our tipsy protagonist a glass of Lagavulin single malt. A woman with a butch cut, an old friend from his college days, approaches him warmly. "Hello, Sara," he says, his voice welcoming like a hand held out. They speak quietly for a while. When she leaves, he abandons his Lagavulin, untouched on the bar, and slips away unnoticed. He barges through the crowd by the door, pushing them aside like curtains. They look back in puzzlement.

He takes a cab to his hotel and lies down on his bed, deep in thought. The baggie of cocaine sits on the table. He'd once told his therapist that the reason he wanted to clean up was for Madison. But that wasn't exactly true. He never told Dr. Goldman about his being a father. He thinks of what Sara told him. And of all the things he should have said in return. He remembers one time watching Crispin at his typewriter, the letters collecting into words—l'esprit de l'escalier. A phrase he often thinks about. The spirit, summoned by the texture of the knob, the tinkle of keys, the shock of a dead bolt, the snap of his heel echoing down the stairwell, like laughter, ha, ha, ha, ha. All the unsaid answers, reassurances, apologies, retorts. He's afraid that when the time comes to make amends, he won't know what to say.

He goes to the baggie, holds it over the toilet, but says aloud, "What's the point?" He cuts himself a few rough lines on the tabletop. They sit there like arrows pointing in different directions.

Later, he has a feeling that he is being watched. Talked about. Judged. A distant cock crows and the sky begins to lighten. His heart keeps time with the cheap clock on the bedside table. It slows until it's normal. Time, too, seems to lessen its pace. The light in the world diminishes.

He is sitting at an Underwood, typing away. Then it becomes a laptop, and he is researching crucifixions for a short story when he comes across a strange name. Archbishop Joachim of Nizhny-Novgorod, found crucified upside down on the Royal Doors of the Sebastopol Cathedral in 1920. Intrigued by its recentness, he checks Wikipedia, only to find the entry reads, "He was a big fat guy who was the best friwnd of Satanand he easts babys, so he was crucified by monkeys." Further research proves this inaccurate. It was Bolsheviks who did him in. Leaving the study, he walks down the hall to discover the blue door wide open. Outside, Jane Street is sandy and blindingly bright. A man is dragging a body across the floor as if it were trash for Monday morning pickup. "You're late," the man says, dropping the wrist of Crispin's corpse. The man pushes him into the crowd. They tear off his clothes. He sees that he has an erection and is filled with deep shame. A security guard in a blue uniform thrusts a heavy beam upon his shoulders. "This is called a patibulum," a woman whispers in his ear. "If you can get free of it, you'll find your child." He is pushed to join the procession. He reaches the top of the hill. Somebody in the crowd is playing Air Supply on a tinny transistor radio. This is a dream. I can control it if I try. He is pushed onto his back and seven-inch spikes are driven between his radii and carpals. His patibulum is lifted onto an upright stipe. Another spike is banged through the intermetatarsal spaces of his feet. Only when he sees the disgust and pity on the faces in the crowd does he feel any pain. It is nearly impossible to breathe. He pulls himself up by his impaled wrists to draw air. I can escape. Fire flashes down his arms, up his legs. He wilts. He pulls himself up to breathe out. I can step down from this thing. The pain is even more horrendous for its new familiarity. The sun grows hotter. Women pass by. They flutter plastic fans with his grandfather's face on them. "Look at his wrinkled peepee," says Anais. "Check out his chicken legs," says Madison. Dr. Goldman, checking her watch, reminds, "Stay away from situations that will lead you to fail." Robert De Niro playing Al Capone comes to stand before him, wearing a tuxedo and brandishing a Louisville Slugger. Capone is suddenly President Estregan, wearing a green satin boxing robe. The bat is swung twice, elegantly. His legs are broken. Unable to hold himself up, he cannot breathe. There's still so much I need to do. The crowd sounds like the recursive sea. To either side, two thieves are nailed to their patibula. He hears the bang, bang, bang, like keystrokes of a typewriter in the next room.

Sitting up suddenly in bed, he looks at the TV, the window looking onto windows, and the teas beside the electric kettle on the counter. For a few seconds, he has no idea where he is. The fall of rain outside reminds him.

*

It's afternoon and my taxi travels north, through the rain. I'm going to a poetry reading and book launch, where I hope some of the literati will tell me more about Crispin. In the deluge, men in yellow plastic cloaks stand on ladders, stringing Christmas lights and wreaths to streetlamps on the road. The torrent is like gravel on the taxi's roof, and I wonder how the men don't fall. The taxi driver curses, opens his door to spit heftily.

From the radio sputters the distorted jingle of the Bombo news report. A voice crackles in Tagalog: "My compatriots, stay tuned for these top stories at the hour: more flooding as rains continue; Reverend Martin, detained at Camp Crame, has his request for bail denied; international environmental activists protest outside the San Mateo munitions and fireworks factory of the Philippines First Corporation; SWAT teams have prepared a battering ram in hope of ending the Lakandula hostage siege; and our own pride and joy, Efren 'Bata' Reyes, wins the World 8 Ball Championship again. Full stories at three on the clock." Then the sanctifying guitar chords of Poison's "Every Rose Has Its Thorn."

I spent yesterday evening and all of this morning recuperating from the other night's coke binge. I didn't want to see anyone. I just couldn't. My link to the outside world was the dozens of text messages I kept getting from people urging me to bring food and water to the protesters outside the Changco home. I sat in bed with my books, searching Crispin's memoir, notebooks, assorted writings, for evidence of his daughter. Nothing specific turned up, though suddenly each of his works has become freighted with meaning—every heroic protagonist is a compensation, every loss now a metaphor, every mention of a father or a child suddenly more than was ever on the page. I fanned his work out on my bed, and looked at it like pieces of a puzzle in which the picture will only be recognized once it is solved. Miss Florentina will be my only chance to learn more. Unless any of the writers at the book launch know something.

The taxi driver turns right onto Edsa. Traffic slows. Stops. Flooding perhaps? The rains cease in an instant. The driver switches off his wipers. Wind rakes the remaining droplets, gathered beyond the wipers' reach, horizontally across the windshield. He keeps looking at me in his rearview. He's young, hair spiked like a sea urchin. He nods his head with feeling to the rock ballad, lips subtly mouth the words. He finally says, "No more rain," grinning as if it were his doing. "My name is Joe," he says, apropos of nothing.

Traffic moves through a corridor of hand-painted movie signs, which rise three stories high and block out the squatter areas like some Potemkin village of celluloid fantasies. It's not too strained a metaphor. Someone in the industry once told me the Philippines has the world's fourth largest film industry, next to Bollywood, Hollywood, and Nigeria's Nollywood. Phollywood, he'd called it, laughing unkindly. These billboards are the iceberg's tip of the melodramatic tradition that links every genre: *Rumble in Manila 4*; *Shake Rattle and Roll Part 9—Christ Have Mercy*; *I Will Wait for You in Heaven*; *Please Teacher Don't Touch Me There*; and *High Skool Hijinks*. In garish, sun-kissed ochre acrylic, the faces of the artistas tower like egos. Gone are the clean-scrubbed teen princesas and gritty heroes of the eighties, icons of my youth—some already passed away, most simply passed on to heavenly political careers or hellish marriages with sons of tycoons.

Keeping to long-standing tradition, this new breed has taken the surnames of the country's elite: Lisa Lupas, Ret-Ret Romualdez, Cherry-pie Changco, Pogi-boy Prieto, Heart Aquino. Others appropriate American culture: Pepsi Paloma IV, Keana Reeves, Mike Adidas. But the one who stands out, again, is the heaving-breasted Vita Nova, whose lithe looks took her from humble Pampanga roots to centre stage of Classmate, the new strip club where dancers don (then remove) the uniforms of Catholic girls' colleges. Her big break, the papers like to highlight, was as an actress in karaoke videos, the first being "Unchained Melody," where she walked by a pond and looked rapt with hungering for her beloved's touch.

Now—on the heels of her success with the Mr. Sexy Sexy Dance, having parlayed her sexual wares wisely—Vita's now a megastar. According to the poster, she's in "her most important role and big-screen breakout ever in the world." That may not be entirely true. If the rumours are to be believed, the tape from the videocam that Nova discovered hidden in her bedroom may take that honour. That is, if it really does contain the postcoital cell-phone conversations that will lead to Estregan's impeachment. Already people are calling it Sexysexygate.

Joe the taxi driver jerks the wheel, barely avoiding a convoy of cars. He makes the sign of the cross. Shouts: "Your mother is a whore!" The convoy (Ford Explorer, stretch BMW, open-backed Toyota Tamaraw filled with scowling goons) parts traffic with the bleeps and squeals of its siren. Cars grudgingly give way. "He thinks he's somebody," Joe explains, his eyes in the rearview mirror forcing me to engage with him. I smile, wrinkling my forehead in complicit exasperation. Convoys like this are a peso a dozen.

But I think I know that BMW. Or maybe it's familiar in that arrogant way of all luxury vehicles. Or maybe I'm just being paranoid again. The beemer bolts ahead. It has a bumper sticker. "PRO-Gun: Peaceful, Responsible, Owners of Guns." Beside it, another. "PRO-God: Praise, Respect, Obey God." I slide down in my seat, quick as an eel. I hide my face with my hands and peek out. The right rear fender is dented. Years ago, learning to park my Corolla in our tight garage, I made a dent just like that. There's a bobble-headed figurine of President Estregan, nodding from the board behind the backseat. A gift I'd given to my grandfather years ago, for his seventieth birthday.

Joe looks at me sympathetically. "Don't be afraid, pare," he says. "BMW. Big Mama Whale. People like that, they're more afraid of us. They're just swimming in the river. You know, de-Nile." He starts cracking himself up and shoves the gear into place. With a proud roar, the car leaps forward into the lane left in the convoy's wake.

"No!" I shout, surprising myself. Joe ignores me, pleased to exhibit his taxi driver guile. We fly along, following the convoy as it wedges its way through traffic. It passes unhindered through a roadblock of soldiers and disappears in the distance, like an apparition from my past.

*

The other night, in the club, when I went to get a couple of fingers of Lagavulin, I saw Sara, an old college friend. I don't know why I'm admitting this. We'd stopped talking years ago, when I'd reinvented myself after my breakup with Anais. Sara had a new buzz cut and I wasn't even sure it was her. She'd been part of Anais's group. I guess I'm ashamed that I rarely admit to myself how often I think of my daughter. Sara approached me warmly. We reminisced quietly. "Hey, did you hear," she said casually, and proceeded to tell me that Anais had gotten married and that their new little family was moving to another city. My child wanted to see me beforehand. A new school, a fresh start, a chance to fill my absence and leave it buried in her past. It was my little girl's idea. I've always been pretty sure that it was never a matter of *if* we would meet, but *when*. But Anais said it was better that we didn't.

Sara asked me: "If your daughter wants to get in touch, what's the best way?" I didn't know what to say. I said: "E-mail's good." It sounded odd, wrong. E-mail? When Sara left, I thought of hundreds of better replies. I left my Scotch and went back to the hotel and just lay there. I couldn't sleep for some reason. A cock crowed and the sky lightened. My heart kept time with the cheap alarm clock by the bed.

I'm paralyzed, I know, by the multiplicity of new beginnings with my daughter. I've thought each through, exploring them in my mind like fingers rubbing their way along old rosary beads. She and I will be in a café, standing in her living room, in the parking lot outside her school, by chance on an opposite escalator in the mall, across a table at a book signing, in an ostentatious restaurant of my choosing, on the musty bed on which I am dying. She will hug me, or she will hit me, or she will cry tears that mean the death of my hope, or she will sob a breath that signifies the birth of my fresh chance. I'll be called, coldly, father, or Miguel, or, precisely, asshole. My child will stare at the gift I brought her and speak of the hate she has for me. My daughter will look away and say she wants to try to forgive me. My girl will play with her coffee spoon and express nothing. My little one will look me in the eye and ask: Why? How could you? Didn't you love me? And despite all my rehearsals, I won't know what to say. If she flees, do I chase her through the crowd, or let her be free? If she says fuck off, shall I bow my head and slink away to weep in the men's room, or should I plant myself before her, arms akimbo, to show that, this time, I mean to stay? Can I tell her that I love her, even if my past actions will always shade future promises with doubt?

I'm petrified, I admit, by the multiplicity of endings for my absence. Should I call her now? Next month? Or when I'm finally a person she can be proud of? Should I post a letter? Compose an e-mail to her mother? I don't know how such simple actions can be part of a choice so complicated. Should I send a present on her sixteenth birthday? Should I write a book, with a hidden message, telling her that I was wrong, that I'm sorry, telling her I'm here for her, whenever she is ready?

*

Yataro came to our rescue a second time, in the final month, albeit indirectly. As the Japs retreated, dishonoured, leaving behind a scorched country, our family had chosen the relative safety of Swanee. One night, three Japanese infantrymen, amputated from the withdrawing main force, found their way to our house, attracted by the light and the sound of silverware on plates, which must have beckoned amid the sizzle of insects and ponderous twilight. The orchestra of crickets at dusk always reminds me of this scene. It was my mother who faced the soldiers as they walked up the driveway. She had heard of the atrocities in other towns, of babies thrown upon bayonets, of women shot where they'd just been raped. The intruders' timing could not have been worse: my father was in the fields with the men, digging up the guns he'd had buried before the occupation.

The soldiers stopped in their tracks when they saw my mother step outside with the best weapon she could find, my grandfather's ancient Holland & Holland double-barrel .450-caliber elephant gun. She raised it and took aim. It jammed and the soldiers laughed. They approached her, one lowering his bayonet, another drawing his sword, the other unbuckling his belt. As Lena and Narcisito watched from the front door, I leaped forward to thrust myself, my nine-year-old body, between the Japs and my mother. I cried out, in Nip-pongo, words I didn't know I knew: "Yagate shini / keshiki ha miezu / semi no koe!" Two of the men laughed. They moved closer. But the one with the sword, suddenly pensive, barked something to the others. They all turned and walked away, disappearing into the forest behind the house. Only years later did I remember the words as a haiku by Basho, taught to me in childhood by Yataro. "Nothing in the cry / of cicadas suggests they / are about to die."

–from *Autoplagiarist* (page 1063), by Crispin Salvador

*

Consider the epic singer. He alone knew the secret beginnings and endings of his tribe: when his children moved to the cities to become janitors and key grips and hotel crooners, he grew hoarse and eventually faded, silently, in his hut. When the singer died, one version of everything was lost.

–from the 1988 essay *Tao* (*People*), by Crispin Salvador

*

Someone is singing badly from upstairs. "Total Eclipse of the Heart." I join the people trickling in to the University of the Philippines's Balay Kalinaw. The two-story multipurpose building, in a pseudo-traditional style, is abuzz with congratulations and congenial laugh-ter. The rain is heavy and loud and everyone yells to compensate. At the top of the stairs, tables are piled with newly minted copies of *And Then the Locusts Came: The Socio-political Relevance of Melo-drama in Philippine Literature in English*. The singer ends her song to sparse applause and breezy electronica music is played in the back-ground. Knots of people stay close to the walls, scarfing down greasy pansit noodles. They joke, chat, squirrel away food in cheeks so as not to miss an opportunity for an interjection, opinion, or punch line. These are the literati of the Philippines: the merry, mellowed, stalwartly middle-class practitioners of the luxury of literature in the language of the privileged. Many are former Maoists. I'm hoping the critic Avellaneda will be here.

By the dais set up in a corner, I spot a writer who had years ago, at my first workshop in college, dismissed my story as "bourgeois angst"; she is sipping a glass of the free sparkling wine donated by, a banner says, the Lupas Landcorp Book Fund. The florid old author of the volume being launched holds court by a big palm plant, young students listening and nodding as if his ideas were originally theirs. "Of course, we must be read by the world," he declares. "If they think we're exotic, give them exotic. But don't forget the responsibility to portray the realities of our society . . ." He flicks absently at a palm frond that tickles his ear. ". . . and the brutal archetypes from life. For example, the richness of our poverty. Boy who loses girl because he cannot win bread for them. Beloved water buffalo dying of inexplicable disease or sometimes run down by the cars of the rich. Every year, floods destroy everything. And then . . ."—he raises his hands like a priest announcing transubstantiation—"and then, the locusts came."

I say hello to a group of writers who remember me. They are clustered in a corner of the room, like the last few Cheerios in a bowl of milk. It's been a lifetime! one exclaims. How long are you here for? asks a second. I tell them a week. Only? says a third. What have you been up to all these years? asks a fourth. I tell them I'm writing a book. They raise their eyebrows and paste on smiles. What's it about? a fifth one inquires. I tell them, to throw them off: "It's a novel about a young writer's death in a flood and how his teacher is moved to redeem the senseless loss by writing about the what-ifs." Fascinating! a sixth one condescends. Where's it set? I reply: "The Philippines." A seventh one asks: How can *you* write about the Philippines?

A pimply young woman saves me from the awkwardness by bounding onto the plywood dais. She barks, "Test, test," into a microphone attached to one of those huge old portable karaoke machines, itself attached to a hand truck by red and green octopus straps. The woman looks like an ugly version of Alice B. Toklas. She wears a white shirt with a stylized Philippine flag and AFEMASIAN silkscreened on it. Shrugging off a backpack made of rattan, she takes out a notebook. She regales us with verse, every word spoken slowly and dragged out at the end, as if the incantation was truly alchemical. Some people listen, most only pretend to while scanning the room, a few groups impolitely continue conversations in politely hushed voices. I float toward the refreshments.

In a corner near the drinks and the cubed cheese and folded

ham on toothpicks, I talk with a pair of writers with whom I once had casual mentor-mentee relationships. Furio Almondo is a jack-of-all-trades scribbler with a perfectly burnished pate, an enduring ambition to be the country's alpha male, and a proletarian pride in his pugnacious body odour; his fiction is consistently infused with Magical Realism and a seventies bravura of one who survived being imprisoned by Marcos. My favourite of his works is a recent prose poem, written as a news report, titled "Borges Disappointed by the Internet." Beside Almondo, at an olfactory-safe distance, is Rita Rajah, the Muslim poetess from Mindanao; her eyebrows are as thin and carefully drawn as her verse, her makeup applied in the generous manner of one who was nearly a great beauty and still savours wistful memories of being so darned close. Her literary fame is based on five poems she wrote in 1972, '73, and '79.

I question the two about Crispin.

"Crispin who?" Furio says, giving me a bewildered look.

"You're so bad," Rita says, laughing and slapping him on the shoulder.

Furio chuckles. "Anyone in this room would have liked to have screwed a tap into his gut and turned it on," he says. "As the saying goes."

"But who had the courage or the means?" Rita says. "Or inclination, really. Let me tell you," she whispers conspiratorially, "most of these people here were just jealous of him."

"Not me," says Furio. "What do I have to be jealous of?"

Rita: "We just wanted the most visible Filipino writer in the world to be more authentically Filipino."

Furio: "Writing in Tagalog, or one of the dialects."

Me: "But Crispin wasn't anything but Filipino."

Furio: "Well, you know . . ."

Rita: "Things were never the same after his autobiography."

Me: "Was it jealousy that caused that scene in the CCP?"

Rita: "No. If we're honest with ourselves, complaining is our national sport. It was just Crispin's turn to complain. We're all crabs pulling each other back into the pot. But Crispy, he thought he was a lobster."

Me: "So you don't think someone boiled him, so to speak?"

Furio: "Not anyone here." (He waggles his fingers in front of him.)

Rita: "Don't look at me."

Me: "Haha. Me neither. But maybe one of the subjects of that book . . ."

Furio: "The mythical *Bridges Ablaze*! Don't you get it, pare? *Nobody* cared about Crispin. He wasn't fucking relevant."

Rita: "What my colleague is trying to gently convey is the sad fact this country doesn't care much about writers."

Furio: "No. What I'm trying to say is nobody cared about that gilded asshole."

Rita: "Crispin and Avellaneda were maybe the only ones who believed that a writer could transform this country . . ."

Furio: "Then a woman came between them. Typical."

Rita (glaring at Furio): "I hate to be the one to put it so bluntly, but those two were the last advocates. I shudder hearing myself say it. But sitting at home, writing stories . . ." (She raises her eyebrow.) ". . . that's a luxury! And to write in English . . ." (She shakes her head dismissively.) ". . . that's the height of luxuriating arrogance! But to sit at home in your Greenwich Village penthouse, living off the Salvador family inheritance, writing in English about the Philippines for the entertainment of foreigners . . ." (She rolls her eyes.) ". . . well, even the young writers here haven't yet invented a slur for someone as heinous as that."

Furio: "It's the height of heinousness."

Me: "But Crispin didn't have an inheritance, and he didn't live in a—"

Furio: "Heinosity, even."

The poet on the stage ends her reading and everyone applauds. I clap, too. I'm glad she stopped. She leaves the dais and is replaced by a fat man wearing the exact same outfit as she. He clasps his hands to his chest and recites a prose poem in the same heightened enunciation as she did, like taffy being made. It's about a welder in Abu Dhabi who sells his soul to a Yemenese fortune-teller in exchange for being able to sing beautifully. The welder sings for his comrades in the workers' barracks and his songs are about the home they are all sick for. His lyrics are so heartbreaking that his comrades slit the singer's throat. The poet bows his head like his throat's been cut. A trio to the side, each wearing AFemAsian shirts, claps enthusiastically. In the back of the crowd, a cell phone goes *chirp-chirp*, signalling a text message. The poet looks at the ceiling and begins another poem, snapping his fingers in time to himself. It's a jazzy piece about cruising for lovers.

"There," reads the poet. "In the Lupas Landcorp Mall . . ."

Rita (voice hushed perfunctorily): "Listen, dear. Do you think a writer writing about corruption will stamp out corruption?"

Poet: " . . . by the men's bathroom stall . . ."

Furio: "A writer writing about sex won't get anybody pregnant. Look, pare. It's nothing to do with Crispin or his infamous *Bridges*. It may have been a brilliant exposé, though we already know our country's a feudal kingdom."

Poet: ". . . by the mart for your shoes . . ."

Rita: "I honestly think it was Crispy's excuse to live abroad, to escape the realities of here and now."

Poet: ". . . by the bee that is jolly . . ."

Furio: "The problem lies in, quote unquote, lit-ah-ra-choor. It just doesn't work. We have to beat our pens into plowshares and our plowshares into swords."

Poet: ". . . by the fruit that is juicy . . ."

Rita: "Hello! Earth to Furio: The revolution will now be streamed onto the Internet. The seventies are gone, comrade. God's been resurrected by Reverend Martin. We threw out our Red Books decades ago, lest our kids read them . . ."

Poet: ". . . by the frozen circle that's for skating . . ."

Rita (continuing): "We've got mortgages. And children's tuition and ballet lessons. Estregan's dictatorship won't last. Marcos is frozen, waiting for a final brownout to melt him completely into our forgetting. Maybe the jellyfish . . ."

Poet: ". . . I see how crooked is every straight guy . . ."

Furio: "I don't know! Ferdinand Marcos, Jr., and the rest of his brood are holding higher office. For Christ's sake, Imelda was a congresswoman. We forget too easil—"

Poet: ". . . encoffined in a closet . . ."

Rita: "Who's forgotten? But in today's *Gazette*, Bansamoro said that the economic boom is around the corner."

Poet: ". . . of macho lonesomeness . . ."

Furio: "Bansamoro's only establishing his own dynasty. The boom's artificial, just remittances from Overseas Foreign Workers. First World dollars fattening a Third World pig."

Poet: ". . . like a beer-battered butterfly . . ."

Me: "I haven't been back here in years, but it does seem like OFW earnings are fuelling investment."

Poet: ". . . in a crystal chrysalis . . ."

Rita: "Not if you're Wigberto Lakandula."

Poet: ". . . on the plate placed before me . . ."

Furio: "Poor bastard. A slave to some pharaoh's pyramid scheme."

Poet: ". . . My mouth, my spoon. My cock, my tremulous fork."

Rita (raising her voice to drown out the poet): "Listen, dear. I'm no aging rebel like Furio here. The truth is, if you want to write something that will elicit change, you have to be a journalist. We haven't had a pure champion of the truth since Mutya Dimatahimik was stabbed outside her newspaper office in 1981 . . ."

Furio: "That was '82. I'm still convinced it was Marcos's bidding. Old Avellaneda was never the same after. If he didn't have their child to look after, he'd have gone the way of Crispy. Batty."

Rita: "I used to think Mutya died in vain. Because there are still reporters being gunned. But that comes with a free press in a lawless country. Crispin, however . . . I mean, nobody's going to the States to murder someone nobody remembers, who's writing a book nobody has seen. As soon as the hit man got to the U.S. he'd be dazzled by the factory outlet sales and disappear."

Furio: "Spotted later managing a taqueria in West Hollywood. Green card in pocket."

Rita: "The only one who'd want to kill Crispin is Crispin."

Furio: "Well, everyone in this room would have, at some point. Honestly. He really gave it good in *Autoplagiarist* . . ."

Rita: "The truth hurts."

Furio: "Only Crispin would have spite enough to kill someone. Himself included."

Rita: "Himself especially."

Furio: "One can only stomach so much failure."

Me: "You really think he was a failure? But he won awards. He brought the spotlight to our nation's literatu—"

Furio: "Awards are just luck in a literary lottery, pare. They didn't make him the bus driver. And even if he was at the wheel for a spell, he didn't have to be a hairy asshole about it."

A third poet takes the stage and begins to read poetry in Tagalog. He also wears an AFemAsian T-shirt, but has a woven tribal sash tied around his head. His poems are translations of Emily Dickinson's. He raps each Tagalog word angrily, his right hand coming down like a lion's claw to emphasize each rhyme.

Me: "So you think maybe something other than literary failure was troubling him?"

Rita: "You know who you have to talk to? Marcel Avellaneda. If anyone will know, it's him."

Furio (snickering): "Yeah. Good luck getting him to talk. Or getting him beyond how much of a hack Crispy was."

Me: "Did any of you like anything Crispin wrote? What about his masterpiece, *Because of—*"

Furio: "*Dahil Sa'Yo?* Not authentic enough. It didn't capture the essence of the Filipino."

Rita: "The trouble with that book is that in its obsession with the new, it was really just being old."

Furio: "I preferred his work when he was merely trying for approval."

Me: "And *The Europa Quartet?*"

Furio: "Elitism! To the max, man."

Me: "The *Kaputol* series was pretty g—"

Rita: "Oh brother! Too Manila-centric."

Me: "*Red Earth?* After all, it was about Marxist farmers . . ."

Furio: "Too provincial."

Rita: "And polemical."

Me: "*The Enlightened?*"

Rita: "Ugh. Postcolonial machismo."

Me: "I suppose you didn't like *Autoplagiarist?*"

Furio: "*That* I liked."

Rita: "Only because it was so bad. Schadenfreude's always delicious."

Furio: "No, sister. It didn't pull its punches. But if you're speaking truth to power, don't bore them. At least try to make them laugh."

Rita: "*Autoplagiarist*'s problem was it was more *about* Filipinos than *for* Filipinos."

Furio: "It's the sort of book Americans love and Filipinos hate. We have to write for our countrymen."

Rita: "Country*women*."

Me: "Then why couldn't he get it published abroad?"

Furio: "The same reason the rest of us Filipinos have a hard time."

Me: "Did Crispin have some sort of hidden regret or—"

Rita: "As I said, ask Marcel. Crispin wasn't the same after the breakup of the Cinco Bravos in the seventies. That's why he left for the States."

Furio (looking at the poet onstage): "I always thought he was a closet gay. He and Avellaneda were lovers. That's why they hated each other so much."

Rita: "Break out the homophobia! Always the Filipino way when they're jealous."

Furio: "Come on, how stage-directed was Crispy's demise? What a drama queen. Spread-eagled. Lacking only a cross."

Rita: "Or pentagram."

Furio (chuckling): "That would make a good book."

Rita: "Hasn't it already been done? Pentagrams only appear in bestsellers."

Furio: "See the sinister connection? Wouldn't you peddle your soul?"

Rita: "What for?"

"Enough money," Furio says, "to buy an Italian villa. Ever seen Gore Vidal's house?"

"Aw," Rita says, "you old sellout." She slaps Furio on the shoulder.

"If only I could!" Furio smiles.

They look at each other contentedly.

"Are you going to the dinner after this?" she asks him, as if I wasn't there.

"Nah," he says. "I've a fete in Forbes Park for Arturo Lupas. I'm ghostwriting his book on the Lupas legacy. They'll be serving canapés and Blue Label scotch."

I drain my champagne so that I can hold up my empty glass. Furio and Rita raise their eyebrows at me and rotate in opposite directions, like automatons, each looking for someone else to talk to.

A fourth reader, gangly and tomboyish, takes the stage. I hurry to leave.

In the bookshop downstairs, I search for books on or by Crispin. The aisles between the shelves are empty. They smell of glue and mosquito repellant. Books are well categorized, though the prelaunch crowd has haphazardly reshelved them, spines facing inward, the clear plastic packaging sloppily replaced. A frumpy shopgirl sits at the cash box, texting on her cell phone. She looks upset, as if blaming me for keeping her there. The poet's verse arrives downstairs in a murmur. Her voice peters out into applause. The clapping blends with the rain. A man comes on, shouting: "Welcome to my launch! Thank you for braving the end of the world!" Laughter and cheers.

A lone copy of *The Enlightened* separates two rows of books on the shelf, its cover facing me. When I reach for it, it jumps backward. The rows of books slump together. "Hey!" I call out. Through the gap, *The Enlightened* vanishes. A figure moves. I peek through. Returning my curiosity is a pretty eye, half hidden behind a lock of black hair. It blinks. A hand loops the hair behind an ear (revealing the sparkle of a diamond stud). A gold charm bracelet tinkles (stirrup, horseshoe, saddle, boot). The eye scrunches. A giggle. "Oh, fuck!" a voice says, like a child who's just learned the word. "Sorry!"

I go to the end of the aisle and peek around the corner.

A cutie-pie of a girl stands before me, smiles, and proffers the book. "You touched it first," she says. She's petite, early twenties. She curls a lock of her long hair around her finger. She's wearing khaki capris and one of those T-shirts printed to look like a tuxedo.

"No, no," I reply, "that's fine. It's not one of his best. Maybe even his most derivative."

"Oh, great. Thanks." She runs a hand over the cover. It is cartoony and features a man on horseback leading a group of riders. There is even a sun-bleached skull in the foreground, its shadow forming the letters in the title. "Nice cover," she says.

"It's an early work. I'd suggest his later stuff."

She gives a crooked grin. "I wish. I'm doing part of my thesis on him, for my undergrad. One more sem, then I'm free. Yay!"

"I knew him, actually. I mean, Salvador. I read all his stuff. He was, um, like a mentor to me in. In New York City."

"You're from New York? That's cool. You actually knew him?"

"I sure did. And I am. I mean, I'm from here, originally. But I've lived in Manhattan for some years. Master's."

"Really? Where?"

"Oh, Columbia. Are you a writer?"

"I wish! I, like, try to write poetry. And short stories. But I wouldn't call myself a writer. Not yet. I need to live first."

"Well, I was doing my master's in creative writing." My hands sweat. She keeps looking down at the book. "I'm actually writing his biography. Maybe I can help you with your thesis?" Is she blushing?

"Are you sure," she says, "you don't want the book? I can get it at the library. I only buy books because they're a justifiable expense— you know, acceptable retail therapy, like classical music CDs. Other girls buy shoes, I buy books. It's how I get away with burning up my parents' credit card." Is she nervous? "I don't even get to read all of them. They're more like the best interior decoration. And I love knowing they're there. Like infinite possibilities, you know? That's why bookstores have become so popular these days. Guilt-free consumerism." She smiles that crooked smile again.

"I know what you mean. I'm *exactly* the same." What a dorkbag I am. "Hey, um . . ."

"Sadie. Name's Sadie."

"Sadie. Cool. Why're you doing your thesis on him?"

"Oh God. Long story. My parents. My mom actually. He's her favourite. Pretty weird, huh? Most moms like Danielle Steele. Or at best, Jane Austen. So I grew up on his books for kids, you know, the *Kaputol* series, about the tomboy Dulcé and her gang? Then graduated to his mysteries. I had a crush on Antonio Astig. For like *so* long it's embarrassing. I wanted to be a detective just like him. I loved his pearl-handled Midnight Special, the groovy fitted barongs and bell-bottoms, and the way he'd say, 'Oh, pare, akala mo astig ka? Astig ako!' What a line, like Dirty Harry! You think you're tough? My name *is* tough! Hehe. I reread those works recently; I can't believe I missed all those double entendres. The metanarrative. My parents encouraged me to read Pinoy writing. They were nationalistic. Blame the seventies."

"My, um, folks were kids of more conservative times. Unfortunately."

"Do you still have family here, or are you just visiting from the Big Apple?" She does jazz hands when she says "Big Apple."

I shake my head again. "No. No family here. Just visiting."

"Why's it called 'The Big Apple' anyway? Is it really the city that never sleeps? Hey, do you smoke? Cigarettes, I mean. Ha. Want to go outside for a bit? The rain's nice anyway."

"Aren't you here for the launch?"

"I did my rounds," she says. "I came for my poetry teacher. No, it's not like that. Haha! Next you'll be calling me Lolita."

"Lo-lee-ta," I say. "Light of my life, fire of my loins."

"Huh? Is that, like, from the book? 'Cause creative writing's my major at Ateneo. Slew my dad, let me tell you. But you know how it is: I like reading, so maybe writing'll be fun, too. Path of least resistance. Hey, I didn't get your name."

"Oh. Sorry. I'm Miguel. Miguel Astig. No, just kidding." She laughs a little. A lot less than I hoped. We go to the cashier and she pays for the book. Outside, we stand under the carport. Rain splatters from its corners in a constant stream. The way the light meets the dark in a neat rectangle around us makes me feel like we're in an Edward Hopper painting. Sadie hands me the book. She puts a Marlboro in my mouth and lights it with a Zippo with a pinup girl on it. I enjoy smoking but I've never properly inhaled. That's probably why I never got hooked, despite my addictive personality. I just like how smoking lets you do something without really doing anything. I don't tell her this. I say: "You know, um, Sadie, John Cheever, he talked about details like smoking. I mean, in an interview he recounted how during a friend's wake, the young widow 'smoked cigarettes like they were heavy.' I've never been able to get that out of my head."

"That's really good," she says. She tries to mimic smoking a heavy cigarette, bringing it to her mouth ever so slowly, her hand shaking ever so slightly.

"Did you know the name Sadie—"

"Yeah. A Beatles song. Please don't sing. Besides, I'm glad they broke up. If not, we wouldn't have those uber-personal songs from John."

"No, I was going to say that Salvador—"

"I know. Sadie's a character in his books. In *The Europa Quartet*. My mom's a *big* fan. She read the series during her last trimester. She dug how headstrong and defiant the Sadie character was. I'm pretty sure that's where I got my name. From a wanton woman. Because I came out of my mom's womb screaming like a buckshot dog. But my dad says it's from the Beatles. At least I'm not named after some saint. Oh, fuck. Sorry. It's just, you know, *I'm* an atheist."

"Thank God," I joke, laughing. "Actually, I quite like 'Miguel.' I was named for the beer, not the archangel. You know that saying, 'There is no god and Mary is his mother'?"

Sadie smiles, shakes her head.

"I think that was," I say, "um, I think Santayana. Right?"

"The guitarist?" Sadie hums "Oye Como Va."

"No, um. Never mind. God's dead, or did he never exist? I bet you're a vegan, too, and you buy fair trade coffee beans. Ever hear that saying, 'Compromise is when nobody is happy'?"

"Nope."

"Actually, Crispin had a girlfriend who was named Sadie. Sadie Baxter, the American photographer. Her work's awesome, actually." I'm getting repetitive. "Actually, you should check the Internet for her. 'Sadie Baxter.' His love for her was so strong it doomed their relationship. Kind of beautiful, actually."

She nods and purses her lips. Is she interested? She's a heck of a lot cuter than Madison. Smaller, like you could pick her up and manfully have your way with her. Plus she's obviously more literary. But man, what's with me always liking the girls I'm sure I can't get?

"Oh fuck," Sadie suddenly says, as if someone poked her from behind. "Do you know what's the time? I have to be home for dinner at seven o'clock."

"It's ten to seven. Is this a ploy?"

"Oh yeah, man, you're absolutely on to me." She drops her cigarette and stubs it out with her flip-flop: trendy red Havaianas, with the Philippine flag on them. My eyes linger on her foot. Her toenails are carefully painted in bubble-gum pink. Her foot is slender. Rabbitlike. Not at all like Madison's. I'm lost for words.

Sadie pops a mint into her mouth. "Curiously strong. Oh, fuck, I'm sorry. It's my last one, and my parents . . . you know. They don't smoke. Well, officially my dad doesn't. Who smokes these days, anyway?"

"Not me," I say, stubbing my cig on the pavement.

"Yeah, me neither. Hey, nice meeting you. I've got to skedaddle." She unfolds an umbrella with a detail of the Sistine Chapel printed on its interior. She runs out of the light and disappears. The clapping of her flip-flops recedes. I pick up her crushed cigarette butt and look at the end where her lips were. It's stained with ChapStick. I smell it. Cherry.

Yeah, I know. I fucking sucked. "Sexy Sadie," I sing quietly, trying to sound like John, "oooh, what have you done?" I watch the rain for a minute.

A car pulls up quick and sudden. What the fuck? My heart begins to race. It's a black Lexus. Should I run? It has super-dark tint. Should I shout for help? The window rolls down. Vintage hip-hop flies out. At the wheel is smiling Sadie, her face lit gently by the instrument panel.

"Hey, nigga," she says. "I forgot something."

I try to hide my relief. I smile cockily. "Did you now?"

"Yeah, son. You have my book."

I look down. I'm holding *The Enlightened*. I hand it through the window. "Sorry. I forgot."

"Nice ploy."

"You're totally on to me."

Sadie is pretty in the soft light, a sheen on her face, still wet from that awkward moment between when one closes the umbrella and jumps into the car. I can smell the leather interiors mixed with mint breath spray and Sadie's vanilla perfume.

"Hey, Miguel. Since you don't have any family here, and since you look so lost there, do you want to come to dinner? Come on. Our cook makes a chicken adobo that will change your life."

6

Lena, Narcisito, our parents, and I returned to Manila from Bacolod to find a vision of the week after Armageddon. Our house was one of the few left standing on our street. Many of our neighbours had been killed. Every family was diminished by at least one. In all, an estimated one hundred thousand civilians died in the liberation of the city.

Parting this sea of sadness one morning, in rode Tito Jason, honking, victoriously, the horn of a battered jeep. He was alive! So very alive. He had changed since that New Year's Eve when he disappeared suddenly. His shiny sidearm, his skin glowing like new leather, his voice loud and happy, were defiance itself among all the death. Many a night I would sit with him after dinner as he relished his Camels on the veranda, in retreat from the family noise inside to which he was no longer accustomed. He told me stories of life as a guerrilla. My favourite was how during the liberation of the city he had served as a guide to the Second Battalion of the U.S. 148th Infantry Regiment, and they happened upon the buildings of the Balintawak Brewing Company. My uncle laughed until he was almost crying when he recounted how he and the others had swum and danced in the knee-high beer, filling their canteens and helmets with the ice-cold stuff that flowed freely from vats the retreating Japs had sabotaged. If he was in a good mood, Tito Jason would show me his bullet-wound scars shaped like war medals. When I asked the right questions, he shared with me his ideas for what makes a man good and a good man better. It was from him that I first learned about communist ideals. I was nearly ten and fancied myself close to manhood. I had never heard anything like what he had to say.

He later returned to the jungle to fight again with the Huk army, this time against a different enemy than the Japanese—the bourgeoisie that the departing Americans had left in power. And despite his second sudden departure, I did not feel abandoned. Tito Jason was my hero. My young imagination certainly turned him into far more than he ever was, but perhaps such things do not matter. When news came that he was shot by government forces in an ambush in Tarlac, my grief at his martyr's death enshrined him as my onyx idol. I've always wondered if my father knew about the attack beforehand.

—from *Autoplagiarist* (page 1088), by Crispin Salvador

*

Cousin Bobby was cleared of all wrongdoing in the rape case, but after several brushes with the law he now finds himself in court again. This time for importing pirated adult DVDs.

Judge: "It's frustrating. Two years later and here we are, together again in this courtroom?!"

Erning, seated behind his cousin, jumps to his feet: "Objection, your honour! Mr. Judge, is not my cousin's fault you have not been promoted!"

*

Sadie goes to her room to freshen up and I use the guest bathroom downstairs.

The Gonzaleses are a typical upper-class family, the type my grandparents would probably approve of. Grapes and Granma had never liked Madison, perhaps because her dad was a foreigner and certainly because her mother was the type of Filipina who aspires to marrying one.

The Gonzales residence, in the ritzy Dasmariñas Village, adjoining Forbes, is surrounded by high walls landscaped into hanging gardens and a grotto enthroning the Virgin and Christ child. The guest bathroom is in rose marble, with tiny shell-shaped soaps, matching candles, and a whimsically painted sign that says, "If you sprinkle when you tinkle, be a sweetie and wipe the seatie." The bathroom reeks of antiseptic, baby oil, and lavender potpourri.

I sit uncomfortably on the couch in the living room. It's all so familiar. My grandmother loved this Filipinized Pueblo-Spanish style—crayon walls and old-wood ceiling beams, capiz light fixtures, Chinois furniture, Buddhist antiques, assorted santo heads in ivory. The carved faces scrutinize me painfully.

I'm so nervous I don't know what to do with myself. Meeting a girl I like *and* meeting her parents in the same day? I feel like I'm next after Caruso at karaoke. Today's paper is on the coffee table. On the society page, Dingdong Changco, Jr., poses with Albon Alcantara, Arturo and Cettina Lupas, Vita Nova, and Tim Yap, at the launch party of the Make Your Own Havaianas week at Rockwell Mall. Dingdong looks greasier than ever. If I posed with him I'd have to rush home to exfoliate.

Sadie comes down the stairs, all fresh and clean. I think she's even put on makeup. "Hey pare," she says, with that crooked smile. "Told you we'd be early. Filipino time. Why don't you come up to my room? I want to show you something."

Her room smells innocent, like a girl before fashion magazines turn her into a woman. In one corner sits a Fender Stratocaster. "Let me find this poem I really want to read you," she says. "Have a seat anywhere." A brass bed is buried almost completely under stuffed animals. I stay standing. A pantheon of Steely Dan, the Spiders from Mars, and a sweat-drenched Neil Diamond stares at me from the wall. Sadie bends down to search a desk drawer, exposing her red thong panties and the tight crack of her plumber's butt. Atop the clutter on her desk is a Hello Kitty diary, a sketchbook, and a plastic pistol case open to reveal blackened rags and a disassembled Glock.

"Hey, cool," I say, looking at the pistol. "You know, Chekhov said that if a gun appears in a story, by the conclusion it has to have gone off."

"You think so?"

"Sure."

"*Where* the *fuck* is my *note*book?" Sadie says. She looks all over, throwing around dirty clothes. I browse the bookshelves along a wall, ordered from Abad and Aeschylus to Zafra and Zola. Piled at her bedside are her current reads: Hobbes, Mill, *Calvin and Hobbes*, John C. Evans, Betty and Veronica Double Digests, *A History of the Ilustrado Propaganda Movement 1880–1896*. "School readings and readings for sanity," Sadie explains.

"Which are you reading right now?"

"That one. *Death of the Sunbird*. The American writer Evans."

"What's it about?"

"The lives of some snowboard instructors in Colorado."

"Is that interesting?"

"Good writing makes anything interesting. Besides, I love contemporary American lit. Call me colonial, but I'm all about it."

On a small table, beside a vase of mums, rises a monolith of Crispin Salvador books. "Yeah," Sadie says, eyeing the pile. "It's like Close Encounters of the Verbose Kind."

"Speaking of aliens, are you sure I can be in your room?"

"Chill out. When I turned twenty-one they eased off on the rules. They're enlightened. Sometimes I think they were like swingers in the seventies. Eew, that was a gross image. Anyway, they said that they'd rather have me be open at home than go off somewhere with something to hide. Whatever. Besides, nothing's gonna happen."

When she turns to look for her poetry diary, I check if my fly is zipped. Whatever thrill I had from being so unexpectedly close, from soon being on the receiving end of one of her poems, all that has suddenly evaporated. Nothing's going to happen? I wipe the inside corners of my eyes to check for eye boogers. I guess now's not the time to kiss her.

"Hey," I say, studying a poster. "I *love* Steely Dan."

"Yeah, me, too."

"I like that guitar part in 'Bad Sneakers.'"

"Which guitar part?"

"You know, uh, the part with, um, the guitars."

"Oh."

"Yeah." Shit. How stupid did I sound? I should've said something about loving Donald Fagen's clever lyrics. Damn spirit of the stairs.

"Hey!" Sadie says, "speaking of Salvador . . ." She sits at her desk to riffle through the mess on it. "I just remembered, my mom was a student of his aunt, at the Assumption. I bet dear old Mummy knows something about that love child you were telling me about in the car. You know how Manila is, everyone knows everyone . . . but where the *fuck* is my poetry diary?"

"Is it the Hello Kitty one in front of you?"

"That's my dream diary."

"How about the one with Fabio on it?"

"That's my diary diary."

"What's the poetry diary look like?"

"It's green and, um . . . oh, here it is! I was sitting on it. Hehe." She opens it and leafs to the end. "You ready? Aw, I hope you like it. Um, I don't know. Be totally honest with me about what you think, okay? Be nice, though, 'kay? *Anyways*, here goes nothing."

She takes a deep breath and reads the poem in a sort of desperate voice that does not become her. She says each word as if it were heavy: "Night falls / like an overwrought theme; / in comes the tide / of a sea of bad metaphors. / O flower, / O rain, / O tree. / Ow! Formulaic poetry! / Will my great epiphany come at my last sentence? / Or is denouement but demented pretense? / What if revelation / has come and gone / and I missed it / while watching television?" Sadie falls silent. She looks like she's going to cry. All the praise I give does nothing to convince her I liked the poem.

*

The four boys don't recognize Cristo when he holds each of them. Narciso Junior squirms, the three younger ones cry. Maria Clara scolds them. She puts her hand at the small of Cristo's back. "Maybe after you've shaved your beard," she says.

In his room, beside the steaming basin, he strops his razor. He peers into the mirror. His face is obscured by a bushy beard streaked with hair of the most vibrant red. Should I, he wonders, be ashamed of my relief at being home? He wets his face. Tonight I will sit at the table and eat a proper dinner. He froths the soap in his cup. Maybe Maria Clara will give me a song. He brushes the lather onto his face. Maybe the boys and I can walk around the estate. He shaves his left cheek. We can look at the stars. He rinses his razor. At least the constellations will still be familiar. He shaves his right cheek. But what shall we do, now that we've lost? He rinses his razor again. My old friends have already ingratiated themselves with the Americans. He shaves his chin, carefully around the curves. Even the ones who'd fought so stalwartly against the Spanish. He shaves beneath his nose. He studies himself in the mirror. Who is this man? he asks. He looks like someone I once knew.

After dinner, Cristo walks with his wife and children. The cool night air is far more comforting than the warmth of the house. The boys are still wary of him, though Maria Clara is lively and lovely. She jokes easily with the children and makes them laugh. He is envious.

On the path home, Cristo sees his house, the windows lit brightly, the boys running ahead. Maria Clara holds his hand. He tells her: "Let's have one more. Let's try for a girl."

She stops and embraces him tightly.

"We will become American," Cristo says. "Our children will learn to speak American. When they are ready, we will send them to America to be educated. Just as I was in Europe. All this land will be theirs when they return. They'll return to make a difference."

"You can finally cease the war inside you," Maria Clara says.

"Yes," Cristo says. "Perhaps."

—from *The Enlightened* (page 270), by Crispin Salvador

*

I remember just before it ended, it had been bad for weeks straight. "What would we do without each other?" Madison demanded. I watched my ice cream melt in the bowl.

For so long we'd made plans. Being in love is all about making plans. Or maybe it was just us. Everything was outlined, researched, and refined. Our nonreligionist wedding ceremony. Our ecofriendly funerals. We wanted to be wed somewhere sacred, yet not under the eyes of any god except our love, our selves, and, as Madison said, the wonderful communion of the humanity close to us. We wanted to be buried outside of cemeteries, under trees, in muslin shrouds, close to the earth that would easily reclaim us; we wanted our relatives to avoid carbon emissions and instead hold secular memorials for us in the cities where they lived. We planned the sound track of our lives (Lakme's aria for her matrimonial march; the bridge in Eric Clapton's "Layla" for my funeral cortege). We talked about adoption as the only moral choice for the world today, and debated about which country we'd rescue an orphan from. Sometimes, though, Madison would say: Maybe I'd like to have one of our own; or, Maybe it would be nice to be married in a cathedral. To which I'd reply with logic and reason.

I looked up from my melting ice cream. "What would we do without each other?" she repeated, this time tearfully. I could answer it honestly and say we'd both be okay. Or I could answer it dishonestly, the way she wanted, and say we'd both be okay. I remember she reached across the table to hold my hands. The sleeve of her white shirt got stained by a glob of ketchup and I watched it soak in. We loved differently. I felt we were blessed by every day together. She took for granted we'd be together forever. "We . . . I mean us," she said, "we'll be fine. I have faith."

Both Madison and I were brought up as Roman Catholics. Our atheism was something we explored together. We led each other through the stubborn questions. How could there possibly be no creator? How could our lives just stop when we die? This struggle toward rationality vulcanized us. Our families, with their inspirational text messages and their shrill e-mails against our decision to be on the organ donor list, made Madison and me feel more alone, and therefore more together. We spent many evenings developing our system of belief, and the only times I ever doubted it was when I was wracked with happiness; I simply couldn't accept that there was no higher power to thank for it.

"Can you just say it? Just say that we'll be okay," Madison demanded. The waitress came to fill up our iced teas but turned on her heel when she saw Madison crying. "Shh. Sweetheart," I said, a bit loudly. "It's fine," I said, hoping people could overhear. Madison never gave a shit about such public displays. We were best friends in a lonely world, and that's all that mattered. "Promise me we will," she said. Often we have to lie to people to make them happy. Yet I told her: "I can't promise." I said the line as if I'd rehearsed it for my first role in a soap opera. Something inside me was happy when she cried.

After I'd moved out of Trump Tower and snipped the apron strings, and allowance, that tied me to my grandparents, Madison and I learned to find perverse pleasure in parsing and paring our lives to the barest essentials. Our frugality—a privileged paucity exclusive to cities like New York—drove us to reject the religion of capitalist consumerism. This was difficult, particularly because we lived in the United States—we loved too much the awe of standing in the aisles of Whole Foods, our minds overloaded by the abundance of varieties of mustards and refreshing beverages. Society, it seemed, tempted us into hypocrisy. I imagined that was how Muslim sleeper cells must feel. We had only to turn on the television, open a magazine, log on to the Internet. But like breaking our dependence on caffeine, shuffling off our tendency to buy things we didn't need came only after two years of necessary cheapness and ontological pondering. Madison, however, still enjoyed going to the shops, to look in the windows at the season's latest, and she'd return home with wistful eyes. I'd accuse her of manufacturing desire. Inversely, Madison could not understand my dedication to meat, and constantly reminded me of the amount of methane emitted by livestock, or how much water, land, food, and cruelty it took to raise a cow for the cheeseburger I was about to go have with Crispin. She started serving tempeh sausages at breakfast, and tofu mince in our low-carb wraps, convinced I wouldn't notice. I didn't.

Madison rubbed my hands. "Why can't you see," she said, "that whatever you're looking for is right in front of you?" It was her familiar mantra, as if our success relied solely on me. A little boy in the booth behind her kept peeking over the seat back. He'd torn off one end of a straw's paper cover and had the straw in his mouth. He squinted over Madison's head, aiming the wrapper at me like a blowgun. "First I thought it was because you're a guy," Madison said. "Uncommunicative. Then I thought you were lost and needed to be found. I don't know what to think anymore."

Like anyone, we were filled with the justifications made to cope with the guilt that comes with failing to adhere to personal aspirations. We couldn't afford now to eat healthily as well as ethically. We didn't have enough time yet to volunteer. We skirted the dreadlocked Greenpeaceniks on the street with their flyers about whaling off Antarctica or the dirty oil-sand mining in Canada—this was New York City, who had time to stop and talk?

"Maybe that's it," Madison said. "I mean, maybe it's New York that's eating us. We have to be so cool, so on, so alive, that we deaden other parts of us." The boy made faces above her head. Madison shook my hands. "Why don't we just go?" she said, hope filling her face like seltzer pouring into a glass. "Grab our passports and take off," she said. "Tonight. We'll go to Penn Station and hop on which-ever train is leaving and we'll see where we end up. Europe. Asia. Africa! I've been trying forever to get us there," she said. "We can make a difference."

In the two years Madison and I were together, what we came to believe in most was the potential of humanity, by way of our faith in each other. We found joy in being free from fatalism. We relished whatever synchronicity allowed us to be alive together for as long as we had been and might be.

"Come on," she begged, "Liebling." Tears streamed down her face in earnest. I wish I knew the moment when we stopped trying to impress each other. But something made me say: "Our problems will follow us." I think there are a limited number of phrases we all use interchangeably for fights. We say the same old things to differ-ent new lovers. Maybe I didn't know the words that would've made things right. I watched her cry.

Her tears always told me I mattered. When you're young, a lovers' quarrel is the sharpest thing in the world. And I loved it. I twisted things around, milked her anguish, to be on the receiving end of her regret. I wish I knew the moment when sympathy died. If I did, I'd write it down, so we could all make sure that it never happens again.

"So, what will we do?" she said, withdrawing her hands, raising herself up in the seat. I looked at her, my Madison. She was about to go from soft to hard, and I had to act decisively or lose my advan-tage. "We'll keep trying," I said. "Don't stop believing." I could hear that old Journey song in my head. I wanted Madison to take my hands again. Holding someone's hand reminds you where you are.

A week later, while making tea, she ended it. I was adrift.

*

Bebot remembers it well.

It was 1955 and Dolores was readying herself before her first summit. He came into her room. I thought you were ready, she told him. I am, he said, I just need to have my barong pressed. That's not being ready, she snapped. When she finished applying her makeup, she went out front to the car. Elmer had the Impala idling, the electric fans whirring full blast. Where's my husband? she said to Elmer as she got in. I don't know, ma'am. Dolores leaned over to the steering wheel and held the horn down until Bebot came rushing out. He sat beside her without a word. As they neared the memorial, he asked her, Are we going to the dinner after? I'm going, she said. Did Leslie telegram from Madrid? he asked. Dolores didn't say anything. I hope her voyage went well, Bebot said.

When they arrived, the sun was low in the sky. The light glinted harshly off the brass of the band near the stage. Two bare flagpoles flanked the covered monument. The crowd was already gathered at their seats. I told you, Dolores said, I knew it. Bebot didn't reply. They walked side by side down the long path through the new lawns. Bebot looked at her intently. It will be okay today, he said. It was a long time ago. Dolores looked at him as if he'd just insulted her. My brother and mother were killed, she said. I know, Bebot said. I know.

The couple rushed to take their places reserved at the front. Dolores's secretary, Tadio, was there. Good afternoon, Congresswoman, good afternoon, sir. Here are your programs. Dolores made Tadio sit between her and Bebot. Tadio looked like he wanted to disappear.

Somebody announced over the loudspeaker, Please stand for the national anthems. Everyone stood. The Filipinos in the crowd put their hands on their chests. The Philippine flag was raised slowly by two soldiers in dress uniform as the band played the "Lupang Hinirang." When the song ended, there was an odd silence. Everyone watched the flag flap at half-mast. Bebot looked over at Dolores. She was staring at a long line of ants making their way over a flagstone in front of her.

Dolores was remembering. She thought of how she and her brother Manito would manufacture wind chimes with the spent bullet casings they collected near their house on Jorge Bocobo Street. And every day, to build strong muscles for fighting, they lifted the large bags filled with the new banknotes, the Mickey Mouse money (one sack bought a cup of rice). Sometimes they even studied their vocabulary for the next day's class, reciting the strange words with eyes made narrow and voices made shrill.

That was how we maintained our innocence, she thought now. When she looked up, the Japanese flag was already near the halfway point on the pole and the band was arriving at the last few bars of the "Kimi Ga Yo."

When Bebot glanced at his wife, he saw that she was weeping.

—from the 1973 short story "Manila Banzai Blues," by Crispin Salvador

*

In Barcelona, Salvador lived in a studio in the Barrio Gótico. The years spent there for his schooling were significant for two vital but different relationships: that with Gigi Mitterand and that with Max Oscurio. He recounted their first encounters, at the same picnic party, in *Autoplagiarist*.

Of Oscurio: "At the entrance to the park, beside Antoni Gaudí's mosaic-scaled lizard straddling the staircases, I saw the two Berties, Roberto Pascual and Edilberto Dario, whom I'd not seen since Manila. Pascual was excitedly telling about a *strip-teaseuse* he'd seen in Paris, a Montréalaise who had simulated sex with a black swan onstage. It was good to share laughter with them again. They introduced me to their older companion, who, despite unkempt hair and sunken cheeks, drew one's interest with his enervating eyes. They seemed to have the blackness of Rasputin's. He leaned against the banister, stroking the lizard's blue head as if it were his pet. This fellow brightened when I greeted their group and he immediately proffered his hand for me to shake. His fingernails were long and painted like a woman's, Tyrolean green. When I tried to shake his hand he grabbed mine firmly, brought it to his lips, and planted a kiss upon my knuckles. I was so taken aback I could not resist. 'Max Oscurio, my beautiful boy,' said he. 'How is it a prince like you has not yet joined our coterie?' Instantaneous was my repulsion."

Of Mitterand: "Trumpets today, and trumpets and more trumpets sounding joy. She was alone, enjoying a cigarette away from the crowds of picnickers. Her hair reminded me of brass just before it tarnishes. Trumpets! She spoke Spanish with a French accent, having difficulty rolling her *r*'s, dragging them on the ground as only the French have the right to do. How do such flaws become beautiful in the right person? She was sitting sidesaddle on the long bench shaped like a Mediterranean kraken, its mosaic matching her ruby earrings as if a prescient Gaudí had intended this very moment. How did I not guess instantly that she was a violinist, with fingers so long, so slender, they were chopsticks of ivory pinching her red-stained cigarette? I found my heart beating so rapidly I felt my lungs would collapse. I asked if she liked the park. She said the survival of Gaudí's work is 'a reprimand to Franco.' Which struck me as one of those strong, stupid opinions that are endearing in their way. But her breasts were monumental in her low-cut blouse, her figure rangy almost to the point of awkwardness. Her white trousers were short above her tanned calves, her ankles of such slightness I wanted to circle my fingers around them, to marvel that they could support her. She explained that the dip in the bench, rolling as it does from the wall and sparkling with tile like the hollow of a wave, was moulded to the posterior of a naked workman whom Gaudí had made sit in the wet clay. I of course did not believe her. She pulled me to sit at her side and we wiggled into the bench's curvature. She smelled of oranges and pastis. Then, standing and looking around, she pulled her trousers down and sank her naked, milk-white posterior into the recess. 'See!?' she declared, taking my flabbergasted expression as a sign I conceded my disbelief. I averted my eyes politely, staring instead into hers, which smiled with magnificent infantile coruscation. She hadn't even given me her name when I silently pledged my heart to her. What a cruel moment that afternoon when she introduced me to Raoul, her Spanish fiancé, an Extremaduran count no less!"

—from the biography in progress, *Crispin Salvador: Eight Lives Lived*, by Miguel Syjuco

*

Things had been strained since they returned from their day trip to the little isthmus off the island of L—. That rendezvous differed vastly from those carefree trips they'd taken last year. Nineteen fifty-eight was a tremendous year, he thinks now, both for that case of Chateau L'Arrosée and for our love.

Pipo watches her brush her teeth. He's always loved observing her when she wasn't looking. As now. His eyes are like a film camera, capturing forever the architecture of her ankles, the way she rises on the balls of her feet to bend like a lily's stem over the basin to spit, the way her arches curve like bows, the way her heels come down to touch the tiles gently, like a kiss. Sadie shakes out her long blond hair and ties it in a chignon. She tightens the towel around her, returns to the bedroom, and looks at him sitting in the leather armchair, pretending to read the three-day-old edition of *Le Canard enchaîné*. Has it really been, Pipo wonders, that long since they'd left the room?

"As I was telling you . . . ," Sadie says. He'll miss the way her British accent makes her enunciate the *s* and *t* sounds. It makes her sound impetuous. ". . . you know well that I'm the sort who stares at a storming sky and thinks 'this rain shall stop, and soon.' And that I believe I will one day return to all the places I have loved, and that the world is small and I shall see you again, inevitably. I know that this something we share will not have ended the next time we meet, even if I don't know what it is that we have. Do you at all understand?" She lets the towel fall around her ankles and lies down on the bed, turning onto her side to look meaningfully at Pipo. He studies the dip at her waist, the deep curve like an autumn valley amid wintry mountains. He catches her eyes with his, then forces her to look at him look away. He doesn't want to say what he's going to say.

"You act as if I should be happy with that." He pauses a moment, for effect. He softens his voice, because he wants to. He knows he shouldn't. "The problem is one doesn't realize what love looks like until you see others who have it, and you realize that you don't. You see lovers—in the street, at a café, in photographs for heaven's sake—and you *think*: that is what it should look like. Ours looks nothing like that. Sometimes it does, then you go away again. You return to your Spanish aristocrat." Pipo spits out the last word. "Then I don't know what I see. That's all." But that isn't all. Yet he holds his tongue.

He stands and looks at her among the big square pillows Europeans love but he could never understand. She sits up, draws her legs against her chest, and rests her chin on her knees, like an origami bird being folded. Sadie stares back. Challenging. Then she studies her hands, turning them over, inspecting them as if they were new. As if this wasn't the end.

Pipo hesitates, in this moment which he realizes will last forever in his mind. Even now he loves how she is a woman who likes to be looked at, even photographed, without drama, not hamming it up, ever, merely displaying, honestly. He has always loved that honesty, even if it meant she refused to decide between him and the Extremaduran count. Then Pipo's hesitation passes and he turns away. The door doesn't make a sound as he leaves.

He knows it isn't over.

The End.

—from *Vida*, Book III of *The Europa Quartet*, by Crispin Salvador

*

At dinner, Dr. and Mrs. Effy and Raqel Gonzales are welcoming. Joined by their son, Toofy, several years younger than Sadie, we sit in their sprawling dining/living room. Raqel catches me admiring a finely painted screen across one wall. "Late Edo period," she explains. "The dealer told me it depicts popular Hokkaido myths." She systematically turns the lazy Susan so that I partake first of every dish as the family watches me fumble with the serving cutlery.

I get this nauseating feeling of déjà vu. But when I look at their faces, I see only strangers. Effy, a greying bear, straight from work in an office barong with a Mont Blanc clipped inside the placket, smelling of cigarettes and Paco Rabanne. Raqel, well preserved by regular sessions at the Polo Club gym, is in stylish Anne Taylor–style linen slacks and tailored cotton blouse. Sadie's brother, Toofy (his name meaning "Effy Jr." or "Effy too" or even "Effy two"—I didn't catch the finer points of Sadie's explanation), is slight and possesses the habit of playing with his lower lip. He didn't shake my hand and seems to shrink from the dinner table.

Sadie sits beside me. I feel her foot rub up against mine under the table. I stare at the linen napkin folded into a swan beside my plate. She keeps rubbing her naked foot against my ankle. Finally, she kicks me hard. I look up and she's staring at me, irritatedly. She leans over to whisper. "Don't forget to ask my mom about Dulcinea."

"No need to whisper! Don't be shy," Raqel says from across the table. "Feel at home. We're so glad you could join us! Really, so glad. Isn't that nice, Daddy?" Her husband is oblivious, busy rolling up his sleeves.

An old man in pyjama pants, terry cloth house slippers, and a too-big yellow T-shirt that says "Don't worry, be happy" shuffles out of the kitchen and circles slowly around the dining table. He's grumbling quietly to himself. Nobody seems to notice. He's holding a spoon.

Raqel continues: "So, Miguel, you're from New York? But you grew up here? Ateneo or La Salle? . . . Ah, good, good."

"Well, I went to La Salle," says Effy.

Raqel: "That's not your fault, dear. But, Miguel, you know, Toofy here is going to Southridge, getting a good Opus Dei education. Did you learn Latin at Ateneo? When did they stop teaching it?

Well, then, Toofy will have to recite some original Thucydides for us later, won't you, Toofs?"

Toofy (reaching for the rice, mumbles): "Thucydides is Greek."

Effy: "This rain is really something, no? That'll stop those Muslim zealots."

Raqel: "I know! I was stuck in traffic nearly two hours, coming home from my Friends of the CCP lunch in Manila. I thought it was another roadblock. There's so many these days. I was relieved it was just a flood. That stupid Bonifacio almost stalled the car passing through it. I was worried you'd have to send your driver with the four-by-four."

Sadie: "Global warming. Maybe all our cars should get those engine snorkels like the four-by-four."

Effy: "That's ridiculous. I don't believe in global warming."

Sadie: "Because you work for Petron."

The old man shouts out: "Listen! It's happening. We must be vigilant." He wields his spoon as if it were a knife.

Effy: "Pop, the war's over. The Japanese surrendered."

Raqel (turning to me): "Don't mind my father-in-law. He's unwell. The maids feed him in the kitchen, but he likes to walk around between spoonfuls."

Toofy (leaning in like a spy in a crowded souk): "We call him Spooky Lolo."

Raqel: "Miguel, excuse me for asking, I'm curious. Who are your parents?"

I tell her.

Raqel: "Ah, I knew your mother from Assumption. She was a few years older. We knew of your dad. They should never have gotten on that plane."

Effy (glaring at his wife): "It was a real tragedy. The country would have been so different."

Me: "Thank you, sir."

Raqel: "I still think it was the CIA. Bobby Pimplicio was too much of a nationalist senator for their liking."

Effy: "The people called him 'Bob Hope.' I still remember his campaign jingle. 'Don't cast your dreams down the drain, cast a vote for Mr. Hope.'"

Sadie: "In history class we learned that anyone could have sabotaged the engine. The administration, the big corporations, even the commies."

Me: "All the explanations never really interested me. All that mattered was that my parents were gone and I never knew them."

Toofy: "Bet it was a spiteful God."

Me (smiling at Toofy): "I tend to agree."

Effy: "How about your lolo, how's he doing? I used to see him at Manila Golf. Haven't seen him in a while, though."

Sadie: "I thought you said you didn't have family here?"

Me: "My lolo is well, sir. Still the firebrand."

Raqel: "How many children are you?"

Me: "We're six, ma'am. My parents kept having kids until they had one they actually liked."

Raqel: "What number are you in the family?"

Me: "Number five."

Raqel: "That's funny! Isn't that funny, Effy?"

Effy: "We're lucky we had a girl, then a boy. We could stop trying."

Sadie: "You know, Miguel is a writer. A damn fine writer, too."

Toofy: "Have you even read his work?"

Raqel: "Oh! What do you write, Miguel? My daughter is a big reader. She inherited her worldly inquisitiveness from me. I used to read her the—"

Effy: "Tell me, how do you earn a living, Miguel? I guess your rich grandparents support your hobby."

Raqel: "Effy!"

Sadie: "Dad!"

(Toofy drops his cutlery on his plate.)

Spooky Lolo: "I taught you better than that. I remember when you killed your puppy because I got angry with you."

Effy: "No, Miguel, I'm just curious. Really. If that's what my daughter wants, that's what she gets, right? I just want to know how much to save for her inheritan—"

Sadie: "Daddy, please."

Raqel: "You must excuse my husband. His art is making money."

Me: "It's a hard art to master, ma'am. Actually, I make enough to support myself. Freelancing and what have you."

Effy: "You can't do that here in the Philippines, no? There's not enough money in it. Maybe in the States yes, but here . . ."

Raqel: "I wanted to be a writer, too, you know. Then I got pregnant and there were so many things keeping me busy. A household to run, my work at the Chosen Children Foundation, Christmas bazaars, Pilates, et cetera."

Sadie: "My mom used to hang with poets and Maoist revolutionaries."

Effy: "You know, speaking of revolutionaries, someone at the office told me he knows the rumours are true. About Sexysexygate. Vita Nova has a videotape that will implicate the president."

Raqel: "That's an example of in flagrante derelicto."

Sadie: "Eew!"

Toofy: "It's *delicto*."

Effy: "The poor bastard, betrayed by his new mistress."

Sadie: "I heard Reverend Martin's backing him anyway. Despite all that 'morality' stuff."

Raqel: "Why can't Filipino men stay monogamous, I don't get it. Like dogs on the street."

Effy: "Because of their wives, that's why."

Raqel (ignoring her husband): "That's the problem with a charismatic order like Reverend Martin's. They're unsanctioned by the Church, but they get away with almost murder . . ."

Sadie: "They deliver the votes."

Effy: "I think they give people hope."

Raqel: "Well, how many millions belong to the El Ohim? Ten? He's a kingmaker. But no matter how populist you are, what kind of Christians are you if the Pope doesn't recognize you?"

Spooky Lolo: "I'm telling you, Satan came as Jesus."

Effy (sounding long-suffering): "Papa. Don't blaspheme."

Sadie: "Mom, Miguel is doing the biography of Crispin Salvador. He's one of your favourites, no?"

Raqel: "Well, just one of my favourite *local* ones. He's no Paulo Coelho. *The Alchemist* changed my life. But it's great that you're writing Salvador's biography. How wonderful for you. Finally, someone's doing it."

Sadie: "Mom, did you know that Crispin—"

Effy: "My wife was once in love with him, Miguel. She had his photograph in her locker at school."

Raqel: "It was a wonderful photo. Salvador looked like a silent-era film star. But Dr. Gonzales exaggerates. I was taking photography at the time, and my teacher at Assumption, the famous Miss Florentina, she asked us to replicate the lighting for our portraiture project."

Effy: "But after that, you went and read all his books."

Raqel: "Oh, you're so funny. Sadie, isn't your dad funny when he's jealous? Well, it'll be a good biography. Salvador was quite the character. I saw him once on campus, giving a talk. Very magnetic. You know, there was always something melancholy about him that—"

Me: "I'll be interviewing Miss Florentina."

Raqel: "Oh! Do give her my regards. If she remembers me. It was so long ago. She was a real dynamo. With her poetry and her travels and her men. She had a joie de vivre that made *us* students feel old. And she was as clever as a mousetrap. She always played the fool in order to control us."

Toofy: "I read on a blog that Salvador, like, offed himself."

Sadie: "Mom, listen. Did you know—"

Raqel: "Did he? Oh my. How sad."

Toofy: "That's why you should read the papers, Ma."

Effy: "Wasn't Salvador a homo?"

Sadie: "Dad!"

Toofy (throwing his fork onto the plate again): "May I be excused?"

Raqel: "No, you may not. We're not halfway through dinner."

Sadie: "Mom, let him go. He's got so much homework."

Effy (looking at his son): "What's the problem? Are there homosexuals here? Of course not."

Raqel: "Toof, stay put. Pray tonight for a coup if you don't want to go to school."

Spooky Lolo: "In the end, somebody else will be telling the truth, and it will all be different."

Raqel (mildly raising her voice): "Papa, please! It's time for your next spoonful. Why don't you go into the kitchen?"

Effy: "Miguel, where did you receive your education?"

Sadie: "Miguel went to an Ivy League school for his master's. For creative writing. Bet you didn't know Ivy League schools had creative writing programs."

Effy: "I went to Harvard for my master's, then to Princeton for my PhD. MBA, then doctorate in economics. And you?"

Raqel: "My husband used to spend his tuition on trips to New York, staying at the Plaza and blowing his parents' money on blond hotsipatootsies."

Me: "Columbia, sir."

Effy: "That's not true. I did that *one* semester. My last. I'd earned a scholarship for students from the Third World, so my tuition money was a bonus."

Raqel: "Lord, how could you go out with white women? White people don't use water to wipe their bottoms after they use the toilet."

Toofy: "That's called 'dry-wiping.'"

Raqel: "Toof! Please, we're eating!"

Effy: "Sorry, Miguel, did you say Columbia? A Little Ivy then."

Me: "Actually, sir, I think it was one of the Founding Four."

Effy: "No, it's Harvard, Yale, University of Pennsylvania, and Princeton."

Me: "I don't think so, sir. I think it was Columbia and not Princeton. I guess it depends on whom you ask."

Effy: "I'm sure it's Princeton."

Raqel: "Who wants mangoes? We had some flown in from the farm in Cebu."

Me: "Thank you, Mrs. Gonzales. I'd love some."

Raqel: "Please, call me Tita Raqy."

Me: "Thank you, Tita Raqy."

(Mrs. Gonzales rings a delicate silver bell on the lazy Susan and watches the kitchen door for the maid. When nobody comes she rings it again.)

Effy: "That bell doesn't work. It's not loud enough. I'll use the remote."

Raqel: "That thing is so crass. This bell is much more elegant."

(Dr. Gonzales reaches for the remote control on the buffet table behind him. He presses the button and an electronic bell sounds in the kitchen—*ding, dong, dang, dong*—like Big Ben on the hour. A second later, a maid comes out with a tray.)

Effy: "If the system ain't broke, don't fix it."

Raqel (speaking in Cebuano): "Inday, please clear the table and bring out some sliced mangoes. One for each . . ."

Sadie (rubbing her foot against mine, then whispering to me): "Ask my mom about Dulcinea."

Me: "I keep trying."

Raqel: ". . . Cut them in halves first, then peel the skin of the pit and stick a knife into the pit. Repeat my instructions."

(The maid repeats the instructions in Cebuano. She returns to the kitchen.)

Raqel: "She's new. We're still house-training her."

Spooky Lolo: "You were so beautiful when you were young. So much idealism it was inspiring."

(Dr. Gonzales rings the electronic bell and the maid reappears.)

Effy (in Tagalog): "I think my father is ready for his next scoop of food."

(The maid guides Spooky Lolo by the arm into the kitchen.)

Toofy (conspiratorially again): "You know, that maid, she washed her feet in the toilet when she first arrived from the province."

Raqel: "Toofy, be Christian, child! You know, Miguel, how these maids are. So hard to find good ones, and tougher to train. You have to tell them thrice how to do everything. Once so that they can forget it, twice so they can get it wrong, three times so they are reminded how to do it correctly. My friend Jessica Rodriguez had this story about her new maid . . . you know the Rodriguezes? They live in Forbes Park also, near the back of the Polo Club. You can smell the stables from their pool."

(Spooky Lolo comes out of the kitchen again, chewing, and resumes shuffling around the dining table.)

Effy: "Doesn't your family own a compound there, Miguel?"

Me: "My grandparents and my aunts, sir. But it's not a compound, just a few properties."

Effy: "Imagine, a compound in Forbes Park! I should have gone into zippers and politics."

Raqel: "As I was saying . . . Jessica was hosting a dinner last week and they were serving lechon. You know, roast suckling pig."

Sadie: "Mom, Miguel grew up in the Philippines."

Raqel: "Ah, I'm sorry. I keep forgetting. You don't have a Filipino accent anymore! Good for you. Anyway, so Jessica Rodriguez, she told her new maid to serve the pig on the large silver platter, but with an apple in the mouth. Of course, who wants to see the fangs and tongue of the pig, no? The maid goes away and the guests eagerly await the entrance of the lechon. When she returns, sure enough, the pig is on the silver platter, and the apple is right there, *plop!*, in the mouth of the maid. Oh my lord, everyone couldn't stop laughing, no? The poor maid didn't know what was going on. Even when she set down the lechon and started to carve it, the apple was right there in her yap."

Sadie: "That's such an old urban myth. It always happens to someone's Tita So-and-So. It's like seeing the White Lady of Balete Drive on a stormy night."

Toofy: "A night like this one."

Raqel: "No, it's really true. It happened to Jessica. She told me when I saw her in the parlor at the Polo Club. Why would she lie?"

(The maid comes with the plates of mangoes and we're all quiet as she serves each of us. Spooky Lolo stops his circling and watches the maid complete her task.)

Me (turning to Toofy): "So, Toofy, what are you going to study in college?"

Toofy: "Dunno."

Raqel: "Inday, serve from the right, and remove from the left. Please repeat to me."

Inday: "Serve from right to left."

Raqel: "No. Serve from left, remove plates from right."

Me: "Do you know where you're going to college?"

Toofy: "Not sure. Far away."

Inday: "Yes, ma'am. Serve from left, remove plates from right."

Raqel: "Good. Now you can go."

Spooky Lolo: "Serve from the right with the right hand, remove plates from the left with the left hand."

Effy: "You know, Miguel, my cousin is in Congress. Maybe your grandfather is his friend? Manoleto Gonzales, second district of Ilocos Norte."

Me: "I'm sorry, sir, doesn't ring a bell."

Effy: "Grew up in Bacolod, but his wife is Ilocana. Changco is her maiden name, from the tycoon family there. Dingdong's second cousin, I think."

Sadie: "Mom, Miguel was just in Bacolod, researching Salvador's life for his book."

Raqel: "Ah, yes, he was from there. But what a modern-day ilustrado, no? From the cane fields of Bacolod all the way to Europe and America! How romantic!"

Sadie: "And Miguel found out that—"

Effy: "My cousin was from one of those rich Bacolod families. Like the Salvadors. All incestuous, everyone related, to keep the money and fair skin in the family. Bad teeth, lazy. He had a third nipple or something. Spoiled as a prince. What kind of kingdom do you inherit there, anyway? Did you like Bacolod, Miguel?"

Sadie: "So, Mom, Miguel met Salvador's sister. Didn't you know her?"

Me: "Bacolod was fine, sir. Quite peaceful, actually."

Effy (leaning onto the table): "See? This cousin, he and his brothers enjoyed guns, and they'd get so bored they used to bring their bodyguards and go with the military and police to hunt. He used to tell me what it was like, waking up while it was still dark, going into the mists before the heat of day arrived. They'd crack Boy Bastos jokes and chew Wrigley's spearmint gum open-mouthed. Just like the movies."

Toofy: "Caricatures of men."

Spooky Lolo: "And Boy Bastos's daughter says, 'The future swims in shit'!" (Spooky Lolo snickers to himself.)

Effy: "My cousin was a bona fide weirdo. He boasted that he loved the smell of gun oil and armpit odour. They were hunting communist guerrillas. Shooting down NPAs like animals."

Raqel: "Oh, Effy, you're so dramatic."

Sadie: "Mom. Wasn't Lena Salvador your choirmaster when you were in college?"

Toofy: "Which ones were the animals?"

Raqel: "Sadie. Darling, stop making chismis like that. Only boors talk about other people, because they have nothing else interesting to say. Why, what happened to her?"

(Toofy takes out his phone from his pocket and starts text-messaging.)

Raqel: "Toofy, please. Don't text at the table. Miguel, please excuse my son, ha? He has cellulitis."

Effy: "I'm telling you, it's true, since he was thirteen. All dressed up with bandoliers and sidearm. I've seen pictures of him as a young-ster, like Rambo or something."

Raqel: "As if you don't like guns, Effy. You even have your chil-dren shooting with you."

Sadie: "Mom. Lena said that Salvador had a daughter. She was named Dulcinea. An artist, apparently."

(Toofy starts texting again, this time under the table. He's obvi-ous, but nobody notices but me.)

Spooky Lolo (raising his voice to be heard): "When you go shop-ping, please buy me a Ped-Egg. You keep forgetting."

Raqel: "Pa, if you don't keep quiet we'll have the maids bring you upstairs."

Effy: "I don't know why you're still against guns. The bad guys have them. Self-defence is important and guns teach you the value of peace. Shooting is like wielding thunder. You think twice before losing your temper. Anyway, my cousin the oddball . . . now he's in government. You know, when he gets new shoes, he makes his bodyguard wear them for a week, so that the leather gets broken in and the shoes don't hurt. It's a good idea, actually. I wonder if Imelda used that trick. Six thousand pairs are a lot of shoes to break in."

Spooky Lolo (mumbling almost inaudibly): ". . . don't know why you didn't enjoy martial law . . . the streets were peaceful again . . . they stole, but at least they gave back."

Raqel: "Effy, that's disgusting. Would you want Ricardo wear-ing your shoes? You don't even let him park the Porsche for you. Besides, I wouldn't want you bringing your feet into the bed after wearing shoes he's worn."

Toofy: "You'll get Chinese Foot Flu."

Sadie: "So, Mom. Mom. Mom, Miguel's now looking for Dul-cinea. She probably has the missing manuscript everyone was talking about."

Effy: "I don't know why it should matter, Raqy, whether my feet are clean or not. It's not as if we share the same bed. You don't even care when I don't come home."

Raqel: "More mangoes, Miguel? Let me ring the bell for you."

(Mrs. Gonzales rings her little bell.)

Sadie: "Mom, are you listening to me? Mom?"

Toofy: "May I be excused? Are we done?"

(Mrs. Gonzales rings her little bell.)

Spooky Lolo: "There's no need for any of this. We're family."

Effy: "You pretend not to notice, pretending to be already sleeping . . ."

(Mrs. Gonzales rings her little bell.)

Effy: ". . . your rosary wrapped around your fist. How many years has it been since we made—"

Raqel (shouting for the maid): "Inday! You bitch, where are you?"

Sadie: "Do you want me to get her for you, Mom?"

Toofy: "Are we goddamned finished?"

(Raqel stands suddenly and goes upstairs. Effy turns the lazy Susan to get more food. Sadie looks to be on the verge of tears. Toofy's cell phone vibrates, signalling a new text message; he holds it blatantly above the table, his thumbs clicking the keys in rapid response. A maid comes out of the kitchen and leads Spooky Lolo by the elbow for his next spoonful.)

*

The year after my Tito Marcelo died was when the fighting began over the fortune. Grapes had sold the zipper company, YKK Philippines, which he'd inherited from his father, both because liquidity was needed for his imminent senatorial campaign and because the business had just settled a costly counterfeiting case with the real U.S. company. (YKK Philippines was sold to Dingdong Changco III, for a record billion pesos, and its name was later changed to TKK Philippines. It is still the largest manufacturer of zippers in eastern Southeast Asia.)

The sale was not as straightforward as Grapes would have liked. He had put the corporation in the names of each of his children— ostensibly to rescue them from inheritance taxes, but more likely to hide his assets from the scrutiny of political opponents. This allowed my aunts to contest the clause that let Grapes administer the company on their behalf. What followed was internecine squabbling, secret meetings to shift allegiance, and round-robin backstabbing. Each sibling sued Grapes. Tito Marcelo's wife sued my aunts. One aunt, convinced the stress would soon kill my grandfather, launched a preemptive case against Granma. Even we grandchildren estimated how much everyone would be receiving (though because my parents were dead, my father's name was absent from the articles of incorporation, and my five siblings and I were exempt from the chaos).

In the end, having funded the appointment of a Supreme Court justice years earlier, Grapes won every suit. The fortune remained his. His children stopped talking to him and Granma, despite living across the street in houses he'd given them when they started their own families. When Grapes was away campaigning, we grandcousins were encouraged to keep Granma company. "She'll probably give us money," we said to each other, though the thought of her sitting alone was what sent us knocking at her bedroom door. She rarely took out her wallet. Usually she told us to choose one thing from the suitcase brimming with fake Rolexes and Omegas she'd brought back from her latest Hong Kong shopping spree. I'd stand in front of the open suitcase, observing the hundreds of second hands ticking out of sync, thinking about how distant I'd become from my grandparents. At first I attributed it to my growing up. But after about a dozen times sitting with Granma, I started avoiding her again. When she knocked on my bedroom door, I didn't answer. I was discomfited by her stories about how rotten her children were.

It even got to the point where, when we saw our titos and titas in public, we weren't sure whether we should greet them. Whose side were we supposed to take in all this? I sometimes wonder if that was what Grapes intended.

One afternoon I saw my cousin Esmie on the elliptical trainer in the gym at the Polo Club. We'd been close once. "Oh my God," she exclaimed. "We just got back from Bangkok with Granma. She treated me and my mom. Grapes doesn't know!"

"I didn't even know Granma was away," I said.

"A hotel maid caught her stealing pens and soaps from her trolley. It was crazy embarrassing. Security was called, and Granma was escorted down to talk to the manager in the lobby. When we came home, Granma came back with like fourteen suitcases, filled with shitty bargain junk. She paid like four thousand dollars in overweight baggage fees. And guess who I saw recently? Tita Baby, last week. She just arrived from L.A. We celebrated her fiftieth at our house. I know, she and my mom are friends now. They both made up with Grapes and he gave them each a small 'pre-inheritance.' Look what I got!"

Esmie held up her wrist to show off a sparkling tennis bracelet.

"Cartier. Anyways, after dinner, we were in the powder room—me, my mom, and Tita Baby—and Tita suddenly unbuttons her blouse and holds it open. And she's like, 'Girls! Don't I look beautiful?'"

"What?"

"I didn't want to look."

"I don't understand."

"She'd gone to Michael Jackson's plastic surgeon!"

"You're kidding. Grapes said she was super in debt."

"Not anymore."

"So did she look beautiful?"

"Oh yeah. She did. She really did."

*

Sadie is like another person when she drops him off at his hotel. They drive wordlessly through the rain. Our stalwart protagonist doesn't know what to say, so he doesn't say anything. They listen to the radio. Suddenly, she switches it off. Asks him, very seriously, when he'll be returning to New York.

"Soon," he says. "Maybe."

"Is it really like in Sex and the City*?"*

"It's better."

Sadie begins to cry.

"What's wrong?" he asks. Sadie shakes her head, bangs the steering wheel, looks away. They arrive outside his hotel. "Come on. What's the matter?"

"I wish you didn't have to see that, you know? Why do they do shit like that, if they really love us?"

"*All families are alike,*" *he says. He takes her hand for the first time. She lets him. "Hey," he says. She looks at him. "Later, if you, you know, end up talking to your mom, do you think you could press her about Dulcinea?"*

Sadie wrests her hand from his. "Please leave," she says. He gets out of the car and stands in the rain, waiting for her to ask him back in. Sadie rockets off, spraying water and splashing some of the GROs huddled in the doorways of the massage parlors. They curse like stevedores.

The boy enters the lobby and shakes the rain off. He knows he should call her cell phone, that he should have acted more sympathetically. But dinner with her family makes him wonder if even his own parents' famous love would have soured. And if it was better to die as they did, before the decline. He thinks of Spooky Lolo surrounded by his family. And the vacancy of Crispin's life lived solely by himself.

In the elevator, a couple is talking as if he isn't there. The man says, "I'm telling you, it was a hoax. Those jellyfish were rubber. The background was staged." The woman replies, "You think it's related to the bombings?" The man says, "To drum up support for you-know-who. They're backing PhilFirst, who is backing President Friendly-Ho Estregan." The woman says, "I think everyone should lay off PhilFirst. They're the country's largest employer, and they drive our economy." The man replies, "That's because they put food on your table. Did you know that the Americans—" The woman says, "I wonder if you can eat them." The man replies, peevishly, "The Americans?" The woman continues, "Feed the poor with them. Jellyfish, I mean." The man looks at her. "I give up," he says. "You're useless!" Then the couple turns to our protagonist and looks at him angrily.

When he gets to bed, all he can do is toss and turn. Finally, he cannot feel his body.

He is washing his hands very carefully, enjoying the ritual. A woman in a headset comes and runs an adhesive roller over his black polo shirt and blue jeans. She leads him down a hall. He is on a Latin American talk show, sitting on an Eames lounge. The host is perfectly tanned and tells him he's much cooler than Pablo Neruda. The boy demurs. The host turns to the crowd and says in Spanish, "Who knew Blanc Neige was so nice?" The crowd erupts in applause. The lights are bright and he can hardly see the audience. Except for Madison, who is in the front row, looking angry. The host stands and goes to an ironing board. He starts pressing a black polo shirt. "Blanc Neige is an international star!" the host says, while turning the shirt over to iron the back. The crowd laughs cruelly. The host goes offstage and returns, dressed in a black polo and blue jeans. The crowd cheers. "Look, all you people," the host says in funny English. "I'm Blanc Neige!" The crowd hoots. After the show, he searches for Madison. The woman with the headset says, "Oye, Blanc Neige, she went with the host into a Toyota LiteAce van." Outside, it is raining hard. The van is in a forest clearing and it is rocking. He goes back into the studio and flirts with a Hong Kong Chinese girl with rabbitlike feet in strappy sandals. She gives him a blow job in a cave by the beach. He goes home to find Madison not there, though Crispin is at the typewriter. He says to Crispin, "Aren't you busy being dead?" The author replies, "Can't die yet. I'm busy writing your story." He leaves Crispin and goes through the blue door into the restaurant he owns with Madison. There she is. She looks beautiful. He helps her clean the shed out back. They bring the summer plates into the restaurant, as well as sangria pitchers. He thinks of what to say to her but doesn't know. He goes outside to smoke a cigarette. When he comes back in, Madison is hanging by her neck from her belt. It's tied to the rack in the kitchen. She gently swings and hits the pans suspended beside her. They sound like church bells after a wedding. No, he says. No, Madison. No. He hugs her legs, buries his face in the space behind her knees. He has nothing left. He knows what's next. His belt will compress the carotid arteries in his neck, cutting off blood to his brain. His brain will swell and plug the top of his spinal column, pinching the vagal nerve and arresting his heart. His eyes will bulge and his sphincter will release. He will suffer. But he will have to do it. He can hear Crispin upstairs. Outside, the metal slugs of type bang like bullets into the white sky, leaving black letters suspended. "Dear Sire/Madame," they say. "First, I request your stricst confidence in this transaction. I am the granddaughter of the statesman and finance minister of the Philippine. I need help from you as a man of God. After the deth of my father, who perished in mysterious circumstance and was found in a flood, I was informed by our lawyer, Clupea Rubra, that my daddy, who at the time was government whistleblower and head of family fortune, called him, Clupea Rubra, and conducted him round his flat and show to him three black cardboard boxes. Along the line, my daddy died mysteriously, and Government has been after us, molesting, policing, and freezing our bank accounts. Your heroic assist is required in replenishing my father's legacy and masticating his despicable murderers. More information TBA." The typewriter continues its banging. "I am looking *for an overseas partner who will assist me in transferring $21,230,000, of which 20% will be given to you, the account owner. Please send your bank details . . ."*

Our slumbering protagonist awakens. Someone is pounding on the door of his room. The glowing hands of the clock say it's four in the morning. The knocking stops. He rushes, bleary-eyed, to answer it. Nobody is there. As soon as he lies down and shuts his eyes, he starts dreaming again.

*

It cannot be doubted that my father, the great Junior Salvador—may he rest in peace—always knew exactly what his purpose was, politically speaking. Thus, he could be slotted anywhere in any administration. Congressman, senator, cabinet minister, consigliere. His skill wasn't making something out of nothing—others were paid to do that. My father's skill was making nothing out of something. This was what he tried to teach me when, newly returned from Europe, my university studies complete, I took to his side in the sixties. And this is what turned me off politics. His specialty, you see, was engineering consent, intuitively taking a page out of the book of Edward Bernays—as you know, Freud's nephew and the father of PR—but twisting it, using localized threats and fear. Martial law, communism, violent social instability, loss of foreign investment, all were used to distract the public from its valid protestations, second thoughts, and objections. Concerns like empty larders, pillaged coffers, debauched leaders, all became third priority to bombs in the streets and guns in the hands of the godless commies or the godfuelled Muslims. With the country watching, not knowing what they were and weren't seeing, my father the political plastic surgeon made himself indispensable to each president. Not by covering things up, mind you, but by sleight of hand, which is always more of a distraction job than a disappearing act. His legacy is that these tactics are still very much employed today. And though he and I had our differences, as I grew to discover his traits developing in me, I both fought those characteristics and used them as a road map in attempting to understand who he was, and therefore who I am and could be if I wasn't careful. For that alone, I owe him everything.

—Crispin Salvador, in a 1997 interview for *The Nation* magazine, on the occasion of his father's passing

*

With the deepening recession, and with Erning saving for an engagement ring for Rocky, he and Cousin Bobby get jobs as security guards at Wal-Mart. Erning, having already learned a lot in life, tries to start a union. But when he finds out that the company would rather shut down a store than allow a union to form, he backs down. Being Filipino, he is eager to keep the status quo. Plus, his life in America has saddled him with debt on four credit cards and layaway payments at Costco. Besides, he enjoys the responsibility of protecting people and their property.

One day, while they are on duty, they hear their supervisor's voice calling frantically over their walkie-talkies: "Guards, a bag snatcher is on the premises. Block all the exits!"

Later, Bobby and Erning sheepishly approach their supervisor.

Bobby (bashfully massaging his triceps): "Eh, sir, the thief escaped."

Supervisor: "How could that have happened?"

Erning (bashfully scratching his head): "Eh, sir, he left via the entrance."

*

"That's a hard question," Crispin said.

We were hiking along the Hudson's edge in Riverside Park, in the heights of Manhattan, where the footpath is set away from the shore. We picked our way over the large stones, like crabs. I could imagine Crispin's answer, and I expected him to go off scandalously about his Filipino peers. I held my breath.

Instead, he fell serious. He stopped on a boulder and took off his spectacles (perfectly round, black plastic frames, usually seen on purposefully hip doctors and Asian architects). Crispin wiped them meticulously. I waited. He replaced them, fished a pocket comb from his overcoat, and ran it through his brilliantined salt-and-pepper hair. Had I upset him? The last edge of the sun slid into New Jersey. The Hudson was slightly aflame, silhouetting his face in shadow. He continued over the rocks. As if the conversation hadn't paused, he began to lecture.

"The beautiful poet Mutya Dimatahimik lay down in front of an advancing tank. She was five months pregnant. The tank led a column of military vehicles going to blockade Malacañang Palace from a march of students, labourers, communists. It was January 1970 and we had our fists raised against Marcos. When you're like that, you observe yourself from outside your body, enjoying the sight of you engaged in heroism among a crowd of fellow heroes. Mutya just went and lay down on the street. I wanted to stop her, but I was being pinned by a cop. The tank pushed toward her. The street shook. The tank didn't slow. A few feet from her small body, it stopped. All of us watching nearly became Catholic again. Three soldiers got out. They dragged her, screaming, to the side. I should say, it was they who were screaming. Mutya didn't say a word. They beat her. She lost her teeth, and nearly lost her child. It was then that we found out that the baby was a girl. In the hospital, I stood by Mutya's side, crying, and asked her what had gotten into her head to do such a thing. She said she'd been thinking of the dedication José Rizal wrote for *Noli Me Tangere*. Imagine?! That part about sacrificing to the truth everything. Death was nothing if her country was dying."

Crispin paused and looked very sad.

"Truly, romantic bullshit, in retrospect," he said. "And yet . . ." He wagged his finger. "And yet, 'No lyric has ever stopped a tank,' so said Seamus Heaney. Auden said that 'poetry makes nothing happen.' Bullshit! I reject all that wholeheartedly! What do they know about the mechanics of tanks? How can anyone estimate the ballistic qualities of words? Invisible things happen in intangible moments. What should keep us writing is precisely that possibility of explosions. If not, what then? A century and a decade ago, Rizal's prose kindled revolution. They didn't have tanks during that time, see? But when he wrote both his great *Noli* and *El Filibusterismo*, he was more concerned about the present than the future, and far more concerned with both those than about the past. An important clue to writers like you. Rizal's books were good, but their lyrics on the page were most certainly futile against the Guardia Civil, not to mention tanks. But their lyrics in the hot head and swelling heart of a young reader, well, Mr. Heaney, there by the grace of God goes your tank buster.

"Now, a hundred and ten years into the future, our present, it's

as if nothing else has been written in our sunburned isles since. Oh
sure, they broke the mould with Rizal, Mr. Malay Renaissance Man
himself. Like China's Sun Yat-sen. Vietnam's Ho Chi Minh. Rizal's
books are *the* literary and historical touchstone, so we still like to
crow about our revolution, the first democratic republic in Asia.
How it was stolen by American backstabbing and imperialism. We
talk as if we were actually there! Aiming our Remingtons. Pow!
Planting our machetes in Spanish cabezas. Shhlock! These are our
greatest accomplishments and saddest tragedies. Since then, has
nothing else happened?"

The sun had disappeared. The footpath's lampposts were far
away, remote, like moons fractured by the branches of the trees.
Leaves and twigs brushed our faces. The city seemed but a rumour.
His silence pressed me to take his question as more than rhetorical.
"Well, what about—"

"Truly!" he said, wagging his finger again. "Don't let's forget
Ferdinand Marcos! His iron butterfly, Imelda! Don't omit her shoes.
How many? One thousand? Three thousand? Six thousand? Does it
matter? Fifteen years ago that story ended. Fifteen years! Truly,
Miguel, as a nation we're overly concerned with the past. Even engaged in the present we lean slightly backward as time forces us
forward. We're like a probinsyano learning English. You know? Before saying anything, we form in our heads the things we're sure
we've learned in class. Aaaapple, b-oy, ca-pi-tul-ism, duh-mock-racy.
That's the problem, we've written one book, and it's been re-bound
again and again. So many re-presentations of the war, the struggle
of the haves and have-nots, People Power Revolutions on Edsa,
whatever. All those Pinoy writers industriously criticizing. All those
critics tirelessly writing. About unsuccessful 1970s rebellions, 1990s
domestic dramas. Or the Filipino-Americans, eagerly roosting in
pigeonholes, writing about the cultural losses that come with being
raised in a foreign country, or being not only brown, but a woman,
and a lesbian, or half-blind, or lower-middle-class, or whatever. Oh my,
what a crime against humanity that the world doesn't read Filipino
writing! This is the tradition you will inherit. Simon Leys, writing
about D. H. Lawrence, pointed out that 'often our imagination cannot fully absorb the truth of a city or of a land unless a poet'—was

it a poet that he said, or a writer?—anyway, 'unless a writer first invents it for us.' So, we realize ourselves in someone else's words. Perhaps we have stopped ourselves from being invented, from self-realization, by blaming others for our wordlessness. Then we wallow in the fact that we, as a people, are not yet whole. Nothing to be done, Pozzo."

I heard elusive voices in the shadows that I'd taken to be plants, ferns, trees whose names I didn't know. A lightning bug flickered across our path and then disappeared. It didn't light up again. The whispers continued. I feigned nonchalance. I prodded Crispin out of his silence. "When you used to write—"

"*Used to?* I still do write. Don't slip on Dr. Freud's banana peel. You might fall into the river. What was it I was saying? Oh, yes, I was saying, it's a global conspiracy. That's why my books are out of print, no? Right out of the *Protocols of the Elders of Zion*. A colonial conspiracy against the Philippines. Poor us. Yeah, truly. Listen, you—*we*—shouldn't foster a tradition of nostalgia, as we have. A retrospective of all the past frustrations. Forget it—it's gone, it's history. Pun intended. Haha! We have to change our country by changing its representation. What is Filipino writing? Living on the margins, a bygone era, loss, exile, poor-me angst, postcolonial identity theft. Tagalog words intermittently scattered around for local colour, exotically italicized. Run-on sentences and facsimiles of Magical Realism, hiding behind the disclaimer that we Pinoys were doing it years before the South Americans. You know I once found one of my books in the Latin America section of a reputable bookstore? I even had a Filipino student who italicized 'fiesta' in one of his stories. Fiesta? There you go. León María Guerrero once told me, 'We Filipinos owe our faults to others, but our virtues are our own.' At first I wasn't sure whether he was being sincere or sarcastic. It can only be the latter. Our heartache for home is so profound we can't get over it, even when we're home and never left. Our imaginations grow moss. So every Filipino novel has a scene about the glory of cooking rice, or the sensuality of tropical fruit. And every short story seems to end with misery or redemptive epiphanies. And variations thereof. An underlying cultural faith in deus ex machina. God coming from the sky to make things right or more wrong.

"First step, get over it, man. I forget which jazz man said that it takes a long time before you can play like yourself. Be an international writer, who happens to be Filipino, and learn to live with the criticisms of being a Twinkie. Anyway, your real home country will be that common ground your work plows between you and your reader. Truly, who wants to read about the angst of a remote tropical nation? Everyone's got enough of their own, thank you very much. Angst is not the human condition, it's the purgatory between what we have and what we want but can't get. Write what you know exists beyond that limited obsession. For now that may include the diaspora, the Great Filipino Floorshow. Fine. But listen, of all those things we Pinoys try so hard to remember, what are those other things that we've tried successfully to forget? Figure that out and write about that. Quit hiding behind our strengths and stand beside our weaknesses and say, These are mine! These are what I'm working to fix! Learn to be completely honest. Then your work will transcend calendars and borders. Goethe called it World Literature. He said, 'National literature no longer means much these days, we are entering the era of *Weltliteratur*.' He said it's up to each of us to hasten this development. How long ago was that? Or, coming full circle, *now* take Mr. Auden's advice: be 'like some valley cheese, local but prized everywhere.'"

We left the river and turned back toward the footpath in the park. We pushed our elbows through the branches, out of the wilderness.

"It's odd, yeah, that I tell you all this? Don't forget, Miguel, wise men are simply those who've made all the mistakes. Oh, I understand now, understand enough for my new book. The evils of one society are all of humanity's evils. I truly wish I could tell you more about *TBA*. I can't. Not yet. I can tell you only this. It's a necessary work. Because it will implicate them all. All those people who said hope was hopeless, and so instead took to begging with their eyes a portion of the booty. Or shuttered their homes, huddled inside, read scripture, and waited, not knowing that God will judge more harshly the sin of omission than the sin of commission.

"I promise you, I'm not as bitter as I seem. Well, perhaps only the truly bitter say that. But let me tell you one last thing. And this is important. I made a mistake. When I was young, I spent my days and nights trying to impress future generations. I spent them. They're gone. All because I was deathly afraid of being forgotten. And then came the regret. The worst thing among all worst things. But from that I gained a small fragment of wisdom. Purpose. Because the past will weigh a lot more once your future becomes shorter. And so, now I'm bargaining, begging, for just one last chance to bequeath a book about all the lessons I've learned painfully over the course of my life. Because it might just make everyone else's that tiny bit easier.

"I once thought *The Bridges Ablaze* would be that masterpiece. I'm not so sure it matters much anymore. You must learn this while you are still young. Live in the crux of the present. And write to explain the world to yourself and to others. Look forward only to the summer of your first convertible. Look forward only if what's in front of you is a mirror. Because one day you'll be so busy looking backward, and everything will feel like winter. If you still don't get it, pare, let me make it abundantly clear. Just write, and write justly. Ezra Pound be damned. Poets lie, though beautifully. Don't make things new, make them whole."

7

It will arrive in the post
in weighty packages, tightly wrapped
in knotted twine.
No return address.
Opened, they are empty.
You are already filled
with what it was,
secrets from an old you
to a future self. Regret
is only realizing
the truth too late.

               —from the 1982 poem "Self-Addressed Stamped Envelope,"
                                     by Crispin Salvador

*

Rocky marries Erning in a small ceremony at the Iglesia ni Kristo church in San Jose, California, with only two hundred friends and relatives attending. Rocky is radiant in the gown she resourcefully picked up from the specialty secondhand shop called Left at the Alter, in Haight-Ashbury. Erning wears the green barong he wore only once before, for his graduation. It is too tight, but he is so happy his smile is contagious. They honeymoon at Disneyland. The picture they have taken of them kissing in front of Cinderella's castle is framed and put on their mantel. A year passes. One night, they sit on the couch watching the Filipino channel.

Rocky: "Honey. I have something to ask. But don't get mad. Okay? Darling, why didn't you give me anything for our anniversary?"

Erning: "Eh, you told me to surprise you!"

*

The little things, you know, eventually become everything. That last week, I was driven nuts by Madison's habitual promiscuity with the mirrors she'd happen across. When I mentioned it, she said she only wanted to look good for me. But I hated her pouting-lipped, three-quarter pose, like some Paris Hilton wannabe. It made me swear that when we made love later that night—my hands choking off her air just as she liked it—I'd lean too heavily and too long, just to see her eyes go wide with panic as she had no more breath to call out our safeword, "Bananas!"

During those final days, we dismissed, once and for all, and completely, each other's finer points for the few nettlesome constancies. We repeated our I-love-yous in the hope they would do something, anything. I think we knew we said those three words less because we believed them and more because we wanted to hear what the other would respond.

That morning—a Monday I think, after a strained weekend alone at the Liebling "beach shack" by an endearing inlet near East Egg—we simultaneously realized we were trying to convince ourselves of nothing. While waiting for the tea to boil, Madison talked about how much she loved being out in the country. How much we needed its space. How much she loved the mornings before I awoke because the peace made her yoga sessions "transcendent."

When the kettle screamed, it was *I* who admitted defeat. It was *I* who spoke up. I expected her to cry again, to beg me to reconsider. But she just sat there, shaking Kokopelli Summer Mist tea leaves into her stainless tea ball. She poured tea into her mug and none into mine. Madison remained as quiet as a victim in a courtroom, the spurned and righteous and therefore the one who'd get our rent-controlled apartment with working fireplace. I said a few more things, then walked to Middle Neck Road to thumb a ride to the city. I kept looking over my shoulder, just in case she tried to follow.

At our home, I packed my things. I was slowed by having to separate our CDs and books. The task took me through the day and into the evening. When I was done, I memorized how the nighttime shadows journeyed across our bedroom and faded on the far wall into morning. When the day came, quietly then loudly, I looked out the window but saw no one. I made lunch, ate it, then gathered my bags. They were fewer than I expected. I double-checked that I wasn't leaving anything important and then I saw it on her pillow. Madison liked to wear my T-shirts to bed after I'd worn them, and my favourite Led Zeppelin shirt was folded where she'd left it after sleeping in it. It smelled of her and me. I put it back on her pillow. Maybe it would make her miss me. Then I pissed all over the toilet seat, kissed our two cats goodbye, and placed my keys on the bookshelf by the entrance. The door clicked behind me. "Don't," it seemed to say.

The next two weeks, Madison didn't call once, and I spent them couch-surfing from one benevolent friend's living room to many sympathetic others'. Then I heard a rumour that despite her need for space, Madison immediately gave up our apartment and moved in with our landlord, who lived directly above us, this goth guy who was rumoured to be the son of Cat Stevens and had yellow contact lenses and fake vampire fangs. I had conversed with him once at a party in the building (he explained he'd had a dentist cement ceramic prosthetics to his canine teeth) and I discovered the fucktard was an aspiring African-wildlife-documentary filmmaker (at the party, he told a group of girls: "The Masai believe elephants are the only other animals with souls. How can we be here in Brooklyn, lounging on our Poäng couches, watching reality TV, while poachers are defiling our besouled brethren?"). I can almost hear Madison's explanation: he understands me, he fills that emptiness, that hole I've had inside me all my life.

I bet.

Yeah. She let us go, easy as that.

✳

The next morning, Sadie won't answer my telephone calls. Outside, there is a strange absence of taxis. I walk to the bus stop. I'm going to be late for my interview with Miss Florentina. A vendor selling barbecued bananas has a radio blaring on the busy corner of Buendia and Makati Avenues.

An American's voice, with its now familiar Brooklyn accent, rings out.

"They will only say that this cowardly act will be punished . . . ," he exclaims; then he calls democracy a pile of bullshit. His vitriol is astounding. He goes on about how the American population will rise up against the Jews. Then he goes on about how the whites should leave and the blacks will return to Africa and how the Native Americans were the stewards of nature and . . .

My cell phone goes *buzz-buzz* in my pocket and I take it out. A text message. Finally, a response from Marcel Avellaneda: Apologies for tardy reply. Been busy directing movie. I'll be pleased to meet. Am free the time you specified. See you at the Metropolitan Theater. I'll show you exactly what Crispin did to make me, and everyone, angry. I put my phone away.

The man's voice on the radio continues.

"Death to the U.S.," he declares. "They are the worst liars and bastards. This is a wonderful day."

Station break. A woman sings the familiar cigarette jingle: "There's a light of hope, when you light a Hope."

Laser sounds, station identification, then a booming voice. A different commentator from the one earlier says: "You are listening to a replay of the September 12, 2001, telephone interview of chess legend Bobby Fischer, recorded live in Baguio following the World Trade Center attacks. We bring you this replay, compatriots, preceding a new live interview after some words from these sponsors . . ."

I'd heard the rumours. Fischer on the run: long wanted by the U.S. government for breaking an embargo and playing a match in Yugoslavia, enraging American authorities by standing in front of international media and spitting on the U.S. order forbidding him to play. Fischer being found: someone had recognized him, despite his shaggy hair and beard, spotted playing chess with the old lolos in Burnham Park in Baguio City, beating them with superhuman ease. Fischer living in exile: staying with the Filipino grandmaster Eugene Torre, who'd introduced him to Justine Ong, a twenty-two-year-old who later gave birth to Fischer's daughter, Jinky.

I walk down the street, his rantings drowned out by the grunts and whistles and yells of street life.

What would Crispin say? He had frothed at the mouth after Susan Sontag was publicly crucified for her reaction to the September 11 attacks. That wasn't a cowardly act, she'd said. Wrong, but not cowardly. Crispin had gotten on his computer to send her an e-mail pledging his agreement and support. When he told me about that incident, I was worried to discover I also agreed. And I grew afraid. What scared me most was the thought of our age's skewed conception of courage and cowardice and the slippery slope in between. I was frightened that my handy idea of heroism was invalid.

The street vendor squatting by her cart is looking at me. She keeps smiling. She has only three teeth—two on top, one below. I look behind me. Nothing strange. The woman smiles wider now. She struggles up to approach me.

The bus arrives, slows. I sprint to catch it.

*

While Salvador's relationship with Oscurio deepened over the following years, his intermittent affair with Mitterand would persist with just enough frequency to ensure he refrained from pursuing other romantic liaisons. According to Salvador's memoir, over his four years in Europe he met with Mitterand whenever she visited Barcelona (which proved often), twice when Salvador overlapped with her in Paris, and on twenty-three different occasions dedicated specifically to their illicit trysts: a rendezvous at the Simplon Pass, skiing on the Matterhorn in Zermatt, summer in Liguria, two "unforgettable trips to London to attend forgettable" plays, a month in the Corsican countryside near Ajaccio, an extended wine tour in the Haute-Loire, a food fest in Essen (ending in a Killepitsch-fuelled public spat in Düsseldorf), and other encounters made possible by Gigi's concert tours and her partnership in Raoul's purveyorship of delicacies for such shops as Fortnum & Mason, El Corte Inglés, and Fauchon.

"How could such a cretin as he have such good taste?" Salvador wrote of Raoul. "His title, after all, had been bought by his father, an Algerian émigré who had shady success in olive oil. It's usually the new rich who have the obsession, and therefore the better ap preciation. Gigi, with her annoying sense of the absurd, would always bring me fancy-wrapped gifts, usually, inexplicably, fresh haggis, which went laughed at but uneaten."

—from the biography in progress, *Crispin Salvador: Eight Lives Lived*, by Miguel Syjuco

*

It was at that particular New Year's party that our beloved friend changed forever. Pipo had just driven down at brakeless speed from a rendezvous with Sadie in a small hotel atop M—. As he later, rather drunkenly, recounted, Sadie had informed him, cruelly, in the dishevelled bed, that this weekend she, his unattainable Sadie, would continue to remain so, as she was returning north to Aigues Mortes, with Raoul, to spend the August holiday with him and her family. It was as if already forgotten was the previous night, or those promissory words they had uttered with clasped hands on the sands of La Concha a month prior. Pipo and Sadie had so wildly secluded themselves those four days in the Hotel Maria Cristina that during his train journey home he had marked the miles with smug grins, satisfied that he had left her finally truly his. This he told me, not seeing the jealousy in my face.

Now, he was slurring more nonsense into my ear. "For what purpose," Pipo demanded, his breath reeking of amontillado and vomit, "is this vexing faith I have in a spoken-for woman, as if the acts of her transgressions upon Raoul—that cuckolded Extremaduran count nearby, attending to business in Hendaya, with his big nose and . . . what was I saying?"

"Acts of transgression," I offered.

"Ah, yes. As if those acts of transgression are my own personal triumphs? In truth, the love of the forbidden has been masquerading as love itself. I'm sure of this. Now. Perhaps it is not that I love her. Perhaps it is that I hate him."

I was trying to stay angry with him, with his recklessness and callousness. From M—, Pipo had driven my Bugatti through a rain shower tinged muddy from the dust storms of North Africa. He screeched the car to a halt, its windshield almost opaque, just before it could plow into the tables outside Els Quatre Gats where we, his friends, sat drinking beneath the full glory of the clearing sky. His irresponsible nocturnal descent had done nothing to sober him. I was, of course, quite incensed. But Pipo's always been too charming, too beautiful, for me to stay angry.

Then he rubbed salt into the wound. Among the large clique he later invited upstairs to his apartment was Max, my own former lover. It was with him, it would turn out, that Pipo later smoked his first opium on the rooftop. Malignant rumours abounded the next morn as to what had happened in the solitude of a moonless sky.

I confronted him over breakfast, trying not to betray myself, trying not to glance at his thigh exposed from beneath the short robe I gave him. Pipo replied: "My dear, we discussed the loves greater than those confined to just one subject or family. Max spoke to me about love, an asexual love, a polymorphous, dutiful love for all of humanity. He recalled the responsibilities we must each shoulder. He reminds me of my uncle, the communist guerrilla, though the two could not in appearance and demeanour be more different. I fear I've misjudged Max on the strength of his eccentricities and ambiguities."

What happened the next evening was the reason I—we—lost Pipo forever.

—from *Amore*, Book IV of *The Europa Quartet*, by Crispin Salvador

*

With the roads free of taxis, the bus makes good time, though the traffic slows on Roxas Boulevard. The sky over Manila Bay is as white and flat as a sheet of paper. On the surface of the water are thousands of dead fish, the size of sardines. They rise and fall with the waves.

There's music. Lively music. And then I see it: the *Paul Watson*. The ship that's been in the news, the one the administration has been trying to evict from the country because of its owners—the World Wardens. It's always strange to encounter in real life the people and objects you first get to know on television. The boat is dull among the luxury vessels at the Manila Yacht Club. Her hulking size and grey hull are ostentatiously incongruent with the sleek white boats around her.

A pair of security guards sit on the dock, back to back on a single monobloc chair. One guard looks out to sea, his expression that of a newly discovered stowaway. The other guard is text-messaging as if he were a war correspondent. A group of street kids, five of them, the eldest probably eight years old, loiters around the gangplank. The smallest is daring the others to board the ship. On the deck, four World Wardens on brightly coloured beach chairs enjoy the break in the rains. They play Monopoly and drink red wine, listening to some sort of world music that's all drums and horns.

The street kids call out to the foreigners. A lanky, balding Caucasian with muttonchops puts down his glass and disappears inside. He resurfaces with an armful of cans of Coca-Cola. Down he goes, the gangplank boinging beneath him. His face is beaming. The children cheer. He passes the Cokes around. The boys put them in their shorts pockets. They begin to pull at the greenie's clothing, tugging at the shemagh scarf wrapped around his neck. The boys' eyes grow bigger and I can hear them sniffling. Their voices are raspy: "Hey, Joe, how 'bout U.S. dollar?" They tug harder at the ends of his shemagh: "Can I have this? Made stateside?" The greenie brushes them off, politely at first, then with increasing panic. The scarf is tightening and his face is turning red.

One of the security guards hisses at the children. "Sssssst! Tama na yan!" he yells, jogging to the gangplank. He holds on to the things on his utility belt so that they don't fall. He slows to a quick walk to make sure. The kids point and laugh. The guard unbuckles the flap on his holster. "Wow, guy," says the World Warden, "that's not necessary, eh?" The other foreigners watch nervously from the prow. The kids flee down the boulevard. The environmentalist is left, scarf dishevelled, one pocket of his cargo shorts pulled out. When the kids are far enough, one turns and does a mocking version of the Mr. Sexy Sexy Dance. He waves his butt toward the security guards and flails his hands above his head. A resounding fart is heard. The kids collapse in laughter. They lounge on the seawall and drink their Cokes. I watch them throw the empty cans at the dead fish rising and falling in the tide.

*

He sits in the bus, watching it all happen. The fish seem like a detail from the places he goes to when he falls asleep. He is distressed about his dreams. Partly for their content, but mostly because he can remember them. Was I better off before, without memory? Have I always had such nightmares?

Last night was the worst. He'd woken up at four in the morning after dreaming of being cuckolded and hanged. When he went back to sleep, he was immediately whisked away again.

He'd been sitting by his window at Trump Tower, overlooking the East River. The hold music on the phone is a song he hasn't heard in a long time. "I'd die for you girl but all they can say is, he's not your kind." Just as he's enjoying it, the music stops and an agent comes on. "Sure, Mister Sigh-joo-chee," the agent says. He corrects the agent: It's See-hoo-coh. The agent says, "Mr. See-joo-cock, I'm more than happy to cancel your account. But let me first ask you a question. Why do you want to stop being one hundred percent safe and protected?" He hangs up on the agent because he realizes he's late. Outside, out of breath, he flags down a taxi. In the backseat, he pulls a photo strip from his pocket, taken in a booth in the Châtelet–Les Halles metro station. He and Madison are sticking their tongues out, or kissing deeply but coyly like silver-screen stars, or making monocles with the fingers of their inverted hands. They had rushed into the booth, giggling. He realizes that they both knew that one day he'd be sitting in the back of a taxi and looking sadly at the photos. The taxi driver watches him studying the pictures. The cabbie is Philip Glass. The composer says into the rearview mirror, "Don't you wish you were relishing first contact with life's offerings, instead of taking snapshots?" He's about to reply when he sees Glass is speaking into the hands-free headset on his cell phone. When he gets to the bar, it is nearly his turn to read. Madison is talking to the guy with the fangs, saying, "I'm reading about Schoenberg and why dissonance is so stressful from the scientific point of view of the eardrum." Fangs says, "Eardrums have points of view?" Madison pulls out a book and says, "Let me read you something . . ." Fangs says, "You know, you're awfully interesting." The MC calls his name and he leaves Madison and Fangs and goes onstage. He reads from his notebook: "At thirty-five, she ran away with a circus geek who actually was a Tuscan count waiting for his nineteenth birthday, the age the oracle had prophesied he would call an army and lead it into a series of clashes against the grandfather who had thrown him as an infant into a pit of impalement and left him for dead, and the count's bloody lost battles before his miraculous victory would birth a new epoch of enlightened peace, re-creating the grandeurs of Rome and the glories of Greece, with she, of course, as queen, her image the people's most loved to the king's most feared, and yet even as monarch, with all her riches and finery, she would lie in her milk bath masturbating to the memory of how they had made love in the curtained carriage drawn by six white horses on the marches between battlefields, he still her beardless Tuscan count, she a dot-commer's daughter from Topeka, Kansas." He finishes reading. He's trembling. His head swims as he walks between the tables. People look at him in alarm, their eyes wide and their mouths like the black holes he saw illustrated in science books as a kid. His old friend Valdes stands up and takes a step toward him. His old friend Clinton holds on to the edge of a table. Sadie throws back a chair while getting up. He sees them watching him fall inexplicably forward. He would be flying, if only he didn't feel so heavy. Everyone stares and points at the table in front of him. Glasses shatter, hesitantly then instantly. A corner of a table strikes his temple. His middle meningeal artery ruptures, causing an epidural hemorrhage. As the blood squeezes his brain, he sees everyone standing over him. Some point, some take photos with their cell phones, some hold their hands over their black-hole mouths. Markus says, "Holy shit, dude, what did you do?" Grapes stands up and says, "You've gone and done it." Madison is where Sadie was sitting and she says, "Now you've ruined everything." Oh my God, he thinks. This isn't a dream. I'm going to die, a simple, everyday death. I didn't make things right.

He awoke. He was crying. His pyjama pants and bed were soaked. He spent the early hours washing the sheet in the bathtub, ashamed of what the chambermaids would think. By the time he was done drying it with the hair dryer, it was time to go see Miss Florentina.

*

Erning and Rocky Isip decide they desperately need a change. They finally squirrel away enough U.S. dollars to return to the Philippines and settle down. Their life's savings are invested in a bubble-tea franchise. Rocky has a baby, whom they name Boy. Still, the couple feel they've so little connecting them, so they have another child, a girl, whom they name Tiny.

Sleep-deprived from caring for the kids, Rocky and Erning fight more than ever. Holding urgently on to the love left between them, they make a pledge to try harder. They spend many cozy nights watching the latest pirated DVDs. They attend Couples for Christ counselling. They forward each other loving and humorous text messages. Nonetheless, they grow relentlessly apart. Even the old joys of walking slowly, hand in hand, in the mall do nothing for them. Since there is no divorce in the Philippines, they file for an annulment and separate.

Erning gets depressed and grows fat. Rocky takes up Tae Bo kick-boxing, loses weight, and dates an event-planner-slash-DJ before abruptly starting a common-law union with a congressman nearly twice her age. Rocky reverts to her maiden name, Bastos, and takes custody of Boy, who becomes a troublesome lad. Erning keeps Tiny, who becomes very religious, the favourite of the nuns at the Assumption.

One day, while out playing golf, poor Erning has a stroke. In the hospital, he is told by his doctor: "Mr. Isip, from now on you can only eat things that can swim." Several weeks pass and Erning doesn't show for his follow-up appointment. The doctor, worried, decides to pass by Erning's house, because, anyway, they are neighbours in Valle Verde. The doctor rings the doorbell and the maid opens the gate.

Maid: "Yes, sir?"

Doctor: "Where is Mr. Isip?"

Maid: "He's in the pool, sir."

Doctor: "Very good! What's he doing?"

Maid: "He's teaching the pig to swim!"

*

I forgot to mention, last night I was feeling a bit crappy about Sadie throwing me out of her car, and I made the mistake of doing a smidge of coke. When I finally passed out, I slept fitfully. At four in the morning, I thought I heard knocking on my door, but it must have been the neighbours screwing. I couldn't get back to sleep for a while. I looked through Crispin's stuff again. Closer scrutiny of a sheaf of photographs underscored this oddity: Crispin tied upon a cross, hands impaled with iron nails, palms open in both supplication and ostentation.

On the reverse of the print was written the name "Sadie Baxter." In the same messy writing, "f/2.8 & 500." Beneath that, the place and date: "March 1994. Pampanga."

In another, a close-up: Crispin's face tilted heavenward, pupils rolled so far back into his head he appears to be contemplating the uncharted surface of his mind.

I woke up this morning with my bed soaked, and that photo still in my hand.

*

My departure from Spain, with Max Oscurio, delivered me to Manila entirely changed. To be precise, I felt no different, but the streets hummed with a new inaudible sound, the acacias hunched more troubled, the stamens of the bougainvillea and gumamela twisted in anticipation. The light was more slothful than on the Continent, perhaps more fecund with possibility, or maybe it was just the humidity that I no longer remembered being so brazen, as if it had been fortified with the centuries of sweat from our nameless brothers and sisters. Maybe that salt of perspiration had become foreign to balikbayans like me. My friends and I in Europe had dubbed ourselves the New Ilustrados—the New Enlightened, taking on the yoke of revolution as our fee for our material advantages.

I had my doubts, of course. If we were following the path of the fathers of the Revolution, could our feet ever reach the proportions of their shoes stretched big by sixty years of history? Like them, we had been ambassadors to and students of the outside world. I arrived in Manila invigorated by my experiences. I had retraced the paseos of General Luna, listened to echoes of the Ramblas where Lopez Jaena and Rizal debated, and taken morning coffee in a sordid café beside which the ilustrados had printed *La Solidaridad*. I hoped I had osmosed the greatness of these men. I arrived, very unsure, for other than Max I was totally alone—the two of us made a pitiful vanguard party—surrounded by family and friends who were still blind.

Almost immediately, Max and I got ourselves into trouble with the authorities. What happened in jail was certainly not pleasant.

—from *Autoplagiarist* (page 1982), by Crispin Salvador

*

Miss Florentina has the world's most perfectly arched eyebrows. "Look at this," she says, pointing to today's *Gazette*. "It's only just the beginning. Can you believe these people?" On the front page, a photographer has used a fish-eye lens to capture Reverend Martin grinning beatifically during a prayer meeting in his cell in Camp Crame. Several police officers, military men, and politicians hold hands in a circle in the cramped quarters. Some are high-ranking Estregan cronies. Grasping Reverend Martin's right hand is Senator Bansamoro, leader of the opposition. Taking his left hand is my grandfather. I recognize him immediately from his thick head of silver hair. The caption beneath reads: "Undying faith, fidelity, and commitment."

Beside it is a smaller article with a photo of riot police arresting protesters in front of the munitions factory of the Philippines First Corporation. A gunboat sits in the Pasig River in a wonderful example of overkill. Amid the higgledy-piggledy of picketers and cops towers a man with long golden hair and sunburns like war paint on his cheeks and nose. He must be seven feet tall. He holds his hands behind his back so that the short cop can reach up and cuff him. The giant bends his knees courteously. His face is raised to the sky. He resembles Saint Sebastian in those old paintings, tied to a stake, seconds before the arrows pierce his chest. The caption says, "'We'll get you yet!'—terrorist environmental group makes threats as they are arrested."

"The appearance of virtue is more important than virtue itself," Miss Florentina says. I'm not sure to which picture she's referring. "Oh yes, I have a letter for you," she continues. "It's here somewhere. I hope." Miss Florentina laughs. It's more of a cackle. On the daybed on which she reclines is a mess of things, like the spilled contents of a bag lady's shopping cart. "Did you hear the latest gossip?" she says. She riffles through the objects around her. "Lakandula sent out the maids but refused to release the Changco child. The couple and their son are the only hostages left. I can't stop following the story. It's amazing. In an instant, Wigberto Lakandula could be national hero or national villain." Miss Florentina's voice is disarmingly vibrant. I am often surprised by people like her. Some internal energy continues in defiance of the decaying body. In the dim light, she seems almost oracular. The darkness gathers in the deep wrinkles of her skin, which sags on her as if she were a child wearing her father's sweater. Her arms are mottled like an old banana. Her hair is long and white.

"*Voilà!*" she says, balancing an envelope on her belly. "But it's the heart of darkness in here." She claps her hands and a lamp lights up. Her eyebrows are tattooed on. "That's better," she says. Miss Florentina is an island in a sea of junk. Books, crumpled letters, TV remote. Lipstick-smeared tissues, contact sheets, transistor radio. Mismatched socks, cordless phone, pad of paper. A ratty wheelchair sits within her reach. For the first time, I notice a disgusting smell. Talcum powder, jasmine, and death. Miss Florentina fishes a letter opener from the jetsam of objects and slices open the envelope.

She squints at its contents through a photographer's loupe tied with hairy twine around her neck. I wait.

"There. That's a nice letter." Miss Florentina claps again. The lamp turns off.

"Can you tell me what it says?"

"It says you want to find Dulcinea. Because you think she has something for you. Because you're searching. Aren't we all? Take, for example, that poor fellow, Mr. Lakandula, searching for justice rarely given. One of the maids he released had a message pinned to her. A manifesto calling for the masses to revolt. Apparently, after that radio report, there were scuffles between police and the crowd. A water cannon was brought in. The pressure was so weak the protesters danced in it. One produced a bar of soap from heavens knows where and applied it to his underarms. Very droll. That's why I still bother with newspapers."

"Miss Florentina, I was . . ."

"Of course one bothers," she says. "Because our days are numbered. I'd like to find out how the story ends." She reminds me of Lena, and of how Crispin could be. Old people act as if they've paid their dues just by living, and can therefore teach you something important. That's why we the young both sometimes listen eagerly and sometimes never visit them. "It will end in tears, I wager," she continues. "It's always the same. One day, they'll smell something odd from this apartment, and all the world's problems will be someone else's. The kids on the list for vacancies in this building will be tickled. You young are held in awe by high ceilings."

"We are," I say.

"I don't know if I should tell you how to find her. She's now free, you know?"

"I'm sorry?"

"Dulcinea."

"I see. You don't think that in the middle of the night, or when she reads her father's name in the papers . . . maybe she wonders?"

"She's out in the world, making it her own. What more can a person ask for? Freedom is the only thing we must demand in life, for all other good things stem from it. I can say this because I well know." She points at her wheelchair. "But that's fine. The world now

comes to me. It tends to when you have something people need."
She laughs. It is discomfiting, almost disingenuous. Miss Florentina
peers at the letter again. She nods and holds it on her lap. Her fingernails are like claws.

She lowers her voice. "I think one of my suitors has been stealing my books. Don't ask me how. Books just go missing. But listen
to me go on."

"What else did the letter—"

"Of course, one must go on! Never rest, lest it catch up. Because
I could not stop for death . . . Though I was never one of those
made frail by that grim obsession. Lena is. Ever since. She simply
stopped trying. Because the afterlife is said to be *so* much better. She
could have done anything with her life. Instead she remained her
daddy's little girl. Constantly pushing his wheelchair wherever he
pointed. How mortified Lena was whenever he'd just stand up, spry
as a teenager. She'd sort of shrink behind him, following with the
empty chair. But I do prefer her gravity to the graceless ones, those
who refer to themselves as 'x-many years young.' Crispin's mother
was like that. Maybe it was the weight of her cancer. We all cope differently. Suddenly these past months I catch myself. I'm ninety-five
years young." She grimaces. "*This* must be purgatory. Though you
don't have to worry yet. Even though we cannot make our sun stand
still, yet we will make him run."

"Marvell. 'To His Coy Mistress.'"

"Very good! I thought kids these days resorted to drink spiking,
not poetry."

"A little of both, I think."

"I like you," she says. "Come live with me and be my love."

"And we will all the pleasures prove."

"Oh, you do remind me of Crispin. He was quite the passionate
shepherd. We used to trade lines of verse in the darkroom. Oh my,
that does sound dirty, doesn't it? He wanted to be a photographer,
but he became a writer, thanks to me."

"Do you think he was killed for his writing?"

"Why do young people enjoy unpleasantries?"

"I was just wondering . . ."

"Do you think it will make people take you more seriously? It doesn't." Miss Florentina looks at the letter again. "I'm sorry, I don't mean to be unpleasant. Tell me, what's it like outside today? I observe the sky through the window, but that's very different. I miss the feel of the first drops of rain. When I'm drawing my last breaths, I want to be wheeled out under the rain and be left there. You know what else I miss dearly? Driving. I used to drive myself everywhere. I had the sweetest little BMW. A 1974 3.0S. Same model as Jacqueline Kennedy Onassis. See, I even know my cars! I sold it to a collector. It became such that I only used it to go to mass. One returns to the Godfulness of youth when the end is in sight. But as soon as I rediscovered the Lord, my legs gave out. As did the building's elevator. The devil, when he makes himself known, always does it subtly. Now I spend my days looking for him in the quiet places. No, that's not true."

"Miss Florentina, did Crispin visit you when he was here last?"

"As long as I engage myself in work, then I'm close to God. Simone Weil, have you read her? She said deep attention is like prayer. I think so is hope. I just had her book somewhere. When Weil was six she refused to eat sugar in solidarity with the soldiers on the front. Children sometimes know best and we chide them for being precocious. Then we grow aged and become again like children, and they call us wise. I did see Crispin the last time he was here. Before his speech at the CCP, that silly little provocateur. He came bearing takeout food from the Aristocrat. When I studied him sitting where you are now, I knew what was eating him. Despite my better judgment, I told him: Go find your Dulcinea. He pretended he was angry, but I knew he was only afraid."

"Of what?" I discreetly take out my notebook and fountain pen.

"Afraid of ruining things. Or change. Altering your life is hard. *I'm* the last person to criticize. But Crispy wasn't free. When you're unhappy with your life, you become more selfish with it."

"Did he want to find her?"

"Of course. Though it was odd. We hardly ever spoke about her. Yet that last time he was here, he asked if I was in touch with her. I told him: Dear, go to her before it's too late. But it was always already too late."

"Then will you help me find her? For him?"

She shakes her head and smiles sadly. With difficulty, Miss Florentina turns to push away the curtain from the window behind her.

Light slants across the room, replacing the shadows with a Victrola in a corner and walls covered with bookshelves, framed photos, paintings by Galicano and Nuyda and Olmeda, and posters of her one-woman shows in Berlin and Barcelona and Buenos Aires. She must find comfort in these repositories of the outside world. Miss Florentina fishes a cigarette from the pocket of her skirt. With steady hands, she lights it.

"Simple pleasures," she says, sighing smoke, "you'll one day conclude, are the most enduring. Listen, child. I adore your persistence. But there are things that are not mine to tell."

We sit quietly. My eyes adjust to the light. Behind her, the sky over Manila Bay remains profoundly white, like a page anticipating your first mark.

"I think," I finally say, "that I understand what Crispin was going through." I don't know why I say this.

"Let's just enjoy our chat and the wine, shall we? You did bring a *bouteille*?"

"I'm sorry? No, I didn't forget. It's only eleven in the morning and I thought—"

"Oh, you haven't changed a bit. Always forgetful."

"Me? I don't understa—"

"What a shame! My two suitors bring me news and nourishment, but my third forgets the wine. You're jealous. Admit it, Crispinito. What do you want from me anyway?"

"Do you want me to go and get a bottle? . . ."

"No! Please don't. Won't you spend the day with me?"

"I'm not sure I—"

"Crispin . . . I mean, I'll tell you all about Crispin. Yes, I'll tell you about Crispin. I taught him the important things, you know? For example, the instant before something comes into focus is more exciting than any sharp certainty. You should write that in your notebook. Photography, child, is about the passing of time. Capturing is the goal of literature. Timelessness is the task of music and painting. But a good photograph holds time just as a vase holds water. The water will evaporate and the vase becomes a memorial to it. What separates a snapshot from a masterpiece is that the latter is a metaphor for patience . . ."

"Yes, but—"

"What *is* your hurry, child?"

"It's really important that I find Dulcinea."

"Can't you just have lunch with me? You'll stay, won't you? Let me see, what else can I entice you with? Crispin died, you know, not because the art left him, but because he gave up on love. Sounds like a romance novel, doesn't it? Angry men have little to live for when their rage becomes ineffective. But how they thrive otherwise."

"So do you think Dulcinea had anything to do with his suicide?"

"You were dead long before you left this world."

"Miss Florentina, I'm not—"

"I mean *he* . . . Oh, I don't know what I mean. What were we saying?" She looks flustered, suddenly withered and bent. Then she smiles. Her eyes spark with shrewdness. The cigarette smoke and that stench from her daybed make me nauseous.

"Tell me, child. Why do you need to find her?" She looks at me carefully. "Do you even know why?"

"I do." I match her gaze. "Yes. I want to ask her what her father should have done."

"Why?"

"Because I think it's important to know."

"It has nothing to do with that infernal book of his?"

"I'm only doing this for Crispin."

Miss Florentina pauses, inhales the silence. A bird flies in the sky behind her—the first sign of natural life I've seen since arriving. It hovers on a current of air, black like a letter on a new page—an *m*. Miss Florentina smiles with painful sadness. "Okay, child," she says. "I'll tell you where." Actually, her smile looks triumphant.

"You will?"

"I believe in you. She lives near the Lingayen Gulf. On one of the Hundred Islands. One of the most beautiful places. Have you ever been?"

"I don't remember it. My grandparents brought me when I was in high school. That's where my parents died and there's a memorial. A big steel sculpture in the forest. An angel with broken wings."

"All the more reason to go."

"Thank you." I realize I'm almost crying.

Miss Florentina nods and smiles. "There is a figure in the *Spoliarium* that I think you should see. A woman in the background, just standing there. Wearing a red cloak half wrapped around her face. The way she looks, it's as if Juan Luna knew Dulcinea when he painted her."

"Thank you."

Miss Florentina digs through the junk around her and produces a little pad.

"Now where are my pencils?" she says.

"I have a pen." I pass it to her.

"I remember this," she says, looking at the Parker. She writes on the pad, like a doctor making a prescription. "Now I have a question for you, Miguel," she says. "Why do you think Crispin didn't seek out his child?"

"He was afraid."

"I think it was more than that. Forgive this analogy, but I'm an old shutterbug. Sometimes one waits too long for the perfect moment before snapping the picture. You never realize that all you needed was to change perspective. That was it. Crispy mistook moving away for moving forward. He lived abroad, thinking it would let him write more honestly. He told me once that he wanted to make himself the best man he could be so that Dulcinea would want to find him. Look what happened."

"What about the mother?"

"What matters is the child. She has her whole life ahead of her." Miss Florentina stares at me purposefully.

"What do you know about *The Bridges Ablaze*?"

"Forget that. Go find your Dulcinea." From her pad, she rips out a page, folds it, and hands it over.

"What about the book?"

"You said it had nothing to do with this." She looks displeased.

"I'm sorry. I just don't know who else to see. I'm supposed to see the critic Avellaneda. But I'm sure that will all be . . . you know. You're the last person who can—"

"Crispin, stop it, child. You never change. Forget our lunch. Just go."

"Just one more question . . ."

"God so commanded and left that command sole daughter of his voice . . ." She turns to me, her back straight, her face challenging. Her smile very self-satisfied. "Your turn."

"I don't understand."

"Hello? Crispinito? *Paradise Lost*?"

"Yes, but—"

"John Milton. Oh, child, you're inutile. What is it? 'Sole daughter of his voice; the rest, we live law to ourselves; our reason is our law.'"

*

"If you believe it, then it can happen," Kap said, his face shrouded in the smoke from his cigar. Dulcé breathed deeply the scent of cloves and lemons. She swung her legs and tried not to look down from the branch. But she couldn't help being scared. From that height, the ground seemed miles away. "Just believe," Kap said, "not that you'll fly, but that you're lighter than air. You may not get it right the first time, or even the second time. But I promise I will catch you." Kap looked at her earnestly.

Dulcé studied him skeptically. Kap wasn't joking.

Kap certainly was impressive enough to inspire confidence, with his huge, muscular black body and his eyes that glowed like magic rubies. And Dulcé had always admired his facility with the branches. In fact, she'd only seen Kap walk on the ground once, because kapres don't leave their trees. Ever. That one time Kap saved her from the neighbour's Rottweiler, Miriam, had been the single exception. And boy, did Kap look awkward, even frightened, even if it was just a sidewalk. It was a deed so uncharacteristic of the kapre race that after Kap swept Dulcé off the ground with a single hand and placed her on the highest branch, after Kap growled at Miriam and sent the dog squealing, after all that, Kap climbed up bashfully and begged Dulcé not to tell anyone. Ever. Kap told Dulcé that he'd know if she betrayed him, because he'd feel it ripple through the airwaves. He'd explained that things like betrayals, lies, even unkind thoughts, send off a shock wave that only those with very sensitive ears and attuned hearts can hear, though every being on earth can feel it, somewhere inside them, even if they don't know it.

So Dulcé trusted him. Kap was her friend and wouldn't let her down. Dulcé took a deep breath and did as she was told. She jumped off the branch. She willed herself to stop falling. It didn't work. The ground closed in. She willed herself harder. The earth was fast approaching. She willed herself hardest. Dulcé felt Kap's huge hand around her waist, pulling her slowly and ever so gently so that the tips of her feet touched the ground as easily as if she had just stepped out of bed.

"We'll try again," Kap said, patiently. "Learning to fly is very difficult indeed."

—from *Ay Naku!*, Book Three of Crispin Salvador's *Kaputol* trilogy

*

The 1960s proved to be a hard decade for Salvador. After his return from Europe, following the bitter falling-out with Oscurio over which would suit their country better, Maoism or Trotskyism, Salvador met Petra Chingson, a University of the Philippines political science student. This was to his parents' chagrin, for she was well known as an activist opposed to foreign involvement in the country. Their disdain for his relationship with Petra, combined with Salvador's disgust at Junior's opposition to President Macapagal's Land Reform Code, pushed the young man to cut ties with his parents for the first of what would be many times in his life. Salvador moved into a one-room apartment above an Ermita noodle house, where he lived penuriously but joyfully with Petra, though gossips talked constantly of how the couple was living in sin.

The effect Petra had on Salvador became evident. As a cub reporter for *The Philippine Gazette*, his stories took on a decided bias. On January 22, 1965, Salvador covered the siege of the Philippine Central Bank building. On March 22 of the same year, he fearlessly reported on the Stonehill government scandal, exposing the Chicago businessman Harry Stonehill and his so-called black book, which listed all the Philippine politicians in his pocket (in *Autoplagiarist*, Salvador writes that his father asked him not to pursue the investigation, lest it implicate the Macapagal administration). Salvador, working for the first time with the young journalist Marcel Avellaneda, won acclaim for the best reportage on the elections in the following months, in which President Macapagal was defeated by the young Ferdinand E. Marcos. Their essay, "The Real Macoy," supporting the new president, is an example of youthful optimism that history would prove overeager.

Salvador hit his stride in 1966. His dispatches on the Culatingan Massacre of farmers by military and police garnered much praise, though for the first time the label of "communist sympathizer" was mentioned, with his detractors quick to cite his uncle Jason's involvement with the Huks as a preclusion to his journalistic objectivity. Later that year, Salvador also reported on the Manila Summit on the Vietnam conflict, and was one of the reporters who broke the news that behind closed doors, U.S. president Lyndon Johnson had bullied leaders and representatives of member countries South Vietnam, Thailand, Australia, New Zealand, South Korea, and the Philippines. Salvador's ballsy coverage resulted in his dismissal from the staff of the *Gazette*. In December, with Avellaneda, photographer Miggy Jones-Matute, poet Mutya Dimatahimik, and cineaste Danilo de Borja, he cofounded the Cinco Bravos, launching what would be one of the most influential artist collectives in the country's history.

In January 1967, Salvador's beloved Petra disappeared while on her way to an anti-U.S. rally outside Clark Airfield. Various rumours abounded, blaming Marcos, Macapagal, American soldiers, the communists, and random brigands for her disappearance. Her battered body was eventually found, its hands missing, but Salvador could not bring himself to identify it. He left their home above the noodle shop, unable to return even to pack his belongings, and moved into the home of his two best friends, Dimatahimik and Avellaneda.

—from the biography in progress, *Crispin Salvador:
Eight Lives Lived*, by Miguel Syjuco

*

On the way to the National Museum, the downpour makes me feel like Chicken Little. I'm soaked, it's farther than I thought, and my insoles are starting to really hurt my feet for some reason. I dash from the shelter of one tree to another. A woman with a black garbage bag on her head passes, staring at me. She's wearing a green surgical mask. I race to the next tree. These are strangler figs. Their branches drop long tendrils into the broken sidewalk. The bark looks like the flesh of wax figures. In curves and hollows, shadows pool like water. I see the faces of kapres, of dwendes, of tianaks. I blink. They are gone.

Up the museum stairs I go, dripping and wet. People look. Two security guards eye me suspiciously. A group of schoolchildren are trying not to point. A man and a woman holding hands by the bag check tighten their grip on each other. They are both wearing surgical masks.

Up the winding wooden stairs to the second level. Signs direct me. I stop by the bathroom to do a bump of coke off my key. I do another, and feel better. I haven't been sleeping well. In the viewing room, tourists take turns reading a notice: Juan Luna's *obra maestra* is "currently unavailable to the public during restoration."

On the big blank wall, the curators have provided a concise history of the painting's creation, significance, and ongoing resurrection, as well as a small facsimile. It's the same size as the print that hung in Crispin's office.

I study the tableau.

In a chamber beneath a coliseum, two corpses of gladiators are dragged across the flagstones by bare-chested servants, who are angled forty-five degrees to the ground from the effort. In the darkness, a pile awaits these still-warm bodies. A heap of dented helmets and armour sits in a corner. A grey-haired man bends over, bony back exposed, sharpening something, presumably a blade, on a stone that sparks. A young woman collapses, exhausted, on the floor. Her pose echoes that of the old man, though her bedraggled hair over her face and her robe slipped from her shoulder attest to a sudden buckling from either overwhelming hopelessness or a seizure of grief. Because the woman sits in the foreground, within the light, she is, in her robes of white and greenish blue, the brightest figure in the painting—a beacon of despair.

I wonder if the painting haunts its restorers.

On the left side of the image, an elderly couple, thin and breakable, hold each other's arms and stare, faces shattered, at a corpse being pulled by a rope looped around his wrist, his head lolling backward, his lifeless body just moments ago godlike with youth. Beside them, a man is being pushed aside by a servant dragging yet another corpse as if it were trash for Monday morning pickup. The man being shoved has recoiled in terror, at once stepping back while his head moves down in recognition and disbelief.

Inch by inch, figure by figure, the restorers must go mad.

Behind these figures, a dim stairway is crowded with innumerable faces, some merely curious, others expectant. The ways they fight their own expressions remind me of the famous mirror in the Van Eyck painting of the Arnolfini marriage: what is reflected is the key to what is really happening.

These are the faces that must follow the restorers home. Appearing in the dim jeepneys on the dark streets, or in the steam of the rice boiling for dinner, or in the void behind closed eyes before sleep comes.

Then I spot her face in the crowd: the woman in the red robe. Her garment is hooded around her head to cover her mouth. She seems to stare at me. Expressionless or serene. Waiting. Hiding or defiant. Patient. The only thing I'm certain of is that she possesses an answer.

*

INTERVIEWER:
Then what do you think must, or can, be done?

CS:
Activism, revolution, violence, even death, will be acceptable, if we are expected to condone the government's neglect and oppression of the people. Because every action will eventually have an equal and opposite reaction. It is a moral balance. Of course, I speak from a country whose systems were imported from other nations. So what is sacrosanct here [in the United States] is not necessarily so where I come from. We're told to trust in the abstract absolutes of faith, politically and religiously. Good in theory. But an abstract like truth is always incomplete truth. Freedom would be wonderful if it was available to all. And democracy is but an experimental system complete with its flaws. Capitalism is the most suspect of these abstracts, made absolute only because of its stamina. Since when has a system of private vice made for public virtue? A lack of options should never force the acceptance of one particular option. Humanity should be more imaginative, more responsible, than that.

INTERVIEWER:

But you yourself came from a privileged background. Some say you are a traitor to your kind.

CS:

Traitor to my class, but faithful to a broad humanity. Ugh, I sound falsely heroic. But heroism and sainthood aren't lofty things. They're usually formed out of self-disgust, opportunism, sublimated fears—which we recognize in ourselves and therefore see, emphasized, in others. When who you are includes what you hate, you carry around your neck a daily reminder of what must be changed in the world. Every good is married to the threat of something bad. Our current president, Corazon Aquino, however saintly she may seem, is married to the threat of what preceded her, the Marcos dictatorship. To exist in the good alone is to suffer from self-delusion and self-righteousness. Concupiscence is part of who we are. Orwell said of Gandhi that saints should be presumed guilty until proven innocent. Just because I was presumed guilty by my countrymen doesn't mean I was or am or will ever be a saint. But it says much about those who make such accusations.

—from a 1988 interview in *The Paris Review*

*

Our naive protagonist runs through the rain, from museum to tree, from tree to bus station. Dripping wet, he takes his notebook from his backpack. Unscrews his pen and curls over the page. The boy writes.

For *Eight Lives Lived*: Salvador once wrote of it as a . . .

He slows. Watches the black ink flow from the nib of the Parker Vacumatic. It's like a river through snow, he thinks. Like necromancy. The words run across the page.

. . . metaphor for the condition of the Philippines under Imperial Spain. The *Spoliarium* is considered a paragon . . .

The boy pauses. He crosses out "paragon."

. . . a sine qua non . . .

He stops, thinks. Reminds himself to check whether he's using the phrase correctly. Resumes.

. . . of Philippineness, though most Filipinos, including myself, have not seen it in person, with it either in Spanish custody or hidden away in our own National Museum . . .

Sculptural letters land in quick succession, the blur of type bars, an old pair of veinous hands move, like a conjurer's, over the keys, the carriage reaches its limit. A bell sounds.

. . . Indeed, the *Spoliarium* is an icon whose inscrutability most Filipinos do not care for or truly understand. Its success is its insolence: the thirteen-by-twenty-two-foot painting won the gold medal in the 1884 Exposición Nacional de Bellas Artes in Madrid, beating the Spaniards at their own game—they who considered us indios and savages . . .

The ink flow lessens and he shakes his pen. It runs smoothly again.

. . . This morbid view of the depths of a lost civilization is our great keeping-up-with-the-Joneses. In this—its historicity, its infamy, the blank wall where it should be hanging, the blurry facsimile and ungrammatical accompanying blurb—within these, in toto, one sees the allegory for the current state of Salvador's nation. Yet in its centre, there stands a quiet figure that may have been of profound meaning to the Panther in exile.

A bell sounds again. The letters continue their staccato pace and on the page appears an asterisk.

*

I hop on a bus heading toward the Lupas Place Mall. I want to find an Internet café to check my e-mail before meeting with Avellaneda. My spam box has been filled with crap and I still haven't received an answer from crispin1037@elsalvador.gob.sv.

The bus is crowded and smells like soggy trouser hems. A pudgy young man holds a handkerchief over his mouth and nose and stares at his high-tech cell phone. It goes *boing-boing*. He presses a button and the screen lights up. The man starts making squeaking noises, bubbles over, and shouts: "Hoy! Listen to this!" He reads from his phone. "Breaking news. Arrests at Lakandula siege. Be the good Lord's vessels for change and stand with brothers and sisters. Tune to AM stations for unfolding events." Somebody calls out, "A radio, who has a radio?" We all turn to the bus driver, who shrugs and points at a brand-new six-disc CD changer duct-taped to the dashboard. The pudgy young man holds up his phone like the Statue of Liberty. It's switched to speaker and a radio commentator says something about the Changco couple. Passengers shush each other until the bus is so filled with shushes that nobody can hear the radio.

Finally, silence, and the reporter's tinny baritone rings loudly: ". . . crowd erupted after a young woman ran in front of the battering ram and was the third person forcibly detained by authorities. During the commotion, shots were heard from within the house. We are awaiting word of any casualties. It is believed Mr. Lakandula still controls the hostages. Police have done their best to calm the crowd. In other news, the Chinese influenza continu—"

The passengers moan in unison and a woman begins to cry hysterically: "My God, my Jesus, my Mary, have pity on poor Wigbertito!" An old office worker in a Christmas-themed Bart Simpson necktie pats her shoulders. A meticulously dressed man shouts: "But he's so handsome!" Another fellow up front tells the driver to let him off at the curb. Five others stand to join him. One raises his arms and cries: "Free Lakandula!" The whole bus cheers as the six of them run into the storm, their hands placed atop their heads in utter futility.

*

When Boy Bastos was still a sperm in Erning's testicle, he was already precocious. One day, he tells his fellow sperms to get ready because he feels the current moving them forward. Boy Bastos, being Boy Bastos, leads the pack. As he is about to shoot forth from Erning's shaft, he shouts, "Go back, go back, it's only tonsils!" The next day, he feels the current moving again and leads the pack once more, this time imbued with an exuberant sense of purpose. At the last instant, he shouts again, "Go back, go back! It's only condom!" The following day, the current flows, and Boy swims forward with temerity, convinced this must be his time to fly forth. Suddenly, he turns back, shouting desperately, "Go back, go back! It's shit!"

*

Overheard on the bus:
   "Pare, have you heard the latest news?"
   "Jellyfish ate Vita Nova?"
   "No! Nuredin Bansamoro met with President Estregan."

"Are you kidding? They're sworn nemeses."

"Well, Bansamoro says to him: Mr. President, please accept this Mercedes-Benz as a peace offering. I hope you'll make me your vice president in the coming election."

"And?"

"Estregan says: Sorry, I don't accept bribes."

"No way!"

"And Senator Bansamoro says: Okay. Then I'll just sell it to you for one peso."

"Wait! Wait! I can guess the punch line! Estregan tells Bansamoro: Fine. At that price, I'll take two!"

*

Thanks for the e-mails guys. Things are well, though lots of rain, and the Christmas season's made the traffic nightmarish. I'm safe and sound, so quit worrying about the bombings. Thanks, Charlotte, for cc'ing everyone re the advice about my feet. I'm pretty sure it has something to do with my insoles getting wet. I appreciate your suggestion, but I can't believe peeing on my feet in the shower will make them smell better. I'll let you know how that goes. (This better not be a prank!)

Honestly, I don't give a sheezy about what's going on with Grapes. It figures that he would get caught up in something like this Philippines First crap. (BTW, did you see his picture with Reverend Martin?) His link to PhilFirst isn't in the papers yet (bet he's paying a shedload to keep it out), but we all know his allegiance with Dinkdong Changco runs deep—PhilFirstCorp's biggest factory is in his province, for pete's sake. Yeah, I know politics shouldn't surprise me. But sometimes I still hope—sometimes when I write about a grandfather (or any father figure) based on Grapes and his crazy ways, I try, for the sake of creating a three-dimensional character, to see things his way. I see him as a patriarch who funded his children and their children (sure, sometimes grudgingly) in anything they wanted to study, become, and do. I see the man whom I played with when I was a child, who was proud of me and wanted the best for me (despite all our differences, *that* was never in doubt). I see someone who, no matter what we did, took us back in the end (sure, he screamed, of course he screamed). I see a man who had big dreams but failed in most through his own hubris. I find myself crying when I write those fictitious father figures into life on the page, and yet I've never been able to allow myself to cry for Grapes. And when I'm done writing, I'm surprised I feel compassion for him, and yes, even sympathy.

Sorry I'm rambling. Thing is, while I try to disconnect myself (as I have), while I try to forget that fight in the hotel room when they kicked me out, and forget my hate, and turn it into empowering disinterest, I find that what returns with the sympathy is this odd feeling of hope. I try to disconnect myself, but I know that when I one day earn my PhD, instead of being proud (though he'll say he is), he'll instead remark: "Oh, I have four," even if they are all *honoris causa* from provincial schools. I know that when I write my book, instead of being proud of my years of hard work (though he'll say he is), he'll remark: "Oh, I've written five," even if someone ghostwrote them and public funds were used to publish them. I know that it's not a competition—and if it was, I'd win by default by simply not caring. And so I try not to care. How can someone *try* not to care?

I'd rather see our grandfather fail with dignity than succeed with such toadying. My view of politics and the opportunities he extended to me would be very different had he ever made a public stand for something nobler than his vested interest and good intentions. Seeing him dragged into this PhilFirst stuff, seeing him drag Granma into politics by making her take over the governorship when none of us wanted it, seeing him drag our good name through the mud by allying one year with Estregan and Changco and the next year with Reverend Martin and Bansamoro, or whoever the revolving door has connected him with over the decades— it all makes me doubt him even more. I think his helping the country is just a way to satisfy his own view of self (Is a selfless act ever unselfish? Can a selfish man never be selfless?). Sure, he's rich enough not to steal, so Granma says. But still. Once, Grapes was a just man of promise. Now, he's just a man of compromise.

No, Mario, I can't, as you say, "fix things for the sake of peace." I don't want to be a hypocrite. (Though, of course, there's our guilt that his failure stems from all those years exiled abroad as he raised us.) I have sympathy, and therefore I have sadness. But what will happen to him when all this PhilFirstCorp business blows up? Probably not a thing. The thing is, *we'll* know about the stands he didn't take.

I'm sorry for this rant. But you guys asked how things are going.

—e-mail from me to my siblings, December 7, 2002

*

The balimbing, known in Spanish as the *carambola* and in English as the star fruit, is a grass green to straw yellow fruit with almost luminescent, rubbery flesh. Growing to about four inches long, it has five longitudinal angular lobes and, when sliced, its pieces form perfect star shapes. The fruit tastes tart and clean and contains iron, vitamins B and C, oxalate, and potassium. A poultice of its leaves is often used to treat ringworm, while a tea of its seeds is a tonic for asthma and intestinal gas. Due to the fruit's many sides, or faces, the term "balimbing" is often used disparagingly to refer to politicians and traitors, though in my mind it can also refer to the versatile, Janus-like character of the Filipino. While our national fruit is officially the mango, arbitrarily mandated by the Americans during their occupation, it is not a long bow to draw to propose the balimbing as the country's unofficial fruit, due to its metaphoric significance.

—from *My Philippine Islands (with 80 colour plates)*, by Crispin Salvador

*

INTERVIEWER:

You've written about regret. It seems to be a touchstone for you. What is your biggest regret?

CS:

What a question! The deepest regrets are the most personal. If I haven't sufficiently shared it via my writing, then maybe it should remain unspoken.

INTERVIEWER:

There must be something you wish you could have done better.

CS:

Fine. Perhaps speaking of it here will help absolve me. My father had an opponent—a nemesis—Respeto Reyes. A good man, it turns out. Very influential, except his uncompromising morals made his political career difficult. If he had not been such a good man he would have become president. Such is our country. But when I started my career as a journalist—this was shortly after I left my parents' home, 1964 I think—part of me wanted to please my father still. You see, it had always been Junior Salvador versus Respeto Reyes, an ongoing Thrilla in Manila. And don't we spend our lives trying to please our parents, even when we're trying to stick it to them? My father raised me to hate his enemies. My first writing job was helping my father with his speeches. We used all sorts of dirty tricks. Insinuated Reyes's homosexuality, which was something completely unfounded. Purported that since Reyes had never been linked to any shadiness or wrongdoing, then he must be particularly vile, better at hiding his own dirt than anyone else. You see the skewed logic, no? Even after I left home, I *still* wrote articles against Reyes. For example, when he was imprisoned and tortured by Marcos in the seventies, I wrote that sometimes even a bad dictator has a good day. I just couldn't understand. Couldn't see, for decades, what a statesman Reyes was proving to be. I tell you, even when you hate your parents, you still end up defending them to the end. It's a hopeful act more than it is dutiful or conciliatory. The truth is that the disappointment you feel toward your parents testifies to the excess of faith you always had in them.

Alas, I've never been able to rectify my actions against Reyes. That is the one and only thing I've ever truly regretted in my life.

—from a 1988 interview in *The Paris Review*

*

My final meeting is in fifteen minutes. Then all that's left is to seek out Dulcinea.

This interview with Marcel Avellaneda may be a scoop. Nobody's ever said what sparked his animosity toward Crispin. They feuded as only former best friends can.

I took the wrong jeepney to the theatre and had to walk. After wandering the labyrinthine streets, my feet really starting to kill me, I found the theatre. First I saw its spires and pinnacles, and then its facade, pink and white like a seashell amid the gray flotsam of buildings. I couldn't get in, its birds-of-paradise grillwork was shut tight. Finally, I found a gate with a rusted lock that opened.

I turn on my cell phone to use as a flashlight.

Inside the lobby, it is like stepping into sepia, with sunlight filtering through stained-glass windows and lingering on the soaring ceiling and Art Deco embellishments. But exposed wiring hangs where fixtures should be, and debris is piled high enough to block entrances to rooms that may well never be visited again. A strange place for a meeting. Thick dust has gathered like snow on the black skin of a reclining statue. I hear something beyond some double doors. An old man's voice.

I go quietly into the main performance hall. In the darkness, the doorways to the lobby are like obelisks of light. Their reach is just enough to frost the proscenium arch with grey. My cell phone, no brighter than a candle, gives the room a sanctified atmosphere more befitting a memorial. A set of footprints in the dust leads to the front of the room. I follow them and stand before the famous arch, the inspiration for Crispin's Palanca Award–winning short story, "One-Act Play." Taking off from the work of Alain Robbe-Grillet, the piece is about a murder committed on this stage and the innumerable possibilities of how the scene could have played out. Framing the drama is Crispin's description of the setting. I've always remembered: "1001 scenes by 1001 woodcarvers, each instructed to succumb to his imagination and recall the stories of his youth. The result is a soaring frieze filled with unobtainable young women, every variety of native fruit, nationalistic flags, a stallion pulling an ornate kalesa, the epic battle in which Lapu Lapu slew Magellan, the two tablets of the Ten Commandments, the flora and fauna of the islands, upheld fists, churches, Intramuros, chubby-bubby sons and roly-poly daughters, Andres Bonifacio leading a revolutionary charge, a roast suckling pig with an apple in its mouth, Jesus on the cross, a woman planting rice in a polished paddy, a crescent moon embracing a single star, a giant spoon and fork, so many other et ceteras and et ceteras."

Fiction, however, sometimes ensures disappointment with reality. The arch only sports carvings of the four Muses—Poetry, Music, Tragedy, Comedy—nothing more. The sobriety of fact. Here, too, was where Crispin had his short run for his disco opera, *All Around the World*. I've seen photos of opening night—the set a stylized deck of Magellan's frigate, the *Victoria*; singing conquistadors in tight polyester pants dangling from the rigging; a disco ball representing the moon in the sky behind the mizzenmast.

I get onto the stage and wait for Avellaneda. The doorways dim. Something rustles among the debris. I call out his name. Dr. Avellaneda! My voice echoes into voices. Like someone's watching. I call his name again.

What was that?

The four faces stare at me. Tragedy and Comedy in equal measure, while Poetry and Music seem indifferent, caught up in themselves.

I don't think Avellaneda's coming.

Nothing—not the years, not Salvador's death—ever seems to satiate the anger. I wait longer than I should. He said he was going to show me what Crispin did. When the darkness is complete, I go my own way.

8

There are only three truths. That which can be known. That which can never be known. The third, which concerns the writer alone, truly is neither of these.

—from the 1987 essay "Crucifictions," by Crispin Salvador

*

Boy Bastos is four years old and quite the talker. Because of his parents' broken marriage, he's a constant source of aggravation to his mother, though she's pleased he's finally taken to calling her lover, the congressman, "Papa." One day Boy sees his mother dressing.

"Mama, what are those things on your chest?"

"Those are my life preservers for swimming."

"Great! Since I can't swim, can I have them for the pool?"

"No, Boy. I need them."

Then, referring to his pretty nanny, Boy asks: "Then can I use my yaya's?"

His mother replies scornfully: "No, son, hers have no air in them."

"But how can that be?" says Boy. "Last night while you were at mahjong I saw Papa blowing them up!"

*

I have dinner near the theatre at a canteen called Beery Good. Rice cakes, a bowl of blood stew, and a can of Sarsi from a dour lady who stands fanning a charcoal grill. You can smell the skewers of assorted things slowly roasting. I'm trying to reach Avellaneda on my cell phone but he's not picking up. The TV in the corner is too loud anyway.

The only patrons are me and a pair of cops. A variety show is on, hosted by a gorgeous Filipina-American actress with a whining Californian accent. She tries speaking Taglish but it's really much less Tagalog than it is English. She mixes up her verb tenses.

Four members of the studio audience are competing to see who can drink the most shot glasses of Datu Puti vinegar. Their faces are contorted and the crowd is laughing. Finally, all but one gives up and she—Queenie, a middle-aged canteen cook from Barangay Quijote, Quezon City—is given the choice between a cash prize of up to ten thousand pesos (three months' salary) or the mystery reward inside the bayong, a woven bag for market produce or the transport of fighting cocks.

The dour lady comes and stands beside me to watch. She clasps her hands and shakes them like she's about to throw dice. I'm worried she'll grab my arm. Queenie chooses the bayong. Camera zooms onto her lips. She's praying. She opens the bag. Pulls out a lollipop. The crowd squeals in delight. Queenie, holding back tears, smiles gamely.

The dour lady wails. "Jesusmariajosep!" She storms into the kitchen. Plates are banged. Her outburst has twisted the cops around. They look at me. One has a hungry face and squints while finishing his Red Horse beer. Bottles litter their table like spent shell casings or illegitimate children. The other cop, dark and movie-star handsome, is contorting his mouth, trying to free with his tongue bits of food from between his gums and cheek.

Cold sweat trickles down my sides.

The gaunt one stands. Stretches. Adjusts his gun belt. He approaches. His smile is strange, as if designed to show off his gold tooth. He stands above me as I look at my food. "Sir," he says, "do you mind?" He speaks with a fake American accent. "Can we change the channel?" He points with his lips at the television. I nod and smile. He smiles back. "You should be getting home," he says. "Something bad is going to happen tonight." He adjusts his gun belt and looks out at the sky.

The channel is switched to a popular news show. A talking head complains: "It's environmental terrorism. Green imperialism." He is a bald man with huge eyeglasses. "How are they so concerned with the habitats of fish, when people—people!—in this country can't afford regular meals? Imagine how poor this nation would be without the leadership of the PhilFirst Corporation! These foreigners should be tried under the laws of *our* country. Instead, they are confined to their ship. Drinking wine and playing games! Is that justice?"

A woman with frizzy hair replies: "What about extradition treaties?"

The man shakes his head. "Inapplicable! In fact, my client is launching an investigation for the public's interest and safety, and will prosecute these so-called World Wardens to the furthest extent possible. That is what laws are for."

*

It had been a long time since she'd done it. Dulcé wondered if she believed enough anymore. All those times before, she was younger. Now, she even *felt* older. The difference between eleven and fifteen is huge, nearly a third of her life! It seemed that with every year the colours of the world faded little by little. Besides, Kap wouldn't be there to catch her.

Dulcé did remember the laws of magic, but she'd also been taught the laws of physics in school. Those were immutable laws. Gravity would always be gravity. But maybe, if one believed enough, one could slow it. Control her fall. Because falling, if you live in the moment, is really just flying, at least until you reach the ground. That's what Kap always said. So what was Dulcé so afraid of? It was just an act of will. Like getting up to go to school when you're too sleepy.

As she'd done so many times with Kap, Dulcé stepped off the branch. She believed she hadn't outgrown the things that mattered. She believed she could be lighter than air again. She believed she wouldn't fall. She believed.

Dulcé fell. She slowed. She sank, gently, like a feather, downward. She reached the ground. The soles of her feet on the soil finally took all of her weight, yet Dulcé felt strangely lighter than she'd ever been. She looked at her shoes. Yes, they were firmly planted on the ground. But she felt like a brand-new person.

The stars above shone as if they were applauding.

—from *Ay Naku!*, Book Three of Crispin Salvador's *Kaputol* trilogy

*

On the way back to the hotel, my taxi is stopped at a roadblock. The elderly driver, shaking visibly, rolls down his window. He tugs and twirls the long hairs growing from a mole on his cheek. A soldier, water pouring off his shiny green raincoat, bends to shine a flashlight in our faces. He's wearing a painter's mask over his mouth and nose. "Licence please." He and the driver exchange quiet words. The soldier goes to the back, knocks on the trunk. It clicks open. The driver turns to smile at me. "It's nothing," he says. "They search taxis tonight. One exploded today near Malacañang Palace." The soldier bangs the trunk shut. Returns.

"Your spare tire is bald," he says. He bends to look at us, his face lacquered with rain.

"If I needed it, it would work," says the driver. "I can't afford a new one."

"I'll have to issue you a ticket and confiscate your licence."

"Can I pay the penalty now?"

"You can instead."

"How much?"

"One hundred pesos."

I pipe up from the backseat: "Are you authorized to be giving traffic tickets?"

"Two hundred pesos," the soldier says, not looking at me.

I roll down my own window. "What division do you belong to? I'm going to report you to—"

"Four hundred pesos." The soldier stares at me.

"Okay, okay!" the driver says, pushing four bills into the soldier's hand.

The soldier returns the licence and motions us through with a swing of his flashlight beam. The driver sighs, his wipers squeaking in reply. He glares at me through the rearview mirror and he resumes stroking the hairs on his mole. I tell him I'll pay. He nods. Tries to smile. "It used to be bribes were fixed," he says. "Fifty pesos, enough for dinner. Very reasonable. Now, it's different."

I turn around to see the glow of the roadblock receding. The taxi has a sticker on its back window. The lights behind us outline black letters on a white field. From inside, it reads ¡FREE LAKANDULA!.

*

A sensational trial found three impoverished farmers guilty of Petra's murder and sentenced them to death. Salvador, convinced the accused were scapegoats, took to the hills. By all accounts, his state of mind at the time was unstable, though his autobiography says he moved with clarity of purpose.

On the evening of December 7, 1967, Salvador packed a rucksack and travelled by jeepney, two buses, tricycle, and finally by foot to a small town at the foot of Mount Banahaw, the mystical volcano renowned for its pilgrimage sites. There, Salvador met Ka Arsenio, the man his comrade in the city said would lead him to the NPA encampments in the mountains beyond. Ka Arsenio barely spoke to Salvador as they hiked. According to Salvador's recollection, "My strange guide could have slit my throat as I slept, or disappeared before I awakened, that is how much he seemed to despise me. And yet, the following morning, there he'd be, boiling water over the campfire for our coffee. During our wordless three-day journey, I never thought he would eventually become my mentor and best friend."

—from the biography in progress, *Crispin Salvador: Eight Lives Lived*, by Miguel Syjuco

*

Consider the rebel I once knew who threw down his arms and took up residence in a remote cave. His thoughts, chromed with the ugliness he'd seen in life, lead his slow evolution into a Bodhisattva. Word gets around of his wisdom. His family, his childhood chums, his former comrades-in-arms, all make a pilgrimage to seek his advice. They are shocked by the things he says. They leave, neglecting his nuggets of wisdom, because they consider his hair shirt, his ascetic mien, his aphorisms, pretentious.

—from the 1988 essay *Tao (People)*, by Crispin Salvador

*

December 7, 2002. Saturday night. I've spent a week in planes, in taxis, in strange dreams and conversations. Tonight's the first night

I actually feel good. Awesome even. As I was finishing my blood stew, Sadie texted to apologize for leaving me in the rain. She promised to make it up to me. I took a nap in the hotel and arrived at the club fresh—showered, nose powdered, and grooving with the certainty of the next step: I know where Dulcinea is.

Tonight, though, I'm free of all that. Tonight, in my pocket, is a throbbing virgin gram. Tonight, even the music is perfect. It's Oknard5 on the deck, in town from NYC for the holidays. He's sampling from electro classics, weaving a tapestry all his own. The crowd is loving it.

And there she is. Sexy Sadie, through the smoke of the dance floor, revealed by the parting crowd. She's leaning up against the bar across the way, elbows propped behind her lackadaisically. She looks at me looking at her. She is hidden by dancing bodies and disco lights flashing red, then blue, then darkness, then green, then orange. The revelers shift and she's revealed again, her gaze unbroken. Sadie smiles.

Her luminescent shoulders are fragile in her black spaghetti straps. Long hair parted in the middle just covers the twin points of her chest, sharp and ostentatious beneath her thin satin top. She reminds me of one of the nymphs in the Pre-Raphaelite painting: heroic Hylas at the water's edge being lured for a swim. Sadie looks down her pert nose at me, her large dark eyes looking up and beckoning. I swear, Waterhouse must have secretly loved a Filipina mestiza. I can imagine Sadie naked in the water, lily pads brushing the undersides of her upturned breasts, a yellow flower in her hair, delicate arms reaching as I bring my amphora to slake my thirst.

When I reach her, she shouts over the music into my ear: "Do you want to tend the rabbits, Lenny?"

"What do you mean?" I yell.

"You looked so lost there. Uncertain as a mouse. Did that guy slip a baggie in your pocket?"

"I thought someone was watching me. I didn't know it was you. I'm fine. Just overwhelmed at being home."

"Me? Watching? What do you think of me, *thinking of you*?" She makes her voice all cute for that mouldy old line.

I play along: "What do you take me for, *granted*?"

"Never. I'm glad you got my text. Didn't think you'd make it, actually. The rains and all. My parents wouldn't let me out."

"Why? All the coup talk?"

"Nah. That's just the usual bullshit. Right? My folks were worried about this freakazoid typhoon. I had to wait for my mom to take her sleeping pills, and my fucking dad wasn't home anyway. Nice pants, by the way. I didn't take you for the—"

"What do you mean?"

"Nothing. I mean, like, rock on, man!" She holds up a hand to do the sign of the horns.

I look down at my tight leather jeans. I'd bought them after Madison and I broke up. I guess I wanted to reinvent myself. Sadie teases, but I can tell she's totally impressed.

"Hey, Sadie, won't your dad . . ."

"No, the driver drops him off under the porte cochere. Tomorrow's my parents' golf day—their together time. Usually they just walk to their balls together. That's how together they are. But with this weather they'll be sleeping in till eleven."

"Can I buy you a drink?"

"*Can* you buy me a drink?" She puts her hand on my chest. Can she feel my heart pounding? It's been so long since I felt the thrill of newness. I think we're such a good match. I'd never felt that with Madison. With Madison it was almost as if need brought us together and exhaustion kept us that way.

"You know, Miguel? I feel really close to you. It's like I've been waiting for you all my life. Buy me a drink, then take me away forever." I almost believe her. Then she raises the back of her hand to her forehead and pretends she's about to swoon. She sure has nice armpits.

I call the bartender over. "I'd like a Swinging Balzac."

"What?" he says. "Single malt on rocks?"

"No, a Swinging Balzac. One part cognac, one part calvados, half part Grand Marnier, splash of lemon. Shaken with ice and strained into a martini glass." The bartender thinks for a second then nods.

"What's that?" Sadie asks.

"Crispin's signature concoction. I think he stole the name from someone more clever. He used to say, 'Fancy a Swinging Balzac?' while waggling his fist like a, you know."

"Like a what?"

"What'll you have?"

Sadie orders a Double Dickel on the rocks. "How very writerly and pretentious of us," she says, grinning.

It is, too. It's great.

*

Our smitten protagonist hears the bartender punch their order into the register. The sound of the bell before the cash drawer opens reminds him of that familiar scene. The old man in his study, at his desk, in a pool of light made milky by pipe tobacco, the type hammers clickety-clacketing until the rewarding ding.

The boy observes himself in the mirror behind the bar, even as he stands beside Sadie in the strobing lights. He stares not out of vanity, but for confirmation. Yes—he thinks, looking himself in the eye—this is real. Even if it's like we're in the movies. Even if it's too good to be true—finally, a girl who gets it; the lighting just right; the sound track soaring; the sensation thick in the throat that a climax is about to be enacted. He shakes his head and thinks, God, I'm high right now.

*

Boy Bastos grows up and has a daughter who looks just like him, whom he names Girly. He chaperones a play date, sitting with Girly and her friend from school. They play luksong tinik, the traditional game involving a pair seated on the ground to form a fence with outstretched hands, over which participants leap. It starts a few hand spans high, then another hand is added once everyone makes the jump. You may have seen that painting by Amorsolo, all bucolic and sun-drenched, often used in pamphlets and books to illustrate an idyllic youth.

The girls hold out their hands, and Boy has no trouble jumping over. He laughs with unexpected glee. Finally, it's his daughter's turn. Boy's stretched hand forms the top of the barrier. Girly makes a magnificent leap, like a pair of scissors opened wide to make a cut.

"You touched!" Boy exclaims.

"No, I didn't," Girly claims.

"I'm sure you did," Boy says. They begin to argue vehemently.

"Papa, how can you be so sure?"

Boy smells his thumb. "Hmmph!" he says. "Like fish! Told you you touched!"

*

Sadie: "What's that smell?"

Our voices echo in the men's room cubicle.

Me: "This is the bathroom."

Sadie: "It's, um, kinda gross."

Me: "Let's finish and get out."

Sadie is timid when she does coke, sniffing demurely as if over a fresh batch of cookies. And after I serve her a bump off my key, she takes it and the baggie and serves me in return. You can tell a lot about a girl by how she does her cocaine. Madison was like a Provençal pig rooting for truffles. Usually she did both the lines I'd cut for her and me. It became her running gag, though I hated it, especially at three in the morning when our supply was running low.

Sadie reaches up and wipes some powder from my upper lip. I feel like I'm in a summer field, standing on the top rung of a ladder, looking over acres of sunflowers. Who needs drugs when you have love, or at least infatuation?

"You know," she says, "in that book I'm reading about the snowboarders, there's this great bit that goes, 'There is something inherently fun about doing coke in a crowded bar with your friends that has little to do with being high. It's the feeling of getting away with something—at an age where it's okay to buy a *Playboy* or see a girl in her underwear, it's like having a hard-on underwater at a public swimming pool.' And you know, I think I'd like to get away with something with you, Miguel, I really think I would." Sadie gives me a kiss on the chin and I feel like I'm a spoon sparking in a microwave. "Let's get some more booze," she says.

I hold open the stall door. I may not be a lot of things, but one thing I am is a gentleman. The curve where Sadie's neck and shoulder meet looks damn delicious.

Laughter and voices approach and suddenly the door opens and some old friends spill into the men's room. I sniff and wipe my nose, to preserve Sadie's honour.

"Dude!" Gabby says. "When'd you get back?" It's great to see him. He still has those eyes like he's got some joyful secret he might just share with you.

Rico: "Good to see you, dawg!"

Chucho (shaking my hand vigorously): "What a guy what a guy what a guy!"

Gabby: "How long you staying?"

Me: "Just a week. Probably."

Chucho: "Not even long enough for a denouement! Why aren't you staying for Christmas?"

Me: "How you guys doing?"

Chucho: "Same same, pare. Same same." He's ballooned since I last saw him. Since his wife got pregnant, I guess. "Nothing changes here."

Rico: "True that, mate." His accent is South London. A few years ago he flunked out of Ateneo Law and was sent to culinary school abroad. His parents knew the Philippine ambassador to the Court of Saint James or something. "Just got back from Heathrow yesterday. Almost didn't make it. But I knew the Christmas parties would be right proper. Got delayed six hours in Narita, waiting for the weather to clear over here. What a bother. Man, can you believe these bombings? Bloody fucking Muslims. And my parents think I'm safer at home than at winter break in Ibiza." He pronounces it "Ibi*th*a."

Gabby: "You know how it is. It's been bad for so long it can't get worse. It's all just the media. These things get blown up."

We laugh at his unintentional pun.

Sadie: "It's not *that* bad." She apparently knows everyone here, in true Manila cosmology. "Manila's one big Rorschach test. You can tell loads about a person by what they think of it."

Chucho: "Sades, why you hanging with this miscreant? Just kidding. I kid, I kid! What a guy what a guy. This motherfucker used to be the Atomic Shaman! Did you know that? Should've seen him dance with glowsticks. But he's moved to better locales.

Look at him. Too much milk and honey and Famous Original Ray's."
He chummily grabs around my waist. I push him away and tousle
his hair.

Gabby (his eyes sparkling): "Dude, you have?"

Rico: "What?" (His face fills with the euphoria of realization,
followed by a goofy look of hope.)

The three guys watch me expectantly.

Sadie looks at me. I look at Sadie. I look at the guys.

"Sorry, fellas. All gone."

We file out of the bathroom together. Gabby's got his arm
around Sadie and I can tell he's teasing her about me. Chucho is
bobbing to the music and starts pumping his fist in the air.

Rico (his arm on my shoulders): "Hey, how's your gramps? He
doing well?"

I've never really liked Rico. He thinks he can be chummy with
me because he worked as my grandfather's assistant after college.
He'd have done well in politics. He's such a dickhead that when he
gets aroused he gets a stiff neck. And because he's recently discovered cocaine he thinks he's extra cool.

Me: "My grandpa's okay. Still at it."

Rico: "You know, your lolo is one of the best men I ever met. He
may be a lot of things, mate, but he's an honest man in a dishonest
line of work."

Me: "Sure."

Rico: "He gave me shit when I worked for him, but I deserved it."

Me: "You shouldn't have showed up stoned so often."

Rico: "Dude, I needed to be. Tough fucking job. I remember
the worst night was when this guy rang the gate at Forbes, looking
for your grandpops. I went out and the guy's like, 'I voted for Governor Salvador. I earned a certificate in caregiving because of his
programs and came to work in Manila.' The bloke's hands were like
all shaking. He goes, 'I tried my best. I have nothing left and nowhere else to go. I need a little help to take the boat home to my
family.' Then he looks me in the eye and is like, 'If the governor
doesn't help me, I don't know what I'll do. I'm afraid of what I'll
do.' He looked like he really meant it. I don't think I'll ever forget
that. He was like playing with the end of his shirt and his hands

were trembling. So I went inside and told your lolo, and he's like, 'They all say that.' So I'm like, 'What should I do?' And your lolo goes: 'Take care of it.' So I go out and tell the guy sorry. You should've seen him. His hands quit shaking and his whole body crumpled and he sat on the ground. I didn't know what to do. So I gave him all the money I had in my wallet. I had to shut the gate, but he just sat there, staring at the fucking pittance I gave him. I wonder a lot about what happened to him."

Me: "You never told me about this."

Rico: "Aw, we weren't hanging out anymore. You were always with your chick and your baby."

Me: "What a fucking hypocrite my grandfather is."

Rico: "You shitting me? I respected him after that. 'Cause he was right. Don't think shit like that doesn't affect your lolo. He just knows what has to be done."

Me: "I don't know. You help wherever you can."

Rico: "Yeah. Try it. Anyways. You sure you can't stay for Christmas?"

Me: "Yeah, I'm sure."

Rico: "Dude, just for the parties, then get the fuck out. Seriously. Every time I come back, I see it. This place is a living ghost town. Innit?"

*

MAGELLAN: Gimme, gimme, gimme some heathens for my Lord
　　Some bullets for our muskets and a whetstone for our swords
　　In ships we come, like a stroke of thunder
　　To live and die, for salvation and plunder
　　We name these lands for our king!
PIGAFETTA: Gimme, gimme, gimme my parchment and my quill
　　The story I have, I know is sure to thrill
　　I'll record our myths and make you legend
　　Our faith in God's empire nothing could rend
　　We name these lands for our king!
　　　　　—from the 1982 disco opera *All Around the World*, based on the life
　　　　　　　of the cartographer and translator Antonio Pigafetta (libretto by
　　　　　　　　　Crispin Salvador, music by Bingbong Cadenza)

*

The music's kicking. Obscure electro remixes. On the mezzanine, we lean on the railing and look down on the dance floor. Sadie points out Vita Nova boogying on the ledge by the DJ booth.

"I have to say," Sadie says, "she sure is hot."

"Yeah. But as soon as she opens her mouth . . . It's that alley accent."

"I hear she's such a slut," Sadie says. "As in really used. I knew this guy who said that fucking her is like throwing a hot dog down a hallway."

"My, my, Miss Gonzales. Watch your tongue."

"I'm just reporting. It's my civic duty. Besides, I hate sluts. They think they're being empowered feminists, but they're so subjugated they're blind."

"Do you really think she's got dirt on the president?" I admit, it's hard to keep from staring at Vita. I'm trying not to, so that Sadie won't notice. But the dancing artista is a bright nebula, it's like the music is coming from her. To a colourful, arcing bass line, a man with a voice like gravity sings about melodies that getcha so: ". . . Where'd they *come* from? *I* don't know . . ." Vita has her eyes shut and is doing this repetitive move where her face goes one way while her hips swing out in the opposite direction. Like a snake. With a killer rack and bodacious ass. The very snake who gave Eve that apple she gave to Adam. The man with the funereal voice calls out in happiness: ". . . But I'd give away the fames of a hundred Henry James . . ." Vita throws her arms above her head in ecstatic display of who she has become. She, too, has great armpits.

Sadie asks: "Looks like you're thinking about dancing. You wanna?"

"I'd love to, but let's drink first. My feet hurt."

"Aren't New Yorkers used to walking?"

"Sure we are."

"Let's shake our tail feathers. Come on!"

"How about we get hammered and do scads of blow?"

"I'm a girl. We just want to have fun."

"And getting hammered and doing scads of blow isn't fun?"

In truth, it's been a long time since I felt comfortable dancing. Yeah, I know, it's the best way to get chicks. One semester even, at Columbia, I paid for three months of hip-hop dance lessons. After stumbling through the Grapevine and the Robocop in the first class, I never went back. I used to think my not going was money wasted. I later realized my not going was money very well spent.

"It's just that my feet really hurt."

"Oh, you're being gay."

"No. I'm not. Gay people love dancing."

"Give me one good reason not to dance with me," she puts her hands on her hips, inadvertently tightening her shirt against her chest. Her nipples are impertinent through the fabric. Or maybe impetuous. Likely both.

"It's just—I've got—Aw, forget it." Either I just dance or I use one of my stock excuses. Thing is, the only way I can find rhythm is by closing my eyes. Then I tend to bump into people.

"Don't be shy. Miguel, it's me. It feels like we've known each other forever, right?"

"Sure." Maybe I'll just dance. Aw, fuck it. I'll make up an excuse. Here I go. "It's just I've got these orthopedic insoles."

"I'm happy for your arches."

"No. They're actually really spleening me. I think the tropical heat melted them out of shape and they're hurting my feet."

"Take them off and chuck 'em."

"I need them for my posture."

"But they hurt you. And we wanna dance."

"They're expensive. And good for me."

"Take them off. I'll put them in my purse."

"I don't want you to do that."

"Really, it's okay."

"That's sort of too intimate. I hardly know you."

"It'll be our definitive bonding experience."

"I'm not that type of guy. I never let a girl touch my orthopedic insoles on the first date. Besides, I think they might smell like pee."

"You're funny. Okay, I get it. I have to admire your inventiveness. You're actually really cute. Let's go get plastered and high as kites. But you owe me a dance next time." We move away from the rail and look for somewhere to sit. I let her lead and I watch her bare back as she goes, and I smirk at the guys who are checking her out.

"Hey, M.," Sadie says, turning, "since you're so keen on chatting . . . I heard Rico talking to you. Are you sure you're leaving before Christmas?"

"Did you hear my reply?"

"I don't eavesdrop."

"No? Just kidding. Yeah, my plan was for a week, before I get sucked in. Why so curious? You want me to stay?"

"On the contrary. I'm like a praying mantis. I prefer that my mates are conveniently disposed of."

"Ooh. Are you going to bite my head off? I should've known you were . . ."

"It's just that . . ." Her face is suddenly serious. She puts her hand on my hip and pulls me closer. "My dad, you know?" She circles her arms around my waist. "He treats me like a . . . aw, fuck." She's scented with baby powder. "You know, my dad didn't like you. What you represent. After I dropped you off, I went to my parents' room, to ask my mom if she knew anything about Crispin's love child. Before I could, my dad like hijacked the conversation and started making fun of you. Don't look that way. It wasn't personal. It was directed at me. At my life choices. And I, I—I don't know. I just, um, I was just wondering . . . I haven't seen New York, and . . ."

"And?"

"And aw fucking fuck. Not him." Sadie points behind me. Albon Alcantara is bounding exuberantly around the room, his camera flashing. He's coming straight for us. "I'm not supposed to be out, remember?" Sadie pulls at my hand. Albon pauses to take a photo by the stairs. The couple really hams for the camera, their smiles carefully careless, looking sick to death of being in the society pages. "Quick," Sadie says, "It's dark there behind the pillar." She takes my hand and tugs.

"Is this another ploy?" I say.

In the shadows I turn to her, fishing into my pocket for my baggie of coke. Suddenly her lips are against mine, feeling and biting. She's leaning her body against me, swaying on her tiptoes, reaching my face with hers. Her arms wrap around my neck, her fingernails scratch against my nape. Oh, jeez. Our tongues touch. Oh, Lord. I hope she's not just emboldened by coke. She pulls away and she's suddenly that coy girl to whom I was first attracted.

But she's crying. It's definitely time for another line.

She kisses me again. Whispers in my ear: "I hope you don't stay."

"Why not?"

"I want you to take me with you."

I don't know what to say. So I say: "Um." Then I say: "Shouldn't you wait to graduate first?"

Sadie pushes me. She's blushing and scowling.

Me: "No, I mean, it's just . . . a college degree is an important thing."

Sadie: "I have to piss."

Me: "You want me to go with you? We can do anoth—"

Sadie: "No thanks, dad. That's an awful lot of Paco Rabanne you've got on. You stink like my father." She picks up her purse and hurries to the ladies' room.

I try to follow, but Albon homes in. A few steps away from me, he flings himself backward, as if swept up by an original idea, to take my picture. Then he hugs me, hefting me off my feet and patting my back. He's always had the demeanour of an Eastern European–born L.A. art gallery owner.

"Ow!" he says, pulling away, holding his forearm. "My new ink." He has a tattoo across his wrist. It says v.i.p. and is made to look like a stamp bouncers give you upon entering a nightclub. It's fresh and peeling a bit. "My gods, though, it's so good to see you," Albon says. "When'd you get back? So long without calling me? Are you staying for good? Why aren't you sure? How long has it been? That long? Are you still decadent? What are you doing these days? . . . Oh! What kind of book is it? I'll throw you a book launch. Why don't you stay and, you know, help us. The scene is growing, people are really learning how to party. Manila's becoming très sophisticated. We need your energy. I mean, my gods, our poor country and its brain drain. In fact, I'm working with the Department of Tourism, to rebrand Filipinos as the Brazilians of Asia. But instead of beaches and samba, we're beaches and disco music. Listen, call me.

Let's play badminton at the Polo Club and we'll talk more. I have to cover this event for my blog. Oh, speaking of. There's a party tomorrow at my club. It's a shindig we call 'Clubbers of the World, Unite!' Gods, I hope this rain will stop. Prada is sponsoring the fashion show, then open bar from ten until midnight. Stolichnaya. All proceeds go to the Philippine Literacy Project, because our kids need to read good. I'll put you on the guest list." Albon hands me his card. "Hey," he says, looking at me earnestly, "that book you're writing, I hope you give it a happy ending. We need more of those." He winks then waddles away, camera lighting up the eager smiles of partiers.

*

The Communist Party of the Philippines had a very strict agenda, which Salvador quickly learned was vastly different from that of the foot soldiers actually waging the "protracted people's war." The time in the hills was, as he called it, "my schooling in the best and the worst of humanity."

From Ka Arsenio, Salvador learned the skills he needed to survive: how to care for and fire his locally made Kalashnikov, which plants were edible, how to navigate by the stars, where to place the butterfly knife between the ribs to puncture an enemy's lung, how to leap through an open window using the Flying Panther technique. In return, Ka Arsenio learned from Salvador how to read and write.

One moonless evening in December, their Sparrow Unit was walking single file between two dried-out rice paddies, sneaking home from a meeting with government soldiers. The rebels had just purchased crates of ammunition from their foes—Philippine Army officers who needed money for the Christmas season. Feeling satisfied and safe after the amiable transaction—and tipsy from the Red Horse Beer the soldiers drank with them—the comrades walked quietly but slowly, intent on enjoying the night air. They carried the boxes on their shoulders while the one woman among them, Ka Helen, balanced hers on her head. When Salvador tried to do the same, his fell and clattered into the paddy.

Shots rang out from across the open space, bursts of bright light bloomed along the far embankment of the paddy. Salvador felt somebody jump on him and hold him down. The bullets thudded into the berm between them and their attackers. Ka Arsenio hissed in his ear: "Did you tip them off?"

The shooting stopped. Ka Arsenio looked Salvador in the eye, unsure of what to do. Salvador could see Ka Helen lying a few feet away, but couldn't tell if she was dead. As he recounted in his memoir: "I'd never heard a night so frightened into silence."

Ka Arsenio kissed Salvador gently on the cheek. Then he held out a finger, then a second one, then a third. They stood up suddenly, took aim, and fired at the shadows moving toward them. Bullets flashed by their heads, "fireflies on a mission, but sounding like killer bees." Salvador sighted carefully at an approaching figure. He saw the soldier was "holding a rifle in one hand and crossing himself repeatedly with the other." Salvador couldn't pull the trigger. The soldier got on one knee and took aim. Salvador fired. The soldier fell backward and lay still. "I hoped he would move," Salvador wrote in *Autoplagiarist*, "but he didn't."

That was the first person he ever killed.

Salvador and Ka Arsenio fired until they ran out of ammunition.

More figures moved across the paddy, rapidly closing the distance.

> —from the biography in progress, *Crispin Salvador: Eight Lives Lived*, by Miguel Syjuco

*

In Sadie's car she acts like nothing happened. "Fuck, I'm so glad we bailed. Same shit, different week," she says. "You really think this party will be cool?"

"They're good friends of mine. Their band's really good. The Cool Kids of Death. Have you heard of them? Punk. Their set starts at four-thirty."

"I'm worried about the weather."

"They've got a hit. You know, 'Sabotage Love! Sabotage Love! This is my reality, I am who I want to be . . .'"

"Um, okay, thanks. Hey, I'm sorry about . . ."

"Sadie, it's okay. Don't be. But if you don't mind my asking, your dad . . ."

"Yeah, really sorry, the driver forgot to put the cartridge back in after I changed the CDs this afternoon. We'll have to stick to radio."

"Oh." How is it possible I can have such a great connection with someone so quickly and that we can become awkward so quickly as well? She ons the radio and navigates static while trying to find a station. The rain hasn't let up. "This storm's something, huh?"

"Don't," she says firmly. "We're better than small talk." Then, warmly: "So, why's the band starting so late?"

"They're gigging at a Christmas party for one of the call centres on Libis. That's when the staff gets off work. They deal with customers in the States."

"Weird."

"Yeah. My friend, he's the guitarist, he told me these people keep schedules like vampires. Some restaurants and bars there open after the workers' shifts. At like four in the morning."

"I've never heard of that. And I live in this city."

"Because you don't leave Makati," I joke. "Hey Sadie, you want another bump?"

"I think you should cool it with that shit."

"I'm okay. I can stop whenever I want to. Listen, you okay with catching The Cool Kids of Death?"

"Sure, it's a different gimmick. Beats going to Where Else? or Venezia. Where the *fuck* are all the stations?" Sadie twists the knob and goes up and down the FM band.

"Are there no streetlights?" I ask. "Or is it your dark tint?"

"Usually there are. I don't know what's going on. Maybe another blackout?"

"Don't tell me more jellyfish."

"Coup d'Etat had power."

"Probably the mall's generator. The Lupases wouldn't want to lose a centavo of revenue."

The lights are on in the hotels. The Peninsula's fountain is lit and gushing. The InterContinental glows obliviously. Shangri-la has a giant wreath of green and red lights on its facade. Other buildings, however, stand like black monuments to the ashy sky. I open my window a crack and hear generators rumbling defiantly. Water comes in and I shut it.

Sadie's cell phone chirps. *Poo-tee-weet*. She looks at it. "A friend passing on a text," she says. The phone is like the moon and her face is being bathed in it. "It says we should stay home tonight because there's shit brewing." Sadie puts her cell on the dashboard.

When we get to Edsa, it is lightless and empty, its wide ten lanes a deserted valley of concrete. The Lexus's headlights slice a pallid, claustrophobic section from the thick rain. Sadie drives slowly. Occasionally, a bus roars past like a train, sending a slap of water against our car.

"Try the AM band," I suggest. She finds Radyo Veritas. The commentator sounds like he's had more than his fair share of coke this evening.

". . . carefully this evening compatriots the roads are flooded in many locations around the metropolis. And returning to our top story Reverend Martin has mysteriously disappeared from his cell in Camp Crame gone without a trace. Authorities are baffled and inquiries are being conducted presently to determine his whereabouts . . ."

Sadie turns the knob. "Makes me nervous, all that bad news," she says. "Aren't there any music stations on AM?" We find one playing a ballad, "Dahil Sa Iyo." The crooner's voice makes love to the Tagalog words. "Because of you, I live. Because of you, until I die." When the song ends, the DJ comes on, whispering seductively in English: "Dat was Julio Iglesias, uh, singing his wonderpul rendition of da beautipul, uh, ninetin-sebenty-tree classics kundiman to keep you company on dis rainiest of ebening. Next we hab—"

Sadie reaches for the radio knob and turns it off. The silence is like a bell.

*

The young man looked at the dead man at his feet, then at the red fedora perched there on the cardboard box. This image in the alley was only his, this young Miguel's, even as he accepted the metal cuffs around his wrists with a steely resolve beyond his years. He reminds himself: This will be forever one of the many things I will be glad is mine. All this, the finality of this one evening, the image of that one hat, the weight of that one stone, the cleaving of two lives on a dark, lonesome road.

—from the 1989 short story "One Stone for Two Birds,"

by Crispin Salvador

*

At the top of the hill where Makati ends and Edsa enters Mandaluyong, we hit traffic. It's at a standstill. "Maybe an accident?" Sadie says.

"Why aren't cars coming south into Makati?"

"Maybe a huge accident."

We spend fifteen minutes in the same spot. Five minutes bitching, five minutes telling dirty jokes, five minutes making out.

"Since we're not going anywhere," Sadie says, clicking open her seat belt. "Let me get that seat belt for you."

"I don't think that's a good idea."

"Push your seat back, sweetie."

"Here, Sadie, let me . . . How do I adjust it . . . There."

"Next is . . . your, fuck . . . grrr . . . buckle . . . it's kinda diffic—"

"Your hands might work better than your teeth."

"There you go. Damn belt. Now I'll just unzip this . . ."

"Ow!"

"Sorry, Miguel. It's these leather pants, they're . . ."

"Just a sec."

". . . really tight. How'd you get them on in the fir—"

"Yeah, hold on. There's a tech—"

"They're stuck for good."

"—nique to them."

"You're free! Why don't you lean back?"

"'kay."

"Miguel?"

"Yes?"

"Nothing."

"What?"

"Nice boxers. I didn't know you liked sailboats."

"That's not what you wanted to say."

"Really. It's nothing. Shhh. Oh, look, a nesting Balzac."

"You like it?"

"Sure. But maybe you'll think less of me."

"Why would I?"

"You know, a prim and proper Assumption girl."

"Maybe I'll think more of you."

"Yeah? Or at least more often. Mmm. Tastes good."

"Oh, God."

"And so hard! Mmph . . ."

Poo-tee-weet.

"Sadie, your cell phone . . . Um, should we get that?"

"Nope."

"Seriously, what if it's important."

"Mmph. You read it. I'm occupied. Mrrph."

"Okay, it's, ah, from, uh, Tita Saqy."

"My mom's sister. Mmph."

"Um, she says—ah that's good—she says everyone should go to the protesters and bring them food and water, or—ah, wow, that's nice—or at least say prayers."

"Fuck that. We've got better things to do. Mmph."

"Oh, shit."

"Mmm."

"Sadie?"

"Mm-hm?"

"Is the car in park?"

"Mm-hm."

"Seriously. The car's moving."

"Oops. Now it's in park. Relax. Mmph."

"Ooh Jesus!"

"You like?"

"I'm getting boosegumps."

"You're funny."

"That feels amaz— Ah! Wow. Ahhrrm! . . . Shit. I . . . uh, I think I just chipped my tooth."

Poo-tee-weet.

"Slurp."

"No, I'm serious, it's so good I'm gritting too hard."

"Mmphmm."

"Wow."

"Why don't you, mmph, bring me to New York, mmph, with you? Mmph. Wouldn't that be nice? Mmph."

"Uh, yeah. Sure. Of course. Ah, that feels amazing . . ."

". . ."

". . ."

"Miguel, what's wrong?"

"Nothing. It's okay. Why don't you rest for a whi—"

"What's the matter?"

"Nothing, it's just . . ."

Poo-tee-weet.

"Am I doing it wrong?"

"No, it's so right."

"Then why'd it stop working?"

"I'm just nervous."

"Is it me? Am I bad at it?"

"No, the first time . . . I always have a hard time."

"Don't make puns."

Poo-tee-weet.

"I didn't mean to. I'm just nervous. Or coked up."

"You didn't like it? Let me just try . . . Mmph . . ."

"Come up here. Kiss me. I'd rather kiss."

"You poor thing. Look, you're blushing. Why are you so nervous?"

"Let's take things slow."

"Okay. We've got all the time in the world."

"Really?"

Poo-tee-weet.

*

Three college girls are walking along the street, one from International School Manila, one from Saint Scholastica, and the third, Girly Bastos, from Assumption. The trio is startled by a large lizard that crosses the path.

Screams the girl from I.S. Manila: "Oh no, an iguana!"

Squeals the girl from Saint Scho: "Ay, butiki!"

Shrieks Girly Bastos, from Assumption: "Shet, Lacoste!"

*

We read the text messages together.

The first is from Ned, Sadie's dressage coach: Rev Mart is free! Rally bhind hm. R rewrd wil b in heaven. He prmses 2 trade hs post as Apostle of da People & run 4 prsidnt. Spred da gud wrd.

The second is from Georgie, Sadie's classmate: "Countrymen! Take to the streets for Lakandula. But keep the peace. Quiet defiance is louder than angry shouts." —Respeto Reyes.

Traffic inches forward about half a mile.

The third is from Pye, Sadie's yoga instructor: Bansamoro, Estregan, and Reverend Martin to stage Christmas play with Vita Nova. Unfortunately, show's cancelled—script called for three wise men and a virgin! Hwehwehweh. A rose, for you @}--;------

We crest the hill to where Edsa slopes down to the bridge spanning the Pasig.

The fourth is from Tita Daqy, Sadie's other aunt: Estregan and Department of Health warn Chinese Flu contagious in crowds. Stay safe @ home n pray for the cuntry. Pls pas 2 as mny ppl as posible. God bless!

A phalanx of red taillights meets us. Extinguished billboards and neon signs glow with what luminosity they can suck from our headlights. Several vehicles at the front of the gathering cast their beams into a river of oily water.

"Fuck," Sadie says. "Where's the bridge?"

"I think it's there. See the lampposts?"

A bus gingerly enters the water and slowly plows through. The water's over its wheels.

"Whoa. It's risen that high?"

The bus makes it to the other side, climbs up the incline, and continues north on Edsa. It's followed by a semi pulling a trailer stacked with sewer pipes. A jeepney follows. It stops midway. Two figures get out, pale in the headlights of the row of hesitating vehicles. The pair tries to push the jeepney across. One of the men falls and disappears. He resurfaces a few yards downstream. The two men clamber to the roof of the jeepney and wave their arms.

"I think we should—"

"Yeah," Sadie says, putting the car into reverse. "But there's no way over the median to the southbound lanes. Should I just turn around on this lane?"

"It's too hard to see in this rain. What if there's an oncoming truck or something without headlights? Try the underpass to the southbound lanes." I open my window and stick my head out. Huge raindrops smack my face. The underpass leads beneath the bridge, a concrete levee keeps the water out. "It doesn't look flooded. Yet."

We skirt around the other hemmed-in vehicles. Some are beginning to manoeuvre indecisively. A few are backing up all the way, hazard lights flashing. Others are U-turning to risk driving into oncoming traffic. It's like bumper cars before the first bump. A bus makes the bridge crossing, slowing beside the jeepney to rescue the two men. Its wake sends a wave against the levee protecting the underpass. Some water splatters over.

"I don't know, Miguel. It's not flooded only because of that cement thingy. I don't want to get stuck in there."

"Just zoom it. If it's flooded we can back out quickly."

Sadie drives down and through the underpass, below the bridge, and out the other end. We're through. "Plato's cave," I say, trying for levity. Sadie doesn't reply. The road inclines to the current level of the river. Over the embankment on our right I see the surface of the water. I could open my window and dip my hand in it.

"Holy shit," Sadie says, switching off her left signal light and nudging me to look. "I don't think we can make that," she says. True enough, the turnoff to the southbound lanes of Edsa is flooded. We can't get back onto the highway.

"Don't worry," I tell her. "Just go straight. This road becomes J. P. Rizal, which follows the river from a height and ends up on Makati Avenue. My hotel is just off it. We can stay there."

Sadie drives on and the road rises slightly. We're in the clear. Sadie gives a sigh of relief and turns on the radio. "Fuck," she says, "I need to relax. That was scary." She puts it onto the music station.

"I think we should listen to the news," I say. "Is that okay?"

Sadie waves her hand dismissively.

I scan for Veritas or Bombo. An excited voice exclaims: "—ots were fired and a group led by Reverend Martin has taken control of the house, overpowering the police, in an attempt to free Wigberto Lakandula . . ."

The road continues. I turn around to look at the river. Its shimmering darkness is lighter against the shadowy embankments. The bridge is lit with the occasional headlights of crossing buses and trucks. The black shapes of buildings line the river. Several miles beyond are lights of a factory. Probably the Philippines First Corporation's munitions factory. It must have a generator for security, especially because of the trouble with the World Wardens.

Sadie's phone goes *poo-tee-weet*. She passes it to me because she's driving. I read the screen. "Who's Maqy?"

"My mom's other sister. Can you read it out?"

The text message says: Avoid protests. Bansamoro warns of armed bandits and antigovernment rioters. Violent factions could start bloodshed.

"I wish we could go," I say.

"Really? It wouldn't make a difference."

The road turns toward Makati. Unlit houses loom on either side, blocking our view of the river. Their heavy iron bars and tall metal gates do make me feel like we're driving through a ghost town. We continue on until the road disappears beneath a flooded portion.

". . . additional troops have been dispatched to stop the crowd which has, it is reported, begun to move from the Changco house on Zacateros down Claro M. Recto, in the direction of Malacañang Palace . . ."

Thunder rolls. The flooded area is like a maelstrom in the barrage of wind and rain. Sadie stops the car at the water's edge and buries her face in her hands.

"Sadie. It's okay. This has nothing to do with the river. It's only collecting between the walls of the properties. It's shallow. See how it's moving? If you constantly rev the engine, the water won't get in. We'll get through. Easy-peasy. But you have to keep the air pushing out of the exhaust so water can't—"

"Let's just wait on the high ground we just passed."

". . . earlier reports of looting have been discredited as misinformation. The crowds so far have been peacef—"

"Wait out here? It's the middle of nowhere. Sadie, come on. This flood can only get deeper."

"It's okay. I brought my gun. It's under your seat."

"Sadie, I'm positive we can make it. Just don't hesitate."

"Fine." She puts the car in gear and revs the engine. We enter the water. It sloshes in the wheel wells and against the underchassis. "I don't know . . . ," she says.

"Come on, Sadie. Keep going."

*

Back at their camp, Salvador helped drag the limping Ka Arsenio into the decrepit building that had once been a Spanish outpost. The place was deserted, but their comrades' rice was boiling in the pot on the fire. The two men went to the window and spotted figures approaching.

"Go," Ka Arsenio said to Salvador. "Escape out the back." Salvador looked at his friend. As he recalled in his memoir: "I knew he wouldn't be convinced to do otherwise than stay. Or perhaps that is a fiction I've created to exonerate myself." Salvador handed his rifle to Ka Arsenio. Then he performed the Flying Panther leap, head-first through the open rear window. He sprinted to the tree line, "fleeing the new chorus of the gunshots I should have faced with my comrade."

—from the biography in progress, *Crispin Salvador: Eight Lives Lived*, by Miguel Syjuco

*

Across the flood and in the distance, lights of cars pass on Makati Avenue. "Come on, you can make it," I say. A section of the road ahead runs along the river, but I don't tell her. It has a concrete embankment anyway.

". . . crowds have also massed at Plaza Miranda, my compatriots, where an impromptu rally is under way . . ."

"Hey, if we stall," I say, trying to lighten the mood again, "you'll have to save me. I can't swim."

"Quit fucking around."

"Sorry."

We push through the water, slowly but steadily. It gurgles beneath us.

"...Among the multitude are prominent national and local
leaders includi—"

"Aw shit, fuck, shit," Sadie says. "Fuck it." She turns the wheel
violently, to make a two-point turn. "We'll just . . ."—she shifts into
reverse—"wait it . . ."—the engine sputters—"out." The car lurches,
then dies.

We sit in silence. Sadie tries to start the engine. It doesn't
turn over. She tries again. Again. She should just quit it already.
Tries again.

"Fuck, fuck, fucking fuck," she says. She hits the steering wheel.
"What are we going to do?"

I try to stay calm. "Listen. Do you have a driver at home? You
do? Okay. Call his cell and have him come with your four-by-
four. He can tow us out, or at least get us to safety while we leave
the car here."

Sadie rings. She bites her lip. Finally, her driver answers. Sadie's
voice is frightened and bossy. She tells him where we are.

"Coolness," she says. "He was just sleeping. He's on his way."
She throws the phone over her shoulder onto the rear seat. Visibly
relieved, she hugs me. "If there's one thing the masses are, it's reliable." She giggles nervously. Her laugh is charming. It sounds like
sneakers squeaking on a basketball court.

We climb over to the back and curl up together. Her hair has the
scent of Gee, Your Hair Smells Terrific shampoo. My yayas used to
use that on us when we were kids. I tell Sadie: "I'd have thought you
use some fancy shampoo."

"Yeah, well. I'm just a simple kind of girl."

I bury my face in her hair. I whisper in her ear: "Smells like my
childhood."

"I hope it was a good childhood."

"Sure it was."

"Hey, can I ask you something?"

"Shoot."

Dark shapes float past our windows. In the quiet of our conversation, the rain becomes louder.

"When we first met, you told me that you didn't have family here. Then at dinner, you talked with my folks about your grandparents. Why'd you lie to me?"

"It was too complicated."

"It sucks being lied to."

"I know. I'm sorry."

Something looms far ahead. When I look, it's just darkness.

"Miguel, you can tell me anything. I won't judge."

"I'm really sorry."

Something knocks on the front of the car. Tops of trees peek over the walls of nearby properties. They look like people spying.

"Can I ask you another question?"

"Of course."

"What happens when you find Dulcinea?"

"I find the missing manuscript."

"That's your only reason?"

"Yeah."

The knocking persists. The trees swoon. The rain on the roof is like a box of bones being shaken.

"Then I think you should leave her alone."

"Why?"

"If she wanted to have anything to do with her dad, she would have."

"It's just not that simple."

Something scrapes on the right fender, like someone trying to come in. A wooden banister floats alongside.

"Are you going to be seeing your grandparents?"

"Nope."

"Why not?"

"It's better that way."

"It's just that simple, huh?" Sadie brushes my bangs from my face. "Sorry," she says. She kisses my forehead. "Are they the reason you left Manila?"

"No."

"Why'd you go?"

Something thuds on the bumper. A San Miguel Beer icebox bobs by. Lightning shatters the dark sky. We wait for thunder. None comes.

"I just don't like who I become here."

The dark mass ahead shifts, as if the night itself is stepping closer.

"Is that my truck? He better not make us wade. We'll get hepatitis or something."

"It's only something in the water."

Rain crashes harder. I raise my voice to be heard.

"You know," I say, "it's not like I don't want to come back and contribute. It just feels so . . . I don't know."

"Hopeless? Do like everyone else. Don't worry about it."

"I don't want to do that, either."

"Then just kiss me."

I kiss her.

"Do you think I'll do okay in New York?"

"You'd do great."

"I won't be shirking my responsibilities? Just leaving, I mean."

"No." I look at Sadie closely. "I don't know." I study her perfect face. Her perfect nose. Her bottom teeth are a little crooked, just to remind me she's real.

"You're still going to go look for Dulcinea, aren't you?"

"Yes."

"When?"

"Tomorrow."

*

BANG! Our car is rocked by an explosion. Sadie and I whip around. My God. Something is . . . The PhilFirst factory is aflame. Fire streaks in all directions. First one, then another, then a lot of fireworks, actual fireworks, shoot into the sky. Green. Blue. Yellow. Popping. Whistling. Hissing. Then they go off simultaneously. Then they take off in spurts. A huge orange flower wilts in the rain. A star studded with pearlescent bursts and a blue cluster in its middle lights the nearby billboard of Vita Nova. A crimson spiral winds sideways into the sign that says JESUS ALONE SAVES, shattering its neon letters in a deluge of glass. Streakers scream vertically one after the other, whizzing high until they burst into balls of sparkles like motes of white cinders. More, then more, rockets fly out. One of the factory buildings becomes a ball of fire—one second there, one second consumed, one second gone. Its incandescent structure stumbles like a skeleton into the water. Flames spider across the river's surface like gasoline alight, tufts of orange and yellow creeping slowly as they spread, rising steadily across the polluted water. The river is ablaze. The water burns, smells like singed hair, sulfur, scorching sugar. The low cloud ceiling, its soft rolls, seem to smoulder from the chemical sun below it. Even the distant horizon is stained red with this false dawn.

*

"I'm not an addict! What are you doing?' Dulcé yelled, pushing their arms off her. "Please, why are you doing this?"

She looked at her mother and stepdad, imploring them with her eyes. Mom was crying, Dad was shaking his head. The doctor and the male nurse forced Dulcé's arms through the straitjacket, then buckled her tight. She couldn't move.

"But it's all true!" Dulcé said. Mom held the diary in her hand.

"Dulcé, dear Dulcé. Just admit it. You made up these stories."

Dad knelt down in front of Dulcé and put his arms on her shoulders. "Babygirl, you're sick. These men are going to take you to the hospital to cure you."

"You're not even my real father," Dulcé said, knowing that those were the worst words she could say. But she was so angry with him for allowing this.

Dad didn't bat an eyelash. "You're my babygirl and I want you to get better."

Mom waved the diary and pleaded: "Dulcé, please, just say those are your fantasy stories. Just say you don't believe them."

Dulcé didn't know what to say. If she said what she wanted to, they would never believe it. If she said what they wanted her to, she'd never be able to believe in herself again. But maybe she could prove it to them!

She closed her eyes real tight and tried to make herself lighter than air. Just believe, she thought. Just believe.

For a second she felt herself lifting up. Her feet left the ground.

I'm doing it! I'm doing it!

But it was only the doctor and the nurse carrying her, lifting her to the bed in the back of the ambulance.

—from *Ay Naku!*, Book Three of Crispin Salvador's *Kaputol* trilogy

*

Sadie jumps to the front seat and turns on the radio. A woman's voice sings: "There's a light of hope, when you light a Hope."

"Is it safe," she asks, "to use the car battery?"

I don't reply. I'm transfixed by the scene behind us. The river courses with fire. Hell must look like this. "Miguel," Sadie says. I snap out of it.

"—everend Martin addressed the crowd just moments ago before we went to station break," says the commentator. "We now come back to you, live. Crowds are continuing to swarm over Jones and MacArthur bridges to join the rallies, while riot police have formed a barricade at the corner of Recto and Legarda, to prevent a march on the Presidential Palace. I spoke earlier on the telephone with Senator Bansamoro, who said the scene is extremely tense. One thrown stone, one gunshot could set it all off. Our reporter Danjen Adapon is on the scene. Hello Dan?! Can you hear me?"

Poo-tee-weet.

"Read it," Sadie says. The message says: Wen u smile the world smiles wid u. When ur down ppl will rally bhind u. But wen u fart u r alone coz ppl will never stand by u! Xcpt 4 JESUS! He died 4 our sins!

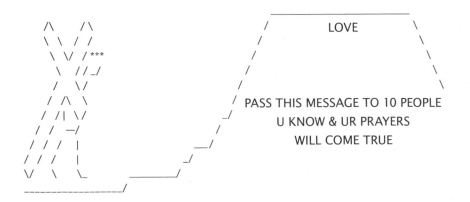

I hand back her phone. "Sadie, let's check the radio for . . ." But she's already busy dialling her driver's number.

"*Fuck!*" she says. "The battery just died!"

"Shit. I left mine in the hotel."

"Loud and clear, Rolly. Loud and clear. The scene here is difficult to describe. I'm speaking to you from the roof of the Chow King restaurant on C. M. Recto. I would say, uh, the crowd numbers as many as, uh, two hundred thousand. Maybe even five hundred thousand. It is an ocean of people. Reports do indicate that various factions have been called here to oppose each other, but from what I see, this crowd has come together peaceably. Most have been here for hours, waiting to see what their leaders will do. More arrive every minute. People are sharing umbrellas and food, many are singing songs. The atmosphere is like a carniva— Uh . . . the . . . Wait. Oh no. There is a confrontation between Reverend Martin and Wigberto Lakandula. They are exchanging words on a stage erected on the back of a truck. Oh my golly, Reverend Martin has pushed Lakandula to the floor! Um, Lakandula is refusing to fight. He is now being led away by some supporters. I recognize the elderly Congressman Respeto Reyes. He is holding Lakandula's hand. Uh, just one minute, please, Rolly." The reporter converses with someone off mic, their voices unintelligible and hurried. "Uh, Rolly, I now understand that Lakandula is leading his followers quietly away. Oh no, there seems to be trouble now. Someone at the other end of the crowd has destroyed a shop window. There seems to be a large group heading toward Makati. A car, no, a taxi has been turned over. They're throwing stones at policemen. At windows with lights in nearby buildings. Oh my golly, they are throwing stones at us . . ."

*

Even as he listens, our fiery protagonist wonders if tonight is the revolution Crispin wanted for so long. He regrets not having joined the crowds.

He thinks of one option for a life. An old man soft and bent over his typewriter while the world changes without him. An old man striking keys in acts of violence without valour. An old man imagining into being a young man's moment, like now. A stormy night beyond closed windows. The threat of mortality far, far away. Decisions to be avoided and never paid for.

*

The river surges with the sudden warmth. The Pasig's waters move toward us, no longer possessing the flat, defeated surface of its former self. The flood in which our car sits flows backward, opposite the river's current. There must be a break or overflow up ahead. The water rises, its level perceptible on the disappearing hood of the car. Bright flashes continue from the factory, slathering everything with colour: the street is red, then black, then green, then yellow, then orange, then black, then orange. A chair floats nearer, thuds on the bumper, passes to our left. Sadie disconnects and reconnects her cell-phone battery. "Power!" she exclaims. She dials. "Shit," she says, "answer the phone. Shit, answer, please answer, you motherfucker. Please. Aw fuck. Battery died. What do we do?"

"The safest place for us is in the car. Your driver'll be here soon."

The dark mass moves closer. Sadie holds her breath. She switches on the headlights, but they are already submerged. What little light they cast skims the surface of the water, as if our car sits on the edge of the moon's broad reflection on a pond. What had been looming now arrives.

It's one of those ice cream carts wheeled around town by bell-clanging vendors. Painted white with jaunty blue and red embellishments, the word STARBUCKS is stenciled along its side. The cart stops, then is moved again by a current that seems to be getting steadily stronger. The shadows behind it shift. A flash of green reveals two children perched upon the cart. A flash of blue shows them to be a girl of around ten carrying her naked toddler brother.

*

Even as he watches, he hears the keystrokes from a distant dream. An old man imagining and typing what must be said.

Poor little rich boy. A side must be taken. If you choose your own, you side with oppression, fratricide, indifference—you will never be content among your own. Rich little poor boy. If you side with the others, you choose treason, patricide, betrayal—you will never be accepted among those unlike you. Religion taught you to revere the family. Education taught you to value the majority over the few. Something to be done, Pozzo. You cannot sit this out. The airplane has landed. The people have clapped. Take a last breath. You're on the stage.

He sits under the lights, thinking of a second option for a life. Patience, however, is just another name for inaction.

*

I watch them float haltingly, the cart catching on the submerged street. They are less alarming as shadows than when lit up and helpless.

*

Even as he thinks, he rationalizes yet a third option for a life.

A splash is made to save the children, to hoist them the few yards to safety, to watch them scuttle back to hidden places, to be a hero engorged with hidden pride, the trumpets crying joyfully, to announce his guiltless return to America, having done his small part, to start a new life in Park Slope with the malleable young Sadie, and with the confidence that comes with being loved by a young beauty, he will sit down and finish my biography, and it will make him feel fulfilled, because he will have written with the vigour of the newly liberated, because he will have, in one single soggy act, absolved himself of our sins.

*

"If you open the door, the car will get ruined," Sadie says. She's crying. "My dad will kill me."

We both turn around. The road that was just several yards behind us is now vanished under the flood.

"My driver will be here any minute . . ."

I look at the water. What if it's too deep? I think of my father, running into the burning airplane. What if he hadn't been so foolhardy? I don't want to go into that flood. What if he hadn't been so selfish to his children? No. We need the people we love to be heroes. We need to know that somewhere someone better than ourselves can save us.

"Please don't," Sadie sobs. She's clinging to the steering wheel as if it were a life raft. "Nobody will see you."

I don't want to go. But I'm afraid of what I would become. "Sadie, come with me."

"I can't," she says. "You don't have to, either."

The door is heavy and won't open. What if she's right? I lean my entire weight against it and it gives only slightly. Water pushes into the car. It's warm and oddly comforting around my feet and ankles. I can't open the door. I'm stuck. I don't have to, go. I look at Sadie. She's tucking her knees up against her chest, Manolo Blahniks in either hand, her feet stacked on top of each other. The water is rising in the recesses of the car floor. I pull the door closed. I open the window. The electric motor grinds down with difficulty. I want it to make it, but I want it to fail. It makes it. The flood is almost level to the open window. When the fireworks light, the surface is glassy, gloomily reflective. I see myself in it, like a mirror, watch myself pulling my body through the window and falling forward, my face meeting my face, into the brown, muculent filth. My feet flay for the bottom. Sadie is screaming. Maybe she's right. I find my footing. Her pleas urge me on. The water is chest high.

An orange firework lights up the sky, then fades. The current is strong. The ground beneath me is reassuring. I stagger toward the children. A red firework paints the distance between us. The sister watches me with a blank expression. She becomes a shadow. The darkness between flashes is interminably private. She and her brother are bright yellow. I smile and wave. What the fuck am I doing? She shifts her brother higher against her shoulder, moves to tighten her fingers and legs onto the ice cream cart. The brother hides his face in her shoulder. Darkness again. Unseen things touch my legs, wrap around my waist, then are pushed away by the current. The children look like ghosts. Everything is too sodden or afraid or exhausted for sound. "I'm nearly there," I shout in Tagalog. Then we're all gloriously blue and I'm close. Five more steps. The little girl whispers something to her brother, who turns. He smiles, his round cheeks and forehead a fading sheen of azure, then a bright and deep yellow. The girl's teeth flash livid lemon. Three more steps. The children stare like statuary, their slick faces brassy from the spectacle in the sky. Something brushes my leg. The children put out their arms to me. Two more steps. Their faces, orange on one side, emerald on the other, smiling like the kids I'd see at Fourth of July celebrations on the banks of the East River. One more step.

My foot searches for ground. My whole body plunges into empty darkness.

9

In the dark emptiness, the light is a rectangle like the corona of an eclipse. The knob is wet in his hand. Maybe it is his hand that is wet. Two lines crease his palm like sister rivers. Or maybe they are different parts of the same river. The door swings. I call to him from inside, "There you are, my protagonist."

He steps gingerly on the sandy floor. I sit in a circle of brightness at my desk. "A dream is a palimpsest," I say. My typewriter steams before me, the fingertips of my right hand embraced by the keys. My other hand I hold out to him. A bloody hole through the palm is where a scar once was. I tell him one of our jokes. "Why can't Jesus eat M&Ms?" The young man shakes his head. I reply, "Because the M&Ms keep falling through the holes."

He turns to rush away, but moves ever so slowly. As if running through water. In the hallway mirror, he is naked. He leans toward his reflection. He sees an image of me, as I once was. He reaches out his hand. Or is his hand following mine? Our fingers touch. The mirror ripples.

*

The surface of the glassy sky shudders. His feet find a bottom, he pulls up, and follows his arm through and out the water, his fingers a rictus gripping a handhold in the air. Our gallant protagonist stands and coughs, lungs heaving gratefully. The warm water tasted like phlegm. The depth is now chest high. The two children are several yards away, their ice cream cart stuck. Floating quickly past are leafy branches, the head of a bald Barbie doll, an empty bottle of Silver Swan soy sauce, plastic bags like jellyfish. He wades through the sludge, his movement ever so slow. Gossamer newspaper pages wrap and disintegrate against his arms and chest. How—he wonders—did the distance between us become so great?

He reaches the children. The fireworks continue, flashing their faces green, blue, red, yellow. He takes the toddler tightly in his arms. The sister clambers onto his back. They weigh surprisingly little. It is our young man who now feels safe.

The riverized road glows suddenly with elemental whiteness. His shadow, stretching against a cinderblock wall, transforms into a three-headed monster. He turns around. It's the twin suns of headlights. A four-by-four vehicle.

*

Mutya slides her hands over Antonio's bare chest. "Mr. Astig," she says, touching his many scars. He sits up before she can ask how he got them. He adjusts the satin sheet around her shoulders. Their sweat still trickles between her bounteous breasts from their lovemaking. He leans in and licks it up.

"Now that you've saved the damsel," Mutya says, running her hands through his hair, "what's left?"

"I have an old iron thumbscrew with Dominador's name on it."

"That's how the story ends?"

"For him. Not me."

"Tony, you held him under a canning machine and he lost his testicles . . ."

"But he got away! What about all those dead women? Life goes on without them?"

"If you want to fight corruption, baby, you have to start with yourself."

Antonio stands and goes to the window. From that height, Metro Manila looks untroubled.

"Antonio, I'm sorry." Mutya wraps the sheet around her and goes to him. She puts her cheek on his shoulder and looks at the grey city. "It's about more than Dominador. I know. But sometimes courage is really just cowardice. Sometimes the bravest thing is to let go."

"There's too much that needs to be done."

"Don't be a hero."

"I never said I wanted to be one."

—from Manila Noir (page 182), by Crispin Salvador

*

Sadie doesn't say a word inside the F150. She just sits as if at the edge of a deep sobbing. Her eyes are so dark they look like they have been gouged out. Her driver has no face and he stops at the police substation behind the Hotel InterContinental. They let the sodden trio out before roaring off without a word. The truck's red lights blur, then fade, then disappear in the rain. The police lieutenant looks surprised. Or perhaps it's more like he's just woken up. He gets blankets for the children, kneels to dry their hair, rub their shoulders, then looks up at the young man. Another cop, wearing fuzzy bedroom slippers and a wifebeater shirt with his uniform's trousers, reclines behind a desk, playing a guitar. The old rock ballad "Patience." A third cop sits on the desk, his bare foot held in his hands as he clips his toenails. The lieutenant carries the children to where they can lie down. He then tells our courageous protagonist, kindly: "Hurry home."

The young man runs in the rain, his limbs loose and free. The puddled sidewalks splash with an irrepressible joy. Suddenly, the hotel is there before him. Its power is out. The desk is unmanned. Upstairs, in candlelight, standing naked and tall in the shower, he stretches his arms up. The bathroom in the darkness looks exactly like the one he and Madison had in Brooklyn, with its peeling paint and Tibetan prayer flags hanging by the window. The water's flow is cold, as cold as can be stood. It is so cold it does not even feel cold anymore, but reassuring, cleansing, clear.

*

"What are you writing?" whispered Millicent.

"Stuff," Dulcé said.

They were sitting beneath the plastic bonsai bodhi tree in the corner of the rec room. Other patients were playing pusoy-dos at the card table, or making portraits of creatures at the art table.

"What sort of stuff?" insisted Millicent.

"Just stuff."

"Let me guess. A letter to your real dad? Or, hmm. Maybe our escape plan?"

"Just stuff I'm making up. Fiction."

Nearby, Ceferina glanced up from her painting of a three-headed cat. She stared at Dulcé, then called out, "Nurse Erlinda! I think Dulcé is talking to herself again!"

The pencils and cards and paintbrushes in the room froze as everyone stared at Dulcé. Nurse Erlinda looked over from where she sat at the art table. She smiled sadly. "Ceferina, Dulcé's just writing silently," she said. Josie, who was painting beside Nurse Erlinda, offered in her mousy voice, "Maybe she's praying."

The quiet activity resumed in the room. A few seconds later, Dulcé whispered carefully, "I told you, Millie, be more quiet."

"Gee! Well excuuuse me." Millicent started pulling at her curly purple hair the way she did when upset. "I suspect Ceferina knows your real dad will break us out of here."

"There's nothing to know. I'm not going anywhere."

"Hey, Dul, when we get out of here, what are you going to do?"

"Nothing."

"I think I'd like to be a pilot."

"I don't think they'll let you be a pilot."

"That's not a very nice thing to say."

Dulcé put down her notebook and studied her friend unrolling the curls in her frizzy hair and watching them pop back.

"I'm sorry, Millie," Dulcé said. "You're right. I'm sorry."

"So whatcha gonna do when you get out?"

"I think I'll be a writer."

"What are you going to write?"

"A book."

"What kind of book?"

"A book of possibilities."

—from *Ay Naku!*, Book Three of Crispin Salvador's *Kaputol* trilogy

*

When he awakens in the midafternoon, he is not surprised that there were no more dreams. It's as if he closed his eyes briefly and night changed to day. Water still sloshes in his ears, like echoes of things familiar. Downstairs, the regular concierge is behind his desk, sleeping with his head on the registration book. The concierge startles awake to greet our serene protagonist as he walks outside. "Hello, Sarge," the concierge calls out. Across the wet, busy street, breakfast at Tapa King is already waiting.

Today's headline in the *Gazette* declares: "Dec. 8, 2002—a morning for democracy as crowds mass for Edsa 5!" The main photograph shows Senator Bansamoro standing protectively beside President Estregan at Malacañang

Palace. Bansamoro is in jeans and a bulletproof vest, and is brandishing an ArmaLite. Estregan—paunch tightening the green satin of his hooded robe from his boxing days, making it ride dangerously high on his legs—smiles porcinely. They are surrounded by special-ops troopers in battle gear. The article explains that the restive masses had come close to overpowering the riot cops and storming the palace. Tear-gas canisters and rubber bullets had been loaded. Rocks had filled pockets and lighters had lingered by the wicks of Molotov cocktails. Blood was about to be shed. But Bansamoro appeared outside the palace with troops formerly of his command and held up his pistol to fire a single shot into the air. (The tabloids dubbed it: "The bullet that saved the country.") The throng surged backward, as if on cue. Before first light the streets were empty.

At sunrise—says another article—police took possession of the Changco house to discover the couple shot dead. Their son was found hiding inside the household's large freezer, where he had lain beneath a large turkey as soon as the gunfight started. He suffered from mild hypothermia. "It was a good thing he is very fat," said Dr. Manuel Manabat, the attending physician at Philippine General Hospital.

The story on page three says the cause of the explosion at the Philippines First Corporation has not been determined. The office of CEO Dingdong Changco, Jr., issued a statement. A leaking roof and faulty wiring in a generator were blamed.

*

I remember the last joke I shared with him.

Boy Bastos's daughter Girly asks her father, "Daddy, what is politics?" Boy is very proud of her inquisitiveness. As he's gotten older, spent and rebuilt the small inheritance his father Erning left him, risen in politics, watched his daughter grow, witnessed his son being born, seen his marriage shed its glitter, he's realized that our greatest doom is to raise children who'll repeat our mistakes. This he knows is something he doesn't want.

He says, "Well, Girly-girl, let me explain it this way. First, I'm the head of the family, so you can call me the President. Your mom makes the rules, so you can call her the Government. We're here to take care of your needs, so we can call you the People. Your yaya Inday works for us, and we pay her for her work, so we'll call her the Working Class. And your baby brother Junior, let's call him the Future. Now think about that and see if it makes sense."

Girly goes to bed, pondering what she heard. In the middle of the night, Girly awakens. She hears baby brother Junior crying, so she checks and discovers he's totally crapped in his diaper. Girly goes to her parents' room to find her mother fast asleep. Unable to wake her because of the sleeping pills taken every night, Girly goes to her yaya's room. The door, however, is locked. Girly peeks through the keyhole and sees her father in bed with Inday. Girly goes back to bed.

At the breakfast table the next morning, Girly tells her father, "Daddy, I think I understand politics now."

Boy is proud. "Wow!" he exclaims. "You really are sharp! Explain to us in your own words how politics work."

"Well," Girly begins, "the President is really fucking the Working Class. And the Government doesn't do anything except sleep and sleep. Nobody ever pays attention to the People. And the Future, well, the Future swims in shit."

Boy Bastos kisses her proudly on the head.

Eventually, Girly grows up. She marries the prominent Attorney Arrayko and becomes the country's most popular economist, senator, and then vice president. When the president at the time is ousted by yet another Edsa Revolution, Girly succeeds him. As she takes the presidential oath of office, she remembers all the wise lessons she learned from her iconoclastic father, Boy, and the legacy of her industrious lolo, Erning. President Girly Bastos Arrayko becomes the hope of the country. The end, however, proves that the joke's on us, and we all know the punch line.

*

The taxi driver asks cheerfully: "Forbes Park, sir?"

"Yes," the young man says. "How did you know?"

The driver whistles the tune from the Marlboro ads, his window down and his hand making content, sinuous motions in the cool wind. "Not yet sun," the driver says, "but no rain."

"Ah. That's why you're so happy."

"Yes, sir. Also, they haven't caught Lakandula still."

As the car sprays its way through a flooded part of Edsa, the young man silently rehearses what he's going to tell them.

*

In Forbes Park, Flame Tree Road has a carpet of red-orange blossoms laid down the length of the street. There are still thick clusters of deep red flowers left on the branches, unshaken by the typhoon. The taxi moves through this tunnel of fire.

When he was a child he would walk with his mother and father to visit Grapes and Granma across the street. This is one of the few memories he has of his parents—the flame tree petals, soft and thick beneath their feet, soaring and burning above them, like thousands of lenses refracting the sunlight of thousands of future childhood afternoons past.

He pays the taxi driver and walks slowly to the gate of his grandparents' home. Wiping his eyes, he rings the doorbell. Slippers applaud beyond the wall. Floyd, the one-eyed houseboy, opens the gate. He is surprised. He tells the young man that his grandmother and grandfather are inside, eating their merienda. Floyd takes the suitcases. In the yard, the acacia tree our wistful protagonist used to climb as a child has surrendered to the storm, its branches wrenched aside to expose the bone-white flesh inside the trunk. Yet the house is as it always was.

The next moment is the easiest scene I've ever typed.

Reflected in the glass of the sliding doors, our protagonist's expression is complicated enough to conceal the emotions within. His purposeful stride trembles. The screen door to the living room slides noisily. Granma looks over from the table to see who's there. She touches Grapes's arm in joyous panic. The two of them struggle up to meet the child whom they thought they had lost. He is unable to find the words he practised. He discovers he would not need them after all.

The words would have come later and the young man would have figured out then what he needed to say. Of the two choices he faced all his life, he would have decided on the benign third. Compromise is when nobody is unhappy, he would have said to himself—a variation on a theme—knowing he'd have to discover if that were indeed so. But his coming home would have been confirmation that, at the very least, he was willing to try—as a child to his grandparents and, yes, having found courage that he could be forgiven, as a father to his own child, however belatedly. Years later, he'd have remembered how it all turned out and he would have written about it as honestly as he could.

10

But first there was a mystery he had to solve.

As the airplane descended from the late-morning sun, from his window seat, flying godlike, our protagonist imagined he could touch the solution, reach out and pick it up and turn it to read the minuscule answer inscribed inside. One of those islands was hers. There was the place Miss Florentina described in her nearly illegible scrawl. The comma-shaped jewel protected by a chain of seven sugar-coated emeralds on a bolt of blue velvet. Made civilized and given a name after millennia remaining nameless. La Isla Dulcinea.

When this day began, he'd mused: This is the last taxi ride, the final airplane journey until it's all whole. Encouraged by the fingers of dawn, he'd sat sleepless with anticipation and stared out the window as they took off, his forehead against the thrumming glass.

The changing terrain had slid away—first shadowy roofs of shanties like a cubist landscape studded with lights, dim horizons of sugarcane, haphazard roads pale like long scars on the dusky landscape, then broken mirrors of rice paddies reflecting the first pizzicato rays of morning. As the sun rose over Pampanga, the enduring devastation of Mount Pinatubo made him gasp.

*

We are liberated by the multiplicity of conclusions to every unfinishing story. How about this one?

The newspaper's front page: The headline reads "Text-Message Revolution—What happened after Edsa 5!" The main photograph shows Reverend Martin in shackles before President Fernando V. Estregan, the commander-

in-chief's face full of reprimand. The pair are accompanied by a stern Senator Bansamoro, who, the caption explains, "personally apprehended the rebel-rousing cleric." A secondary article asks: "Bansamoro: Estregan's fighting cock for VP next election?" An editorial cartoon shows a man being bonked on the head by fellow commuters after asking: "How can it be Edsa 5 when it didn't happen on Edsa Blvd?" In a sidebar piece, Wigberto Lakandula is said to be at large, with sightings reported from Baguio to Mindanao.

*

Our assiduous protagonist took out his fountain pen and wrote in his notebook, remembering 1991.

After four centuries of slumber, a mushroom-cloud eruption sent wet ash as far as Singapore and Pnom Penh. The region was rocked by earthquakes. A typhoon descended on the mountain to transform ash into lahar—a monstrous dough that advanced inch by inch, to bury five hundred square miles of arable land beneath a foot of tephra and pumicelike sediment. To stem the flow, emergency superdams were built, though those were made brittle by kickbacks. They cracked against the lahar's glacial persistence.

Down there was where Crispin had his wrists swabbed with rubbing alcohol, invited nails into his flesh, listened to the hammer falls, bang, bang, bang, until he was raised on crossed planks above the crowd. An Easter ritual more promissory than penitential. Do the promises we ask for matter as much as those asked of us? Can any of us alter those things that life will change anyway? The woman who gave you life will one day fade, of something never truly understandable. The man who raised you, his power freshly withered, will offer his hand in mutual forgiveness, and you will hesitate to take it. A lover, deserving, whom you still wish you'd known how to love properly, will be wrested from you forever. And you will regret not making that defining decision that would have lifted you from the dead into a life you once thought probable. When God takes what he gives us, is our anger justified?

These are the thoughts that ran through his head as he watched the familiar desert below. He wondered, too, if déjà vu unsettles because it tells us that each moment should be appreciated more than it is. It reminds us that every instant is worth remembering.

He took out photographs from a folder. Harsh, contrasty duotones. Oversaturated colour prints. A Roman soldier wearing white Adidas shell toes. Hooded, shirtless flagellants, blood blackening the waists of their Levi's jeans. A close-up of a sanguineous bamboo rod, bending ever so slightly in the motion of the wielder's devotion. Lines of men and women dressed like Jesus, waiting like understudies in a Lenten play. Red and blue pennants strung up, ends tied to a sign that reads: LOCATION OF CHRIST'S SECOND FALL—PROUDLY SPONSORED BY SAN MIGUEL BEER. Sadie Baxter, Pentax slung around her neck, her blond hair a Caucasian halo against the brown skin of the crowd beside her.

He studied a photo that had bothered him a long time. Crispin on his cross, arms spread to the sky, eyes rolled back. What did Crispin see? At his feet, two old women and a fingerless leper stretch handkerchiefs up to catch his blood. In the crowd in the background, noticed for the first time, a man sticks his tongue out at the camera, thumbs in his ears and fingers frozen in their waggling.

Our faithful protagonist gazed out the window. This is also—he said to himself—the last landscape my parents saw in their final hours. But now it is entirely different.

A jeepney below sent up dust as it made its way across the wasteland. The plume rose, pillared, dispersed into a cloud. Ahead of it, the top half of a church buried in sand. In Tagalog and Sambal, he remembered, Pinatubo means "to have made grow."

Look! There's the shadow of our plane. Why is that still a thrill to spot? Maybe it confirms that we're still tethered to home, even if only by shadows.

*

Or this one?

The newspaper front page: The headline reads "Text-Message Revolution—What happened after Edsa 5!" The main photo shows police escorting Dingdong Changco, Jr., into his cell in Camp Crame. Farther down, a secondary photo shows President Fernando V. Estregan and Reverend Martin raising each other's arms on a stage surrounded by a multitude. The article explains that after the riots, Estregan declared a state of emergency. The military arrested various prominent figures, including the president's saviour, Nuredin Bansamoro, who was sitting for breakfast with his wives and children. All detained were charged with conspiracy and treason and linked to the recent bombings. In an "Exclusive!" account along the bottom of the page, Reverend Martin says his appointment as the president's spiritual adviser is "a gift from Above." He describes the urge to speak in tongues as he led his followers—millions strong—in a "Thanks God" rally outside the palace. The sidebar article reports that Wigberto Lakandula received a presidential pardon and was declared a hero of the people. He is intending to run for Congress, tapped to fill the seat of a retiring Respeto Reyes.

*

The plane began its descent. He felt it in his stomach. He thought, too, of how we almost always overlook these waypoints, the everyday transformations that occur between milestones, crises, epiphanies, and deaths. It went by so quickly, is what we say of our youth, of our loves, of our wedding days, of the childhoods of our children, of our very lives.

Somewhere he had read of that mystery of how we retain our consciousness, memories, personalities, when every cell in our body is replaced every seven years. Is nostalgia—that sense of wonder and grief at how far we've come—only intuited mourning for that self we've molted, felt so wholly in our every atom that we cannot intellectually perceive it, only feel it? The things a father did, or didn't, or imagined, or feared doing to his child—all those are gone forever, their loss honed by memory. The fingers held out one by one as her age is counted; the count is always doubted and must be started again. The Internet searches. The questioning of common friends: "How is she? What does she look like now?" That time at school, when her mother pulled her away, and the little girl looked back at him, confused. Those letters that were planned but never written, or written but never sent. The oblique hints in a book that he hopes she'll one day read when she is old enough.

If only we could go back and reverse the things we did wrong, better the things we did right. We can't. Not because time doesn't move that way, but because we ourselves would be entirely different. It would not be fair. You've had your chance. You're no longer on the stage. The clapping has subsided. The trumpets are silent, packed up in cases already gathering dust.

*

Or maybe even this one?

The newspaper's front page: the headline reads "Text-Message Revolution—What happened after Edsa 5!" The main photograph shows Vita Nova, primped and proper in a red pantsuit, giving a press conference, a smiling Senator Nuredin Bansamoro at her side. She has finally revealed the evidence to a senatorial inquiry—transcriptions of a postcoital conversation on the infamous sex tape—proving President Fernando V. Estregan masterminded not only the bombings, but also the riot led by Wigberto Lakandula (whom the army says they've killed, though no body has been presented). "Clearly, the president wished to destabilize the nation," Bansamoro is quoted as saying, "in order to declare martial law and avoid the coming elections." An impeachment is under way. Another article explains that Reverend Martin has broadcast a prayer rally from his cell in Camp Crame, urging his followers to throw their support behind Bansamoro "in our country's darkest hour." A sidebar article says the Catholic Church continues to support Estregan, despite evidence of his wrongdoing, because Nova is "morally suspect for her corrupting films and recent television commercial endorsing contraception."

*

The plane descended into one of those cold, brittle mornings that are perfectly blue. The green hills roiled up and away from the ivory strip running the length of the coast. The South China Sea ran westward, transparent then deepening into a glissando of indigo.

He stumbled down the steps onto the tarmac. The other passengers were already embracing relatives or text-messaging on their phones. He shivered and hugged himself.

Outside the airstrip was a dusty road with a sari-sari store and canteen. Nobody was behind either counter. The place looked like the ghost towns of the movies, with attentive flies and a pair of dogs loping down the street in search of scraps. The other passengers disappeared. No signal on his cell phone. The sun, overhead, destroyed all shadows. A road stretched in either direction. The sky was scented with fish. The sea he could hear somewhere.

A shade appeared in a doorway. "Where you go?" a little woman asked.

She watched with her dog face, with such intensity her irises appeared to quiver, to recur from somewhere earlier, perhaps a dream, or not.

"Where you go?" she asked.

He told her.

"I bring," she said, then faded into shadows.

He waited.

In the passenger compartment of her trike, he put his backpack on the floor and his feet on the backpack. Leaned his head out the door, like a dog in a car window. The wind still cool, but softening. The road straight and proverbial, though dusty. He shut his eyes. The motorcycle hummed. The driver whistled an unforgettable shapeless tune. The air smelled of two-stroke oil and seaweed. He nodded off.

*

Or perhaps this one will eventually make most sense:

A blank page rises up to receive black letters, fingers pushing and resting in the warm curls of the keys of an old Underwood, the decanters of sherry and water sounding like bells with every hammer fall. I transform memory into fiction. Outside, beneath the window, a door opens, voices tumble out atop each other, meat grills, cutlery scrapes on plates, music from a jukebox communicates only two bars before I can name the tune, a man's voice singing: "I'd die for you girl and all they can say is, he's not your kind." The door closes. Silence. Only the cold city breath on my face. I transform fiction into memory.

*

Slowing brought him back, brakes like a kettle at boil. Eyes closed, trying to hold in the dream. He could make sense of it but then it was gone. The wind changed, now humid and sticky. The trike stopped. He stumbled into the light. Foliage alongside the road was interrupted by a worn path leading to a spot of blue as small in the distance as a postage stamp. He turned to pay the driver. The trike was gone. So, too, was the backpack. That familiar panic cleared what was left of the drowsiness. Did I, he wondered, even bring a backpack? There answered only an urgent hushing from the sea. Nothing to be done. Shadows grew long toward the west. He followed the path.

From the beach he saw the island chain. A man stood on the prow of an outrigger pump boat, its name emblazoned in festive letters on the wooden hull: *Pekod.* The boatman watched him wade through the surf. Started the motor when he climbed aboard. He told the boatman: "Isla Dulcinea." But the engine was already roaring. They tilted through the water, bouncing over waves. Am I dreaming? he thought.

They passed islands connected loosely by long sandbars. Each island un-inhabited. How is it possible—he wondered—for there still to be places un-claimed by people? If I could only take one myself, start over without having to fix the things that need to be fixed. But the dangers of self-reliance terrify him, just like getting what you wish for. He counted: one, two, three, four, five, six. And the seventh. There's its comma. The boat stopped on its tail, the closest point to the mainland, and he stepped onto a stone landing beside a post planted deep into the ground. A squashed tire hung from it, bleached gray and half submerged in the water.

The island was perfect: shaded by large trees, many fruit-bearing, and sheltered by taller limestone promontories of the surrounding islands. The craft shuddered against the tire. The boatman proffered a hand thick with calluses and a weeping welt across it. Our adventurous protagonist had nothing except what was in his pockets. Wallet, cell phone, passport—all had been in the backpack. What—he wondered—had the backpack even looked like? Should I ask the boatman to bring me back to shore? The windows of the house, wide open, had white lace curtains waving in the breeze. I'll stay. I've come so far. Listen. Is that . . . Yes. Music. He fished in his pocket and pressed his last coin into the boatman's hand.

The house was a simple bungalow of whitewashed cement block walls. It was a place he'd seen before. Wasabi-green shutters were latched against the facade. Grey smoke streamed northward from an aluminum chimney. A sarimanok weathervane pointed south.

He made his way to the house, watching the sand spray before him as he walked. This is paradise, he thought. This could be my heaven.

The front door was ajar. He knocked. Called out. Hello! No answer. Is anybody here? That song. A tango. I know it. Vintage Bingbong Cadenza. "Cadenas de Amor." It sounds like a beautiful woman lying down to remember. A phonograph in the corner declared, "Tenía una cara tan bonita como una bendición y ella me dijo: Toda la vida es un sueño. Para lograr lo imposible, hay que intentar lo absurdo."

He knocked and called out again. Hello! A welcome mat read: "Come In If You're Good Lookin'." Cadenza repeated the refrain in Spanish: *She had a face like a blessing and she told me: All of life is a dream. To attain the impossible, we must attempt the absurd.*

Everything seemed familiar.

The interior, spare but comfortable, was as quaint as the outside. More of a large shack with an open plan. French doors on three walls. A fancy iron daybed in the centre, facing the doors which framed the edges of two islands, themselves framing the sea. If I could walk on water—he thought—I could make my way into Asia, then Africa, then America, then back home to here. A soft mackinaw blanket was crumpled on the bed and a book lay facedown on the floor. An old brass bason cradled mangosteens, guyabanos, a durian. A stove held a stainless-steel kettle, which was boiling, though the whistle was broken. A faucet dripped water from a plastic drum. He went to it and tapped it. It sounded like a bell underwater. In a corner, a shotgun slouched like a bully outside the convenience store. Across the room, atop a desk: a short-wave radio, a pile of documents, an alarm-red fedora, a picture frame.

By the door, an unfinished portrait on an easel, its features not yet filled in. The artist obviously possessed a capable hand. Beside the painting, a full-length mirror.

Outside, footprints in the sand. He followed them into the warm sea. Fish the size of sardines bobbed in the tide. When he touched them, they sprang to life and darted away. He walked around the house. A generator. An outhouse. A shed containing drums of diesel. Regular things. Real things. A small parliament of chickens clucked inside a coop. He looked repeatedly out to the comma. Is that her boat at the dock? No. Just the tire against the post. It's beginning to get dark.

He sat on the bed. What it must have looked like when they transported it by outrigger, its disassembled panels fastened by ropes, a rolled mattress atop trunks and boxes, all weighing the boat in the water, and a still-beautiful woman straddling the windy prow—bare feet pointed like a maiden's, her soles touched by waves.

A book lay at his feet. *The Approach to Al-Mu'tasim*, by the Bombay lawyer Mir Bahadur Ali.

Perfectly framed between the French doors, like the solstice sun at Stonehenge, a blood orange descended in a valley of stratocumulus.

The voice from the gramophone taunted: "Para lograr lo imposible, hay que intentar lo absurdo."

The kettle on the stove sizzled. He rushed to it. The water had boiled away. The vessel sighed when lifted.

He stood before the portrait. Beneath a red cloak, the unfinished visage seemed to mock him with its emptiness, like the eyes of Greek statuary at their most reprimanding, lupine, dead. His reflection in the mirror, though complete, seemed sucked of its own significance.

He went to the desk to radio for help. The shortwave's battery was dead.

There, beside the red hat, a picture frame. That girl with hazel eyes. The one from the photo album, but a few years older. First Holy Communion. Behind her, Marcel Avellaneda and Mutya Dimatahimik, each with a loving hand on her shoulders, all smiling proudly.

He picked up the orange notebook, its cover soft and satisfying, in places

worn to the gloss of warm caramel. Beneath it lay three black cardboard manuscript boxes. He could hear his heart beat faster. On the beach, still nothing.
Horizons empty as only horizons can be. The music died. The record crack-
led. How could it have lasted these hours? The needle scratched persistently,
like an old clock's second hand stuck.

Is that an outboard motor? He peered out the window. Gramophone
clicking in time with his heart. Calm down. Calm down. Listen.

That's the engine of a boat.

No.

It is.

It faded in and out. In, then out. Whatever it was, heard or imagined, it
was lost in the waves. Gone. He held the notebook closed. Fingertips feeling
the side, enjoying the smooth coarseness of paper gathered for a single purpose. He glanced out the window. Listened once more. His thumbs caressed
the nap of the book cover. He looked over his shoulder. Somebody is watching.
He looked at the manuscript boxes.

I won't find Dulcinea.

Our protagonist opened the first box. It was empty. He opened the second. Empty. The third. Empty.

He was not surprised or disappointed. That which was missing only outlined that which was not. Their emptiness contained the entirety of what had
been lived, and the certainties of how it ended, how it must end for each of us.
Our last moment in a string of final moments, the last look you take backward
before going forward to the light: that pinprick of dawn, the horizon turning
vertical, the sun and the moon in the same sky. The rhythm of a breath we've
known always and the terminal sequence of heartbeats. The concave heavens
and the convex earth. And in the curve between, the dangling end of a rope,
that long cord of life, its loose ends frayed, its individual sinews, moments
insignificant on their own, woven together, for strength.

Standing thus where the beginning and end circle to meet, one cannot
help but look at what has just been made whole, and the small things loved
that made it all worthwhile: the last-minute epiphany, the relief after pain, the
consolation of yesterdays, your old chair at your desk, loading a typewriter,
recollections seasoned by time, a window looking out on someone else's
across the street, the confidence of deep experience, satisfaction at no one
else's cost, unfolding a newspaper, the entropy of love, turning the tuning
knob of a radio, admiring young women who know you're too old to be any

harm, dovetailing, the selfish sacrament of forgiveness, the vibrations of Greenwich Village, the felt of a good Borsalino, sin and all its involvements, retrieving your mail, the tinkle of house keys, good tobacco, firm handshakes, the relief of rationalized blame, shoeshines, the earnest musk of library stacks, answers to questions that should not have been asked, a piece of music heard for the first time, a young couple embracing out of grief, the fuel of oedipal dissatisfaction, perfumed letters not yet opened postmarked far away, the comforts of religion, the long dip above her waist, the optimism of airplane rides, *schadenfreude*, transatlantic crossings, the portability of aphorisms, calvados, the utopic mouthfeel of political theory, breaking a sweat, the breathlessness of not yet knowing its success or defeat, ballerinas, eavesdropping, foreign supermarkets, that first sip of a cold beer, the freedom of taxis, newly minted ambition, visiting your first tailor, blank notebooks, imagining your first kiss, the smell of hamburgers and cut sugarcane, puberty and its efflorescing complexities, old Manila, the shush of a pencil being sharpened, the tang of a bell, mother's voice calling you for dinner, reading aloud carefully, soft chill on cheeks and the ticking of bicycle gears, challenges still unengaged, choosing a flavour through frosty glass and watching it scooped on a sugar cone, running jumps in the house where you grew up, implacable imagination, dust motes spinning in sunbeams in the waking from a nap, the plump scent of shampoo, hearing someone sing your name, seeing faces to whom life will soon ascribe meaning, warmth, the discovery of your first word, the oblivion of not yet knowing there would ever be your last.

EPILOGUE

My suitcase set down in the hallway, that anonymous morning in February, I leafed through the stack of mail that had arrived during my absence. This particular letter was thin, without a stamp, though on university letterhead. I assumed it had been hand-delivered. I opened it straightaway. Its contents were so striking, I could do nothing but stare at my image in the hall mirror. Such news always reflects our own mortality.

I had seen, you see, something of myself in him. Beyond our coming from the same place and our complicit understanding of what it's like to be away from it. The news of his death—a drowning—convinced me I had known him better than I did. Perhaps it was just my age, or my loneliness, or both, for those two circumstances, eventually, cannot be separated. The fact is, I didn't know him as well as I should have. Only from our classes, a few consultations in my office, and the profile he said he wished to write. On two occasions we had stilted conversations over cheeseburgers. That was all. He was just another face in my workshop, and I envied and pitied him as I do all my students. Perhaps a bit more. So I was surprised that the letter had affected me so deeply. The simplicity of random accidents is often too painful to bear, and I began to wonder what had happened.

Life, as it does, went on, perhaps too easily. There were the quotidian tasks of a new semester, a string of anxious appointments with my proctologist, the afternoon naps deserved by we of the creaky limbs, and the continued effort to finish the manuscript to which I'd long kept faithful, like a guilty spouse. Atop a pile on my desk lay the unanswered questionnaire he had asked me to ponder before the interviews that never happened. Weeks passed and I was disturbed to find I could not stop thinking about him and the short stories he had submitted in class: one was about grandparents raising a grand-child; another was about a failing relationship with a girlfriend; the last story, his most convincing, presented a protagonist working out the permutations of his first encounter with his child whom he did not know.

One afternoon, I found myself unscrewing my old fountain pen and writing answers on my young student's questionnaire. His generic queries, and my premature obituary that *The Philippine Sun* had run—which I'd framed and put by my desk—weighed heavily. Amid the blessings of another spring—while sitting at a bus window, walking to class, even midsentence during a lecture—I spent an inordinate amount of time glancing at what I realized, for the first time ever, was the short road leading through the winter of my life. I sat at my desk and looked at the manuscript pages etched with words and gathered together in three black boxes: my masterpiece, my great return, my honest song for my homeland.

To make sense of what was happening to me, I obsessed on what had happened to him. I kept returning to the single article devoted to him on-line—a brief of such brutal brevity, elucidating the moment the world would first move on without him. I became scared of crossing the street. Avoided soaping the soles of my feet in the shower. And so, with the relentlessness of Sisyphus, I locked myself in my oubliette and threw myself into revising—salvaging—that long-awaited book. But I was like one of those men who every day dons his suit, jokes with his kids over breakfast, kisses his wife, and goes out the door to the job he lost long ago—all that's left to a man like that is habit.

Days became weeks. Pages became chapters. Weeks became months. But with every sheet of paper I filled, I doubted more and more the utility of chronicling ancient sins. What were those spent leaves but shed days?

One night, before dawn, I staggered from my desk to vomit violently into the wastepaper bin. The rest of the day I was ill, unable to stand, the heat of a circuitous dream waylaying my thoughts to the things I never talked about. Through eyes made young—no, through *his* eyes—I saw what I'd become. An angry man doomed to failure, a failure of a man damned to anger.

The moon had set, or perhaps it hadn't yet risen, or perhaps it wasn't to have come at all, when I went to that familiar trash receptacle near the Hudson River and burned the three manuscript boxes—that old albatross, that old cormorant, that old vulture. I watched the book ablaze. It transformed into smoke. I knew that if I had left it for our children, all I'd be leaving was a list of our shame. That night, I slept. A deathlike sleep the likes of which I'd not had in years.

Morning arrived, I returned to my desk, and rolled a blank sheet into my trusty old Underwood. I didn't know what I wanted to write, though I wanted it to be—this time, finally—a memorial. Complete with attendant promises.

I sat there, closed my eyes, my fingertips resting in the warm embrace of the typewriter keyboard. Outside, beneath my window, a door opened infinitely, voices tumbled out atop each other, tangled with music, the chimes of cutlery, and familiar, treasured, scents. The memories of my young student sluiced, flowed into one, which carved its way into a geography it had never traversed.

For youth was all he had. Boyish in the manner of those who pass seamlessly from adolescence to old age, he moved with self-conscious uncertainty but wrote with abandon, almost always to a fault. He favoured torn bell-bottom jeans, pinstripe double-vented jackets, and T-shirts that he'd clearly hoped would project his personality, sporting slogans like YOUR CHIVAS OR MINE? or JIM LEHRER FOR PRESIDENT. He was perpetually late for my workshop and his excuses felt like lies. He often spoke too quickly, looked out of the sides of his eyes, and was aggressive toward the ideas and writing of his classmates. I don't think he was well liked.

I found myself typing with the rhythm of a storm on your roof. I presented him as a father, as a son, as a holy ghost. To imagine the mystery of his life, I started with the certainty of his death. He was found floating, spread-eagle and faceup in the brackish overrun of the Pasig River.

From the possibilities, a story was selected, unfolded. The world losing that boy through its complicated mechanics began to hint at parallels, at symmetries, perhaps because the telling of a story imbibes the chaos of our own days with a certain elegance, a comprehensible beauty. When you're old and lost, is it really pathetic to search for connections to explain our choices to ourselves?

The boy became a man. A young man—a description that encompasses all the promises of living. When I finished writing, spent, after four seasons at the typewriter, I had knotted his being forever with mine. And with this fiction of possibilities, entwined with the possibilities of fiction, I've woven in my own unlived life.

And so, my return. I write these final words as I approach my first day home.

Home to what remains of my family.

Home to my child, for whenever she's ready.

Home, with the discovery that we are only enlightened at a new beginning, at what we perceive to be the end.

—Crispin Salvador, en route to Manila, December 1, 2002

ACKNOWLEDGMENTS

My gratitude has no order, and it will not fit on this page. But in true Pinoy fashion, I'll try.

My deepest thanks go to Mom and Dad, for giving me my life; and to all my siblings (in-laws included), for making that life loving, secure, and filled with laughter.

To my coach, comrade, and pal: John C. Evans, who was there before the beginning, who edited this work through all the drafts, and who has taught me more about writing than anyone else.

To my editors: Eric Chinski, my ally in the trenches, who helped, pencil brandished, patiently make this book all it could be; to Nicole Winstanley, Paul Baggaley, and Meredith Curnow, who have such faith in my work I can't help but be enlightened; and to my editors in other languages—as we say in Tagalog, *Salamat*. And, of course, I can't forget all the people (copyeditors, assistants, translators, designers, and others) who made my manuscript a book.

To my agents: Peter Straus and Melanie Jackson, my indispensable guides and reliable friends in the world of publishing, and to Laurence and Stephen and the good folks at Rogers, Coleridge, and White, for bringing my work across the planet.

To my teachers: the Ateneo de Manila, my light in dominoes; Columbia University's Writing Division, which taught the tools of the trade; and, of course, the University of Adelaide, whose support made this book possible. Whatever I achieve is the success of all my teachers, especially Paul Go, Rofel Brion, DM Reyes, Danton Remoto, Jing and Tony Hidalgo; my master's guides Jessica Hagedorn,

Jaime Manrique, Jonathan Dee, Victoria Redel, Alan Ziegler; and my PhD supervisors Di Schwerdt, Brian Castro, Ben Marcus, and, especially, Nick Jose.

Thanks, too, to those behind the Palanca Awards and the Man Asian Literary Prize, who saw the merit in my book long before it was published.

My gratitude goes to Dr. Deberah S. Goldman, for teaching me that within the extraordinary first exists the ordinary, to Clinton Palanca, for being a brother in arms, and to Manuel Quezon III, whose tireless work helps explain our country to ourselves. To Conrad and Laurent, *pour l'amour sans condition*. To sweet Mary Jane, for always reminding me. And to my friends, for being a big part of this life from which I draw inspiration.

Of course, I save the best for last. I thank my Edith—my mate, *ma vie, aking pangarap*—without whom all this work would be impossible, without whom I would not see this world for how wonderful it can be.